I0819540

ALSO BY VIRGINIA HUME

Haven Point

LIBERTY ISLAND

LIBERTY ISLAND

A NOVEL

VIRGINIA HUME

ST. MARTIN'S PRESS
NEW YORK

This is a work of fiction. All of the names, characters, organizations, places, and events portrayed in this work are either products of the author's imagination or used fictitiously.

First published in the United States by St. Martin's Press, an imprint of St. Martin's Publishing Group

EU Representative: Macmillan Publishers Ireland Ltd, 1st Floor,
The Liffey Trust Centre, 117–126 Sheriff Street Upper, Dublin 1, D01 YC43

Printed in the United States of America. For information, address
St. Martin's Publishing Group, 120 Broadway, New York, NY 10271.

www.stmartins.com

The Library of Congress Cataloging-in-Publication Data is available upon request.

ISBN 978-1-250-28564-5 (hardcover)
ISBN 978-1-250-28565-2 (ebook)

First Edition: 2026

10 9 8 7 6 5 4 3 2 1

To my mother, Clare Hume

Part One

Late in the afternoon, the girls were on the beach—a bit grubby and tired, but the good kind that comes after a long, merry day.

At first, they had been so terrified that Aunt Phillipa would discover that they didn't have a chaperone after all, they thought every passing boat was coming to fetch them.

To ward off the possibility, they tried holding their breath until the boats went by, like one does when passing a cemetery, but it turned out that a carriage passes a cemetery a good deal faster than boats passed islands, so they had to give that up. Audrey came up with an incantation to use instead: "Please make that boat go another way, for on this island we wish to stay." It worked like a charm. (Well, it was a charm. So it worked like it was supposed to.)

Now that it had been a whole week, they were finally comfortable.

"I used to want to grow up," Sally said, as she watched the gulls wheeling overhead. "Not anymore."

"Me neither. You have to get married or be a spinster," Audrey replied. "If you marry, you have to be domesticated, and your husband might not even keep his hair. And nobody wants to be a spinster like Aunt Phillipa."

"Not all spinsters are crotchety," Victoria said. "Some are

young and wear smart hats. Of course they go to committees all the time."

"Well, if it's going to committees, or doing chores and watching your husband's hair fall out, I'd rather stay here on this island where I have some liberty," Sally said.

Lucy, who was making sand angels with her arms and legs, said, rather idly, "I suppose that's what we should call it. 'Liberty Island.'"

They'd been trying to settle on a name for days, but four girls with lots of ideas can't always agree. This felt like a fact, though, not an idea. So "Liberty Island" it was.

From *Liberty Island*, by Miss Crane

CHAPTER ONE

November 1910

New York City

JULIA

It's wonderful to be among people who know you so well (or most of the time, at least).

FROM *LIBERTY ISLAND*, BY MISS CRANE

Finally, nearly three months into her first semester at Barnard, Julia Demarest had landed at a gathering of the smart set—and yet there she was, standing alone by the wall, feeling stupid.

It seemed so promising, too! The four flights of stairs she and Mina climbed to reach the apartment had sagged in a most encouraging manner, and halfway up, they'd heard laughter and argument, and the muffled, doleful strains of what sounded like some Moorish air playing on a phonograph.

The door had opened to a marvelously bohemian scene—women in shapeless silk tunics, and men with low, loose collars and all manner of beards. Even the more conventionally dressed gave off a whiff of heedlessness. And while Julia could not say she *liked* the smell of Turkish cigarettes, the smoke was indisputably atmospheric.

Julia had come with Mina Ellis (a fellow freshman, though Julia thought she seemed years older). Mina had finagled a job as a general factotum at *The Current*, a new and thrillingly radical magazine. Not two minutes after they arrived at the party, the host, an editor there, pulled her away, leaving Julia to fend for herself.

Other than a passing greeting from "Stella the Anarchist," one of Mina's roommates (the others were "Jane the Socialist" and "Vera the Dancer," of unknown political affiliation), Julia had spoken to no one.

She finally screwed up her courage and sidled up to a nearby cluster of people, hoping they might open the circle for her. One woman made eye contact, but no invitation was forthcoming.

Julia sighed inwardly. *Probably for the best.* From what she could hear, they were in a heated discussion about behaviorism and syndicalism. (Or behaviorism *versus* syndicalism? Beyond a vague and appealing sense of subversiveness, Julia knew little about either.)

Mina towered over many of the guests, so Julia caught an occasional glimpse. When she slipped out of view at one point, Julia hoped she was finding some circuitous way back to her. A moment later, she spotted Mina again and realized she had merely moved on to another conversation.

Worse, a shift in the crowd revealed that Mina was now talking to Pelham Stewart, the very man Julia had hoped to meet this evening.

Mr. Stewart, a senior at Columbia, was one of the promising young writers whose work appeared in *The Current*. Julia knew better than to expect her friend to part the seas to beckon her over. Mina had not even glanced in her direction.

Julia had only laid eyes on Pelham Stewart once, when he gave one of the informal talks *The Current* hosted in the restaurant below their offices. He had not struck her as particularly attractive at first. Ruggedly handsome, maybe—with his broad shoulders, dark disobedient hair, and those thick brows that almost met at the worry lines between his eyes—but too brooding and intense for her tastes.

She had been riveted by the talk, though. His theme was "Smashing the Idols." When he declared, "We must abandon the tired notion that piety and restraint are the highest virtues," Julia had almost cheered. As a girl, she was constantly told she was insufficiently restrained ("hoydenish," to use her brother William's favorite word).

"And what of this absurd urgency about 'assimilating' immigrants?" he continued. "Nobody clings to the old country more than the Protestant aristocrat. Culturally, we're practically a British colony—the old church, the old literature, the old snobberies." (Julia tucked that away to pull out next time Father and William complained about foreigners besmirching America with their alien ways.)

Mr. Stewart relaxed when he took questions from the audience, and when one exchange made him laugh, his face completely transformed. Gone was the forbidding expression. He suddenly seemed youthful, charming, eager to be amused.

Julia was smitten, though she tried to disguise it when she and Mina went to a nearby teahouse after the talk. Mina was too perceptive. She leaned back, one long leg crossed over the other, and raised an eyebrow.

"Handsome, isn't he?"

"I suppose." Julia shrugged.

"You can't fool me, duckie. I saw how you looked at him. I must orchestrate an introduction."

Julia promptly abandoned the act and leaned forward eagerly. "Oh, would you?"

On the way over this evening, Julia asked Mina what sort of women Mr. Stewart liked.

"Don't you dare change a jot for any man!" Mina had scolded.

"Not to change myself. Just for the purpose of conversing."

"Well, in that case," she replied, with a mischievous smile, "perhaps leave off that you're playing basketball."

"Will you never banish that image from your mind?" Julia laughed.

"Never. It is burned into my memory." Ever since she spotted Julia racing to her dormitory in bloomers and a middy blouse, Mina had been ribbing her about joining the freshman basketball team.

As it happened, this advice was unnecessary. Julia found Mina's friends so terrifyingly sophisticated and blasé, she would never have mentioned anything as "rah-rah-sis-boom-bah" as basketball.

"Do I look all right, at least?" Julia had put on a simple blue silk dress with covered buttons, which looked nice with her eyes, and wrapped an ivory Persian-embroidered scarf around her waist. Her dark hair was in a low, loose knot.

"Anything goes, really. You're terribly aristocratic-looking, but there's nothing you can do about that." She paused a moment, as if in thought, then added, "Come to think of it, I'm going to call you 'Duchess' from now on instead of 'duckie.'"

It pained Julia, watching her friend and Mr. Stewart in an animated conversation. She knew Mina would tease her tomorrow. *Why did you not join us? You said you wanted to meet Pelham!* But not everyone was comfortable elbowing her way through a crowd in such a manner.

Nor was Julia comfortable continuing to stand in awkward solitude. Defeated, she headed to the bedroom to get her cloak. But then she felt a tap on her shoulder and turned to see a face that was as welcome as it was familiar.

"Hello, Jules. Imagine seeing you here." Smiling down at her was Michael Seaborne, Columbia junior and dear old family friend.

Julia placed a grateful hand on his forearm. "How glad I am to see you, Michael! I was feeling quite friendless a moment ago."

His eyes frowned. "You, Jules, friendless? I can't imagine it. But I was just leaving, if you'd like to join me."

Julia looked back at the crowd. Mina, with that sly look on her face Julia knew so well, was whispering something in Pelham's ear, and he was laughing appreciatively in response.

"Yes, please," Julia said.

"I'm sorry you had an unpleasant time of it," Michael said, as he took her arm and they headed up Amsterdam Avenue, ducking their heads against the icy headwind that whooshed down the street. "What brought you there?"

"My friend is working at *The Current*, but someone grabbed her when we walked in, and I didn't know a soul. Or I didn't think I did, at least."

Julia battled her disappointment by reminding herself how fortunate she was to have run into Michael. He was like a taste of home, but better, since he was not actually *from* home. Michael's mother grew up with Julia's grandmother in Concord, Massachusetts (though a generation apart, Julia's grandmother was only seven years older). But while Julia's family was in Boston, Margaret Seaborne had married a newspaper publisher and settled in Washington, DC.

Michael was such a comfortable sort of person, too, with an easy, loose-limbed way of moving, and big brown eyes that turned down at the corners, giving him a look of kind sympathy.

"Where does your dorm mistress think you are?" Michael asked. "She can't have known you were at that party."

"Oh, heavens, no. I am now at a violin concert at the Lyceum, which I am finding most edifying. It ends at ten PM." In order to get around the strict rules in Brooks Hall, the girls lied shamelessly about where they were going and with whom.

Michael laughed. "I'm glad you're enjoying it. You've got some time, then. I'm meeting friends at the Astor. Care to come for a bit? They're nice enough, though perhaps not as clever as the crowd we just left."

"You know I think you're terribly clever," Julia scolded. She paused, and with customary candor added, "Though I was surprised to see you there."

He chuckled again. "I'm on the staff of the *Columbia Spectator* with a few of the writers for *The Current*. I hope I don't disappoint you when I say I'm not terribly revolutionary."

"Oh, you can't disappoint me, Michael, but what *do* you consider yourself?"

Michael shrugged. "Merely chary of anyone claiming to have all the answers. Son of a newspaperman, you know. The skepticism is bred in. Don't let it stop you from being curious."

There was no danger of that. At some point in the past few years, Julia had realized that, outside the snow globe that was Boston society, smart young people were reimagining *everything*. They were determined to toss out old, rigid notions and make a better world, one with more freedom and opportunities, especially for women.

Once Julia was aware of it, she saw it everywhere, in newspapers and magazines, and especially in Father and William's grumbling comments (a good sign that these young thinkers were onto something wonderful). She wanted nothing more than to be a part of this grand, thrilling spectacle. The very reason she wanted to attend Barnard was that she knew New York was where it was all brewing.

When they reached the Astor, Julia followed Michael toward a table of three men and one woman. When the woman turned, and Julia realized it was Florence North, a Barnard senior, she stopped in her tracks. Upperclassmen were terribly hard on "freshies" who broke the rules.

Miss North cupped her hands and called out, "Don't worry, I'm not a snitch!"

Julia laughed, and feigned wiping her brow.

They made room for the newcomers, and Michael introduced Julia.

"Seaborne, I never thought to see a scapegrace like yourself with such a charming-looking young lady," Michael's friend George Atlee said.

Michael leaned back and looked at Julia appraisingly, as if just noticing her. Julia sat up straighter and raised her eyebrows, awaiting a compliment.

"Splendid frock, Jules. You do look fetching." He looked at his friends and added, "Don't be fooled by those blue eyes. She once threw a dead fish at me."

"The fish was not thrown, but catapulted," Julia said. "And it didn't even hit you. Besides, you deserved it for being in league with my older brother."

Naturally, an explanation was demanded, so Julia told them about the summer idyll she and her friends created on an island off their coastal Maine summer community, Haven Point.

Julia was ten at the time of the incident Michael mentioned. When the girls saw the boat sailing by, close to the shore, they knew it was a spy mission. Julia's stuffy older brother and his friends were forever trying to figure out what they were up to. The girls ran to the beach, filled their skirts with whatever they could find, loaded the catapult, and let loose their arsenal.

"You girls built a catapult?" Mr. Atlee interrupted.

Julia raised a finger in correction. "My parents' *caretaker* built a catapult. And a lookout tower. In hindsight, I believe he was reliving his own childhood."

"It sounds just like the *Liberty Island* books," Florence said, admiringly.

Michael and Julia exchanged an amused glance. "Funny thing about that," Michael said. "Julia's aunt wrote the *Liberty Island* books."

"And Michael's mother illustrated them," Julia added.

Florence's eyes went wide. "I adored that series! Were they based on you, then?"

"Very loosely! We never saved passengers from a wrecked ship, or faced down sharks, or anything like that," Julia said. She was proud of her aunt's books, and of the island that inspired them, but it felt boastful to bring up the subject herself. Michael never hesitated, though, and she invariably enjoyed the reaction.

When Michael and his friends fell into conversation about the Columbia rowing team, Florence turned to Julia. It turned out she was born in Boston, too, but her family moved to New York when she was in high school.

"They'd never have let me attend Barnard if we didn't live here," Florence said. "How did you convince your family?"

"That wasn't the first hurdle!" Julia said. "First I had to persuade them to let me go to college at all. Once they were convinced I was serious, I conspired with my aunt. She went to Radcliffe, where I couldn't have gotten in on a bet, but she knew some high-society Barnard alum, who wrote my parents and told them how respectable it was."

"And how closely they keep an eye on their students," Florence teased.

"Precisely," Julia replied primly. "I believe her exact words were 'Our girls are never, ever at the Astor when they're meant to be at a violin concert.'"

Florence laughed, and repeated her vow not to snitch; then the orchestra returned from a break. Julia enjoyed a turn on the dance floor with Michael, and another with Mr. Atlee, after which Michael pointed at his watch, and Julia reluctantly bade everyone goodbye.

"I feel like an infant," she said with a sigh, as Michael walked her toward Morningside Heights.

"I am fairly certain they did not see you in that light," Michael said. "In fact, I should ask if you are keeping your vow to remain unattached, as I think Mr. Atlee was quite interested."

"I remain determined." Julia tried to sound resolute. She had told Michael at the beginning of the term that, having miraculously been admitted to Barnard (a beneficiary, she knew, of the school lowering standards to attract girls from outside New York), she was determined to see it through, which meant no romantic entanglements.

She did not feel the need to mention that a certain Pelham Stewart might have challenged that notion. After all, she still had not even met the man.

An hour later, Julia sat opposite her dearest friend, Louisa Murphy, drinking cocoa by the little fireplace in the living room of their suite.

At barely five feet, with a smattering of freckles over her nose, Louisa looked almost like a child. Their classmates made that common mistake at first, treating Louisa like a younger sister, but they quickly learned that she was more like a wise aunt. It was her stillness, the way she had of training her clear green eyes on you and listening so carefully. Louisa was terribly funny, but with her fine Irish wit, she said a great deal with very little.

Louisa, an orphan, had always been sickly, and when she was eight, a social worker brought her to Haven Point for the fresh air her doctors recommended. She and Julia had spent every summer together since.

"How was it that you went out with Mina and ended up with Michael?" Louisa asked.

Julia knew Louisa was wary of Mina, so she answered carefully. "The party was crowded and smoky. Michael happened to be there, so I left with him."

They had met Mina a few days into the semester when she appeared at their door, swished in, and flopped into the wingback chair. Rather than the standard-issue ankle-length black skirt and white shirtwaist, Mina had worn a gray skirt in some flowing material, a blouse with kimono sleeves, and an Egyptian scarf wrapped around her head.

"I'm in hiding, and you duckies looked like fun. I'm Mina Ellis. What are your names?"

They introduced themselves; then Julia asked what sent her into hiding.

"I fear I irritated my roommate, Miss Marvin," Mina said, feigning a sorrowful expression.

"What happened?" Julia asked. Isabella Marvin was the only girl on their floor whom she could not abide. She suspected it would not be a hard task to annoy her.

"She was putting up more dried flowers, and I happened to mention that I thought it was an odd custom."

"Oh, my!" Julia laughed. Isabella was very rich, very pretty, and—if the row of dried flower arrangements hanging from their curtain rod was any indication—also very much admired.

"But it *is* odd, is it not? A beau gives one flowers, alive and fresh with scent. They shrivel and die, then one smashes them between the pages of a book or hangs them upside down. I merely said it struck me as an inapt metaphor, all this desiccated vegetation."

Mina shrugged, as if she had just been innocently commenting rather than firing a shot directly at Isabella's considerable ego. Even Louisa had to laugh.

After Mina swished out the door again, Julia slumped into the chair she had just vacated.

"Oh, she is just how I want to be—so languorous and sophisticated. Like a cat!"

"You want to be . . . *languorous*?" Louisa was clearly straining to hold back laughter.

"Yes!" Julia closed her eyes and waved a lazy hand. "Languorous, with an air of mystery that makes people burn to know my hidden secrets."

"Well, all right, then." Louisa shrugged.

Julia knew Louisa, who did not have a particle of envy in her, was not jealous of Mina. She had merely noticed that Mina was a rather elusive sort of friend, and she did not like Julia being treated cavalierly. Julia also knew that Mina was not terribly reliable, but Mina had told Julia a great deal about her dreadful mother and her sad childhood, which Julia felt at least partially explained her erratic ways. Louisa was not privy to any of this, as Mina had shared it in confidence.

"By the way, I mentioned to Michael you made me join basketball because I'd become obnoxiously restless."

"Did he find that hard to imagine?" Louisa raised an eyebrow.

"He called it Newton's fourth law: 'Julia Demarest must move.'"

Julia's effort to become more Mina-like had mostly consisted of avoidance of any activity that seemed too "college girl." Louisa took it in stride, as she did all of Julia's fancies, until one rainy afternoon in early November.

They were in the living room, Louisa doing homework at her desk, while Julia sat at her own, trying to disentangle two necklaces. She let out another exasperated groan. "I swear this one necklace is a predator! It eats all of the other ones."

Louisa smacked her pencil on her desk. "If you don't join the basketball team and get some exercise, I'm moving out."

"You don't mean that," Julia scoffed, still struggling with the knotted chains.

"I know you wish to adopt the blasé attitude of a serious intellectual, but you are not making allowances for your nature. You are not a house cat, Julia. You are a sheepdog."

Julia finally looked up, aghast. "A sheepdog!"

"Or a collie, if you prefer," Louisa continued, unapologetic. "Any of those intelligent breeds that eat your furniture if you don't work them hard enough."

Julia paused for an outraged moment and then began to laugh. "We have been in this dormitory for more than a month, and I have not consumed so much as a table leg!"

Julia could not be angry. Louisa took Julia's desire to shed her patrician Back Bay skin and remake herself along more intellectual lines with the same equanimity she had Julia's childhood aspiration of becoming a pirate or a smuggler. Her concerns were purely practical.

"Well, just as you must move, I must sleep," Louisa said now, rising from her chair. "I have to work tomorrow."

Louisa's professional ambition was to help poor, wage-earning women, but she was pursuing a teaching certificate as a backup. Given that she'd already landed a part-time job assisting a labor expert at a foundation, Julia knew she'd never need her backup.

Once Louisa was in her own room with the door closed, Julia grabbed the blanket off the back of the divan, dragged a chair to the window, opened it, and sat with her chin resting on her hands. (Louisa was accustomed to Julia hanging out of windows, but she objected when it was below freezing.)

Julia loved their view of Milbank Quadrangle. During the day, she watched girls walking arm in arm, or sitting on a bench reading, or listening to the noontime stump speakers. At night, she liked to look out at the inky darkness. The breeze was from the west this evening, and it carried a briny smell, and occasional sounds from the night boats on the Hudson. She could hear the city, too, another layer of sound, comfortably far off.

Julia's sociability and innate buoyancy fortified her against lingering disappointment. "A hummingbird," Mr. Atlee had called her this evening, having observed her turning from one person to another, eager to catch all the interesting and amusing things people had to say.

Julia's tendency to exist in the present was not well suited to achieving her goals, however. She was determined to be more deliberate and felt it was time to consider where things stood.

Her first months at Barnard had mostly been wonderful. Julia was awed by her brilliant classmates and loved being on intimate terms with girls so different from those she knew growing up. They often piled into her and Louisa's suite, lounging on the divan or among the downy pillows on the floor while Louisa fixed something in their chafing dish.

But while Julia had dreamed about such "dorm room spreads," she had imagined debating interesting intellectual movements. In reality, they chewed more on fudge and Welsh rarebit than ideas. To realize their ambitions, her classmates had to do far better in school than the men, which left little time for causes. Julia hoped to find stimulating conversation at the Suffrage Club, but when she tried to join, she learned they did not even allow freshmen.

From the first, Julia sensed that Mina Ellis could be her ticket to the smart set, so she was disappointed when she moved to an apartment a few blocks from campus.

"It was a nice experiment, living in Brooks Hall, but doomed to failure," Mina had said. "I'm a terrible college girl, not up for all these dorm room shenanigans."

When Mina approached Julia after botany class one day and asked if she'd like to skip the stringy meat in the lunchroom and have a bite at a nearby restaurant, Julia accepted eagerly, and their friendship was launched.

Julia was flattered that the most fascinating girl in their class had taken an interest in her, and when Mina landed a job at *The Current*, it seemed to validate her instinct that Mina was in the thick of the intellectual and artistic movements that she found so alluring. Still, progress was lagging. Julia had to peg away at her studies, just to keep her head above water, and her hopes for this evening had not been realized.

Mina was her only real connection to the smart young intellectuals bent on changing the world, and as Louisa pointed out, she was not terribly dependable.

Julia closed the window with a defeated sigh, but as she got ready for bed, she scolded herself. *Where is your initiative?* She had always despised being at someone else's mercy, and not all avenues to stimulating conversation required Mina's unreliable patronage. It took little time to hit on an idea. *The Suffrage Club!* An advantage of Julia's hummingbird nature was that she had gotten to know just about everyone in her class. If anyone could start a movement to challenge the Suffrage Club's silly prohibition of first-year girls, she could.

CHAPTER TWO

May 1898

Boston, Massachusetts

ANNA

Anna Bradley entered the house on Commonwealth Avenue, just as her sister, Elizabeth, emerged from the parlor, where she was directing preparations for her mother-in-law's birthday luncheon.

"Oh, dear," Elizabeth said, eyeing Anna's soaking wet gown.

"I know. I was two blocks away when the sky opened up," Anna said. "I might as well have stood in front of a fire hose. I wish I were a dog. I'd just shake."

Elizabeth smiled sympathetically. "I'll send Millicent up. She can help you get ready."

Anna headed upstairs, almost grateful for the sorry state of her gown. Had she been outwardly presentable, Elizabeth might have detected her rather wretched internal state.

Three days ago, Anna's father, a professor of philosophy at Harvard, had told her he was retiring.

"Does that mean you'll be able to devote more time to our book?" Anna asked, a hopeful question that was belied by the stab of anxiety she felt in anticipation of the answer.

"Oh, no, I'm afraid I won't be continuing with that, dear," he said blithely. "You're welcome to complete it yourself, of course."

For years, she and Father had been working together on a scholarly biography of Margaret Fuller, the great thinker and writer from the intellectual heyday of Concord, Massachusetts. This book was everything to Anna. Completing it would establish her as America's preeminent scholar of Margaret Fuller. The rewards she would reap—magazine articles, lectures, textbook consultations, and more—would not make her wealthy, but they would give her the independence she craved.

Working together, she and Father could have finished the book within a year. It would have been done ages ago, in fact, had Anna's stepmother not thrown up so many roadblocks. Ignorant, possessive Clarissa resented how much time and energy Father devoted to his career, and particularly this project, which honored a woman whom Anna's late mother had idolized.

Anna had no idea how long it would take her to complete it on her own. The prospect had left her in a rather despondent state, which was exacerbated by an extremely unpleasant morning.

There was no time to wallow now, though. Anna had to get ready for the luncheon for Elizabeth's mother-in-law. When she entered her room, prepared to submit herself to the ministrations of Elizabeth's maid, however, Anna found she had company.

"Hello, Jules." Anna smiled, her spirits rising at the sight of her nearly five-year-old niece. Julia was lying in her favorite position—on her back on the floor, feet resting on the seat of Anna's desk chair—but her arms were crossed over her chest and her eyes narrowed.

"Hi, Anana," she grumbled, using the contraction for "Aunt Anna" she had invented when she was littler and not yet relinquished. "I am hiding."

"Have you been up to some sort of roguery?"

"No ro-gree!" Julia replied, indignant. "But everyone is cross."

"Everyone meaning William?"

"Everyone *everyone*. Even Rosemary."

"Well, that is something, then," Anna acknowledged. Unlike her ancient and short-tempered predecessor, whom Elizabeth had ejected in a rare show of defiance, Rosemary had the minimum requirements for the job of Julia's nurse: youthful vigor and endless patience.

Julia always ran instead of walked, and never on the ground if some higher avenue was available—a wall, a fence, and once, memorably, a cow. Anything that resembled a foothold she considered an invitation to climb. At two, she fell while scaling the bookcase in the library, bringing herself and several shelves of books down with her. (Unhurt, but afraid of a scold, she hid under a rug. Evidently she thought because it was flat, she would be, too, rather than the Julia-shaped lump that Elizabeth found when she heard the noise and came to investigate.)

More recently, Julia had developed a bad case of sticky fingers. Her older brother, William, was her most frequent victim. Yesterday he burst into Anna's room, where Julia was taking refuge, and demanded she return his fire truck. Julia disclaimed knowledge of its whereabouts, but she scampered out the door when William threatened to look in her room. Knowing she would retrieve the toy, put it under his bed, and claim he had merely misplaced it, he gave chase.

"Why do you have to be so freakish?" he yelled, as he raced down the hall after her. "You shouldn't play with fire trucks anyway!"

Despite her daring gymnastic feats and occasional petty theft, Julia was a true original, and quite the most popular member of the Demarest household.

"Shouldn't you be getting ready to see your grandmother?" Anna asked.

Julia's face darkened. "Why doesn't William have to go?"

"Because it's a ladies' event, and he is not a lady."

"I'm not a lady either!"

"Well, you're a female, and that's close enough. You need only to come in and greet your grandmother, and then you can be on your way."

"Grandmother Lillian will be cross, too." To some extent, Julia was just sticking to a theme she had warmed to—in this case, crossness—but Lillian *was* often cross with Julia.

"If you are worried your grandmother will be cross, perhaps it's time for . . ." Anna waited for Julia to finish the sentence.

"Princess Phronsie?"

Anna nodded. She and Julia had invented the game together. Anna came up with the story, while Julia had supplied the name. (Or, rather, the book *The Five Little Peppers* supplied the name. Phronsie was the baby of the Pepper family.)

Princess Phronsie knew that preparing to reign over a great kingdom required many daring adventures, but the people of the kingdom, including the king and queen, seemed not to understand this. They expected a princess to behave with perfect decorum. Her adventures, therefore, had to be kept secret. Publicly, she would display pristine manners.

The game was more fitting than Julia realized. The First Families of Boston, of which Lillian was a member by both birth and marriage, operated like an alliance of hereditary monarchies. Given the keen interest in the royal progeny, meddling grandparents were hardly unusual. And since Lillian was widowed after producing one son, Elizabeth's husband, Jerome, this household had the dubious pleasure of all her concentrated attention.

That said, Lillian's criticisms of Julia went well beyond the already excessive standards of the Boston Brahmins, and Anna had noted with some dismay that they were only intensifying with time.

Though Julia was irked at times by her grandmother, thus far she did not seem in the least intimidated by her. Anna would not wish it otherwise, but Lillian, who lacked the coercive power of an actual monarch, relied on fear and intimidation to get her way, so Julia's nonchalance only contributed to her agitation.

Anna adored her niece's independent spirit and mostly let Julia do what she wished within the confines of this room. And while Julia could not perfectly adhere to the Princess Phronsie program, it had helped her manage creditable demonstrations of etiquette during many encounters with her grandmother.

"Shall we try walking?"

Julia nodded and stood up straight. Eschewing the book they ordinarily used for such purposes, Anna placed a red felt slipper on Julia's head. Soon they were both laughing at Julia's attempts to move while keeping the rebellious object in place.

After this enjoyable interlude, Julia resumed her earlier position, on her back with her feet on the chair, just as Rosemary appeared, with Elizabeth's maid Millicent hovering behind her, prepared to make Anna presentable.

"Come, child," Rosemary said, holding out a hand. Julia arched her back for an upside-down assessment of the nurse's mood.

"I will come if you will not be cross," she said, a wary look in her eyes.

"I will be genial." Rosemary smiled. Julia groaned, got up, and let herself be led away. Forty-five minutes later, with Millicent's help, Anna was in her simple navy silk dress, with no adornments other than a small pearl bracelet.

Anna considered it fortunate that she was plain—medium height, with medium brown hair and an unremarkable complexion. Her only redeeming feature was a pair of large brown eyes ("speaking eyes," Mother had always called them). Anna did not doubt that Elizabeth was happy to have her, but four years in this house had taught her a good deal about the complex architecture of this family. She knew her continued welcome required blending into the woodwork.

An hour later, Anna sat at the long dining table, thinking about the final conversation she had with her mother.

"I hope the traditions live on," Mother had said. She was referring to the traditions of her own family—the Newbolds, from Concord, where she had grown up among the Emersons, Alcotts, and Ripleys. When Mother was little, her family even lived on the Transcendentalist commune, Brook Farm. She raised Elizabeth and Anna to revere simplicity, nature, and beauty, to reject materialism, and to believe that women deserved equal rights and opportunities.

"You will help Elizabeth, won't you?" Mother asked.

"Of course," Anna had promised. But now, surveying her sister's home—the blood-red silk walls, Gobelin tapestries, and the table adorned with silver bowls and Royal Worcester china—Anna reflected that she'd had no idea what she was signing up for.

Elizabeth sat at one end, with their vulgar, socially ambitious stepmother to her right. Clarissa's spot would normally belong to the guest of honor, but Lillian did not consider herself a guest in this house. Though Jerome had moved his mother to a fine house on Louisburg Square when he and Elizabeth were married, Lillian considered her son's residence to be an extension of her royal palace.

Lillian—silver-haired, stout, and haughty—was enthroned at the other end of the table, opposite Elizabeth, with her goddaughter, Judith Fairchild, to her right. Mrs. Fairchild had recently returned to Boston after a number of years abroad, and Anna had been observing her with a mix of apprehension and grudging respect for her audacity.

"Judith, dear, what do you hear from Emily?" Lillian asked, referring to the stepdaughter Judith had deposited at a Parisian boarding school before returning to America. (Unfortunately for Judith, Emily was thirteen, too old to be swaddled in blankets and left on the convent steps.)

"She is marvelous. I am so very glad she is with the Sisters at Sacré Coeur." Judith clasped her hands together and beamed at the ceiling, like a saint in a Renaissance painting. Though Reginald Fairchild had been dead for years, Judith still wore mourning, which lent her an air of devotion to her husband's memory that she certainly did not feel. (The blond, fair-skinned beauty likely also knew how well she looked in black.)

"I know some worry they make Papists out of their students, but there are many nice Protestant girls there," she continued. "Emily is growing up pure of heart, blossoming into a perfect specimen of Christian womanhood."

"And you credit her school with this?" asked Annette Patterson, one of Elizabeth's cleverer friends. Her face was the picture of innocence, but Anna knew what she left unsaid . . . *Or did this moral purity result from the vast ocean that separates you?*

"Oh, I do indeed. I must say, I fear for American girls. Mothers have become so consumed with the intellectual standards of their daughters' instructors, they fail to investigate their morals."

Touché. Annette Patterson's daughter, who had inherited her mother's cleverness, attended a demanding school far more focused on academics than moral training. Anna violently disagreed with Judith, but she could not help being impressed by the way she had made a virtue of her choice for her stepdaughter, and a vice of any other.

Meanwhile, Lillian looked on her goddaughter with unblemished fondness. Anna had long suspected that Lillian once hoped her son and Judith would make a match. When Jerome married Elizabeth instead, and Judith hastily attached herself to the widower Mr. Fairchild (richer than Croesus, with one foot in the grave), it suggested she had harbored the same hope.

A notorious flirt before her marriage, and a famous philanderess during, Mrs. Fairchild had left for Europe with her reputation in tatters. Now she was back, having artfully recast herself as an expert in "Christian mothering." Lillian recently rhapsodized about a pamphlet Judith had written on the topic and presented at the Chilton Club.

Anna had felt sorry for Mr. Fairchild, as she assumed he was the only man in Boston unaware of his wife's behavior. (Lillian Demarest was the only woman.) When he died, it emerged that, in fact, he had not been so blind. He had tied up all of his money in a trust for Emily and Henry, the son Judith had managed to produce before he died. To extract anything beyond her meager allowance required Judith to appeal to the trustee. Though no one was sure of the precise terms, the trust evidently contained provisions regarding his widow's moral conduct, which explained her recent transformation.

"I cannot comprehend all this ambition for our daughters," Mrs. Fairchild continued. "What more could a woman want than to preside over the household realm, to make her home a sanctuary, to fashion and mold the souls of their children? Why, civilization rests on our feminine shoulders!"

"Not all women marry, Mrs. Fairchild," Annette said, a touch of remonstrance in her voice. A few of the women glanced at Anna.

"Well, of course not, but there are vocations for such women," Lillian cut in. "Eugenia Lockwood, for example, is doing marvelous work at her settlement house. Elizabeth, you are volunteering there, are you not?"

"Yes, and she is indeed doing good work. In fact, my sister attended her conversation series this morning. I'm sorry I have not asked, Anna. How was it?"

"Quite interesting," Anna replied, resisting the temptation to throw her salad plate across the room.

Anna generally avoided Eugenia's "conversations," which were inspired by a similar series sponsored by Margaret Fuller fifty years ago. Anna's and Eugenia's late mothers grew up together in Concord, and Anna was irritated by Eugenia's proprietary attitude about all things relating to that town's rich history, particularly Margaret Fuller. Anna only went this morning because it was the one chance she had to see her friend Irma Bellingham, who was in town from New York.

The event started off well enough. Anna entered the sumptuously decorated Trustees Room at the public library, which Eugenia had secured through some connection. Looking around at the marble wainscotting and mantel, and the paintings of Charles I and Benjamin Franklin, she had the marvelous feeling of having invaded some masculine sanctum.

Irma waved her over, and Anna slid into the seat she had saved.

"It's like a gathering of Cee-Bees, but with gray hair and spectacles!" Irma whispered. Anna smiled at Irma's use of their old college term for the "career-bound." Girls at Radcliffe had been supportive of each other, regardless of whether they planned to marry or pursue a career. They faced enough hostility from the multitudes who disapproved of women attending college at all. That said, since career and marriage were mutually exclusive, except in the rarest circumstances, the girls who were firmly committed to pursuing a profession had shared a special bond.

Eugenia stood at the front of the room, looking, as always, like a cartoon bluestocking in her severe dark skirt, thick round glasses, and hair pulled back into a tight, no-nonsense bun. Anna had timed her arrival to coincide with the beginning of the meeting. Eugenia never failed to ask Anna about the Fuller biography (in a tone that would be appropriate for a thesis advisor speaking to a doctoral student), and she was too raw for unwanted questions.

Naturally, she got one anyway.

For the benefit of those attending for the first time, Eugenia briefly described Margaret Fuller's "Conversations" from the 1840s, then gestured to Anna.

"I see Miss Bradley is here. She and her father, Professor James Bradley, have been working on a biography of Margaret Fuller." She looked at Anna and added, "I heard your father is retiring. I hope he will see this through to completion."

Anna felt her face grow warm. "I'm certain he will continue to help." She figured it was true enough. After all, if she asked Father a question, Clarissa might at least permit him to answer it. Eugenia's brows came together, suggesting she was not satisfied with Anna's response, but she moved on.

As the session was coming to its close, Anna gestured to Irma that they should slip out immediately, but they were no match for Eugenia, who made a beeline for them.

"Anna, can I speak to you about the Fuller biography?"

"I'm afraid I must go, Eugenia. My sister is expecting me."

Eugenia ignored the rebuff. "You sounded uncertain about your father's involvement. The fiftieth anniversary of Fuller's death is two years away. I hope it will be finished by then."

Anna managed a smile and a mumbled "As do I," and she and Irma made their escape.

"That woman has the social instincts of a mountain goat," Irma said under her breath, as they walked down the grand staircase.

Anna saw Irma to her train and then walked home, with a literal dark cloud over her head. (That the cloud then opened up and drenched Anna struck her as an extremely overwrought metaphor.)

Meanwhile, Judith had turned the subject back to the virtues of convent life.

"Until she was old enough to go to Sacré Coeur, I made sure Emily was exposed to only the purest books. I was relieved to learn that the Sisters do not permit the girls to read anything, not even letters from their mothers, before they read them themselves."

"What do you think we should read to our little girls?" Serena Lawrence asked anxiously. "My Ruthie is nearly five." Serena, a contemporary of Anna's, was a great beauty and a bit feather-witted, but Anna had always liked her.

"You are right to ask, Mrs. Lawrence. It is astonishing what poison is being poured into our daughters' minds!"

Poured into their minds? Anna wondered. *How? Through their ears?*

"As it happens, I am writing a pamphlet on the subject, but in the meantime, I recommend Sophie May's books, *Little Prudy* in particular. When Emily was little, she found it utterly captivating."

Anna held back a laugh. Since Elizabeth was not much of a reader, Anna had slipped into the role of Julia's personal librarian. Lillian had given her granddaughter a copy of *Little Prudy*, and Julia was not in the least captivated by it. Moral instruction always made her wiggle, and while delivered with a lighter hand in *Little Prudy* than some books, the lessons in piety, virtue, and self-sacrifice were not subtle enough for Julia's sharp ear for didacticism.

"At least Prudy is naughty sometimes," Julia had conceded, though she considered the character's transgressions so minor, she found her penitent tears and prayers for forgiveness to be very tiresome.

"And when your Ruthie is a bit older, I naturally recommend Mrs. Howland's books," Judith said. Her smile hinted they should all understand her emphasis on "naturally," though Anna did not see why. Mrs. Howland's books were popular twenty or thirty years ago, but they were so pious they made *Little Prudy* seem racy and had fallen quite out of favor.

Reading had come easily to Julia, and her tastes were beginning to emerge. Unfortunately, she seemed most attracted to William's dime novels, the more elementary of which she could now tackle.

They were terrible dreck, but Anna understood why Julia liked them. Boys in books went on adventures, faced down dangers, while girls were depicted leading proscribed lives. *Why are they so excited about a stupid picnic?* Julia would ask.

Julia had also begun to pick up on some common themes. Last week, she sat on her bed in her nightdress while Anna read her a story. Suddenly, Julia slumped back onto her pillow, closed her eyes, and groaned.

"What is it?" Anna asked.

"Why are girls *always* reading at someone's sickbed!?"

Anna was growing tired of Judith's preening and Lillian's fawning, so she was relieved when Elizabeth announced it was time for dessert and led them from the dismal dining room into the gothic parlor, with its ponderous velvet sofas, gloomy oil paintings, and surfaces cluttered with gilded gewgaws.

On a round mahogany table stood a three-tiered cake, with pale yellow fondant and Lillian's initials at the center. After they all applauded the accomplishment of Lillian blowing out a single candle (Elizabeth knew better than to have the representative number), the guests moved to seat themselves about the room.

Clarissa followed Lillian so closely in an effort to claim a spot beside her, Anna wondered if the birthday girl could feel the breath on her neck. In the end, Lillian sat with a triumphant Clarissa to her left and Judith to her right.

Soon after the cake was served, Rosemary escorted Julia into the room. Lillian eyed the child closely, but fortunately, there was nothing in Julia's appearance to add evidence to the case she seemed constantly to be building against her. Julia, who had her mother's dark hair and blue eyes, looked tidy and pretty in a white cashmere dress with navy ribbons at the shoulders.

Julia approached Lillian, planted a kiss on the proffered cheek, and said, "Happy birthday, Grandmother Lillian, and many happy returns."

"Thank you, Julia."

"I like your gown. It's very beautiful!" Julia added. (Unlike most Boston Brahmin women, who were known for their thrift and lack of interest in fashion, Lillian was terribly vain. Anna always advised Julia to compliment her.)

"Very pretty of you, Julia," Lillian said, with a nod. Her approval was provisional, of course, but better than the alternative.

Julia moved on to greet Clarissa with a similar cordiality. She looked over Clarissa's ensemble, a rather hectic chiffon-and-silk affair in varying shades of green, with many frills and flounces.

"Your gown is so pretty, too, Grandmother Clarissa. Like a cucumber!" Fortunately, Julia's tastes were not well-developed, because her seemingly genuine admiration mitigated the effect of her words.

"Oh," Clarissa said primly.

Elizabeth had a good sense of humor, but her meticulous manners would never allow her to betray amusement in such circumstances, and she maintained an impassive expression. Other guests, however, were clearly struggling to contain laughter. Julia made her rounds, politely greeted the other women, and then bade them all adieu, with only a brief, longing glance at the cake in the corner of the room.

"Well," Clarissa sniffed, once Rosemary had escorted Julia out.

"Oh, don't be absurd, Clarissa," Lillian said. She turned and looked Clarissa up and down, then returned her attention to her cake, muttering, not quite under her breath, "She was not off, really."

Anna said a silent prayer of thanks that Julia had bestowed her wayward compliment on Clarissa. Elizabeth would have had an earful later had Julia's cucumber comment been directed at someone Lillian actually liked. She also could not help but enjoy seeing her stepmother get her comeuppance, even if it was at Lillian's hands.

If her life had depended on it, Clarissa could not have done a more thorough job of erasing all evidence of Anna's mother. Within a year of marrying Father, she had transformed their home in Cambridge, which had been simply decorated but warm and welcoming, into a bad imitation of the Borghese Palace. She persuaded Father to sell the little lakeside cottage in Western Massachusetts where Elizabeth and Anna spent all their childhood summers, and buy a "snug little property in Newport."

Worst of all was her interference in Elizabeth's relationship with her longtime sweetheart from the lake, Calvin Stannarius. They discovered Clarissa's deceit in rather dramatic circumstances, but by then, Elizabeth was married to Jerome Demarest, with a two-year-old son and Julia on the way.

Having finally cajoled Father into retirement, Clarissa had officially prevailed in her battle against all Anna's family had once held dear. So there was some consolation in Clarissa's failure to realize her other chief ambition: advancing herself in society through friendship with Lillian Demarest.

After the other guests left, Lillian and Judith lingered in the parlor. Anna glanced out the window and spotted Julia, who was supposed to be in her room, sitting in the tree in the corner of the backyard, talking over the fence to Katie, the servant girl next door.

It was unfortunate that Lillian chose that moment to approach the window and see if the rain had let up, as Julia was breaking several of her grandmother's cardinal rules by escaping the confines of her room, perching in a tree in a most unladylike fashion, and consorting with a person of "the lower orders."

Lillian spun around and glared at Elizabeth. "What is Julia doing out there?"

Anna would dearly love her sister to look out the window, smile innocently, and say, *It seems she has climbed the tree*, but as usual, she said nothing.

"Where is her nurse?" Lillian demanded.

"Rosemary went to pick up William at a friend's," Elizabeth replied. An instant later, they heard the front door close. "That must be them."

When Rosemary and William appeared at the door of the parlor, Lillian wagged a finger out the window and addressed Rosemary without preamble.

"The child is in the tree," she said sharply. After the nurse left to fetch Julia, Lillian scowled and said, "Why you have that Rosemary looking after Julia, I cannot fathom." (She always referred to her as "that Rosemary," as if it were a double name, like Mary Ellen.) "Mrs. Stith was vastly more qualified, and had a far firmer hand, which the child needs above all things."

Elizabeth virtually never stood up to Lillian. She had kept the house as a museum to Jerome's childhood, and allowed Lillian to behave as if she still owned it. (Lillian once pointed to a worn spot on one of the velvet sofas and said, "My man is coming to fix that next week"—the sort of attention one welcomes in a landlord, but not in a mother-in-law.)

Anna had been so proud of Elizabeth when she got rid of Mrs. Stith, whom Lillian had foisted upon her, but she soon learned her sister might not have taken a stand after all.

"But Father didn't like Mrs. Stith," William said, as he shoveled a bite of cake in his mouth.

"What's that?" Lillian spun around, evidently also surprised.

"He said she was an old sourpuss, and he didn't like having her around."

Lillian looked at Elizabeth, who merely shrugged, leaving her (and Anna) to wonder if Mrs. Stith would still be in residence, if not for Jerome's interference.

Judith, meanwhile, had been observing these proceedings from the settee with a look of keen interest. As Anna watched out of the corner of her eye, Judith deliberately softened her expression.

"I am sure you wonder why I go on and on about Emily's school, but I cannot say enough good about it." She spoke with saccharine sympathy, as if the "problem" with Julia was so self-evident, it made perfect sense to begin discussing the solution.

"The child is not five years old!" Anna said before she could stop herself. It was too infuriating. Prior to this infraction, which anyone but Lillian would consider barely worthy of comment, Judith's only experience of Julia Demarest had been the child's unimpeachable behavior a half hour earlier. Judith was a quick study, though. She had shrewdly perceived Lillian's fixation on breaking her granddaughter's spirit and decided to help.

"It's never too early to begin thinking about her future," Lillian remonstrated. "Especially for a child as willful as Julia."

Elizabeth flushed but said nothing.

Later, Anna lay on her bed, looking up at the ceiling.

Anna had promised herself she would only live with her sister as long as she felt useful and welcome. She knew she was useful, at least to Julia, but she had begun to worry about whether she was truly welcome.

Elizabeth had taken it as a given when Anna finished college four years ago that she would move in with her and Jerome. Unmarried women were expected to shelter with family. No siren song had called Anna to another city, and she had no bachelor brother who needed her to manage his affairs. She could not return to Cambridge. Thanks to Clarissa, living at home during college had been almost unendurable.

Anna also knew her sister would never treat her as the servile resident spinster, a trial that many of her unmarried friends had endured at the hands of their relations.

When Anna first moved in, however, Lillian had tried valiantly to force Anna into the role of obsequious poor relation. To Anna's great amusement, Elizabeth had unwittingly foiled her mother-in-law. Whenever Lillian remarked on Anna's good fortune to live with her son and daughter-in-law, Elizabeth invariably jumped in and said, with great earnestness, *Oh, no. I am the fortunate one. It is a great comfort to have my sister with me!* If Lillian tried to get Anna to run a little errand for her—*Oh, dear, I seem to have forgotten my scissors. Anna, would you mind . . . ?*—Elizabeth handled the task herself or called for a servant.

Elizabeth was exquisitely sensitive to Lillian. She simply had no frame of reference for what her mother-in-law was trying to accomplish. Their own mother had not taught them that unmarried women should live lives of grateful self-abnegation, and Elizabeth married so young, she never even contemplated spinsterhood.

That, however, had been a rare defeat. Lillian was desperate for her son's attention and deference, and to remain the central authority in this family.

Jerome was a man mostly concerned with his own comfort, and he was largely impervious to his mother's criticisms. That said, he reflexively deferred to his mother on domestic matters (*Oh, I daresay Mother's right . . .*), and Anna was definitely a domestic matter.

She rose and went to the stack of boxes that had been delivered from Father's office, which contained the sum of their research into Margaret Fuller. She opened one, noted the disarray, and felt like closing it again, but she knew she had to press forward.

If Lillian turned against Anna, Jerome would likely accede to her judgment, if only to stop her badgering, and there was no reason to believe that Elizabeth would put up a fight.

Anna needed to get on her own two feet, and soon.

CHAPTER THREE

March 1913

Washington, DC

JULIA

"I feel sorry for them," Victoria said, peering at the clams in the pot. "They live their whole lives in a shell, hiding under the sand, hoping nobody notices them, and now this."

"How's that different from being a girl?" Lucy grumbled. "Isn't everyone always telling us to stay at home and do nothing to attract notice?"

"We don't get boiled over fires, though," Victoria said.

Lucy nodded, though she privately thought Victoria was setting the mark a bit low.

From *Liberty Island*, by Miss Crane

Julia had her first moment of anxiety when she looked down from the Capitol steps. The suffrage parade was supposed to start in a few minutes, but spectators still swarmed Pennsylvania Avenue.

She and Louisa were staying with the Seabornes, and before they left the house, Michael's mother had given them a warning: "They were clever to plan the suffrage march on the eve of the inauguration, given the ready-made audience. But inaugurations are such spectacles, girls. The crowd will not be very respectable. Do be careful."

Julia promised, but she had not been worried. The police department had announced that they planned to assign more men to the suffrage parade than to President-Elect Wilson's actual inauguration. Perhaps they had, but the officers seemed awfully lackadaisical.

Louisa also looked concerned. "I can't make out what the policemen are doing. Whatever it is, they're not in much of a hurry to do it."

"I'm sure it will be fine," Mina said, but the glint in her eye was as much a sign of trouble as Louisa's wrinkled brow.

The start was delayed by almost a half hour, but the police eventually moved the crowd back, and finally, Julia, Mina, and Louisa were walking arm in arm down the broad avenue.

Julia felt a thrill at the pageantry. The floats were elegant, and the women, who had come from all over the country, representing so many different groups, were proud and dignified. It was marvelous to finally be taking some action.

Two years ago, Julia had taken up the fight to allow freshmen to join Barnard's Suffrage Club. She wrote an editorial for the *Barnard Bulletin*, arguing that it made no sense to create a barrier against women who were not just willing but actually yearning to stand arm in arm with other women, to immerse themselves in the cause.

When she circulated a petition, however, Mina refused to sign it. In addition to her usual excuse—*I'm not a joiner, Duchess*—she insisted it would be "all talk."

Julia's campaign succeeded, but while she'd never admit it to Mina, the meetings were a bit unsatisfying. She sensed that many of the club's members lived in fear of people recoiling in horror at their demands, and they spent much of their time crafting hypothetical responses.

Julia's father and brother were routinely horrified by women's desire for new freedoms, so she had developed some immunity against this particular fear. She never felt like she needed perfect arguments to counter their bluster. She would merely ask, *But why* shouldn't *women have equal rights?* Their inevitable pathetic stammering felt like a victory.

Parade organizers had warned the women that many spectators would be unsympathetic, and to expect some jeering. A large crowd, even if hostile, would bring lots of needed publicity, and as long as the spectators stayed behind the wire stanchion, they could even welcome the boos and hisses, knowing it was helping the cause.

But the spectators did not stay behind the wire stanchion.

Julia, Mina, and Louisa had made it a few blocks before progress began to stall, and a half a block later, they came to a complete halt. Julia could not see what impeded them, but word soon spread through the procession.

"The crowd broke through the barriers at Fourth Street," a woman ahead called back. "The police are making a wedge with motorcars to lead us through."

"What? That will be even worse for everyone in the back," Louisa said. "They have to get people behind the curb line again."

Julia agreed. The police acting as an ice cutter would only protect those at the head of the procession.

"Oh, this is an adventure!" Mina said, her eyes alight.

They began to move again, but sure enough, while those in the front followed safely behind the police escort, the crowd simply filled in behind them. As they neared Fourth Street, Julia could hear the din of shouting and jeering, and soon she saw hordes of men pouring onto the parade route from every direction.

What at first was a mass of people, a cacophony of voices, soon became individual men's angry faces and clear, furious insults. *Go home where you belong! Disgrace!*

Though they were surrounded, an instinct seemed to move telepathically through the women. *Keep moving forward. Maintain your dignity.* Somehow they pressed ahead, though very slowly, and while they previously had taken up the entire breadth of the wide avenue, now they had to walk in twos or threes.

It was afternoon on a broad thoroughfare, but it might as well have been three o'clock in the morning in one of the worst neighborhoods in Boston or New York. The rage, taunts, and sudden, uncertain movements of the crowd, along with the ubiquitous odor of alcohol, gave it the feel of a massive incipient barroom brawl.

Julia felt something hit her skirt and looked down to see tobacco juice. A mounted policeman nearby not only seemed disinclined to intervene on their behalf but looked downright amused. The only assistance came from Boy Scouts armed with batons. They tried valiantly to push the men back but were hopelessly outnumbered.

Julia raised her chin, tightened her grip on Mina's and Louisa's hands, determined to stick together and press on, but the crowd hemmed in tighter and tighter until Julia was forced to release Mina's hand.

The jostling, spitting, and jeering continued. Louisa's expression was resolute, her spine straight, but she was pale, and Julia felt a stab of worry. Louisa was so small, and she had never outgrown her sickly constitution. She ushered Louisa behind her and held tightly to her hand.

A moment later, someone knocked into them. Julia felt a yank, and Louisa was pulled away by the force of the crowd. She turned, her instinct to move forward overcome by the greater need to find her friend.

"Louisa!" Julia yelled. "LOUISA!"

Ignoring the menacing laughter and mocking faces, she stood on tiptoes, leaning one way and then another, trying to see over the wall of men. When she spotted a gap in the crowd, her heart seized, as a vision of Louisa trampled flashed through her mind.

Propelled by panic, she pushed her way back until she reached the edge of the open circle she had detected. At its center was Louisa, crumpled on the ground, blood pouring from a wound on her head.

"Oh, dear God." Julia fell to her knees by Louisa's side. Louisa groaned, and she felt a wave of relief. She looked up and scanned the faces to see if anyone looked helpful. The men had taken a few steps back—not out of common decency, she suspected, but rather to distance themselves from the catastrophe.

"Somebody, please get help!"

Julia shifted to sit mermaid style, lifted Louisa's head onto her lap, and gingerly brushed her hair aside to better see the wound. She knew head cuts bled a great deal, but this was gushing. Unsure if Louisa might have sustained other injuries, she dared not move her.

Julia removed the yellow scarf from around her neck and blotted at the wound, then looked up again, her anger boiling over.

"Why are you all just standing there?" she yelled. "Is there not one decent man among you who will go for help?"

Suddenly, Mina appeared, stopped dead in her tracks, and then looked around at the circle of men who were still gawping at them.

"You beasts! You . . . you *monsters*!" Mina yelled, as other women from the procession began crowding in. Julia sighed. This was so unhelpful.

"Mina, keep the girls moving. Tell them to look for help." At Mina's equivocal expression, Julia's exasperation overflowed. "Mina, please! Keep them MOVING!"

Finally, Mina began taking women by the arm, one by one, and leading them back to the procession. "Keep going, look for help," she repeated, over and over.

Louisa's eyes opened. She blinked at the sky, and then took in Julia's face.

"Keep going, Ju," she said weakly.

"You are such a goose," Julia said, stroking her head.

The Barnard group had been toward the rear of the procession, so the crowd mercifully began to thin out. Unfortunately, this also had the effect of making Julia and Louisa more visible. Seconds after Julia spotted a Red Cross van coming from one direction, she saw a photographer worming his way toward them from another.

She prayed the ambulance would get to them first, but they arrived at the same time. Two men jumped from the back of the van, and as they prepared to load Louisa onto a stretcher, the photographer raised his camera to take a picture.

"Please don't," Julia said.

"No, let him," Mina said. "People should see what these men have wrought."

"Don't show her face, then," Julia begged.

As she got into the ambulance with Louisa, Julia scolded herself for her stupidity. She had spent enough time with Michael's newspaper family to know that a photographer only cared about requests from one person: his editor.

Early that evening, Julia sat beside Louisa's bed with a feeling of unpleasant anticipation. Julia's brother had come to town for the inauguration, and the Seabornes had invited him and his fiancée, Pauline Powell, to dinner.

Julia had known she would not have a prayer of getting to know her future sister-in-law in William's domineering presence, so she had called on Pauline yesterday at her family's home in Alexandria, Virginia.

Louisa could tell Julia was not looking forward to the visit. "Give her a chance," she said.

"I promise I will"—Julia sighed—"though it's hard to imagine developing a fondness for anyone with judgment so dubious as to marry William Demarest."

"I'm just glad he found someone." Louisa was not blind to William's faults, but she had long believed he envied Julia's social ease, and she felt some sympathy for him. (If that was the case, Julia thought a good first step would be for him to stop being such a prig.)

William would never confide in Julia, but Boston was small enough for her to have learned that her brother had experienced a few romantic disappointments. He met Miss Powell through a Harvard friend who hailed from some ancient Virginia family, and reportedly pursued her with a single-mindedness that even Julia acknowledged sounded almost human.

Father had grudgingly said William's fiancée was a "pretty little thing." When Pauline opened the door to her family's townhome with a welcoming smile, Julia instantly saw the accuracy of his assessment. Miss Powell was just a few inches above five feet, with exquisite posture, glossy brown hair, and pleasant, even features.

Father had also said she was "poor as dirt, with a dozen younger siblings." Julia took this to be hyperbole, but noise from behind a pair of double doors off the hallway of their small house suggested the number might not be far off.

"Follow me, Miss Demarest. We will hide back here, where we might hear each other."

She led Julia to a library at the back of the house. It was tiny, just two chairs by a fireplace and a desk under a window that overlooked the back garden, but it had a cozy feel. Book-filled shelves lined three walls, a warm fire burned in the grate, and tea awaited on a little table.

"How many brothers and sisters do you have, Miss Powell?" Julia asked.

"I am the oldest of eight, though I know it sounds like twenty." She laughed, as she gestured for Julia to sit. "They are in a particularly pitched battle at present. Every few months, some cousins send us a big barrel with all their castoffs. We complain bitterly about the insult, but as soon as it arrives, we spend days in protracted arguments over the contents."

"I imagine it has been very hard since you lost your father." According to Father, the Powells, while socially prominent, had been left land-poor after the Civil War and never quite recovered. Their circumstances deteriorated further when Pauline's father died a few years ago.

"Yes, terribly. My mother is a darling, and I regret she is visiting my grandmother and not here to meet you, but I'm afraid she is dreadfully impractical. We must take in boarders, and she and I have grand rows." She smiled and added, "Mostly about butter."

"Butter?"

"Mother lets the boarders use as much as they wish. I get angry, seeing the great quantities left on their plates. Then Mother asks, 'When did you get to be such a Yankee?' And round and round we go."

Julia laughed. Before long, Miss Demarest and Miss Powell were Julia and Pauline. Julia admired Pauline's clarity, candor, and humorous perspective on her family, who, even in their penury, clung to their First Families of Virginia pride.

"I argued with my grandmother once about Charles Darwin's theories," Pauline said. "She insisted we cannot be descended from monkeys because we know for a fact we're descended from Charlemagne."

By the time Julia left an hour later, she quite liked her new relation-to-be, and the family's straitened circumstances helped her understand Pauline's decision to graft herself onto William.

Julia and Louisa were staying in the two-story ivy-covered cottage, which had once served as Margaret's studio, in the Seabornes' backyard. Julia stiffened when she heard the door, followed by footsteps ascending the stairs toward the bedroom.

William knocked, and when Louisa beckoned him in, he entered with his chest forward, his entire bearing even more insufferable than usual. Father had a thick brown mustache, while William was clean-shaven, but they otherwise looked much alike—tall, with broad shoulders, and impeccably combed dark hair, parted in the middle. Father carried it off better, though.

Pauline followed him into the room, but she went straight to the bedside, quietly introduced herself to Louisa, and spoke to her with the ease and sympathy of one accustomed to attending to younger siblings.

"May I speak with you alone, Julia?" William said, his voice barely controlled.

"Well, hello, William. Lovely to see you, too," Julia replied, but she followed him out to the staircase landing, where William handed her a copy of the afternoon paper. It was folded back to reveal a picture of Louisa, eyes half closed, head wrapped in Julia's bloodstained scarf. In addition to ignoring her request to keep Louisa's face out of the picture, the photographer evidently had raced to a darkroom to develop it.

"You allowed Louisa to become a spectacle. And what were you thinking, putting her in such danger? Mother will be furious."

Louisa's voice came through the door: "Don't fix this on Julia, William. I chose to go!"

"And why should we have anticipated danger?" Julia unfolded the newspaper, scanned the page, and then pointed to another headline. "Look at the criticism being heaped on the police for failing to provide the protection they promised! *Reasonable* people blame them, not the peaceable women who behaved with dignity and restraint in the face of a marauding band of horrible men."

"You should not have been consorting with those people," William huffed.

Julia put a hand to her chest and adopted a scandalized expression. "Why, William, are you suggesting we were *consorting* with those horrible men?"

"I was not referring to the *men*, Julia," he said, impatiently.

"Oh, so by 'those people,' you meant women who believe they should have the right to represent their own interests in this country?"

"No, I meant socialists and radicals, but I see there is no talking sense into you." William turned and went back downstairs, leaving his fiancée behind. Julia took a deep breath, then returned to the bedroom. Pauline, still by Louisa's bed, seemed quite calm.

"I am sorry you had to hear that, Pauline."

"Perhaps he is overwrought, thinking what might have happened to you."

"Perhaps," Julia said. William probably would not have cared if Julia had been trampled by the crowd, but no one wanted to believe that a brother and sister shared no bond of affection.

"For what it's worth, I think you're very brave, marching as you did today and speaking your mind so freely," Pauline said.

Julia looked at Pauline, a question in her eye. "Do you not, Pauline? Speak your mind, I mean."

Pauline paused and looked out the window. "Sometimes I wish I could," she said finally.

"What stops you?"

"Oh, everything . . ."

Louisa shot her a warning look, but Julia had no intention of pressing Pauline on the matter. It was not hard to fill in the blanks.

"I heard you and William went to Newport," Louisa said, kindly changing the subject.

"Yes. I met William and Julia's grandmother there," Pauline replied. "I suspect I made very little impression on her."

"I'm sure that's not true, Pauline," Julia said.

"You mean to console me, I know," she replied, with the hint of an impish smile. "Rest assured, there is no need. It was my dearest wish to make as little impression as possible."

Julia laughed. "Pauline, you are very clever. It is also one of my chief ambitions to ensure that my grandmother takes as little notice of me as possible." When she was little, Lillian was forever trying to mend Julia's ways. *Never say, "You bet." This isn't a saloon . . . Comb your hair. You look as if a gale was blowing . . . You'll never get a husband if you don't put on better looks . . .*

Julia doubted she had ever spent more than ten minutes with her grandmother without hearing her abbreviated "ugh," paired with a minute shake of her head.

Pauline had to marry someone eligible, and William certainly qualified. As horrifying as it was that she would have to mold herself to William's wishes, if nothing else, it reminded Julia of why they had marched today.

Margaret called in her own physician, who said Louisa must rest another day before returning to New York. A lifetime of indifferent health had taught Louisa to take things as they came, but she seemed worried. Louisa's scholarship required her to be "straight as the roads of Kildare," as she always put it. Missing class for illness was one thing, but this injury had resulted from her choice to attend a march of which many faculty members disapproved.

Of all people, it was Mina who put her mind at ease. She came by the studio the next morning with flowers, and handed Louisa a newspaper. "Nice words from your dean in there."

The Teachers College dean was quoted in the story as deprecating the violence at the march, and expressing pride in his student Louisa Murphy and his hopes for her full recovery. Louisa was relieved, and Julia was glad her friend had a glimpse of Mina behaving with normal human sympathy.

Julia, meanwhile, was to enjoy the unexpected pleasure of a day with Margaret Seaborne. She did feel some compunction about this, however. Though Woodrow Wilson had eschewed the usual inaugural balls, considering them too frivolous for such a solemn occasion, the ceremony itself would be attended by the usual pageantry. Mr. Seaborne was not only a prominent newspaper publisher but also a graduate of Princeton, like the incoming president, and would likely enjoy the royal treatment.

"Margaret, I feel guilty that I am keeping you from the festivities today," Julia said, when she joined the Seabornes at their breakfast table, having left Louisa to rest.

Robert Seaborne looked out from behind his paper and chuckled. "As regrettable as the circumstances are, they have provided my wife with an excuse, and a noble one, at that, to skip events she had no desire to attend."

"Well, I will miss being with you, darling," Margaret said, filling Julia's coffee cup.

"A very pretty piece of perjury, my dear." Robert smiled at Margaret affectionately.

At first glance, Robert and Margaret Seaborne looked oddly matched. Margaret, in a plain green dress, dark hair falling from a braided coil, still looked like the professional artist she had been. Robert, silver-haired and distinguished, looked as if he had never met an artist in his life. They were obviously smitten with each other, though.

Julia's and Michael's families got together every few years, but it was almost always in summertime, either on Haven Point or at the house the Seabornes owned on Gibson Island in Maryland. Julia had not been to their home in Washington for many years and had forgotten how perfectly it reflected Margaret's earthy charm. It was spacious, but not overly grand, with an eclectic collection of art and a hodgepodge of furniture that somehow harmonized.

When Margaret led her to a little sitting room at the back of the house, Julia noticed framed prints of two *Liberty Island* illustrations on the wall.

"Louisa and I love these!" Julia smiled at them fondly.

"Mr. Carruthers" showed Lucy, the character loosely based on Julia, standing on a bluff in too-large fishing boots and waders. She was wagging her finger at a harbor seal, basking on the ledge below, haughtily impervious to her scolding.

Though many *Liberty Island* stories sprang from Anna's capacious imagination, Julia and her friends actually *had* known a seal on Liberty Island, old and rotund, with silvery gray fur and white whiskers. Julia had named him Mr. Carruthers, after Father's banker, to whom he bore a striking resemblance.

The other illustration was of the four girls lying on their backs under the night sky, heads together, so they formed a plus sign. Lucy was pointing at a star.

"They're my favorites," Margaret said.

"I know Anna got you to come out of retirement to work on *Liberty Island*. How did she convince you? By my math, you had four little boys when the first book was published."

"Well, as you know, the stories were serialized first, then bound and sold as a novel. All Anna had to do was send me the manuscript, along with the magazine containing the first installation. I was so indignant by the poor job their illustrator did, I dashed off a letter instantly, telling her I would take the commission."

"What made them so awful?" Julia asked, intrigued. She had seen the serialized versions, but other than noting that the book's illustrations were far better, she had not paid much attention.

"The girls might have been plucked from some sentimental Victorian tale. Rosy cheeks, tidy pinafores, big ribbons in neatly combed hair. In every picture, they appeared either frightened or contrite. Although always with perfect posture."

Julia laughed. "Inaccurate, to the extent *Liberty Island* was drawn from reality. We ran around like savages and slumped like old miners. Did Robert mind your taking the job?"

"He was not terribly pleased that I accepted without even consulting him." Margaret smiled ruefully. "But I told him I owed it to your grandmother's memory to do the story justice."

Julia sighed. "I wish I had known my grandmother."

"I wish you had, too. Winifred Newbold was so intelligent and creative, and so very kind. Though I was far younger, she had no idea of the usual stratifications. I took terrible advantage and followed her around like a puppy."

Eventually, the conversation turned to Julia's plans for after college.

"I'll probably teach," Julia said. She had discovered no other grand ambition, and it was not difficult for Barnard graduates to get teaching jobs. Besides, Julia not only loved children but felt she understood them. Though most of Julia's teachers had tried to tamp down her imagination and exuberance, she had as models the rare few who actually appreciated these qualities and knew how to channel them.

"Will you return to Boston?"

Julia raised an eyebrow, and Margaret smiled.

Julia knew Margaret could not say much, lest she find herself crosswise of Julia's parents. Father, at least, expected Julia to return home after graduation. Why would she ever live anywhere else? However, like Anna, who helped Julia navigate to Barnard without ever explicitly acknowledging that the goal was to get Julia out of Boston, Margaret likely understood that if Julia returned to her hometown, the powerful undertow of Boston society would pull her inexorably into its current.

"Would you like to stay in New York?"

Julia paused, thinking. "I love a lot about it. The energy, how much there is to do. And I've met such interesting people."

She told Margaret about all the smart young thinkers she had met through Mina. (However tiresome Mina's theatrics and attention-seeking could be, she had been generous in taking Julia to gatherings and making introductions.)

She described some of their adventures in Greenwich Village, where all the young artists and writers seemed to be moving. Julia was enchanted by the neighborhood, with its shabby brownstones, and the way the predictable grid system vanished as soon as one entered the district. It was as if the streets themselves had rebelled, dodging and weaving until planners threw up their hands and left them to their anarchic ways.

"All that said, as a student, I always have Morningside Heights to return to. The thought of a cramped apartment on a busy, treeless street fills me with dread. I want to *want* to live there, but I confess I don't."

"I felt the same, actually. Washington wound up being a good compromise, a busy city that felt more *expansive* somehow. It's the height restrictions and broad avenues, I think."

Julia nodded. "In New York, breezes have an artificial, almost menacing quality, as if the tall buildings compelled them to gather and charge down the streets."

"Given all that, I wonder why you'd even consider living in New York?" Margaret said. It was so like her to get straight to the nub of things.

"I suppose it's because people I admire . . ." Julia began, then hesitated.

". . . cannot understand living anywhere else?" Margaret smiled. When Julia nodded, Margaret leaned forward. "It's a good thing you've always gone your own way, then, isn't it?"

The next day, while Louisa slept, Julia looked out the window of the parlor car as the train sped past factories and muddy fields, and reflected on the events of the past few days. Julia had always sensed that her mother and aunt found it hard to speak of their own mother. She understood why it was a painful subject. Far too soon after she died, their father had married Clarissa, a perfectly dreadful woman.

Though she was glad to have learned more about Winifred Newbold, the conversation with Margaret left Julia feeling wistful. Disappointed, even.

A memory floated into her mind, from Mina's visit to Haven Point the summer after their freshman year. It was during a terrible heat wave, when everyone who could do so had headed for the coast, like animals escaping a forest fire.

Julia had expected her friend to behave shockingly. Not that she minded—the prospect afforded her some perverse pleasure. Her greater concern was how Mina would react to Haven Point. Would she pick up a whiff of what she always called the "stale air of gentility"?

Julia also wondered what Mina would make of her friends Maudie and Ruthie. Mina had lost touch with her own childhood friends. She said she no longer had anything in common with them, "now that they're setting up their little households." Meanwhile, Maudie was already engaged to John Franklin, her longtime boyfriend, and Ruthie was seeing the very eligible Vernon Scott. Ruthie's mother, like Julia's, had married after her first debutante season, and Julia expected her friend to follow suit.

As it happened, while Mina did not dress or act in a conventional fashion, she behaved with relative propriety. She would never be particularly ingratiating, but she was perfectly pleasant to Julia's family and friends.

She even managed to charm William and Father. Upon learning that Mina worked at *The Current*, William had sniffed and said, "Isn't that a socialist rag?"

"Terribly!" Mina replied, eyes wide, as if it was only upon working there that she learned the magazine's editorial stance. "But the place is so dreadfully chaotic, I suspect we have little to fear from the socialists!"

Julia had felt some anticipatory embarrassment about Fourwinds, their house on Haven Point, which she considered far too large, but Mina had nothing but compliments. She was charmed by the stone foundation and gray shingles, the asymmetrical rooflines and differently shaped windows. "It looks like it popped out of the ground and grew whichever way it liked!"

The one sticky moment came after Julia introduced Mina to Anna.

"Your aunt is fascinating," Mina said. "She seems so different from your mother. Isn't theirs the side of the family that came from Concord?"

"Yes. Anna was the scholar of the family, and Mother the athlete," Julia had replied. She tried to keep the defensiveness out of her tone, though evidently without success.

"I don't mean to insult your mother, Julia. She's lovely!" Mina said.

In truth, Mina had only put words to something Julia herself had noticed. Julia did not see in her mother a hint of the freethinking Concord spirit that Margaret had described in Julia's grandmother.

It was hard for Julia not to feel robbed. As much as she loved being around Mina's irreverent, creative, forward-thinking friends, it felt like a club she could only visit on a guest card. No previously undiscovered artistic or literary ability had announced itself during Julia's years at Barnard, and she had neither the audacity nor genius for making oneself indispensable that had given Mina full membership.

Though Julia had not told Margaret as much, another reason she resisted staying in New York after graduation was her sense that she would never really belong. Her connection to Concord might have been an asset, given the admiration that many modern thinkers had for their nineteenth-century counterparts in Concord. Pelham Stewart (whom Julia still had not met!) had mentioned both Emerson and Thoreau in articles he wrote.

That, however, would have required Julia's mother passing along that legacy. Instead, Father spotted Mother on a tennis court, and reputedly fell in love on the spot. They were married a few months later. By all appearances, Mother had molded herself to the tastes and wishes of Julia's other grandmother, a typical wealthy and narrow-minded Boston matron.

Like those British aristocrats who had to close off wings of the ancestral home, Mother had sealed off her Concord roots. It was hard not to wonder what it might have been like if she had kept those doors open, allowed Julia to explore the old rooms.

Julia was so lost in thought, she was surprised when she heard Louisa's voice.

"What are you fretting yourself about?" she asked sleepily.

Louisa's loyalty to Julia's family was so firm, Julia knew she would not understand all she had been pondering, so she stuck to one reflection.

"I was just thinking about my parents," Julia said. "Father saw

Mother on a tennis court and fell in love. It seems like so little to build a lifetime on."

Louisa shrugged. "Mr. Sweeney down the street married his wife because she made good doughnuts. They were married fifty years."

Julia laughed out loud. "What would I do without you, Louisa?"

CHAPTER FOUR

July 1898

Boston, Massachusetts, and Haven Point, Maine

ANNA

Anna sat in the conversation room at the Athenaeum Library, though she was not "in conversation" in any normal sense of the word. She was, rather, listening to Mr. Thatcher Winslow Wimborne, a foppish man of about fifty, as he talked perfect nonsense in his nasal, upper-crust New England accent.

"I believe there are many hidden Oriental influences in Boston architecture, and we shall begin by checking the curve of various banisters. I am persuaded there are also pagodas hidden in some gardens."

So she was now to peer over garden walls? Anna would not be surprised. At this point, nothing this preposterous fellow suggested would surprise her.

And I thought I was so clever, too, Anna thought ruefully. Weeks organizing the Margaret Fuller materials had taught her that she would not earn a dime from this project for years, and she would not even see that unless she could figure out a way to access resources that were not available at the public library.

When she saw the advertisement for a research assistant to an amateur historian, it seemed like the perfect solution. The Athenaeum

Library was so close to home, and while nonmembers could not check books out (and virtually no women were members), with Mr. Wimborne's sponsorship, Anna would be permitted to review materials while she was on the premises.

Mr. Wimborne, however, had been evasive on the subject of sponsorship, and Anna had spent her time chasing one absurd idea after another—ships' figureheads, tea chests, signal flags, and whatever whim bounced into the silly man's disorderly mind—all vaguely related to his revered ancestors' involvement in the China trade.

Worst of all, she had yet to be paid. Anna would soon decamp to Maine with her sister's family, and she was determined to extract her payment before they left. She waited until his incoherent lecture was finished, and they were packing up their notes.

"Mr. Wimborne, you said that you would have my check this week."

"Oh, come now. Why are you so eager for money?" he said, in the sort of teasing tone one might use with a six-year-old, before gently chucking her on the chin.

"I am eager to be paid for my work, per our agreement," Anna said firmly.

"But you live quite comfortably with your sister. Lots of women who do not need the money are willing to donate time to an interesting project."

"Where I live has no bearing on the matter," Anna said, trying to keep the anger from her voice (and refraining from pointing out that, while bizarre, the work was not at all interesting).

Mr. Wimborne looked unmoved. Anna, her frustration increasing, added, "As it happens, I do need the money."

"Whatever for?" Mr. Wimborne stopped putting his things away and looked at her, curious to hear the answer to what he seemed to believe was a perfectly legitimate question.

"If you must know," Anna replied, her tone hinting that she did not actually believe he "must" know anything at all, "I need to buy my stepmother a birthday present."

His eyes lit up. "Oh? Does your stepmother have good taste?"

Anna's anger bubbled over. "No! It's appalling," she snapped. "She recently added a 'Turkish corner' to the parlor of my childhood home. Perhaps you should meet her, Mr. Wimborne. She insists she has a great passion for the Oriental."

Anna regretted it instantly. She was prepared to give this job up today if she was not paid, but she meant to do so with professionalism and dignity, not intemperate sarcasm.

Mr. Wimborne, far from affronted, threw back his head and laughed. "Well, then, I know the perfect place! It's just around the corner." Noticing her hesitation, he said, "You will get your money, and I will pony up for the gift, too. Come along, girl."

Anna was speechless, but she supposed if jumping through this hoop would get her paid, then jump she would. She sighed and followed him into the hallway.

To her dismay, as they were heading to the door, she saw Mr. Harley Lockwood, Eugenia's older brother, at the receiving desk. Anna had always been baffled by Eugenia's worshipful attitude toward her older brother. He was in the popular crowd at Harvard, and seemed like a typical frivolous, football-playing prankster.

Of more contemporary interest, while Anna was not certain of the exact nature of it, she knew he had been romantically involved with Lillian's goddaughter, Judith Fairchild. For all she knew, he still was. Anna had not only heard their names whispered together, but had also seen the two of them with her own eyes.

It was on the last night of Anna's (long, painful) debut season. Clarissa had pressured Mr. Lockwood into signing Anna's dance card. When the band struck up the first notes of the dance, however, Mr. Lockwood was nowhere to be found.

Anna had slipped out of the ballroom, afraid Clarissa would embarrass her by hunting the man down. As she headed for the sitting-out room, she detected motion in the foyer. She peered around a pillar and spotted Mrs. Fairchild clinging to Mr. Lockwood's arm, staring up at him in a *we are so star-crossed* manner. Mr. Fairchild had only just died, so Judith merely being out of her home was a shocking transgression, never mind this scene.

Now, as they passed the receiving desk, Mr. Lockwood looked up. His eyes took in Mr. Wimborne, then traveled to Anna. Clearly surprised, he quirked an eyebrow. Anna lifted her chin and ignored him.

They had just reached the vestibule when Mr. Wimborne realized he'd forgotten his umbrella. While he was inside fetching it, Mr. Lockwood came out, holding several books under his arm.

"Hello, Miss Bradley." He nodded.

"Mr. Lockwood." She nodded back.

"Wimborne just told me you were working for him. He called you his 'library girl.'" He uttered the last two words with obvious disdain.

For the second time in twenty minutes, Anna felt herself on the precipice of losing the reins of her tongue. Before she could issue a sharp retort, reminding Mr. Lockwood that being choosy about professional opportunities was a luxury women could hardly afford, Mr. Wimborne appeared at the door.

"Come along, dear," he said, taking Anna's arm and leading her to the door. "Good day, Mr. Lockwood."

An hour later, Anna was back at Elizabeth's house, looking at the brass samovar that Mr. Wimborne had unearthed at a shabby little shop two blocks from the Athenaeum. It was a perfectly hideous specimen that Clarissa would love. True to his word, Mr. Wimborne had purchased it, with great good cheer, and had paid her for her work.

He had also given Anna a gratifying little tidbit.

"So, you know Lockwood, do you?" he asked, as they walked down Tremont Street. Anna replied that she did, and that their mothers had grown up together in Concord.

"Fine fellow, but I do feel some pity. What a coil, that situation with Mrs. Fairchild!" he said.

Mr. Wimborne was maddening and ridiculous, but his attitude toward Anna had been almost fatherly, so she was a bit taken aback by his mentioning the scandal.

Of course society had obviously deemed Mr. Lockwood and Mrs. Fairchild fair game for gossip, as evidenced by the fact that even Anna, who was not at all social, had heard the names linked.

"A coil indeed," Anna said calmly, as if she were conversant in the subject. She was curious to know if Mr. Wimborne was referring to something past or current.

"Well, Mrs. Fairchild is a persistent little somebody," he said. "And she certainly has her wiles."

Present tense, Anna thought.

For some reason, she felt vaguely disappointed.

Two weeks later, Anna sat on the deck of a massive yacht, anchored in Haven Point's small harbor.

Mr. Sears patted the arms of his rattan deck chair. "We thought Bertie had the right idea about painting these white," he said, as if he and the Prince of Wales were great chums. "Nice effect, don't you agree?"

They all nodded politely. Rhinelander Sears, Ambrose Lawrence's cousin, and his wife, Vesta, had stopped on their way from Bar Harbor to Newport, and Anna was one of a group who had been invited to tour the vessel. Mr. Sears had highlighted its many virtues—electric lighting, a grand piano, an auxiliary steam engine, and an array of additional features Anna could not recall, as she had lost interest at the very start. (The tour began with a lengthy explanation of how they'd achieved the bright whiteness of the sails—*something, boiling repeatedly, something else*—which Anna felt any reasonable person would agree was empirically boring.)

That said, she could not help picking up a peculiar obsession with the various species of wood used throughout the interior. *Different in every room! Black walnut in the library! Oak in the family salon!* When they entered the dining room, Nora Graham leaned toward Anna and, with a look of feigned curiosity, whispered, "What sort of wood, do you suppose?"

Not thirty seconds later, Mr. Sears gestured grandly at the walls.

"Hand-carved East India mahogany!" Anna and Nora assiduously avoided eye contact.

"So, how's this little experiment of yours going, Amby?" Rhinelander asked, a mocking edge to his tone, as he waved a hand toward Haven Point.

"Quite well," Ambrose replied stiffly.

"I heard Penrose and Williams had to pull out."

"The panic, you know. We still have a number of the most select families purchasing lots."

The most select families. Anna groaned inwardly. Such comments were unhelpful in the extreme, especially when George Graham had worked so hard to avoid such an outcome.

As wonderful as the past few summers had been, Anna was beginning to wonder if they were a flash in the pan.

Eight years ago, Anna had sat in the ornate dining room of the Demarests' house in Newport, keenly feeling the loss of the lakeside cottage that Clarissa had tolerated (barely) for one summer before insisting Father sell it. They had just been served their soup when Jerome mentioned that he was considering building a house in Ambrose Lawrence's new summer colony in Maine.

Lillian looked frantic. "Why would you go up to that wilderness?" she sputtered. "What is wrong with Newport?"

"What's wrong with Newport?" Jerome scoffed. "Have you not noticed the crowds? Nouveau strivers coming in the windows. You can't even get a tennis court!"

Oblivious as always to the effect he had on his mother, Jerome looked up thoughtfully, spoon suspended between bowl and lips. "I think Ambrose is going about it the right way. No hotel means no riffraff. From the start, it will be populated with the right sort."

Earlier that summer, George Graham, a friend of Jerome and Ambrose's from Harvard, had invited a group of college friends and their wives to Maine. It was meant to be a swan song of sorts. For more than a century, the Graham family had owned Haven Point, a peninsula on

Maine's Casco Bay. After countless offers from speculators interested in purchasing the land for a hotel, they had finally decided to sell.

As it happened, Ambrose, also tired of the crowds in Newport, had been touring other spots in New England in search of an alternative, but nothing had appealed to him. "Too much new money," he said. According to his diagnosis, the problem was that the genesis of most summer colonies was a hotel. ("And anyone can go to a hotel!") The cottage lots and communities were an afterthought.

Ambrose had hit upon the idea of building a community from scratch and had just begun searching for land when they all descended on Haven Point. He took one look and made the Grahams an offer on the spot. George and his family would keep their house and a large piece of land around it. Ambrose hired a surveyor to carve up the other plots, as well as a lawyer to handle the legal niceties, and became Haven Point's unofficial mayor and pitchman.

Jerome, ignoring his mother's almost histrionic reaction, had been one of the first to purchase a lot. He hired an architect and builder, and two summers later, Anna paid her first visit.

"I think you will like it, Anna," Elizabeth had said. "It might even remind you of the lake."

Anna was skeptical. Ambrose Lawrence was awfully starchy, and his rationale for the project suggested Haven Point would be another Newport, only smaller and gossipier. Her first impression when she arrived at the steamship landing was not favorable.

She had looked up at the enormous houses glaring down at her, listened to the screech of seagulls and almost violent sound of the waves hurling themselves against the granite cliff, and wondered how Elizabeth ever thought this place was anything like the lake. There, nature had whispered and crept. Here, it roared and rampaged.

On a map, Haven Point looked as if it had tried to tear itself from the north shore of Casco Bay but was held fast by a spit of land on the northern part of the peninsula. From this tenuous connection, it gradually sloped upward until it reached the high cliffs on the southern edge.

Fourwinds, Elizabeth and Jerome's house, stood on an irregular outcropping on the southwestern part of the peninsula, affording views east into the Atlantic, and south and west into the island-studded bay.

Though it was hard to get past Fourwinds's sheer scale, Anna did soften a bit upon seeing the shingle-sheathed house with its quirky rooflines and windows, a sign that Elizabeth and Jerome had at least departed from the extravagant architecture of Newport houses. Inside, the first floor was dominated by one large room that stretched almost the entire length of the house, with a wall of windows facing the ocean. Large stone fireplaces and comfortable seating anchored the ends, and a long dining table was in the middle.

Anna was also touched that Elizabeth had used much of the furniture from their lake house. Her favorite old hickory rocker was on the south porch, and she spotted other pieces throughout—drop-leaf tables, several of Mother's paintings, and a brass bed frame.

Houses that blended into the landscape were very much in fashion, though, so it did not necessarily say anything about the broader community. It was that evening when Anna truly began to feel that they had gotten lucky.

As it was a weeknight, Jerome and the other Boston husbands were away. George Graham, however, was an attorney in Portland, and he and Nora had invited them for dinner. On the way, Elizabeth pointed out cottages that had been built on the interior of the peninsula, and explained that George had persuaded Ambrose to carve out these smaller lots, promising that he knew plenty of wonderful families who would snatch them up. This proved true. A dozen houses had already been built, and more lots had been sold.

"George Graham sounds like a good counterbalance to Ambrose," Anna had commented.

"Indeed," Elizabeth chuckled. "Ambrose wants to change the name from Haven Point. George agreed, but he wanted to have a say in the matter. Ambrose keeps proposing outlandishly pretentious names, and George counters with the most commonplace thing he can think of."

Nora Graham greeted them at her door, and Anna liked her on

sight. Everything about Nora, from appearance to personality, seemed wonderfully proportional. She was a little taller than Anna, sturdy but not stout, with thick brown hair and fine, even features.

There was nothing miserly or withholding in Nora's interactions—she smiled when amused and unostentatiously attended to her guests' needs. In conversation, she directed her hazel eyes at whoever was speaking, responding with sympathy where appropriate. She seemed sensible, steady, and immune to excess.

George Graham was the more expressive of the pair. He often poked fun at himself and good-naturedly teased his wife, whose eyes twinkled, even when she rolled them at his raillery.

The rest of the company, mostly George and Nora's friends from Maine and New Hampshire, were intelligent and genial. The women's skirts and shirtwaists were well-made, but had minimal trimmings, and their hair was simply arranged. When Anna asked what she should wear, Elizabeth had said the women agreed they deserved a break during the summer.

"Everyone loosens their corsets here."

Like Elizabeth, Serena Lawrence was spending the summer on Haven Point, while Ambrose went back and forth. Serena, as always, was dressed to the nines, but she seemed comfortable with the other women, and they with her.

After dinner, the women moved to the living room, and the conversation naturally turned to children. Serena was a new and nervous mother, and Anna immediately saw how much she depended on the wisdom of Nora Graham, who had two children already.

"When Amory sleeps, he sometimes pulls his lower lip in," Serena said, her brow wrinkled in worry. "I read babies do that when they are suffering from abdominal pain."

"That might be. If it's serious, though, I suspect he would also let you know when he's awake."

Anna thought it was kind of Nora to give the appearance of earnestly considering the theory (which she likely believed had no merit at all), and Serena seemed relieved by the indulgent response.

Later, at the request of one of their guests, George got his fiddle and played, while Nora sang "Annie Laurie" and "Comin' thro' the Rye." Anna was struck by Nora's sweet, clear contralto, and by her and George's modesty when everyone praised their performance. They seemed to see their talents as something to be shared and enjoyed, but which they had not earned. It was so unlike Jerome and his friends, who were determined to view their accomplishments as the result of ferocious effort.

Anna soon learned that this had been a typical evening event. They had simple dinners, played cards or games, and sang songs. Days were filled with lawn tennis, sailing, or gathering with their children on the beach. She began to feel that Haven Point was a place where they might be able to heed their mother's exhortation to keep the old traditions alive, and she was grateful that Jerome and Ambrose had broken with Newport and committed to this quieter, wilder landscape.

The financial panic had put a pause on development, though, and Ambrose had grown anxious about selling the remaining lots. His concern was not the financial investment—he had more money than he could spend in two lifetimes—but, rather, the massive investment of his ego.

Rhinelander could not have hit his mark better than by mentioning Leighton Penrose and Bud Williams. The two men, brothers-in-law, had to pull out while their houses were still under construction. The unfinished homes were on the east side of the point, visible to all who sailed by on their way to the more established summer communities to the north.

Ambrose had been in a frenzy, courting wealthy friends and acquaintances, among them Rhinelander and Vesta, who were supposedly interested in building a house—in addition to their Newport cottage, of course.

After lunch, Vesta talked over the idea with Elizabeth, Serena, and Anna.

"I suppose it might be fun, rusticating. Far from the madding crowd and all that," Vesta said, with a wave of her hand. "The land is so cheap. We could have a big house party, give our friends a taste of wilderness."

She turned to Serena. "I wonder that you and Ambrose did not keep your Newport cottage. I would feel so bereft of society if I had to be here all summer."

"Oh, but I'm so fond of the people here!" Serena said. Anna knew she meant it, but she picked up a hint of uncertainty. Women like Vesta always flummoxed Serena.

"I am sure they're nice, but I would worry that I was robbing my children of the opportunity to get along in society." Vesta turned to Elizabeth. "I understand your little William will be making a long visit to his grandmother in Newport. Very wise."

"Yes, he is going," Elizabeth said. Lillian would arrive that afternoon, and would take William with her when she departed. Anna was glad her sister responded only to that fact, and ignored the supposed wisdom of it.

Vesta cocked her head, as if an idea had just come to her. "Why, Serena, since Ambrose's parents still have their cottage, you should do the same with Amory!" She made this sound like a brilliant, novel idea, rather than a very obvious one that Serena had considered and rejected.

"Maybe someday," Serena said weakly.

"I would not like to hide my children away." Vesta shook her head. "We must set them up for success, and in Newport, they are among the future leaders of business and industry."

When Elizabeth and Vesta went to the rail to better observe a passing yacht, Serena's brow creased. "Perhaps I should send Amory to Newport, as Elizabeth is doing with William."

"Does Amory wish to go?"

"No, not really."

"Well, William does. His grandmother dotes on him so, as you know." Anna sighed. "I suppose it will do him no harm."

Serena was anxious but also very suggestible, easily swayed by anyone who spoke with an air of authority. Fortunately, reeling her back in only required Anna to refute Vesta's assertion with the same certitude with which it had been made.

"Why would you think Newport might cause William harm?"

"I suppose it's not harmful, per se," Anna said, sounding as if she was being maximally charitable. "But Newport has nothing like the same beneficial effect on children."

"Oh, I am so glad to hear you say so!" Serena had an almost pleading look in her eyes. "I think you are quite right, but I wish you would tell me more, because I confess I am unable to articulate precisely what it is about Haven Point that is so marvelous for the children."

"Children have more freedom here, whereas in Newport, their amusements are mostly arranged for them. And while Newport is lovely, there is something so wholesome about the raw beauty of Haven Point."

Serena looked at Anna eagerly, hoping to hear more. Anna thought for a moment.

"Our mother had a theory about summer. We lived in 'society' the rest of the year, but summer was for freedom, for following our affinities, as she called them. You might recall that we had a little lakeside cottage in the western part of Massachusetts. We knew many fine people in that community, but it was not at all ostentatious. People entertained simply, and nobody promenaded in their finery, showing off to each other like they do in Newport.

"Our mother, you know, lived on the Brook Farm commune as a girl. While she remembered her time there very fondly, she knew one could not entirely leave the world behind. The cottage was her compromise, a way to give us a flavor of what she had enjoyed."

"But what about meeting important people?" Serena said.

"I think meeting and knowing *good* people is what matters, don't you?"

Serena nodded, satisfied. "How well you say it. Your mother would like the people here."

"Yes, she would. You and Ambrose should be proud of what you have built." Until this moment, when Serena's distress compelled her to do so, Anna had not really thought it through, but what she had said was true. Earlier, in fact, she had imagined how Mother would have viewed the scene on this deck—the conspicuous flaunting of wealth, the gossip and vacuous conversation, the petty rivalries. That would not have appealed to her, but she would have liked this community.

The women on Haven Point could certainly be said to be "in society." They lived in nice homes, made social calls, subscribed to charities, and supported the arts, but they were of a different stock from Elizabeth and Serena's circle in Boston. The fashionable notion that women were sensitive by nature, in need of protection from the rough world, seemed not to have taken hold in northern New England. Anna could not imagine any Maine woman cultivating the air of an invalid like some Boston society women did.

Haven Point women were also thrifty and resourceful. Many of their families still owned farms, and Anna often heard them speak of being pressed into service when they were young, helping out at harvest time.

Julia, in particular, seemed to thrive on Haven Point, where she was among people who loved her and found her amusing, rather than constantly standing in wait, ready to pounce on any transgression.

Just yesterday, Anna and Elizabeth ran into Nora at the steamship landing, where they were all picking up their mail.

"Nora, I hope Julia came by to apologize," Elizabeth said. Julia had come home with a bouquet of dahlias, whose pale peach color marked them as being of Nora's carefully cultivated variety. When asked, she confessed to having picked them without permission.

"She did. This morning, in fact," Nora said, then chuckled.

"I suspect I will regret asking, but what did she say to amuse you?"

"Rest easy, Elizabeth. It was a most sincere apology," Nora said. "But by way of explanation, she said they leaned toward her and smiled, so she knew they wanted to be picked."

Anna laughed. "A reasonable interpretation."

"She promised that next time, no matter how much they beg, she will not listen."

"She is the most fanciful child." Elizabeth shook her head. "Last night, I went into her room and asked why she was still awake. She said her eyes did not wish to close."

Julia, who ascribed human emotions and motivations to all things, animate and inanimate, often implied that parts of her body operated of their own volition. How could she help it if her hand grabbed what was not hers, or her legs carried her where she was not meant to go? (Rosemary had tried to use this tendency to her advantage. "But Julia, your stomach likes spinach." Julia shook her head and said, "Oh, no, it doesn't! Not even a little.")

However, while their own mother would have indeed liked it here on Haven Point, there was a difference. Mother had actively sought out a summer refuge for her daughters, while Elizabeth had stumbled into it, by the sheer luck of a sporting-mad husband who had grown tired of the Newport crowds impeding his ability to play golf and tennis. Elizabeth's reclamation of summer had been largely accidental, the result not of intention but rather of the good offices of Nora and George. Anna was not sure her sister even recognized her good fortune.

The easygoing, accepting character of this place would be utterly destroyed by people like Rhinelander and Vesta Sears. Worse, Anna could not imagine Elizabeth lifting a finger to impede such an outcome.

Lillian arrived that afternoon. She walked in the house, looked around, and said, "You still haven't put paper up?"

Jerome looked around, too, as if seeing it for the first time, and said, "Yes, when will we, Liz?"

Elizabeth, who had no intention of papering the unfinished walls, murmured something noncommittal in response.

That night, Elizabeth and Jerome hosted a dinner at Fourwinds. The meal was tolerable, as Elizabeth kindly seated Anna beside George Graham, but after dinner, the ladies joined Elizabeth on the south porch.

"Why is there no hotel here?" Vesta asked.

"We believe it is more wholesome without one," Letty Stinneford said. "And we do like our peace and quiet."

Odd, Anna thought, noting Letty's uncharacteristically prim tone.

"What do you do with your time?"

"Oh, we have plenty of amusements," Nora said. "Why, we sing, and we play Fox and Geese on the beach, and every Sunday evening, we have Vespers."

"And we always have our needlework," added Letty.

Now Anna knew something was up. Letty Stinneford hated needlework.

And then it hit her. *They're trying to bore her to death!* It seemed to work, because before long, Vesta turned her attention to Lillian and discussions of Newport.

At one point, however, her voice rose above the others. "Consuelo Vanderbilt wore a wonderful cream-colored silk frock, with a yoke of Venetian lace." She looked around and spoke in a teacherly fashion. "Dotted muslin is *everywhere* this summer. It looks *wonderful* with a black hat and a splash of color in a *corsage*."

Anna glanced around at the assembled group and almost burst out laughing, belatedly noticing the sobriety with which they had dressed for the evening. It seemed that their scheme to appear as drab as possible had succeeded, given that it had convinced Vesta Sears that they were in dire need of her fashion counsel.

After a while, the men joined them, filling in the seats and leaning against the rails. After Elizabeth ensured everyone was comfortable, Anna moved over and made room for her on the ottoman.

The conversation was rather desultory, since Rhinelander and Vesta had rubbed everyone the wrong way, and the Haven Point women were making a concerted effort to appear uninteresting. While the group was in desperate need of a distraction, it unfortunately came in the form of Julia, careening onto the porch with great flourish.

She wore a woolen coat of William's that was far too long. To remedy this, she had tied a scarf around her waist and bunched some of the material over the top. The cap she wore, also William's, came down over her eyes, requiring her to tilt her head back in order to see. Needless to say, the child presented an extremely odd appearance.

"What is she doing up?" Lillian asked sharply.

There was a moment of terrible silence. Anna wished she could sweep Julia into her arms and lovingly spirit her away, but Lillian already mistrusted Anna. As a member of the Demarest household, presumably living under its strictures, Anna would look as if she were usurping her sister and brother-in-law's authority, an authority Elizabeth seemed too paralyzed to exercise.

As usual, a word from his mother acted as an alarm clock, awakening Jerome to whatever was amiss. He looked at Elizabeth.

"What *is* she doing up?"

As if by way of answer, Julia flung her arms out and began to sing.

Over the water, over the lee, over the water to Charley
Charley loves good ale and wine, Charley loves good brandy
Charley loves a little girl as sweet as sugar candy

When Julia finished, she peered around from under the brim of the hat, her expression triumphant. The few seconds that followed felt like an eternity, but the silence was broken by Nora Graham.

"Brilliantly done, Julia!" Nora applauded, and the other women from Haven Point immediately joined in. Nora pulled Julia to her side, then addressed the group. "She's been planning it for ages. She wanted to surprise everyone."

"Well, she did that," Jerome said, with a boozy laugh.

Rosemary appeared at the doorway, looking harassed and embarrassed. Nora looked her directly in the eye and said, "Julia was *brilliant*. Thank you!"

Though Rosemary could not possibly know what precipitated this comment, she seemed to understand that it fell under the category of Management of Julia's Reputation. She nodded, smiled formally, and held out a hand to beckon Julia.

"Come along now, child."

Julia looked around the room, as if evaluating whether she might continue to enjoy the unexpected hospitality. When her eyes reached Anna and Elizabeth, she took in their warning looks and tight smiles, sighed dramatically, then went to the door and took Rosemary's hand.

"Good night, darling," Elizabeth called as they exited.

Julia looked back, smiled, waved, and called out, "Good night!"

Letty Stinneford beamed around the room. "Was that not marvelous? We do like to encourage the children's theatricals."

Before anyone could notice the incongruity of Letty's comment with the boring, lifeless community she and others had thus far been depicting, Serena spoke up.

"So, you gentlemen sail to Monhegan Island tomorrow?" she asked brightly.

Dear Serena, Anna thought. On some intuitive level, Serena must have known the men could not ignore her. They certainly never had.

"Heading out first thing," Ambrose said, and the conversation turned away from Julia, and toward their planned excursion.

Anna felt a rush of warmth at the women's performance. Mothers here agreed that their children deserved a break from rigid rules, and with most husbands away during the week and summer staff limited, they deserved a break from enforcing them. Under no interpretation, however, did this indulgence extend to welcoming a fugitive child to an adult party. In any less fraught situation, it would have prompted a scold. But with that collective and protective instinct, ancient as mankind itself, these women had sized up the circumstances and done what neither Elizabeth nor Anna could: pretended Julia's appearance was not only permitted, but worthy of celebration.

The next morning, Anna headed to Nora's house. As she passed the Grahams' garden, she spotted a wide-brimmed sun hat and looked over the stone wall.

"Hello, Nora."

Nora turned, saw Anna, then stood and waved her in. "Come have something to drink, Anna. I need a break."

Anna had not seen Nora's kitchen garden before. When she entered the gate, she looked around in wonder. "How do you coax so many vegetables out of such inhospitable soil?"

"Wisdom of earlier generations. My mother's thumb was far greener than mine." Nora shrugged, then nodded to the stone stairs. "Sit. I made some ginger punch."

She returned with two glasses and lowered herself to sit beside Anna.

"Thank you for helping Julia after her performance last night," Anna said. "And I was grateful for *your* performance, too."

"Performance?" Nora asked, with such a poor imitation of innocence, Anna had to laugh.

"Nora Graham, you must credit me with some intelligence. You cannot pretend that you and the others were not intentionally trying to bore the Searses to tears."

"Oh, all right," Nora said, with a resigned sigh. "But any deception was well-intentioned. Rhinelander and Vesta Sears assumed they would find no one interesting here, so we gave them the satisfaction of thinking they were right. And now Vesta has some ammunition, should her husband persist in his supposed interest in purchasing a lot."

"Was Ambrose pleased, do you think?" Anna asked.

"Is it your observation that his cousin's presence pleases Ambrose?"

Anna thought for a moment. "It actually seems to set his hackles up."

"That is my perception as well. Far more important, of course, is how it affects Serena."

"How so?"

"George and I always knew Ambrose and Serena were more, well . . . *formal.* That's fine. We like them." Nora raised her chin in feigned affectation and added, "And I always thought it spoke well of Ambrose that he is so devoted to George."

"Well, of course." Anna smiled. George was not an obvious member of Jerome and Ambrose's set, and she, too, was glad their usual prejudices had not blinded them to what a fine man he was.

"We knew we'd have some grand people building grand houses on Haven Point. We hoped they would follow the example of Serena and Ambrose, who hold no one else to their social standards. But as much as I like Serena, I worry about her at times."

"What worries you?"

"With husbands coming and going, it's the wives who set the tone, most of us being here all summer. It's bad enough when you get a passel of women together, being what we are. Just one woman's poison can get into the groundwater."

"But Serena isn't poison!"

"Oh, no. Of course not. I was referring to women like Vesta Sears." Nora shook her head, her brow creased, then picked up her spade and returned to her gardening before she spoke again. "Ambrose is anxious about selling the lots, and he has a blind spot for his sort. Serena does not care for Vesta, but if he persisted in selling to them, I'm not sure she would stand up to him."

"So you thought you would help her along," Anna said. "Very clever."

Nora shrugged. "I suspect Rhinelander Sears was not that interested in the first place."

"He mostly seems interested in provoking Ambrose, but last night was a good insurance policy," Anna said. "I do have one question, though. Did Elizabeth know what you all planned?"

Nora paused again, thinking. "Given a choice," she said finally, "I don't believe we must tell people what would make them uncomfortable to know."

Anna's heart sank a bit, but she thanked Nora and headed back to Fourwinds.

Anna was encouraged by the recognition of the special nature of Haven Point, and the desire to preserve the community as it was. It was dismaying, though, to learn that Nora saw that Elizabeth was unwilling to participate in a scheme, no matter how harmless, without her husband's consent. The other women could gather like a fleet of ships, hoist their sails, and head into battle, but Elizabeth, unfit for the task, was left behind in the harbor.

When Anna returned to Fourwinds, she found that the Radcliffe newsletter had arrived. She took it upstairs to her room. Flipping through it, she was surprised to come across her own name in the class notes: "Anna Bradley is spending the summer with her sister's family on Haven Point, Maine."

Hers was not the only such entry, but it caused her a terrible pang. In college, Anna had never thought she was better than her friends, but she knew she was comparably fortunate, and everyone else knew it, too. She arrived at Radcliffe knowing precisely what her future held: She and her father, the revered Harvard professor, were working in partnership on a great scholarly work, which would, in turn, launch Anna as a writer and thinker in her own right. She had been envied for her certainty, and for her clear path to achievement and independence.

Now, having been abandoned by her father, Anna was years away from finishing the book. And without the book, what hope did she have of establishing her own career?

In the meantime, if Elizabeth was the boat left behind in the harbor, what did that make Anna? Just a dinghy attached to her side. Untie the knot, and she could be cut loose in an instant.

CHAPTER FIVE

July 1913
Haven Point, Maine

JULIA

At first, it was just a small dark shape, interrupting the surface of the water. Only when it got closer did they recognize the delicate head and slender neck of a deer. The girls hid when it got close (because you know how deer are), but they watched through the bushes as the deer emerged from the water, sniffed around, chewed on some plants, then dozed for a bit before swimming away again.

It was wonderful to learn that deer could swim, but to discover that they did so with no evident purpose? That was beyond anything!

FROM *LIBERTY ISLAND*, BY MISS CRANE

Julia entered her aunt's house without knocking. Anna peered out of the kitchen. "Julia!"

"I am petitioning as a refugee."

"Oh, dear." Anna approached and gave her a stout hug. "What is happening at Fourwinds?"

"Mother is tense. Lillian is questioning her every move. William is wearing his best lord-of-the-manor ways, and poor Pauline seems overwhelmed. Oh, and Louisa is helping in the kitchen, and getting much reverence and glorification." Julia half laughed, half groaned.

"I imagine that rankles."

"Not really," Julia said, waving that away. "I think I was still in hot water from the suffrage parade. Then I got mad at William for making poor Mrs. Powell travel up here, and snapped at Mother, too. It was not well received."

"You're welcome to take refuge," Anna replied. "Care for some tea?"

Julia accepted gratefully. Anna returned to the kitchen, and Julia sat on the window seat and looked out at the water. She was ashamed that she had not thought to wonder about the location of the wedding until Pauline's mother arrived that morning, pale and exhausted. Julia went looking for Louisa, who, having arrived several days before, likely had a better sense of things. She finally hunted her down in the pantry.

"Why are William and Pauline marrying here, rather than near her home in Virginia?"

Louisa, a touch of apprehension in her eyes, leaned out of the pantry, looked around for servants, then ducked back in and pulled the door closed.

"I gather it is what your brother wanted." She spoke in a low voice. "He said Pauline would love the Maine coast, and he'd pay her mother's way."

"That beast!" Julia said, fury rising.

"After seeing Mrs. Powell, I cannot disagree that it was selfish. But your mother is short on help and overwhelmed, so it would not be wise to go off half-cocked."

Too late. Julia was full-cocked. She stalked off and found her brother in his room, putting on his collar.

"How could you make that poor woman come all the way up here, William? Have you seen her? She looks positively ill!"

William did not even turn from his mirror. "I didn't make anyone do anything," he said, in that maddeningly composed way of his. "Mrs. Powell had first-class tickets all the way."

"I wonder, William," Julia said, mimicking her brother's slow and deliberate tone. "If Pauline's mother had offered you first-class passage to Virginia, would you have gone, so Pauline might have married out of her own home?"

Collar in place, William finally turned to Julia.

"I do not see why I should entertain this hypothetical. She did not." William reached for his waistcoat. "And I daresay she could not have done so. This allowed us to be married in some comfort with friends present."

"*Your* friends, William!" Julia's anger bubbled up again. "I see what's afoot here. He who pays the piper calls the tune."

"You are aware, I assume, that not everyone wishes to be a 'New Woman'?" William snarled, his face reddening. He was so proud of what he considered his manly self-control, Julia felt some pleasure at forcing him to drop the mask.

When he spoke again, however, he had reverted to his air of long-suffering condescension. "I hardly think this discussion is fruitful now."

He left the room without another word. Julia, blood still boiling, marched off to find her mother, who was at her dressing table, pinning up her hair.

"How could you let William drag poor Mrs. Powell up from Virginia?"

With what looked like maximum restraint, Mother turned to face Julia. "We are down two servants with a houseful of guests and a wedding tomorrow, Julia. If you do not mind, I would prefer to stick to problems that are not too late to address."

"Can I just ask you this? Did you at least suggest to William that it might be easier for Pauline's family if they married in Virginia?"

"Pauline wanted to get married here, too."

"Because she is powerless to say otherwise!"

"Again, Julia, what good does this do now?"

Julia turned on her heels and walked out, disgusted.

When Anna returned to the living room with the tea, Julia resisted the temptation to tell her about the argument that morning. Though far more modern than Mother, Anna's sororal loyalty was positively Victorian.

Even without fully unburdening herself, it was a nice reprieve from the tension at home, and Julia enjoyed sitting in the cozy old cottage with an aunt who had never showed her anything but perfect acceptance.

She was tempted to skip the rehearsal entirely, but Julia knew that would solve nothing. And since the only thing worse than truancy would be arriving in her current disheveled state, she eventually returned to Fourwinds to dress.

The rehearsal went smoothly, and while Julia's two-hour absence might not have made hearts grow fonder, the edge was off, at least. On the way to the post-rehearsal clambake, Julia filled Louisa in on the various conflagrations since they met in the pantry.

"William evidently thinks it's very cutting and clever to say that not everyone wants to be a 'New Woman.' Has he only just learned the phrase? It's been bandied about for more than a quarter century!"

"Perhaps it took that long to penetrate the walls of the Somerset Club," Louisa said. "You know how hard it is to get into that place."

Julia laughed, grateful for the tonic of Louisa's wit.

Guests from out of town had already arrived at the beach. Julia spotted Michael and his family and headed in their direction. Robert and Margaret had come, along with two of Michael's brothers and their wives. Knowing Mother was overburdened, they had chosen to stay in a hotel in Portland. Julia chatted happily with them until Father beckoned them to meet Mrs. Powell.

"We don't leave until Tuesday," Michael said. "Time for a sail on Monday?"

"Absolutely!" Julia said.

"Good. I want to see Liberty Island from the eyes of a defender rather than the invader."

Julia moved to the bonfire, where William and his friends had gathered. Bull Trumbull, one of William's cronies, who had inherited a fortune and was evidently making the spending of it his life's work, was extolling Pauline's virtues to a few friends who had not yet had the pleasure of meeting her. He glanced at Julia as she approached.

"So, Miss Demarest. Where's that friend of yours who was here a couple of summers back?" Bull asked.

"Miss Ellis? She is in New York."

"Now there's a 'New Woman' I might like," Bull said, his voice thick with champagne and meaning. He and William had obviously been talking. "Not to get leg-shackled to, of course. But she seems like a game one."

"Game, Mr. Trumbull?" Julia looked up at him innocently. "What do you mean by that?"

"Up for some fun." Bull smirked.

"Doesn't everyone like to have fun?"

"Julia . . ." William said, in a tone of warning and frustration.

Julia smiled brightly at Bull. "Miss Ellis is working for women's suffrage." She hoped to irritate him, but unfortunately, Bull did not bite.

"Oh, a man-hater now?" He shrugged. "Shame."

The conversation soon shifted to one of Julia's least favorite subjects, the Great Causeway Controversy. Julia had given Mina a full tour when she visited two years ago. When they reached the footbridge that led to the mainland, Julia explained that some residents were agitating for a causeway. The connection to the mainland was underwater except during low tide. Even then, it made for a squishy walk, and some also wanted to have their motorcars on Haven Point. The causeway idea, however, was meeting with much resistance.

Mina had burst out laughing.

"What's so funny?" Julia asked.

"It's just that, of course there's resistance! Don't you see? This is a fortress." She made a sweeping gesture toward Haven Point and then toward the high tide rushing under the footbridge. "And this is a moat! I'm surprised nobody has proposed a drawbridge."

Julia laughed, too. "Keep out the barbarians!"

"Exactly. It's a fortified village. A citadel."

Julia, depressed by the fact that William and his friends could spend hours on such a petty issue, escaped and headed down the beach toward an empty picnic table. The sun set on the other side of the peninsula, but as it did, it painted pink and mauve onto the sky and water on the east side. It was like hearing the muted strains of a distant orchestra. By the time Maudie appeared, Julia was in a better humor.

"What are you doing here by yourself?" Maude asked.

"I thought my family would disapprove of my killing my brother the night before his wedding."

"Brothers . . ." Maudie sighed as she plopped down on the opposite bench.

"The worst."

As if summoned, Maudie's older brother Owen appeared, greeted Julia with a warm hug, then sat beside his sister.

"Did Maudie tell you about the tourists on Gunnison Island?"

Julia looked at Maudie, who grimaced.

"Some fans of the books put two and two together," Owen said. "They figured out that Gunnison was the likely inspiration for *Liberty Island*, and people have been sailing over, ignoring the NO TRESPASSING sign, and tramping about."

"We should get the catapult working again," Maudie said.

"I still can't believe we were fooled into thinking you girls were over there learning how to garden and cook outdoors," Owen said. "Mother acted like she was doing us this great favor, getting you out of our hair. All the while you were preparing to battle the enemy."

"Which was you!" Maudie said.

"And who started it?"

"You did!" Julia said, laughing. "Taking over that old schoolhouse!"

William, Owen, and a few of their friends had been allowed to use the old stone building on the mainland as a clubhouse. Green with envy, seven-year-old Julia and Maudie had responded to this development with a range of tactics, including espionage and vandalism.

"That was not sufficient justification for war," Owen sniffed. Maudie smacked his arm, and he elbowed her in return.

"I'm joking. We really were horrid to you girls. I am sorry about that," Owen said, charmingly penitent.

"You are forgiven," Julia replied.

"I'm not so sure," Maudie said. Owen cuffed her again, then left to get a drink.

"I envy your relationship with Owen," Julia said, after he walked away.

"Owen and I fight like cats and dogs!"

"No, you don't. Or maybe you do, but it's . . . I don't know . . . *playful.* It's not like me and William." It pained Julia when brothers of her school friends came to visit. They all said the same things. *Oh, we had the most bitter fights, but now we get along like a house on fire.*

Julia and William had never been smack-and-elbow siblings. As long as Julia could remember, it had been censorious, condescending William versus rebellious, stubborn Julia. It was impossible to imagine their relationship improving. They were worlds apart in temperament and attitude, and the gulf had only widened.

Ruthie Lawrence had just arrived on Haven Point, and soon she and Louisa joined them at the picnic table, rounding out the Liberty Island reunion. Ruthie had been a rather waiflike little girl, but while she was as pretty as ever, with her golden hair and lovely features, she had developed a passion for tennis in her teen years and become quite accomplished. She had just come from a tournament in Rhode Island.

Julia had expected Ruthie would have gotten married by now, and evidently Serena and Ambrose were eager for her to do so. But while she was still seeing Vernon Scott, she was not racing to the altar.

"I like being able to travel to tournaments all over the country," Ruthie said with a shrug. "If Vernon can wait, then my parents can wait, too."

After the clambake, William's friends had planned some horrid stag event, so Maudie invited the girls over to the cottage on the

Grahams' property that she and John Franklin had occupied after they married last summer. Pauline was spending her wedding eve there, so they planned to toast the bride and look over her trousseau.

Julia was grateful to Maudie for how well she had taken Pauline in hand. It seemed such an unlikely friendship—sturdy Maudie, a Yankee from almost as far north as one could be and still be American, and the pretty Southern orchid that was Pauline.

They all admired Pauline's sheets, pillowcases, tablecloths, nightgowns, and handkerchiefs, most of which had been sewn by Pauline and Mrs. Powell's clever hands. Pauline might have had to sell herself, but her habit of thrift would not be so easily broken.

The Powells were teetotalers, and Pauline always declined wine at dinner, so Julia was surprised when she accepted the glass of champagne Maudie offered for a toast.

"To the bride!" Maudie said.

They had an amusing evening, singing songs and telling stories. They told Pauline about Liberty Island, and Pauline related amusing tales about her family's old retainer, whom they called "Uncle Robert," and who, in turn, called them "broken-down 'ristocrats."

There was a good deal of laughter, and Julia finally felt she had put her troubles aside. By the end of the evening, however, Pauline was very tipsy.

"Think you'll be able to get up for your wedding?" Maudie asked.

Pauline straightened her back, looked at Maudie with feigned hauteur, and said, "Well, I hertainly sope ho!"

They all dissolved into laughter again, but Maudie declared it time for the bride to get to bed.

Ruthie and Louisa left, but Julia lingered.

"Was this the first time you've seen Pauline have a drink?" Julia asked Maudie, when she returned from Pauline's room.

"Yes, but it is not her first. When I talked about serving champagne, she told me she adores it, though she never drinks in front of her mother. Did you see how she looked at that glass? It was as if she had met the man of her dreams."

Julia thought Pauline looked a bit pale the next day, but to anyone who had not been present the night before, it could be easily written off as maidenly nerves. In fact, it was almost becoming.

Monday sparkled, a perfect day for a sail. Mina had no interest in childhood memories (she refused to believe she had ever even been a child), so Julia had not taken her to Liberty Island. She looked forward to showing it to Michael.

As soon as they were around the back of the island, with Haven Point out of view, Julia felt something slacken inside.

"It feels good to escape."

"Was a trip to Liberty Island always an escape?"

"I thought so, though it was arguably a banishment." Julia laughed as they turned about, tacking into the cove. "We used to call it Jumaru, by the way, after Julia, Maudie, and Ruthie. Once Louisa arrived, she refused to let us change it to Jumarulou, so when the books came out, we relented to Liberty Island."

They had sailed the dinghy over, so when they reached the shallow water, Michael rolled up his pants, jumped out, and pulled the boat onto the little comma-shaped beach. He grabbed the picnic basket, and Julia led him up from the rocky shore, through the trees, to the clearing where she had spent so many happy hours.

Michael looked around in wonder. "You'd never know it was here!"

"They think there was a farmhouse here at some point, and that the trees were cleared for grazing, though nobody knows for sure."

Gunnison Island stretched from northeast to southwest, fitting the pattern of most Casco Bay islands, which, on a map, looked like a great deity had thrown a handful of rocks sidearm into the bay. Spruce trees blocked the view of the clearing from Haven Point. "We could be neither seen nor heard. Which was the idea, of course."

Julia pointed out the circle of rocks where they'd had their fires and showed him the old lookout tower. Michael's eyes scanned the south side of the clearing, then pointed to a spot between two spruces.

"Is that where you launched the catapult?"

"Perceptive! It was like a turret. Room to launch our projectiles, and undergrowth to hide behind." After she led him over the rest of the small island, they returned to the clearing for their picnic.

"Who came out here with you?"

"My aunt Anna for the first two summers, then our caretaker's niece took over. She was back from the West, having left her good-for-nothing scoundrel of a husband."

"Her words?"

"A direct quote." Julia explained that when the scoundrel took up with a Harvey Girl, a waitress from one of the famous Harvey restaurants on the Santa Fe line, she scraped some money together and came home. "She was gratified by how indignant we were on her behalf."

"Your aunt gave me a cryptic message. She said you can tell me the bootlegger story."

Julia clapped her hands together, delighted. "She must trust you. This is a great secret!"

"I will take it to the grave."

Julia explained that when they were eleven, after years of pleading, they were permitted to stay overnight on Liberty Island by themselves. Maine had been a dry state for many years, and there were rumrunners all along the coastline. One foggy night, they heard boat engines and yelling, followed by what sounded like a gunshot, then some cursing.

One engine grew more distant, but the other seemed to be drawing nearer. The girls scrambled to a spot where they could see between the spruces, just as a boat appeared through the fog. A man was at the wheel, holding his arm, moaning and cursing.

"So we did what any good pirate does and ran down to the shoreline."

"Brave!"

"I believe 'idiotic' was the word Anna and our caretaker used. We called out and asked if the man needed help. He said he'd been winged by the revenue man. Having frequently played smuggler, we were familiar with both terms," Julia said. She added, "We were always the rumrunners, by the way. Never the revenue men."

"You knew who the good guys were."

"Our parents' comments on the subject had led us to see them as a rather genial sort of criminal."

"That you are standing here today suggests this man did not disabuse you of this."

"He was a perfect specimen, a credit to the breed. We yelled to tie up his boat. Maudie and I rowed over and fetched him. As it happened, Ruthie had taken an earnest interest in nursing, and as her mother is a committed hypochondriac, she always had plenty of bandages and the like. We'd spent many hours pretending to be gravely wounded while Ruthie treated us."

After Ruthie and Louisa fetched the supplies, they returned to the beach, whereupon Ruthie began ordering everyone around like an army general. She instructed Julia to hold the lantern as she cut the man's shirt, checked the wound to confirm that he had just been winged and that no bullet had lodged in his arm. The man offered a flask to clean the wound, but Ruthie, affronted, informed him she would properly sterilize it.

"His name was Clem, by the way."

Michael nodded. "Well, of course it was."

"Honestly, I'd have preferred something like Demon Dan, but anyway . . ."

Julia explained that Ruthie had cleaned the wound, applied ointment and a bandage, and commanded him to lean against the rowboat and rest his arm on the gunwale. At that point, Clem finally seemed to notice that they were four eleven-year-old girls, and asked what they were doing out there alone at night with no adults watching over them.

"A belated concern, but quite paternal. We told him we'd been camping out here for years, and that we could send up a flare if we had any trouble. Clem told us about the new revenue man in Portland. At one point, he referred to him as a 'sneaky bastard,' but he apologized, saying he knew he shouldn't speak so."

"Why did you need permission to tell this story?" Michael asked, laughing.

"To this day, none of our fathers know it. At the time, my aunt said we'd never be allowed to stay out here again if they found out. Maudie almost turned her against the idea entirely when she said we'd be perfectly safe if we only had a couple of pistols."

Michael was rolling. "Now I know why this wasn't in the *Liberty Island* books."

"I should ask your mother to do an illustration anyway," Julia said. "We never saw Clem again, but for years after, he left us little treats on the island."

Julia saw Michael off at the wharf, but rather than returning to Fourwinds, she made her way to the beach, lowered herself onto the sand, and watched the waves deposit pebbles and shells and then, with a great crackling sound, pull them away.

I know how you feel. Julia felt the same tug, toward this shore and away from it again.

When Mina spoke of having nothing in common with her childhood friends, Julia suspected they might not have had much in common to start with. Like a fish does not know it's wet, when Julia was little, she had no idea how special her childhood summers had been.

It was the readers' reaction to *Liberty Island* that taught her. They wrote of their envy, not just of the girls' freedom but also of their friendship. Louisa was like a sister, and Julia knew she would always feel close to Ruthie and Maudie, too.

But now Maudie was married, and while Ruthie had held off, she would not be too far behind. Though Julia did not look down on them for it, they were following the pattern their parents had set, and she feared their lives would soon be unrecognizable to her.

And William is even worse than Father, Julia thought bitterly, considering Pauline's fate. Jerome Demarest was materially indulgent, occasionally amused by his daughter's antics, but like all the fathers Julia had known growing up, he was not particularly forward-thinking.

What was William's excuse, though? Other young men were open to new ideas, and not just radicals either. Michael Seaborne, for example.

Of course Michael was just a boy when his mother gained such fame for her *Liberty Island* illustrations. Under those circumstances, Julia supposed, he could hardly be anything other than open to women's opportunities.

Julia sighed, got up, brushed the sand off her skirts. As she headed up the hill from the beach to Fourwinds, she was struck by a troubling thought. If Michael Seaborne's character could be credited to his mother's influence, what did that say about the formation of William's?

CHAPTER SIX

July 1899
Haven Point, Maine

ANNA

William, face red and his fists clenched, stalked onto the side porch, Owen Graham in tow. Anna set aside her book, and Elizabeth looked up from her needlework.

"What is it, William?" Elizabeth asked.

"Mother, you must do something about Julia! She and Maudie are ruining *everything*." He practically spat the last word. Anna thought, not for the first time, what a shame it was that such a handsome boy so often wore such unhandsome expressions.

"Oh?" Elizabeth asked mildly. "What happened?"

"We were coming out of the clubhouse and got pelted with tennis balls. Julia was shooting them at us, I know she was. She can't throw for anything, so she obviously stole my slingshot!"

"You did not see the person?" Elizabeth asked.

"We saw a coupla kids running away," Owen said. "They wore boys' clothes, but they didn't look like boys."

"She probably nicked the clothes from me, too. You know what a thief she is," William added. "She steals *all* my books."

"I'll speak to her," Elizabeth said. She used the same mild tone, which obviously infuriated her son. He bent forward, his face contorted by rage.

"You can talk 'til you're blue in the face, Mother! It won't do a bit of good. She needs to be punished!"

At this, Elizabeth raised an eyebrow. "That, William, will be *all*."

William stood then, face flushed. His jaw was still set, but he knew he had erred. Owen, for his part, looked abashed. (Anna had noticed that he seemed rather more uncertain about this confrontation from the start.)

"Sorry," William mumbled. "Come on, Owen."

Anna was tempted to laugh at the picture that had formed in her mind, of Julia and Maudie trotting down the road in oversized boys' clothing, but she refrained, since Elizabeth showed no sign of sharing her amusement.

"This is growing intolerable," Elizabeth said, with a weary sigh.

"I am sure it is very difficult for you," Anna said consolingly.

A war between the sexes was underway on Haven Point, and Julia and Maudie were both instigators and primary combatants. This latest report was consistent with their tactics, which were decidedly guerrilla in nature—sabotage, espionage, and (of course) theft.

As with all wars, the causes were many and varied, but to Anna's thinking, they all fell under the umbrella of envy. Julia and Maudie felt they were constantly being hemmed in, while the boys were enjoying unparalleled freedom.

It was bad enough when William and his friends took over the old stone building on the mainland, which had once been a school, and turned it into a clubhouse. What really drove Julia to the edge was the great Rough Rider Controversy.

The Ballantines' nephew, a Harvard man who served under Colonel Roosevelt in the Battle of San Juan Hill, had come to Haven Point to recuperate from malaria, and held an informal talk from a hammock on the Ballantines' porch.

Julia was obsessed with Teddy Roosevelt's Rough Riders, and Maudie had been infected by her contagious enthusiasm. They were livid when they were prohibited from hearing him speak, while the boys were allowed to go, and William did not help things when he returned late that afternoon.

"It was the *most* glorious talk. I shall never forget it. What stories we heard!"

Julia was slumped on the sofa, one arm dangling over the edge, looking at him through lazy eyes—a valiant and utterly unconvincing attempt to appear indifferent. Finally, her curiosity won out, and she swallowed her pride.

"What sorts of stories?"

"I can't tell you!" William said haughtily. "The things he told us are not fit for a girl's ear."

Julia glared daggers at him. Things had been going downhill ever since.

A few days after Elizabeth reprimanded William, Anna was outside when Julia emerged from the forest at the center of the point, covered with dirt.

"Oh, dear, Julia. Where have you been?" Anna asked.

"Maudie and I were training the goats," she said. Unfortunately, William had chosen this moment to emerge from the house. He caught sight of his sister, and his nose wrinkled.

"Look at you! What a mess you are. And what on earth are you training goats for?"

"For a circus," Julia replied, as if this were obvious.

William made a disgusted sound. "Why do you have to be such a little hoyden?"

He went back inside, the screen door slamming behind him. Julia shrugged.

"And how did it go, the goat training?" Anna asked.

Her shoulders slumped, and she sighed. "Not well. They won't listen."

A moment later, William reappeared at the front door, holding up one of his novels. "I found *this* in your room," he said, furious.

Julia rolled her eyes dramatically. "So?"

"So, you took it from me, and you shouldn't read it anyway, because it's not proper."

"Well, you can have it back now."

William let loose another disgusted groan and went back indoors.

It was unfortunate timing for Julia to develop a fatal addiction to dime novels. Thanks to Judith Fairchild, her reading material had become quite a bugaboo of Lillian's. Only a few months ago, Lillian came upon Julia in Jerome's library, lying on her back reading a similarly dreadful book.

"Julia Demarest, you should not be reading such vulgar novels!" She turned to Elizabeth. "How can you allow this? Those books feature the most *degenerate* men. Children who read them look upon criminal behavior as not only common but desirable."

"But Grandmother, this book is about Spotter Shrimp, a boy detective," Julia replied, her tone consoling. "He helps *catch* criminals, who go to jail, and jail is not desirable."

Seeing that Lillian was not appeased, Julia added, "And Spotter has a sister named Annabella, who is . . ." She stopped, scanned the page to find the words, then looked up eagerly. "'Matrimonially hopeful'!"

Lillian sniffed, then wagged a finger at her daughter-in-law. "Good books make good children, Elizabeth." She departed in a huff, and Julia shrugged as if to say, *I did my best*, and returned to her reading.

Over the last year, Mrs. Fairchild had carved out a niche for herself within the world of Christian mothering. Anna already knew she was shrewd, but this move was a true strategic masterstroke.

Boston's Watch and Ward Society had been banging the drums about the dangers of illicit literature for years. However, that organization focused on adult literature (with some attention to dime novels for boys, which were thought to encourage criminal activity). Seeing that mothers of daughters in Boston were being left out of this very fashionable panic, Mrs. Fairchild spotted the opening and seized it.

Her pamphlet on the effect of books on girls' moral formation proved so popular, she began producing a regular newsletter called *Our*

Daughters' Reading, which, in turn, led to essays for the *Evening Transcript*, lectures to librarians, and even a spot in a roundup of "experts" on the subject in *Harper's Magazine*. It was a charade, of course, but one that had earned her social indemnification. To criticize her was to align oneself with impurity and purveyors of smut.

Anna was not remotely worried about Julia's reading material, but she was concerned about William's keen attention to it. In a few weeks, William would go to Newport to be with his grandmother. Lillian was a ready audience for his complaints about his sister. Now "theft of unsuitable literature" would be added to the list.

A few nights later, at a gathering at the Ballantines' cottage, Nora proposed an idea to Anna.

"You know what a sore spot the boys' clubhouse has been for the girls. I think we should let Maudie and Julia get something similar going on Gunnison Island. They could sail over and run a little wild. Supervised, of course, and just on fine weekdays."

Anna smiled. "I think that's a wonderful idea." Gunnison Island was part of the property Ambrose Lawrence had purchased from the Grahams. It was uninhabited and close to Haven Point's shore.

"Well, I'm not sure you will once you hear me out," Nora warned. "You see, I was hoping you might go with them. Julia has spoken of all the pretending you two do together, and I thought you might help them get up some make-believe games and whatnot."

"I am not much of a sailor," Anna said. "Frankly, for the most part, I am a bit, well . . . indoorsy?"

Nora smiled. "That's all right. I've spoken with Duncan Douglas, and he said he would help. We should tell the girls it's a secret so we don't end up with the same problem in reverse, with the boys angry the girls are getting such a treat."

Mr. Douglas, who acted as caretaker for both the Grahams and the Demarests, was extremely competent, but while relieved on that score, Anna was not sure Julia would be able to keep her mouth shut for long.

"Maudie won't either," Nora replied, when Anna said as much. "I'll tell Owen we are getting the girls out of their hair. We can say they're learning to cook outdoors or something equally unappealing. Elizabeth will do the same with William."

"Elizabeth agreed to this?"

"We're both fed up with all the fighting."

"All right." Anna still felt unsure about her fitness for this role, but she was willing to give it a try. She also appreciated that Nora evidently believed the girls had a legitimate grievance, and while she suspected Elizabeth was merely "fed up," as Nora had put it, she had consented, at least.

"What about Ruthie? She'll wonder where her friends have gone."

"We can ask Serena. Perhaps she will allow it."

Anna thought that was unlikely. Serena was fully in the clutches of Dr. Frazier, who had attended her mother for decades, treating even the most minor complaints with great interest and seriousness, and offering many gratifying pronouncements about the particular delicacy of her blood and liver.

To Anna's surprise, Serena thought it was a grand plan.

"That sounds splendid!" Serena clasped her hands together. "Ruthie is already sturdier from the swamp root I have been giving her this summer. More fresh air will only improve her delicate constitution."

In typical fashion, once the plan was incubated, Nora wasted no time in getting it hatched. When, two days later, Anna climbed aboard Duncan's motorboat, she experienced some trepidation. The girls had only been told that their mothers felt they deserved their own retreat. Anna knew she was here to help them "get up some pretend games," but she wondered if it would feel contrived.

As they motored around to the southeast side of the island, where the irregular shape of the cliff created a small hidden cove and a little beach, she scanned her mind for ideas.

As it turned out, her presence was all that was required. The moment Duncan pulled the boat onto the beach, Julia jumped out and said, "Let's pretend we've been shipwrecked!" Anna made them carry the picnic baskets from the beach up to the clearing at the center of the island, but once that was accomplished, the girls were off.

The island was ringed by spruce trees. While spots were visible from the mainland, the clearing was mostly sheltered from view and wind, and the girls were never out of earshot. (Anna's earshot, at least. Fortunately, they were well out of earshot of Haven Point.)

They had a string of fair days that first week. Duncan dropped them off every morning and returned to pick them up later in the day. The girls christened their arcadia "Jumaru," after Julia, Maudie, and Ruthie. They were in heaven.

Since they were effectively stranded, Anna's one nagging worry was what they would do if a sudden storm came up. On the third day, however, Duncan arrived early.

"We need to pack up and go. Some weather is coming," he said.

The girls grumbled at what they considered an unreasonable prognostication. Other than a few clouds in the sky, the day had been perfect. Not thirty minutes after they returned to Haven Point, however, a thunderstorm came out of nowhere. Assuaged by Duncan Douglas's occult powers of weather prediction, Anna was now free to enjoy watching the girls play on Jumaru.

A few days later, it rained again, and Elizabeth took the children to Portland, so Anna had the house to herself. She sat at her desk and arranged her notes for the Margaret Fuller biography. An hour later, she had written one paragraph, and she did not even like it.

What is wrong with me?

Anna had told herself that the reason for her lack of progress was that she could not feel truly ready until she finished the research. She finally wheedled Mr. Wimborne into sponsoring her to use the Athenaeum Library and spent many late afternoons there, perusing books and papers and taking copious notes. She had been so diligent, she thought it would be an easy matter when she sat down to write the unfinished chapters, but her progress had lagged.

Anna sat back in her desk chair, looked up, and sighed. *I'm sorry, Mother.*

Anna was fourteen when she began helping organize Father's notes for classes and scholarly papers. They had begun talking about the Fuller biography a few years later, not long before Mother died. They both knew how deeply Mother admired Fuller, and that she worried her contributions would be forgotten. What better way to keep alive the values and traditions Mother held dear than to honor a woman who embodied so many of them?

That said, in their last private conversation, Mother had tried to ensure that Anna did not feel obligated.

"I think Father will struggle when I am gone," she said. "I know he likes working with you, and the idea of this book brings him comfort."

"I hope so. It brings me comfort, too."

Mother was quiet for a moment, and Anna saw a wrinkle in her brow. "Only if it is your inclination, Anna," she said finally. "I want you to follow your own affinity."

Anna understood. Mother did not want her to feel as if she had made a deathbed promise. She was leaving room for a future day when Anna might have different ambitions. Anna, who knew that day would never come, had replied with certainty: "Don't worry, Mother. I promise to follow my inclinations."

It had not occurred to either of them that someday it might not be *Father's* inclination.

Anna's work for Mr. Wimborne had done little to help Anna focus. His directives were as incoherent as ever. Just last week, in fact, Anna had received a letter from him, requesting that she visit some grizzled old man in Bath who had once carved ship's figureheads. Fortunately, Anna happened to grumble about it to Nora.

"You'd have to see him at the cemetery," Nora said. "He's been dead ten years or more."

Anna had at least learned how to extract payment from the man, who persisted in asking why she needed money.

"I need to see a fortune teller," she told him one week. (If he would not be honorable, she felt no need to be honest.) When Mr. Wimborne, predictably, asked why, Anna cast her eyes down and said, "It is a very deep secret. I cannot tell you."

"Is it a man, Miss Bradley?"

Eyes still on the floor, Anna shook her head and tried to make herself blush. Whether she succeeded in changing the tint of her cheeks, she could not say, but she got her payment. The next time, she told Mr. Wimborne that the fortune teller had told her she must purchase a red scarf and hat.

"To be worn at a particular moment?"

"Yes, but she instructed me not to speak to a soul about it."

When that particular line felt exhausted, Anna invented a friend in "desperate trouble." In response to his inevitable questions, she twisted her handkerchief and said, "Oh, please do not press me. I would not wish you to be involved."

"Why, Miss Bradley! Your life is far more interesting than I ever imagined."

Only because I am imagining it to be more interesting than it is, she thought, as she took the proffered check.

Anna had managed to save some money, but acting as a research assistant to Mr. Thatcher Winslow Wimborne was neither satisfying nor a sustainable path to independence, and she needed that path.

Though Anna did her best to absent herself when Lillian was around, that was not always possible. Thanks to Judith, who hung on her godmother's sleeve and watched everything like a hawk, Anna's sense that she was an object of suspicion had only increased.

That said, Mrs. Fairchild had actually given Anna an idea. Irma Bellingham's older sister Sally, a fellow Radcliffe graduate, worked as a reader for their uncle's publishing firm, Fanning and Scott, which put out a number of successful magazines. One of these, *Young Friends*, targeted children of Julia's age and older.

Send me stories! Sally often said. A three-thousand-word story, if accepted, could fetch fifty dollars.

Anna did not entirely relish the idea. Writing children's stories felt like an official declaration that she was not a scholar, or even a serious person. She needed the money, though, and if she wrote under a pseudonym, no one would need to know she had stooped so low.

She also found some pleasure in the thought of anonymously thumbing her nose at Judith Fairchild, whose latest newsletter extolled stories that "encourage girls to aspire to the womanly virtues of domesticity, docility, piety, and submissiveness."

It seemed worth trying, at least. Anna put her notes aside, got some fresh foolscap, picked up the fountain pen Elizabeth had given her for Christmas, and did not put it down again for three hours.

Using Julia and her friends as inspiration, Anna wrote about four girls on an island, two pairs of sisters who were cousins. Their mothers had died, and their fathers, who were off fighting in the Spanish-American War, had left them in the care of a spinster aunt. (For the aunt's character, Anna borrowed a good deal from Lillian Demarest, with a few dollops of Clarissa thrown in for good measure.)

The girls' liberal-minded fathers agreed to let them camp on an island with a chaperone. Through various mix-ups and a bit of chicanery, the girls ended up on Liberty Island unchaperoned, where they had many adventures.

Anna looked it over and felt satisfied with the results. The girls had given her so much material to work with, and she had read enough children's stories to know that it would at least entertain her hard-to-entertain niece. (Whether Julia was at all representative of the average reader—or the average anything—she could not say.) And as her characters were untainted by "domesticity, docility, piety, and submissiveness," she had succeeded in thoroughly transgressing Judith Fairchild's rules for girls' fiction.

I'll shine it up, send it off, and leave it to the publishing gods, she thought. If it turned out she could make money this efficiently, it would be something worth knowing, a bit of security in her back pocket.

Anna sent the story to Sally, asking that she be called Miss Crane (the maiden name of Margaret Fuller's mother). She resolved to tell nobody at all, including—perhaps *especially*—Elizabeth. Jerome was only vaguely aware of the girls' adventures on Gunnison Island, and Anna suspected her sister would like to keep it that way.

So thoroughly had Anna surrendered the story to the publishing gods, she very nearly forgot about it until the letter came from Sally.

I was thrilled with your submission, and my uncle shared my enthusiasm. So much so, he made room for it in the next issue. The check is enclosed. My uncle would like to see more of your work, and so would I!

Anna looked at the check. As with Mr. Wimborne, she was making up stories for money. This was a far more straightforward and efficient transaction, though, and vastly more enjoyable.

Anna could do this until the cows came home.

CHAPTER SEVEN

June 1917

Washington, DC

JULIA

The girls often pretended there was a naval blockade and practiced daring maneuvers in the cove. They watched for enemy spies on the shore, charged up San Juan Hill, pantomimed firing cannons, and captured Guam without firing a shot.

So, you see, they had not actually forgotten about their fathers, off fighting the war.

FROM *LIBERTY ISLAND*, BY MISS CRANE

Julia threaded her way around tables, dodging servants carrying bowls and platters to the buffet table at the center of the Seabornes' backyard. All was in preparation for the large group of war reporters about to descend upon them.

Mr. Seaborne approached Julia, a glint of mischief in his eyes.

"Margaret wants your help in arranging flowers, and then I believe she's assigned you to the punch bowl. Your real job, however, is to keep her away from the war photographers. If she gets talking to any of them, I'm afraid she'll run off to France herself."

Julia laughed. Margaret had taken up photography, and had even set up a darkroom in their cellar. Margaret was at the back of the yard, standing at a table piled with cut flowers from her garden, but when

Julia joined her, it was clear that she did not have war photographers on her mind.

"I am so glad you are here, Julia. I'm a nervous wreck," she said under her breath.

"About this party?" Julia asked, surprised.

"No, no," Margaret whispered. When she looked up, Julia saw the circles under her eyes.

"Oh, of course. You're worried about Michael," Julia said. "I'm sorry. I was not thinking. But I feel certain he will be all right. It is a relief, is it not, that he will be reporting?"

Michael had been torn between enlisting and going to Europe as a war correspondent. It was only when General Pershing said he'd rather have one good reporter over there than a whole battalion of men that Michael made his decision.

"I don't want Robert to know how worried I am. I am comparatively fortunate, of course, not having any of my sons enlisted as soldiers," Margaret said, as Julia picked up stems and greens and began arranging them in vases.

Ever since the United States officially entered the war in April, men of all ages had been signing up, but the older Seaborne "boys" (if one could use the word *boys* for married men with children) were working at their papers, immune to the pressure to enlist.

"You know Michael, though. He will take any risk presented," she continued. "That boy has always grabbed the happy skirt of chance, but luck and daring only count so much in this awful war."

"Michael is adventurous but sensible," Julia said. She realized then that she had been a bit blithe in thinking this, but she used her most reassuring tone. She knew the war was particularly hard on Margaret. In addition to having a son heading to France, Margaret tended toward pacifism. Even without a husband in the newspaper business, she would have had to be terribly guarded in what she said. There was no tolerance for even the mildest expression of doubt, since the whole city—indeed the whole country—seemed to have gone war-mad.

The boys in Julia's third grade class were no exception. Every recess during the spring term, Julia had been treated to the sound of their voices as they marched about the playground, holding sticks like guns. *Shoulder arms! Forward march! Hep-hep-halt! Mark time*... (Given that Julia had been obsessed with Teddy Roosevelt's Rough Riders at their age, she could not really fault them.)

An hour later, Julia stood behind the same table, the stems, greens, and vases replaced by a large bowl of punch and small glass cups. Though she was greeted cordially by many of the men, they had a clear preference for beer and whiskey.

The reporters stood about in clusters on the lawn, the younger and greener listening, as the more seasoned offered their opinions about the censorship rules they had learned about that day. Though arguably young and green, Michael naturally knew a great deal about the newspaper business. While his parents greeted the arriving guests, Michael circulated among them, spreading his usual good cheer.

As Julia was ladling a cup of punch to one of the rare takers, she heard his voice.

"Do you know Miss Demarest?" he said. "She went to Barnard."

"I don't believe I do."

When Julia looked up and saw Michael's companion, she almost fell over. *Pelham Stewart!*

Mr. Stewart had spoken the truth when he said he did not know her. In all these years, they had never met. Julia never missed his articles in *The Current*, where he still worked, though, and nothing she had read indicated he was going overseas.

After the long-awaited introduction, Michael was pulled away, leaving Julia and Mr. Stewart alone.

"How did we not know each other?" He cocked his head, as if this were a great mystery.

She smiled. "Oh, I knew you. You just didn't know me!"

Julia had not forgotten Mina's counsel. Men like Pelham Stewart were accustomed to sophisticated, worldly women, not eager ingenues.

But given the circumstances, where he was going, it did not feel right to pretend.

He shook his head, as if in wonder.

"You look as if you just found a long-lost puppy." Julia laughed.

"Perhaps I have, though . . . not a puppy." He returned her smile, leading her to imagine what other "long-lost" thing he might be thinking of. "I know I'm taking liberties as a man off to a war zone, but are you permitted to leave your post? I was going to get a plate, and I would love if you would sit with me."

Julia nodded at the full punch bowl and smiled. "I think I can be spared."

He filled a plate at the buffet, then led her to a wrought-iron bench outside Margaret's studio.

"How did you know me when I did not know you? I assure you, if I had seen your face, I would have remembered."

"I saw a talk you gave once, downstairs from *The Current*."

He groaned. "Was I dreadfully pompous?"

"Oh, not at all! You spoke about the old Protestant aristocracy and their puritanical ways. I remember thinking, 'When did he meet my father and brother?'"

Mr. Stewart responded with a gratifying laugh.

"I went to Barnard thinking I would be steeped in exciting modern ideas, but I was not really picking them up in Latin or botany. I was thrilled to attend that talk—quite dazzled, really." She shrugged, hoping that between her use of past tense and her mild expression, she would avoid giving him the impression that she was throwing herself at him.

"But I never met you!"

"We were supposed to meet once after that, but it did not come to pass. I think I've read everything you've written, though."

"You read *The Current*?"

She straightened, and with a tone of mock seriousness said, "I do, and have done ever since my brother mentioned it was run by"—she lowered her voice to an ominous pitch—"*dangerous radicals*."

He laughed again. "By which you inferred it was worth reading?"

"An indication, at least." She smiled. "I don't know much about politics, really, but I'm terribly interested."

He shifted to face her, arm on the back of the bench, his plate of food forgotten on his lap.

"Why, you're darling!" His expression was one of curiosity, perhaps even astonishment.

Julia's memory had not been overly charitable. He was still ruggedly handsome, with his broad shoulders and that tendency to pull his dark brows together. His blue eyes were softer than she remembered, though, and his hair, now cut close, had lost that unruly look.

"You look surprised," Julia said. "Do I make a very forbidding first impression?"

"Not at all. I noticed you were beautiful, of course, though I hardly need to tell you that. But you're so fresh and unaffected, so marvelously yourself. When were we meant to meet?"

"Your senior year. I was a freshman. Mina Ellis planned to introduce us at a party. I went, but it was quite crowded, and I left."

"You and Miss Ellis are friends?"

"Again, you seem surprised."

"Well, she's quite worldly. And you seem quite . . ."

". . . Unworldly, I know." Julia sighed. "Her friends were all so sophisticated, and I was determined to worm my way into her set. Mina did her best to help me tamp down my exuberance, but to no effect."

"Well, I am glad she failed," Pelham said with a frown. "And I wouldn't say 'unworldly.' *Otherworldly* would be more suitable."

"You flatter me, Mr. Stewart," Julia said, feeling a not unpleasant tightening in her heart.

"Ugh," he groaned. "Mr. Stewart is my father. I am again abusing the privilege, as I know you won't deny me, but can I ask that you call me Pelham?"

"Certainly. I'm Julia, then."

Pelham smiled broadly, his face transforming just as it had when she first laid eyes on him all those years ago. "So, Julia, what other advice did Miss Ellis provide?"

Julia figured she might as well open her budget to him. "I was under strict orders not to mention that I was on the basketball team."

"You played basketball? It gets better and better! Why did she think you should keep this a secret?"

"Too 'rah-rah-sis-boom-bah.' Do not mistake me. I was eager for her advice. I aspired to a languorous, mysterious air. Basketball was not in keeping with that image."

He laughed, then asked about her relationship to the Seabornes, and was delighted to hear about Julia's Concord roots, especially when it emerged that Julia's grandmother had lived on the Brook Farm commune in West Roxbury when she was a girl.

"It's a shame Brook Farm did not succeed," Pelham said. "I suspect under other circumstances they could have made a go of it. Did your grandmother enjoy it?"

"Very much, I gather." Winifred Newbold was very little at the time, and Brook Farm was indeed idyllic for children. However, Julia knew she emerged from it with no illusions about the practicability of such ventures. But if Pelham Stewart, on the eve of departing for the front lines, wished to believe Brook Farm might have had a chance, Julia was not about to disabuse him of that notion.

"They were among the first to recognize the importance of beauty and simple living," he said. "Now that you mention it, I caught a whiff of that as I walked through the house earlier."

"Yes. I love the Seabornes' house. Margaret is an artist, in fact."

"Is your home in Boston similar?"

Julia could not hold back a laugh, thinking of her comparatively lavish home in Back Bay. "Let's just say my paternal grandmother had more influence there."

Pelham looked at her closely, as if intrigued by the window she had opened. Julia, however, mentally slammed it shut.

Three years ago, when Julia announced that she had accepted a teaching job in Washington, Mother had taken it with equanimity. Father, however, still firmly believed that Boston was the hub of the universe, despite it not having been so for decades.

"Why go there instead of coming home?" he asked.

"Jerome, dear, she does have something like a home in Washington. The Seabornes are there."

The comment had stabbed at Julia's heart. Little did Mother know, Julia often felt more at home with the Seabornes than she did with her own family in Back Bay.

Father remained mystified by the decision, although it helped when Louisa took a job with the Department of Labor. (Her parents pretended to believe that Julia was looking after Louisa, though Julia knew that any comfort came from the reverse.)

Julia shifted to more comfortable conversational ground. "Mrs. Seaborne is actually named for a famous figure of Concord, Margaret Fuller."

"Ah, I know that name," Mr. Stuart said. "Fuller was an early advocate for women's education and rights, was she not?"

"Yes. Far ahead of her time."

Among Mina's friends, Julia was always the asker of questions. She never knew more than anyone about anything. It was refreshing to be able to tell Pelham Stewart a bit about this idol of her family.

"Did she live at Brook Farm?" Pelham asked.

"No, she was not a resident," Julia replied. When Pelham's brows went together, Julia detected a hint of disappointment and added, "She was a frequent visitor, though. In fact, they had a building there called Fuller Cottage."

This seemed to satisfy him, and they moved on to talk about matters of more contemporary interest. Pelham explained that *The Current* could not afford to send him to France, but *The New Republic* needed another war reporter, so he was going under their auspices.

Pelham asked what brought Julia to Washington. She explained that she had many friends there—the Seabornes, but also her best friend, Louisa, among others—and that she had been attracted to the opportunity to remain active in the suffrage movement.

She worried that her job at a public school a few blocks from the Seabornes might make her sound unambitious. Julia enjoyed teaching third grade, and she was happy at the Morgan School, but many Barnard alumnae had more interesting occupations, and those who became teachers generally aspired to jobs at better schools, teaching older students.

As it turned out, though, Pelham was interested in elementary education. "I think it's wonderful you're working with younger children. They're still moldable, so you have a chance to make a difference, help them become good thinkers."

Julia appreciated that her students were still at a socially uncomplicated age, even as they were beginning to leave their egocentricity behind and develop the ability to understand other people's perspectives. She did not wish to disappoint Pelham, however, by telling him that with nearly forty children in the classroom, her "molding" opportunities were limited.

The crowd had begun to thin out, so Julia and Pelham headed across the lawn toward the house. Halfway there, Pelham stopped abruptly and turned to look down at her.

"I am again being terribly forward, Julia, but I do not wish to say goodbye quite yet. I have time tomorrow afternoon. Can I see you?"

"I would like that," she said, and suggested a ride in Rock Creek Park. Julia kept no horses in Washington, but several friends who had gone overseas as nurses or ambulance drivers had given her permission to exercise their mounts in their absence.

They made their plans, and Pelham squeezed her hand and left. After Julia helped Margaret clean up, she looked around for Michael, hoping to say goodbye, but she could not find him anywhere. She gave up and got her cloak, but when she opened the door to leave, she found him sitting on the porch stairs, looking uncharacteristically somber. Julia sat down beside him.

"Are you all right, Michael?"

"I suppose," he replied, with a little shrug.

"Nervous?"

"No, it's not that." He took a deep breath, and then turned to look at her, a sad smile on his face. "I just fear I might have delivered you into the hands of a competitor this evening."

"Oh, Michael . . ." Julia said, her heart sinking.

"Don't worry, Julia. I have always adored you, and I suppose I always will. But I have also always been your friend, and I will always be that, too." He smiled again, reassuringly. "I am glad you know now. I'd hate it if I never told you and didn't make it back. But please, you are not to feel uncomfortable."

As if to underscore his point, he offered to walk her home, and as they made their way toward Connecticut Avenue, he kept up a steady flow of innocuous conversation. When they reached her row house on Mintwood Place, he turned to her and took her hands in his.

"I will miss you, my friend," he said, smiling down at her.

"I'll miss you, too, Michael," she said.

She said goodbye with a firm hug and her best wishes, but as she walked upstairs to her apartment, she felt terribly dismayed.

Michael had always been warm and supportive, but she'd had no idea that he felt anything beyond brotherly affection for her. He had squired her about Washington, just as he did during their two overlapping years in Morningside Heights. He took her to Monday evening dances at his country club, showed her all the best spots for good, long tramps through the woods, and made her his partner for all the Washington Canoe Club's mixed paddling contests.

Several of Michael's friends had taken Julia out, and she wondered why that never seemed to bother him. Thinking it over, though, it occurred to her that in those cases, he might not have felt he was "delivering her into the hands of a competitor." He would have been right, too. However eligible, none of Michael's friends had captured her heart.

Julia's row house, in the aptly named Pretty Prospect neighborhood, was narrow, but it was at the end of the block, and as she had the third floor to herself, she had windows on three sides. She went out to the sleeping porch at the back, lowered herself onto the cushion-covered daybed, and watched the sun set between the two large elms in the backyard.

In thinking about Michael's declaration, she began to wonder if it might have been the product of circumstances. Going off to war, even as a correspondent, surely made one sentimental. And on the eve of his departure, Julia was right there, as she always had been.

Conscious though she was of the contradiction, Julia elected not to apply similar skepticism to Pelham Stewart's interest. She had waited years to meet this man. Finally she had, and he seemed taken with her—the real her, too, not the intellectual imitation she'd tried on during her Barnard years. Their connection seemed meant to be, and she refused to believe it was mere eve-of-war sentiment.

Julia put on a navy worsted jacket over a white silk shirt and breeches, tan gloves and boots, and a simple straw sailor hat. She felt she looked effortlessly smart, despite the not inconsiderable effort that she put into selecting the outfit.

She arrived at the stable to find Pelham leaning against a fence, waiting for her. He approached and looked at her searchingly.

"So you weren't a dream."

"Flesh and blood." Julia smiled, and her heart quivered.

She got the horses, and they mounted and ambled down the bridle path that ran alongside Rock Creek. The woods were alive with the scent of spring, new leaf and flower. When they reached the old mill that now operated as a teahouse, they tied up the horses, ordered tea and biscuits, and sat beside the waterfall that ran from the mill dam. Everything else, the war and worry, might have been a million miles away.

Julia quickly gathered that Pelham Stewart was a man of many intellectual enthusiasms. Like all reporters, he was frustrated with limitations that had been placed on the war correspondents, and worried they would be used as tools for the military. He confessed that he would rather be going to Russia, as he had taken an eager interest in events there in the wake of the revolution in February.

He had also taken an interest in Sigmund Freud, the Austrian doctor, and even undergone psychoanalysis. "Freud exposed the constraints of bourgeois morality, the limitations that society puts on us. He helped me see how harmful my parents were to my development. My mother is obsessed with society's opinion, and my father has a very narrow view of what constitutes an appropriate occupation for his son. They're both very repressed."

Julia did not know many people who spoke candidly about their families. Mina was an open book, often talking about her awful mother, and she never hesitated to ask people probing questions about their own families. But while she practically rubbed her hands with glee at any interesting revelations—*Oh, now this is getting really good!*—Pelham's curiosity seemed more genuine. "I just want to know what sort of soil produced such a perfect specimen," he said.

Thus encouraged, Julia abandoned the reticence she had felt the previous evening.

"My father and brother subscribe to all the old notions about a woman's place, and have little patience for modern feminine rebellions, as they call them," Julia said. "I cannot say that I see the same sort of social ambition in my mother that you see in yours, though. I suppose if she had it, it was satisfied by her marriage. She is very contained, though. And so different from my aunt . . ."

Julia told him about Anna, the adventures she orchestrated for Julia, and the *Liberty Island* books that they inspired.

"It sounds like you found many ways to escape the harmful influence of Boston puritans," he said, laughter in his eyes.

"Oh, yes," she replied, cheerfully. "Though I cannot say I was harmed."

Pelham smiled gently. "Even if not harshly conveyed, expectations can still cause harm."

Julia felt uncomfortable, as if she were speaking out of turn. "I suppose I do not like to think of my family, particularly my mother, in this way."

"I understand. Perhaps I seem terribly disloyal in comparison."

"No, no. I did not mean that."

"Try not to feel guilty. Even if not intended in this way, guilt and family loyalty are tools that prop up archaic social constraints."

There was nothing of the condescending teacher about Pelham. He did not talk down to Julia, or seem like he was showing off what he knew. He was both passionate and compassionate, eager to share his interests.

Julia felt as if she had taken an intoxicant of some kind. Not for a moment did she feel she must pretend to know more than she did, or to be anything other than who she was. He seemed enchanted, delighted by her curiosity.

She was a bit flummoxed by one comment he made. His parents, he said, "perfectly illustrated why marriage is an outdated institution." She wondered if he opposed marriage entirely, or merely thought it was in need of reform. The latter would align him with Louisa, who objected to marriage laws that harmed poor working women. But afraid he would mistake her curiosity for personal interest, Julia did not probe further.

They reluctantly rode back to the stable, and after they dismounted and handed off the horses to the stableman, she walked with him toward the parking lot, where he had a borrowed car. He had offered to drive her home, but as she lived just a few blocks away, she declined.

He stopped in the shelter of some trees, looked around, and, seeing no one about, took a step closer to her.

"May I take one more liberty?" His expression was sweetly pleading. She nodded, and he pulled her toward him, put a hand behind her neck, then bent and kissed her.

Julia had been kissed before, though her career had not started auspiciously. (When she was fourteen, and Llewelyn Montgomery kissed her behind one of the great elms near the Frog Pond at the Boston Common, Julia had pushed him into a snowbank.)

She'd had better experiences since, however. Charlie Singer, for example, a friend of Michael's who took Julia out several times before she decided he was not quite for her, had kissed her quite nicely. He had nothing on Pelham Stewart, though. Julia felt this kiss like fire.

He pulled back, took her hands in his, and shook his head.

"I cannot believe I have only now met you," he said. "I am telling myself it bodes well. I have a reason to come home again."

"I'd like very much for you to do so," she replied. "So be careful?"

"I will write," he said, and they parted.

CHAPTER EIGHT

September 1899
New York City

ANNA

Sally Bellingham emerged from a door off the reception area. "You've come!" She threw her arms out wide, to the evident consternation of Fanning and Scott's formidable receptionist.

"I could hardly not! Your uncle bade me." Anna laughed, accepting her friend's embrace. Sally led her back through the door, which opened onto a long hall.

"I was treated to quite a tableau while I waited," Anna said.

"Were you? Tell!"

"A tidy, eager young man came in with a large envelope and was ushered into an office. Not thirty seconds later, a gentleman was disgorged from another. He was stooped and shaggy, much older, and very discouraged. I feared I was watching the metamorphosis of a fiction writer."

"You are endowing this with far too much metaphorical significance." Sally laughed. "But it can be a dispiriting business. That's why it's best to come with an attitude like yours."

"And what attitude is that?" Anna asked, as they stopped before the last door, with a window that bore the name GREGORY FANNING in large black letters.

"Deep reluctance!"

Anna opened her mouth to protest, but Sally held up a finger. "I have not forgotten your plans for the future, and juvenile fiction was nowhere in them." Sally lowered her voice. "But I hope you'll give my uncle a listen."

Anna assured her that she would not be there otherwise, though she could promise nothing else. In his letter, Mr. Fanning had said only that he wished to discuss "the reception of 'Liberty Island,' and possible future opportunities."

Sally knocked, and a deep voice beckoned them in.

Two hours later, Anna sat with Sally at a teahouse, her head spinning from the meeting. Mr. Fanning was businesslike, but not unfriendly. Pleased with the reception Anna's story had received, he proposed that she write an entire series set on Liberty Island. They would run one in *Young Friends* every month, and then publish it as a novel next summer.

"I will certainly give it some thought." Anna was glad to hear the story had done well, but she was not certain about making such a commitment.

Mr. Fanning smiled gently. "Sally has told me your ambitions run in a more scholarly line. I gather you are one of our accidental authors, which, as it happens, are often the best sort." He handed over some papers. "Perhaps this will help."

Anna took the proffered contract. Her eyes scanned over legalese and deadlines and then settled on the bottom line.

"Oh!" she replied, stunned by the numbers before her.

"It has been many years since we received so many letters from young readers in praise of one of our stories."

"*Rhapsodic* praise," Sally interposed.

"May I ask, Miss Bradley, how long it took to write the story?"

"Not a great deal of time, if I'm honest."

"Would it be difficult to come up with more ideas?"

"It would not." Anna could not hold back a chuckle. After sending off the story, she'd had another month on Jumaru, so she had loads of material.

"Well, then, it sounds as if this project would not be too much of a diversion from whatever else you would rather be doing."

This was certainly true. It would not take much time, and if the novel did well, it would set her up nicely, and then she could get back to the Fuller biography.

"All right, Mr. Fanning. I will accept the offer," she said. "On one condition."

"What is that?"

"A different illustrator," she replied.

Mr. Fanning looked at Sally, a question in his eye.

Sally laughed and held up her hands. "On my honor, we did not conspire!" She looked at Anna. "Did you and I discuss the illustrations?"

"Not a word passed between us on the subject," Anna said.

Mr. Fanning sighed. "All right. I accept that you came to the same conclusion independently. It will cost us more to hire an illustrator who is not already in our stable. Do you have someone in mind?"

"I do, in fact. Margaret Seaborne."

"I thought she had retired," Mr. Fanning said.

"She is an old family friend. I believe she can be persuaded to come out of retirement for this."

"If she can be convinced and doesn't try for highway robbery, I will consider it. Presuming she accepts, or we find another you are comfortable with, do we have a deal?"

"We do," Anna said.

Sally cheered, quite unprofessionally, and then laughed at her uncle's raised eyebrow.

"I must thank you, dear Anna," Sally said now, raising her teacup in a toast. "My stock has risen quite precipitously. My only fear is that my uncle is now under the impression that I can pull more rabbits out of the hat, when I know you are a rare bunny."

"I can't imagine that's true," Anna said. "Surely others have equal or better skill."

"I am not sure you understand how unique your story is," Sally said, shaking her head. "You might single-handedly revolutionize children's literature."

"Sally!" Anna laughed.

"I read children's stories all day every day, and I could not be more serious. It is not just that you took girls out of the domestic sphere and set them on adventures. It's also your style." Sally put her hands together in prayer and cast her eyes toward the ceiling. "Lord, deliver me from wise adult narrators talking down to the child reader."

"I have noticed that tiresome tendency," Anna conceded.

"And those few who do write from a child's point of view have obviously forgotten their own childhoods. Such idealized, sentimental pap. But your characters are so real, so true to life! How did you do it?"

Anna thought for a moment. "I confess I did not think it out. In addition to drawing inspiration from my very real niece and her friends, I suppose I was also responding to Julia's very real literary aversions."

"Perhaps I should hire her. Does she despise domestic stories?"

"She certainly prefers adventures. She is terribly addicted to dime novels." Anna thought some more and added, "And it's not that Julia minds *feelings*. Indeed, she has loads of them. But she cannot bear mawkishness."

"That reminds me, we did get a few complaints. One of our authors stormed into Mr. Scott's office and complained that the story was a 'dime novel masquerading as literature.'"

Anna smiled. "I accomplished my goal, then. Who was that author?"

"Mrs. Howland," Sally groaned.

"Oh, I know her books," Anna said. "I didn't realize Fanning and Scott was her publisher."

"We shouldn't be. Her tone is too moralizing, and her novels do not sell well anymore. She's also a terrible shrew. Mr. Scott has known her forever and puts up with her, though I don't know how. With every new book, we print fewer copies, and she invariably gives him an earful."

"What were the other complaints?"

"I'm sure you can guess." Sally shrugged. "The girls have too much license and behave in an unattractively masculine manner. Portraying girls outside the home gives them unrealistic expectations, which will lead to dissatisfaction. Oh, and the pacing will cause unhealthy vicarious excitement."

"And neither you nor your uncle is troubled by these concerns?"

"All the hand-wringing in the world will not keep girls from reading what they wish."

Anna returned home to find that Julia was in hot water. William, it seemed, had infuriated Julia with some comment. In retaliation, she snuck into his room, found his geography text, and wrote "Wee Willie's Book" on the inside front page.

This might not have been so bad, had his friends not seen it and called him "Wee Willie" all day. Julia had hit William where it hurt the most: his pride. He had learned his lesson on Haven Point, though. Rather than demanding his mother take some particular course of action, he came home and presented the evidence without comment.

As punishment, Julia would not be allowed to go with her school friends to *Brownies in Fairyland* at the Music Hall on Saturday, which she had looked forward to.

Anna found Julia in her room, quite impenitent, angrily railing about the injustice, but she could do little more than listen. The child was not ready to hear that she had brought this on herself.

When Saturday came, Julia's spirits were so much better that it aroused Anna's suspicions, and she wished she did not have an appointment with Mr. Wimborne at the Athenaeum. (He had been so forlorn when she announced she was quitting, she agreed to meet with him twice a month.)

When she returned two hours later, Lillian's carriage was outside, and upon entering the house, she saw her niece being led upstairs by Rosemary. Julia's face was scraped, her hair tangled, and her petticoat had a large rent through it.

Rosemary turned, and Anna shot her a questioning look. She whispered down the stairs, "Meet me in the library. I'll be down shortly."

Ten minutes later, Anna and Rosemary were huddled together behind the closed door of Jerome's library. Julia, it seemed, had concocted a plan to see the show at the Music Hall after all. She waited until Rosemary left to take William to a birthday party, then sat by her window until she spotted Katie, the servant girl next door. Julia opened her window, waved until she got Katie's attention, then gestured for her to stay put. Julia had written a letter, wrapped it around an apple, and then somehow tied it with string. Katie soon saw the missile flying from Julia's room, over the fence, and onto the ground a few feet away.

In the letter, Julia claimed to have been kidnapped by a bad old lady, and begged Katie to bring a ladder to her window. Katie, as addicted as Julia to adventure stories, had no trouble believing the tale. Rosemary was not sure how the girl pulled it off, but Katie somehow snuck out of her yard, found the ladder, dragged it to the side of the house, then scurried back to her own side of the fence.

"Julia would not have gotten far, of course, but she might not have fallen into the bushes had she not been carrying a valise with her party dress and shoes in it."

Franklin, the coachman, spotted Julia clambering out of the bushes. When he came over to help, Julia burst into tears. He took her hand and led her to the stable, promising he would give her a fair listen.

Julia, who was great friends with all the stable hands, had a very friendly audience for her tales of woe, after which Franklin commenced negotiations with the fugitive. He finally persuaded her to return to the house through the kitchen door, where she would be left with Cook, while he spoke to Elizabeth privately.

Unfortunately, Lillian had chosen that moment to arrive in her carriage. She was speaking to Elizabeth in the parlor when they spotted Franklin out the back window, leading Julia back to the house.

"What was Julia's plan for after the performance?" Anna wondered.

Rosemary shook her head with a sad chuckle. "She is a dreadful scamp, of course, and she has the most fantastical ideas. But she does not think very far in advance."

Rosemary went back upstairs, but Anna, hearing Lillian's voice emanating from the parlor, took a few steps closer to the door.

". . . do not take some action to improve that child's behavior, I will be forced to speak to my son about it," Lillian was saying.

As far as Anna could hear, Elizabeth did not reply.

"I wonder at you, Elizabeth! There is a grave danger that the child will become utterly incorrigible. She has no respect for authority. She is entirely too familiar with the servants. I'm sure she picks up that abominable slang she uses from the stables. And her reading! The most unsuitable and improper books. I gave her two improving stories for Christmas, but I do not think she has even cracked the spine of either."

Lillian was not wrong about that last point. Julia was practically allergic to "improving" stories.

"A child like that must be kept on the tightest of leads. She must be by your side as much as possible so that she might learn how to go on. And I do mean *your* side, Elizabeth, not her aunt's. I know she spends a good deal of time with your sister—entire days in the summer, I gather.

"I did not object when my son took your sister in, but I am increasingly concerned about her influence over my granddaughter, and I believe she displays a sad want of gratitude for someone so well circumstanced."

Though Anna had long sensed that Lillian held her in suspicion, the confirmation was rather unsettling.

"To what influence are you referring, Lillian?" Elizabeth asked. The touch of crispness in her tone was very slight indeed, but Anna was still gratified to hear it.

"Who can know, with that secretive air she has about her? Oh, don't act confused. Judith has noticed it, too," she said, impatiently.

"It is not too early to begin thinking about where Julia will be educated," Lillian continued. "She will need far more discipline than she will get in any school in this city. You and Jerome will come with me to Mrs. Fairchild's presentation about the Parisian school that has done such wonders for Emily."

Done wonders in removing the responsibility from Mrs. Fairchild's unwilling shoulders, Anna thought bitterly.

There was a pause, during which Lillian was evidently expecting some sort of answer. "Well, Elizabeth?" she said finally.

"We will consider it," Elizabeth said.

A telltale grunt suggested Lillian was lifting her considerable bulk from her chair, in preparation for her departure, and Anna took a few steps away from the door.

"Julia also needs the civilizing influence of Newport, so it is fortunate that she has reached the age William was when he began spending August with me. If you are unable to tear yourself away from that god-awful wilderness in order to accompany her, I will keep her by *my* side for the month, and ensure she has a full regimen of activities that will put her among better, more cultured influences . . ."

Lillian's voice throughout this speech was getting closer to the door, so Anna crept to the staircase and up to her room, where she sat on her bed, wondering what, if anything, she could possibly do.

Lillian's condemnations of Julia had always been absurdly disproportionate. It felt as if it was getting worse, though, and now bordered on an obsession. Bullies were not deterred by submission, and Lillian was nothing if not a bully.

Anna was mystified by her sister's passivity. Elizabeth had not been a particularly willful child, but nor had she been overly docile. She'd had some independence of spirit. When had she lost that?

Anna was tempted to conclude, *The moment she married Jerome*, but she quickly realized that was not correct. At least once in the intervening years, Elizabeth had showed remarkable spirit and resolve and a willingness to do the right thing, even if it meant keeping a profound secret from her husband. Anna remembered it like it was yesterday.

• • •

They were on Haven Point, and Elizabeth was well along in her second pregnancy. Other than the usual restlessness she felt when prohibited from swatting at tennis or golf balls, Elizabeth had sailed through it. That week, though, Anna had noticed that her sister seemed listless and distracted. Despondent, even, which was unusual for someone of such even temperament.

Even the enormous storm they had one evening had not roused her from her torpor. The next morning, Duncan Douglas came over to check for damages. Anna was sitting with Elizabeth in the living room when he came downstairs after looking over the attic. Fourwinds had come through relatively unscathed, but according to Duncan's description, Portland had not been so fortunate. The harbor was a mess, and trees and telegraph wires were down everywhere.

"A shipwreck, too," he said. "Commercial vessel on its way south."

When he left, Elizabeth's stupor was gone, replaced by a strange agitation. Out of the blue, she announced she had to go to Portland. Anna offered to go in her place, but Elizabeth insisted she needed to go herself.

"I'll come with you, then," Anna said.

Though Elizabeth finally agreed, it was with obvious reluctance. On the steamer, Elizabeth gazed out the window, silent and preoccupied. It was only when they disembarked that she finally turned to Anna.

"I just need to check something," she said.

With Anna in her wake, they headed to the office of one of the shipping companies. A crowd had gathered, and Elizabeth approached a man on the outskirts.

"Pardon me, but I gather one of the ships met with grief. Could you tell me which one?"

"The *Margaret Ann*," he replied. "Dashed on the rocks off Cape Elizabeth. Some made it to safety, but four or five died. Did you know someone aboard?"

Elizabeth shook her head, but her ashen face said otherwise. They moved a few feet away. Anna looked at her sister, a question in her eyes.

"Please," Elizabeth said, her voice strangled. "I promise I will explain later."

A young man, clearly a sailor, emerged from the office and approached a young woman who stood beneath a tree about fifteen feet from where Anna and Elizabeth stood. She wore a cloak but was obviously with child, even further along than Elizabeth. The man shook his head, and she let out a cry. He took her by the arm and led her inside the office.

After a beat, Elizabeth followed, Anna again trailing behind. Inside, a number of people were waiting to speak to the clerk, but they had evidently made way for the poor woman, who stood with her hands clasped before her, speaking with great urgency to the man behind the desk.

"I am sorry, but as I told Mr. O'Brien here, if you weren't wed, Mr. Moore won't pay out."

"Come now," the man, presumably Mr. O'Brien, said. "Calvin had the ring in his pocket!"

Calvin? Anna felt a terrible clutching sensation in her heart. Could this be *Elizabeth's* Calvin, her childhood sweetheart from the lake? As far as Anna knew, her sister had not spoken to him since he broke her heart more than five years ago. With his next words, the clerk confirmed his identity.

"Sounds like Mr. Stannarius planned to do right by you, but I'm afraid it won't change anything," the clerk replied, his tone as sympathetic as it was certain.

The woman's shoulders slumped, and Mr. O'Brien led her back outside. As soon as the door closed behind them, Elizabeth approached the clerk.

"This Mr. Moore truly will not help her?" Elizabeth asked. The clerk looked at her a bit oddly, clearly wondering why this elegant woman was taking such an interest in the case.

"Afraid not—stickler for morals, he is. He won't be helping an unwed woman who got herself in a family way."

Elizabeth managed a faint "Thank you" (while Anna refrained from asking how a woman could "get herself" in a family way).

Outside, Elizabeth stopped on the top stair, shaded her eyes, and looked about until she spotted Mr. O'Brien and the woman. He patted her shoulder and walked away, and the woman lowered herself onto a bench.

When Anna and Elizabeth reached her, she had her face in her hands.

"Excuse me," Elizabeth said.

She removed her hands and looked up, her eyes wet. She was small, fair-haired, and pale, with a roundish face. From afar, Anna had thought she looked plain, particularly in comparison to Elizabeth, who was all elegant contrasts—lush dark hair, blue eyes, and thick lashes against her creamy complexion. Now Anna saw that there was something taking about her, a dignity in her brown eyes and direct gaze.

"Yes?"

"I could not help overhearing you in the shipping office," Elizabeth said. "I apprehend that you are in some trouble. I wondered if I might serve you in some way."

"I don't know if anyone can help me," the woman said, sorrow giving way to weariness.

"Have you no family?"

The woman's face crumpled again. "My mam turned me out."

"Oh. That is very hard on you, I'm certain," Elizabeth said. Not waiting for an invitation, she slid onto the bench beside the woman. "Do you think her position will alter, given the sad news of what happened to the child's father?"

"She'll tell me to go to the Sisters." She raised her chin. "And I won't do that. I won't!"

Among the Irish, Anna knew, going to "the Sisters" meant putting one's baby in an orphanage.

"I understand," Elizabeth said, with a kind smile. "Again, I would like to help."

The woman looked confused. "I'm sorry, but who are you? Why were you in the office?"

"We knew of someone on a commercial vessel and thought it might be the same one."

"But it wasn't," the woman said, in a flat tone that suggested she envied Elizabeth her good news. As it was a statement and not a question, Elizabeth was spared the need to tell a lie.

"This is my sister, Anna Bradley," she said instead. "And my name is Elizabeth Demarest."

Elizabeth had waited a beat between the two names, and Anna suspected she was wondering if the name Bradley might elicit a spark of recognition. Cal had been so reserved, it seemed unlikely he would have mentioned Elizabeth to this woman, but she needed to be sure.

Indeed, neither Anna's name nor Elizabeth's seemed to register.

"My name is Johanna. I've . . . I've been going by Stannarius," she said, her eyes dropping.

"Of course you have," Elizabeth said. "I think I can help, if you would permit me."

"Why would you want to help me?" She seemed more confused than suspicious.

"In one regard, I have occasion to be sympathetic." Elizabeth smiled gently and glanced down at her own midsection. "I am fortunate in my circumstances and think it most regrettable that Mr. Moore is unwilling to do his duty. I have a summer home not far from here, and a dear friend there whose family has lived on this coast for generations. They know the sorrow of losing loved ones at sea. I will need to speak to her, but I am certain she will assist you. May I ask where you're staying?"

The woman did not speak for a moment. Anna suspected she resisted becoming an object of charity, indebted to a woman she had never before laid eyes on. However, as she had made clear, she was without choices. She closed her eyes and let out a defeated sigh.

"At a boardinghouse. I don't know how long I'll be there. We were there as a married couple, but you know how word gets 'round. The landlady will probably turn me out, too."

"I think you are safe tonight. Will you let us walk you there? I will speak to my friend and come back tomorrow."

Clever, Anna thought. Elizabeth could have just asked for the name of the boardinghouse, but being seen in Elizabeth's respectable company would mitigate against the outcome Johanna feared.

She shook her head slightly, as if she wanted to reject Elizabeth's offer, but once again, she acquiesced. "All right. Thank you."

The boardinghouse was in a shabby quarter of town, but it had a small, well-kept yard. Several people were gathered on the porch.

"You may tell them I knew the father's family," Elizabeth said in a low voice. "That I heard what happened and came to see you. Do you understand?"

The woman nodded, unaware it was the truth, but able to see the advantage. When they reached the gate, Elizabeth turned to her and took her hands in her own.

"Again, I am very sorry for your loss, Mrs. Stannarius, but I am glad I saw you, and we will be back tomorrow." Elizabeth spoke with a hint of familiarity for the benefit of the spectators. They watched as Johanna ascended the stairs, nodded somberly to the people on the porch, and entered the boardinghouse.

Elizabeth said nothing as she and Anna returned to the steamship landing and purchased their tickets back to Haven Point, but she was the picture of agonizing grief, her face slack, her inside brows turned up.

On the steamer, they found seats in a quiet corner of the ladies' cabin. Elizabeth sat by the window again and looked out, silent and deathly still. It was not until they had left the harbor, and the steamer began to wend its way among the islands, that she finally turned to Anna and took a deep, shaky breath.

"I saw Calvin in Portland a few days ago."

"Had you seen him since . . . ?"

Elizabeth shook her head. "I had not laid eyes on him since he left that summer."

Anna knew she meant the summer he stopped writing her.

Elizabeth's mouth trembled, and she looked out the window again. "I can hardly bear to think of how I behaved when I saw him. He was so kind, so earnestly curious to know how I was, but I was stiff, formal. Finally, he said, 'Liz, why are you being this way?' I said I knew it had been many years, but I could hardly forget how he had ended things with me, without even the courtesy of an explanation."

Elizabeth turned to Anna now. "He looked at me a moment, and then it was as if something had dawned on him. He said, 'Liz, I never stopped writing you.'"

With a terrible, blinding clarity, Anna understood what had happened. "So, Clarissa . . ." she began, a dangerous edge in her voice.

". . . intercepted the letters," Elizabeth said. "Cal even tried to call on me in Cambridge that September, but she said I was engaged to Jerome Demarest. We weren't, not yet. She merely told him what she wished to make manifest. When Cal later heard we were married, what was he to think, other than that she had spoken the truth?"

A tear ran down her cheek. "He asked, 'How could you have thought that of me, Liz?'"

"Oh, no . . ." Anna put her hand on Elizabeth's forearm. Before Mother died, she and Father had told Elizabeth they approved of the union, but only wanted them to wait until they were a little older. Calvin and Elizabeth were all but engaged by the summer in question.

"It was fair of him to ask. The only answer was that my pride got in my way."

"But you were so young, Liz. And what an act Clarissa put on!" When Calvin's letters stopped coming, Anna immediately suspected their stepmother. Clarissa, however, had acted angrier than anyone. She even threatened to see Calvin's family and demand justice, which Elizabeth forbade her to do. "She was too clever, too wicked."

Elizabeth did not look convinced.

"You were looking for Johanna today, weren't you?"

Elizabeth nodded. "Calvin was alone when I saw him outside the shipping office, but I spotted them later when I was waiting for the steamship. They did not see me."

"What do you hope to do for her?"

"The Grahams have that cottage on the other side of the peninsula. It's not occupied now. She could stay there." The cottage, built by some ancient Graham relation, was rarely used, but George had kept it up with an eye on selling it when the economy improved. They'd had guests there as recently as last summer.

"We have doctors on call, with Serena, Nora, and I all expecting, so plenty of help when the time comes. There's not much reason to go to that side of the point, and presuming Nora is amenable, we can come up with some explanation."

"What do you plan to say to Clarissa?" Anna relished the prospect of the confrontation.

Elizabeth shook her head. "Nothing."

Anna was stunned. "But you must!"

"What good would that do?"

It was her standard response when Anna suggested they confront Clarissa about some overreach or urged Elizabeth to stand up to Lillian. Anna was dismayed for a moment, until she realized that this situation was different. Elizabeth could not risk Jerome learning anything about her encounter with Calvin, or what she hoped to do for his fiancée and child. (Anna was not sure Jerome had ever heard the name Calvin Stannarius, never mind knowing what Calvin had been to Elizabeth. Either way, he was hardly likely to approve of Elizabeth's plan.)

"You are very kind, Elizabeth. Mother would be proud," Anna said.

Nora came through, and arranged everything in her usual competent way, and after the baby came a week later, Johanna's mother relented and agreed to take her daughter and granddaughter in. As far as Anna knew, Jerome never heard a word about it, and Elizabeth had never spoken of it again.

Anna wondered if something in Elizabeth had broken when she learned what she had lost through Clarissa's deceit. She could not remember seeing an ounce of spirit in her sister since.

Anna was glad she had found a way to earn some money. If Elizabeth was not even willing to fight for her daughter, she certainly wouldn't fight for her sister.

CHAPTER NINE

August 1917
Washington, DC

JULIA

When the tide was right, and only the tops of the rocks they'd placed along the water's edge showed, they played Cross the River. They leapt from rock to rock, careful not to slip into the water, lest they be pulled into dangerous rapids or get eaten by an alligator.

There weren't really alligators, of course, and it was only a few inches of water, but it's easy to persuade yourself of something when everyone else acts like they believe it, too. (Grown-ups do it all the time, only they don't admit it's pretend.)

FROM *LIBERTY ISLAND*, BY MISS CRANE

The curtain had closed, but Louisa was still laughing.

"Now you know why I insisted we sit in the rear of the theater," Julia said to Bess Riordan, her fellow third grade teacher at Morgan. "Take Louisa to a comedy, and she'll barely crack a smile. Dramatic films? In hysterics, beginning to end."

"It was too absurd." Louisa was still mirthful as they gathered up their things and left the theater.

"It was rather ridiculous," Bess said. She stopped and read from the poster on the wall outside, one hand on her chest, the other stretched out dramatically. "'Theda Bara's Camille is a comet of Exalted Passion rushing brilliantly across the firmament of life!'"

"See?" Louisa said. "High comedy."

They headed down Columbia Road until they reached Bess's corner. They bade her goodbye with a hug; then Julia and Louisa continued toward Mintwood Place, where they would dress for Mina Ellis's housewarming party.

The suffrage effort was heating up, and Mina and several of her friends from New York had taken jobs with the National Woman's Party. "We're storming the barricades!" Mina said in her letter announcing their plans. Julia had been glad of the news, but she had a few concerns.

Julia and Louisa were as close as ever, and though jobs in different parts of the city made it impractical for them to live together, their more separate lives had only expanded both of their circles. But Louisa and Mina had never gotten along very well; Louisa still maintained that Mina was not a good friend to Julia, and she felt her teasing was too hard-edged.

That said, she had readily agreed to attend the housewarming, so Julia had reason to hope that Mina's presence would not cause problems in her most treasured friendship.

"Does Mina know anything about you and Mr. Stewart?" Louisa asked, naming another of Julia's concerns.

"Well . . . she knows that I met him," Julia said.

"Only that?" Louisa raised an eyebrow.

"I know. I know . . ." Julia sighed.

Mina was proprietary about people, and it would irk her that Julia and Pelham were communicating without her knowledge, especially if she learned about it from someone else. It had not felt so consequential when Mina was hundreds of miles away in New York, but now she would live in Julia's neighborhood.

Pelham's first letter had come not long after he left for France.

I think of your bright eyes and eager shoulders, how pleased I was that you did not touch your hair when you removed your hat. You were so unselfconscious, and your hair so charmingly tousled. I can still picture the ringlets the damp air made about your face.

I wish I had not wasted an hour of the twenty-four between meeting you and my departure on something so mundane as sleep. I could have spent them with you, basking in your sun, appreciating your youth. (We were nearly the same age then, but every week here adds a decade to my years. Soon I will be old enough to be your grandfather.)

Pelham did not write of battles or troop movements. He sent his observations of people, places, and ideas. His letters had a discursive quality, as if he was continuing the conversation they had begun during their brief time together. Julia was already familiar with his beautiful prose, and his brilliant, incisive thinking. She was flattered that these skills were being put to use for her sole benefit.

As she and Louisa dressed, Julia again considered telling Mina, but ultimately she decided against it. She and Pelham were nurturing something in their letters, like an egg in an incubator, and any disturbance could crack the delicate shell. Mina was so indiscreet, Julia could easily imagine her making public property of what was, for the time being, theirs alone.

"I must say, Mina is awfully lucky that you love dogs," Louisa said, as they headed down the block. "She'd never have found this place otherwise."

"Perhaps I should patent it—the Canine Method! The answer to the housing shortage."

Finding places to live in the capital was a famous challenge, especially for unmarried women. Many advertisements explicitly forbade "Bachelor Girls." Fortunately for Mina, Julia had befriended Zeke, a large, homely creature who was often in the fenced yard of a row house she passed on her way to and from school.

Zeke's owner, Mrs. Palmer, occasionally rented rooms to young working women. When Mina announced she was coming, Julia asked if she had any available, though she thought it best to be candid. "They're moving here to work for women's suffrage, and they're a bit . . . *unconventional*."

Mrs. Palmer narrowed her eyes in thought. "I can take your one friend," she said finally. "Not sure I can stomach a houseful."

When Julia and Louisa reached the gate, Zeke galumphed over to greet them. Julia scratched the back of his neck, and his tongue lolled with pleasure. The door opened, and they looked up to see Emmeline, Mrs. Palmer's maid.

"You've come to see your friend?" she asked, a rather haughty expression on her face. Julia smiled. Emmeline had an aristocratic bearing, and Mina and her friends had clearly outraged her sense of decorum (which Julia had observed was far stricter than Mrs. Palmer's).

"It's good to see you, Emmeline. And yes, we're here to see Miss Ellis."

"Just follow the noise," she sniffed.

Julia and Louisa, thoroughly amused, climbed the stairs to Mina's door. There was music coming from inside, some twangy Hawaiian tune, but to Julia's relief, it was not terribly loud.

"Duchess!" Mina stood in the middle of the small living room, arms out, a large bottle of gin in one hand. She wore exotic harem pants in a brown-and-gold pattern, and a loose peasant blouse. Her dark hair was bobbed short.

"I think you've shocked Emmeline," Julia said, laughing.

"I've shocked *who*?" Mina asked.

"Emmeline. The maid?"

"Oh, well—" Mina waved a hand, and Julia cringed inwardly. Mina's head was often in the clouds, but it had not escaped Julia's notice that her friend was particularly oblivious to servants, streetcar drivers, and others in unexalted professions.

Clothes spilled out of an open trunk in the corner, and cardboard boxes were serving as coffee tables. The ukulele strains Julia had heard came from a little Victrola in the corner.

Looking beyond the messiness, Julia felt a little thrill, a sense that she had found something she had been missing in Washington. On the wall behind Mina hung a giant unframed painting of a woman in a kimono, holding a corset out her window, preparing to drop it into a trash can below. Painted in large black letters at the top was the message “Can the mind be enfranchised when the body is enslaved?” On the other walls were illustrations from *Rogue*, a satirical fashion magazine where Mina worked for a spell.

Three other guests had arrived, two of whom Julia and Louisa already knew—Mina’s former roommates Vera Markwell (“Vera the Dancer”) and Jane Varney (“Jane the Socialist”). The third guest, Mitzy Warren, was one of their illustrator friends.

“Is Vera all right?” Julia asked, nodding toward the divan. Vera, in a loose, silky dress, a batik scarf tied around her head, was stretched out, with one long, thin arm dangling off to the side, and one long, thin, bare leg thrown over the back.

“She got herself tangled up with Bernard Fulton,” Mina said. Bernard was a writer who lived with his wife, Francine, in Greenwich Village. (Despite their iconoclasm, Greenwich Villagers did occasionally get married, though as Mina once said, they were “usually quite apologetic about it.”) Francine, also an illustrator, had created some of the *Rogue* covers gracing Mina’s wall.

“Mystifying to all of us, as the man dances like a rudderless barge,” Mina said. “Francine supposedly believed in free unions, but she reneged when she had a baby. Bernard now calls himself an ‘experimentalist.’”

“Sounds very scientific,” Jane said. “Six syllables, when the two-syllable *cheater* would be just as apt.”

More guests arrived—mostly women, as was the case with all gatherings of young people these days, but a wonderfully shaggy older gentleman, a sculptor friend of Jane’s, showed up, as did a young writer who happened to be in town, and a couple of other men who were working on labor issues in the capital.

As Julia had expected, there was much grumbling about the fact that Washington would be a dry city in a few months. Julia had never been much of a drinker, so she did not have quite the same dread of Prohibition as others did, but she had always found mild inebriation to be contagious. Mina's guests gave the impression of getting all the liquor they could into their systems, like bears preparing for hibernation, and Julia's spirits rose as people loosened up and grew more cheerful and amusing.

Evidently tourists had discovered Greenwich Village, and Mina and Jane staged an impromptu skit, pretending to be the "rich plutocrats" peering at the residents of the village like they were animals in the Central Park Zoo.

The drinks were not having an enlivening effect on Vera, who was only growing more maudlin. Her friends tended to her in shifts, and Mina even managed to get a smile out of her with a pitch-perfect charade of Bernard and Vera on the dance floor, alternating between acting as Vera (graceful gliding) and as Bernard (awkward shuffling).

Mina and her friends had plenty of other complaints about Washington, but Julia had been prepared for those and mostly took them in stride (though it did irk her to hear Mina complain about living in the "suburbs," given how fortunate she was to have this apartment).

Julia, for her part, had been pleasantly surprised by Washington. Though her hometown had a larger population, between Boston society's obsession with family lineage and the layout of the city, which allowed affluent families to wall themselves off in Back Bay and on Beacon Hill, it had always felt cramped.

Washington was more transient, and the neighborhood divisions were not so distinct, so it felt more porous socially. The "cave dwellers," as the old Washington families were called, were known for their clannishness and disdain of "official Washington," but even that set contained a number of smart, broad-minded young women.

Julia also met many interesting people through the Seabornes, who hosted a never-ending parade of diplomats, artists, writers, and politicians, and she'd found a group of outdoorsy women with whom she regularly went canoeing.

While it compared favorably to Boston, however, she knew Washington was not New York. It had no bohemian enclave like Greenwich Village, and Julia relished the vibrant conversation and rapid-fire exchange of heterodox ideas.

That said, she was also reminded of some things she had not missed.

"Will you be joining the protest outside the White House?" Jane asked.

"Julia can't possibly," Mina teased. "She'll lose caste."

"You mean lose *my job*," Julia said with a sigh. The suffrage movement had long been divided between the moderates and the radicals, and the war had only deepened the divisions. The moderates were committed to supporting the president and having their members do war work, while the radicals were staging protests outside the White House.

Mina and her friends had little patience for the moderates, but Julia and Louisa pitched in when they could, with little regard to which group was sponsoring a particular effort. They often rolled bandages at a nearby toy shop, which converted to a surgical-dressing station every evening after closing, and they also had spent many hours at the National Woman's Party headquarters, helping with mailings.

Participating in public protests, however, would likely cost both Julia and Louisa their jobs.

"I'm just teasing, Duchess!" Mina said. "Oh, you must tell everyone what your grandmother said about suffrage."

This was the dance Mina had always done with Julia. One moment, she would tease, and the next, she would pull Julia into the conversation and set her up to be amusing.

"My grandmother insisted that any reasonably attractive woman can get what she wants from men without having the vote," Julia said. "I replied, 'But Grandmother, what about unattractive women?' To which she said, 'Julia, you are not unattractive. If you would just behave, I am sure *some* man will have you.'"

This did get a laugh, after which Mina, as usual, inserted a bit of her own commentary. "Julia's grandmother is the epitome of the blue-blooded Bostonian, straight from a Henry James novel."

Among Mina's friends, Julia always felt like a visitor to a foreign country, someone who had learned the language but could not be expected to speak like a native. Between Mina's comment about her grandmother, whom she had never met, and her liberal use of "Duchess," Julia could not help feeling that she was being marked as an outsider.

In need of a change of scenery, Julia joined Louisa, who was at the kitchen table with Mitzy and a few people from the labor world.

Mitzy was describing a book she was illustrating, designed to get children interested in socialism, when Mina popped into the kitchen for more glasses and caught a few words of the conversation.

"Julia's aunt wrote children's books. That series . . . What was it called, Julia?" Mina said.

Mina knew very well what it was called, but being ignorant of "all things children" was part of her image.

"*Liberty Island.* Our family friend Margaret Seaborne was the illustrator."

"Oh, yes. I'm familiar with Mrs. Seaborne's work. Nicely illustrated. And good books for their time, I suppose."

"For their time?" Louisa asked. Between her diminutive stature and big clear eyes, Louisa could make a pointed question sound like it had no edges at all.

"They're just a bit dated. I know it's only been fifteen or twenty years since they came out, but things have changed so much."

"Better than all that sentimental Victorian nonsense, though," one of Louisa's labor friends said.

"As it happens, I think that is a problem," Mitzy said, with a hint (very slight) of apology in her expression. "The style is more contemporary, and the girls are depicted as enjoying some freedom. It gives off a deceptive whiff of modernity."

"How so?" Louisa asked.

"The characters obtained their so-called liberty through duplicity, and at the end of every book, they slip back into their conventional lives. Portraying female freedom as illicit reinforces bourgeois norms. I mean no offense, but I actually think it is quite harmful."

"I see," Louisa said. Through all of this, she wore her usual placid expression, but Julia knew she was fuming, a fact that was confirmed when they left a little while later (the remaining guests having transitioned from the cheerful inebriation Julia found enjoyable to the sloppy version she did not).

"Absurd, what that Mitzy woman was saying about *Liberty Island*."

"Hah! I knew she got your goat," Julia said. "Don't you think she has a point, though? What freedom did we really have on the island? We always came back to Haven Point."

"Julia, you know what we had was unusual."

"Of course, but the point is, it should not have been. Remember how we were discouraged from talking about it, and how at first we only went on weekdays, when most of the fathers were away? That was because they weren't to know how wildly we behaved out there."

Louisa shrugged. "Right. They probably wouldn't have approved."

"But has anything changed on Haven Point? I don't begrudge Maudie and Ruthie their marriages, which I am sure will be happy, but do you not see them as just conforming to bourgeois norms?"

"Julia, I know all these ideas about completely upending society are alluring," Louisa said. "But there's a danger of throwing the baby out with the bathwater."

"Oh, let's not argue." Julia gave Louisa's shoulder a squeeze. Liberty Island was one of the few subjects about which Louisa was very sentimental. And while modern in some ways, she was still a traditional, old-fashioned Catholic girl.

Julia had not been as offended as Louisa by Mitzy's observations, but she was troubled by the idea that the *Liberty Island* books could be harmful. She told Pelham all about the evening in her next letter, how she had felt among Mina's friends, and about the exchange with Mitzy.

His response was somewhat encouraging.

I was sorry to read of the discomfort you felt at that party. How I wish you could see yourself as I see you. Your mother might have cast off the spirit of Concord in her effort to please and conform, but it is obviously in your blood and bones. Your curiosity, tolerance, and liberality of spirit shine through in your letters, as do your reverence of nature and beauty, and your ability to share in your students' childlike wonder.

Every letter you write gives me a glimmer of hope in this dark horror. If you felt uncomfortable in a room I suspect was full of sharp tongues and hard edges, I can only rejoice!

Julia smiled. Pelham never made her feel like she was pressing her nose against the glass, looking in from the outside. She did not have to wear a sack dress or write modernist poetry for him to treat her as a fellow traveler. Her membership in his world was her birthright as a child of Concord.

Regarding your aunt's books, I understand what Mitzy was getting at. We are in a pitched battle against the stale old morality, and ingrained habits of society. Her concerns, though, were overwrought. As Sigmund Freud has taught us, children are perfectly able to distinguish fantasy from reality. They do not become what they read.

All that said, I wish your mother had not felt the need to hide you away! A perfect world would celebrate the freedom-loving, imaginative, and expressive child that I know you were, but you did not grow up in that world.

Julia was reassured by Pelham's very sensible analysis. Just as girls could read *Little Women* without thinking that the March family's world was, or should be, their own, they could read *Liberty Island* and know that it was written at another time.

It was a bit sad, though. Julia had not realized it until Mitzy's comment, but the books *were* dated. The depictions of girls of such independent spirit, venturing beyond the domestic sphere, actually caused a minor uproar when *Liberty Island* first came out. But while women still had miles to go, things had changed enough in the last seventeen years to render the books a bit quaint. *Liberty Island* would continue to please girls, thanks to Anna's clever writing and Margaret's brilliant illustrations, but they were stories from another time.

When Julia reread Pelham's letter, however, she had a disquieting revelation. It was in the contrast between Mitzy's comment about how the girls in *Liberty Island* used trickery to gain their freedom and Pelham's remark about Mother "hiding Julia away."

Julia had always been proud that she and her friends had inspired the characters in her aunt's books. But had they? Their fictional counterparts seized the island, but in real life, these adventures had been orchestrated for them.

Perhaps Pelham was right that children could distinguish fantasy from reality. Now that she was grown, however, Julia began to wonder how much she had been conflating the two.

CHAPTER TEN

July 1900
Haven Point, Maine

ANNA

William and Julia were on the dock, getting ready for the boat parade, while Elizabeth and Anna sat on a bright red carriage quilt, looking down upon the festivities. The lawn of the yacht club was like a green sea dotted by blanket islands, with children darting between, accepting treats offered out of large wicker picnic baskets.

George Graham's reading of the Declaration of Independence had been followed by a few speeches, and now the musical portion of this rather homespun Independence Day celebration was underway. Some small children were playing horns and harmonicas, and Anna perceived with some amusement that at the moment it might be a touch *too* homespun.

"I assume it's a patriotic song?" she whispered to Elizabeth.

"They're so dear," Elizabeth whispered back. "But they sound like a flock of geese."

The children finished to loud applause (in part for their effort, and in part from relief that the performance had concluded).

"By the way, did you see the letter from Father I left on your bureau?" Elizabeth asked.

"Yes, thank you. Brimming with personal insights and warm sentiment," she said dryly.

Elizabeth let loose an unladylike snort. Father, his mind benumbed by his years with Clarissa, had adopted the efficiency of writing joint letters to Anna and Elizabeth. They read like telegrams: *Clarissa and I went here and there . . . Clarissa and I saw him and her.*

One line at the end of the otherwise uninteresting missive had caught Anna's eye, however: "We look forward to seeing Julia in Newport in August." Anna had felt a spasm of anxiety when she read it. If Julia went to Newport, it would mark the first time Elizabeth had handed her daughter over to a grandmother who had made no secret of her disapproval of the child, or of Elizabeth's manner of raising her.

Anna was not privy to all of Elizabeth and Lillian's conversations, but she had heard enough comments over the months to discern that Lillian had grown quite insistent upon the idea of sending Julia off to a convent school. Anna felt certain she was amassing evidence to bring to Jerome.

A month in Newport under her grandmother's watchful eye would surely add to the dossier of Julia's sins, but Anna had yet to see a single sign of resistance from Elizabeth.

"I noticed what Father said about Julia. Is she going to Newport?"

"William was her age when he began going," Elizabeth replied.

"Do you *want* her to go?" Anna persisted.

"I'd rather Julia be with me, of course, but she might wish to go."

Though her sister's evasiveness was both irritating and worrying, Elizabeth's next question reminded Anna that she, too, was keeping her own counsel about important matters.

"I saw you also got a letter from your friend Sally Bellingham. How are she and Irma?"

"Oh . . . they're fine," Anna said.

Now that *Liberty Island* was being shipped to booksellers, Anna had longed to tell her sister about it. She had not forgotten Nora Graham's wisdom, though: Sometimes it was better not to reveal to someone what might be uncomfortable for them to know. While each new installment of the serialized version in *Young Friends* had brought an ever-greater number of readers, they had also garnered a corresponding number of complaints.

According to Sally, the letters came from "rich, bored women," usually in cities or towns where some crusading figure had successfully stirred up a panic. Given that Judith Fairchild was Boston's very own "crusading figure," and that Lillian had latched on to the issue as another cudgel against Julia, it would put Elizabeth in an uncomfortable position to know that Anna was the author of a book that was likely to gain infamy in moralizing circles.

Ambrose and Serena were entertaining a large house party, and when Anna's eyes wandered to where they were set up, she thought she recognized a familiar set of broad shoulders and fair hair beneath a hat. She could only see a bit of his profile, though.

"Is that Harley Lockwood with the Lawrences?"

"Yes! He just arrived today." Elizabeth sounded pleased. Considering that the last time Anna laid eyes on him was at the Athenaeum Library, when he had behaved so condescendingly about her work with Mr. Wimborne, she could not share her sister's enthusiasm.

Oh, well. At least his sister isn't here, Anna thought.

"Mr. Lockwood has also persuaded Eugenia to take time off work," Elizabeth added brightly. "She will be joining him soon."

Anna refrained from audibly groaning. Eugenia Lockwood's inevitable questions about the Margaret Fuller biography and her endless yammering about her settlement house would be constant reminders of the Very Important Work others were doing, while Anna frittered her life away writing children's stories.

She consoled herself with the idea that she need not interact with them much, but minutes after Elizabeth went down to the dock to help with the children's boat parade, Anna felt a shadow blocking the sun and looked up to see Mr. Lockwood.

"Hello, Miss Bradley. I am pleased to see you," he said. "May I join you?"

"Um . . . yes, of course," Anna said. He lowered himself onto the blanket, wrapped his arms around his knees, and they exchanged civilities. Anna inquired about the Lawrences' agenda for their guests, and Mr. Lockwood rattled off some planned amusements, before mentioning what she already knew, which was that his sister would arrive soon.

"Wonderful!" Anna said, then compounded her mendacity by adding, "I look forward to seeing her."

There was a certain awkwardness in Mr. Lockwood's manner that made Anna think he had some particular purpose in approaching her. As they waited for the boat parade to begin, he finally revealed it.

"Miss Bradley, I am not sure you remember the last time I saw you, but I do, and with some regret, as I believe I behaved badly."

"Oh, I remember," Anna said in a breezy tone, her eyes still on the water.

"I confess I am not . . . well, *fond* of Mr. Wimborne, and knowing you were Eugenia's most intelligent classmate, I suppose I was surprised to see you working with him. It was none of my affair, of course, and I hope you will accept my apology, both for my behavior and for how long it has taken me to express my remorse."

Anna did not like Mr. Wimborne either, of course, though she was not about to give Mr. Lockwood the satisfaction of knowing that. On balance, it seemed best to get it behind them.

"I was a bit miffed, I confess. Women cannot always afford to be particular about their opportunities. But I appreciate and accept the apology." Anna concluded this with a nod, which she hoped, like a period, would put an end to the conversation.

He thanked her for being gracious, and his shoulders seemed to relax a bit. Fortunately, the boat parade was getting started, which provided a distraction.

"Ambrose tells me they're thinking of changing the name of this place from Haven Point," Mr. Lockwood said after a few minutes. "I gather he and his friend Mr. Graham are struggling to reach agreement."

"Yes. It's been a years-long debate."

"Ambrose had a thought earlier." Mr. Lockwood's eyes were on the children paddling by in a decorated canoe, but she saw a smile playing at the corner of his mouth.

"Oh? And what was his latest?"

"'L'Haute Falaise.'"

Anna stifled a laugh. "Of course, 'The High Cliff.' I assume he has not yet presented this to Mr. Graham."

"Not that I know of."

"If past is prologue, George will not be enthusiastic. At one point, Ambrose wanted a name that evoked restfulness. When he suggested 'Locum Pacificum,' George said, 'But we're on the Atlanticum.'"

Mr. Lockwood chuckled. "Perhaps we can help. How does this place see itself, its essence?"

She mirrored his faux earnestness and pretended to give the question careful thought. "It's not aristocratically standoffish like Newport," she said.

"Excellent." Mr. Lockwood nodded his approval.

"But not as democratic as, say, Saratoga."

"Well, one would not wish to go off completely half-cocked. So, in other words, neither ostentatious nor excessively rustic. Somewhere in between?"

"That is the consensus," Anna said.

He snapped his fingers. "What about 'Girondinia,' after the moderates of the French Revolution?"

"Well, that is very . . ."

"French!" Mr. Lockwood interposed, eagerly.

"Oh, entirely French. But perhaps an unfortunate association, given that most of the Girondins were executed?"

"I suppose you're right." Mr. Lockwood sighed, feigning disappointment.

"'Girondinia' does have a nice ring," Anna said consolingly, then she looked up, thoughtful. "Come to think of it, 'Guillotine' rolls right off the tongue, too."

"*Where are you off to, Mr. Lockwood?*" he said in an exaggeratedly robust tone, before answering in another. "*Why, I'm heading to Guillotine!*"

"*I hear that is a nice place*," Anna supplied. "*On a neck, is it not?*"

When Mr. Lockwood laughed heartily, Anna felt a surge of pleasure, followed almost immediately by vexation.

Anna was not accustomed to conversing so comfortably with men, but she could not forget that this was the sort of clever banter that attractive men of Mr. Lockwood's type were known to have. (Not that she *felt* attracted to Mr. Lockwood, of course. It was merely an observation of fact that his face was a pleasing, squarish shape, his jawline well-defined without being aggressive, and his blue-gray eyes were striking, capable of conveying both earnestness and skepticism.)

Oh, well, she thought. Provided she did not become silly, if he wished to amuse her, she saw no reason not to be amused.

Late the next morning, Elizabeth's maid Delia knocked on Anna's bedroom door.

"Miss Bradley, there is a gentleman here to see you. A Mr. Lockwood."

Harley Lockwood is calling on me?

"I'll be right down, Delia. Thank you."

Anna looked in the mirror above her dresser. Her hair was twisted and pinned at the nape of her neck, and she wore a simple gown of lavender dimity. Despite the wide-brimmed hat she always wore outside, her cheeks had acquired a hint of color. It was not unattractive, however. In fact, it made her eyes stand out.

Anna! she scolded herself, and then went downstairs to greet her guest.

He stood in the living room, holding a book, which he handed to her after they exchanged greetings. It was a copy of a novel he had mentioned yesterday.

"It's very clever," he said. "I think you'll enjoy it."

"That was good of you, Mr. Lockwood, thank you."

"Also, Eugenia arrives tomorrow. She looks forward to seeing you."

Ah, so that's why he is here. "I look forward to seeing her as well."

Mr. Lockwood looked up at the portrait that hung above the fireplace. It was of Elizabeth and Anna as little girls, walking through a meadow with their feet bare and daisy chain crowns on their heads. (Lillian was incapable of looking at it without ostentatiously sniffing.)

"A lovely painting. You and your sister?"

"Yes. Our late mother painted it."

"She was quite talented. Do you paint?"

"Neither Elizabeth nor I have any aptitude whatsoever," Anna said. "My father used to joke that they taught us the Three *A*s—athletics, academics, and art—in hopes of producing well-rounded children. By the time he realized they had produced one athlete and one scholar, it was too late for them to have the artist."

Mr. Lockwood smiled. "Did your mother feel that way, too?"

Anna thought for a moment. "I do not remember her expressing that same thought, but nor do I recall her contradicting him." She looked at him, curious. "What an interesting question. I wonder what made you ask it."

Mr. Lockwood shrugged. "I was just thinking of Brook Farm. My mother did not live there, but she attended the school and took a lively interest in the place, and I know she admired their principle of following one's affinities. I suppose I thought if your mother did, too, she might be delighted that you and your sister found your individual interests."

Anna nodded. "I believe you are right. She was never one to put a thumb on the scale when it came to our pursuits."

However frivolous he might be, Anna was realizing, Harley Lockwood was not without powers of observation.

Later that afternoon, Anna was reading on the screen porch when Elizabeth came in, picked up a magazine, and flipped through the pages in an unconvincing charade.

"So, I heard Mr. Lockwood came by," she said, a hint of meaning in her voice.

"Lower that eyebrow, Liz. He wanted to tell me that Eugenia would arrive tomorrow. A fact he seemed to believe would thrill me no end."

Elizabeth's brows now puckered in obvious disapproval. "You are very severe. I realize Eugenia is a bit . . ."

"Pedantic? Officious? Domineering?" Anna offered, helpfully.

Elizabeth sighed. "Yes. But you might be more charitable, considering she has neither your countenance nor your social address."

"I have neither countenance nor social address!"

"Of course you do!" Elizabeth seemed genuinely surprised Anna would think otherwise. "You are not only attractive, but you have wit and keen intelligence. Just because you choose to share these gifts with family and a small circle of friends in no way diminishes them."

Anna was so surprised, it took her a moment to reply.

"Oh. Well, thank you," she managed finally. "I suppose I don't see myself that way."

"And, to my original point," Elizabeth said, her voice softening, "I know Eugenia goes on about her research and settlement house, and she can be overbearing, but try to remember that her work and her brother are her entire life."

"Oh, all right," Anna relented.

Though she thought Elizabeth was being too generous, Anna could acknowledge that she got along better in the world than Eugenia Lockwood, who seemed unaware of how off-putting she could be. She could see how such obtuseness would make life a trial at times.

Her resolution to be kinder to Eugenia was put to the test the very next day. Elizabeth was showing Anna some flowers she had planted in front of the house, while Julia sat on the flagstone entry steps, writing in a diary.

Anna looked up and saw the familiar square figure heading briskly in their direction, using a closed parasol as a walking stick. Anna and Elizabeth moved toward the road to greet her. When Eugenia reached them, she nodded, and offered a no-nonsense "Good day."

"It is good to see you, Eugenia. We were pleased to learn you would be joining your brother on Haven Point," Elizabeth said. Anna echoed this with what she hoped was credible cordiality.

"Thank you, yes. Difficult to leave my work, but Harley persuaded me that the seaside air would do me good. Hence this constitutional I am taking."

"May I introduce my daughter, Julia?" Elizabeth said, gesturing toward the house.

"Of course. I should like to meet her," Eugenia's expression suggested a clinical interest, as if she were about to be shown a rare shell or exotic plant.

Julia generally preferred to be excluded from adult social calls, but she was not utterly without manners. When she saw them coming, she put her diary aside and moved to rise.

Eugenia put her hand out, palm down, as if motioning a dog to sit. "Do not get up for me, dear." She spoke in the dictatorial tone that Anna found so irritating, but Julia cheerfully plopped back down and looked up at the visitor with some curiosity.

"I am Miss Lockwood, Julia. I am pleased to meet you. Is that a diary you're writing in?"

"Yes. My grandmother gave it to me."

"What do you write about?"

"Mostly about things I did that day." She went back to the beginning of the diary and began flipping through pages. She stopped at an entry that she presumably considered representative and read it out loud: "'Climbed the oak, went skating, raced Miles Farlow and beat him cold. He got mad and pushed me. I laughed.'"

"That seems like a good way to hold on to memories," Eugenia said.

Julia nodded primly. "Yes. And I also write down the mean things my brother says to me, and what I wish I could say back to him."

"Julia, your grandmother gave you that diary so you might reflect on how to be a good girl," Elizabeth said.

"It is helping me be good!" Julia pointed at the book. "I write them here instead of saying them."

"Those are not the only two options," Elizabeth remonstrated.

Julia, eyes wide, shook her head. "Oh, yes, they are!"

Eugenia observed this exchange with a rather strained expression on her face. Rosemary appeared at that moment to fetch Julia, and once they were inside, she burst out laughing so heartily, Anna and Elizabeth could not help joining in.

Anna could not recall ever hearing Eugenia laugh. She rarely saw her smile. It was a revelation, discovering the sense of humor underneath all that pedantry.

"Well, I must thank you," Eugenia said when she caught her breath. "That was the most amusing thing I have heard in a long time. And we must credit the child for her good sense. What a clever way to keep uncharitable thoughts to oneself! Well, I must be going. Goodbye."

Eugenia turned on her heels, raised her parasol in a farewell salute, and was on her way.

Elizabeth turned to Anna, eyebrows raised.

"Oh, all right . . ." Anna said grudgingly. "She's not so bad."

Later that week, Anna was at a party, talking to Elizabeth, when Serena approached them.

"Anna, that gown suits you so well!" Serena said, with genuine admiration. "You look lovely."

"Doesn't she?" Elizabeth said. "Anna is forever trying to camouflage herself. I am glad it was otherwise tonight."

Anna felt her face grow warm. She was not embarrassed by Elizabeth pointing out her preference for blending into the background. Her family had always teased her about that. It was rather that the habit of repelling attention was so fixed, she felt uncomfortable attracting it tonight.

And while she had not been entirely conscious of it, Anna had taken pains with her appearance, choosing a green linen gown with a silk underskirt, which was simple but becoming, and arranging her hair in a looser fashion, so some strands fell about her face.

When Mr. Lockwood entered the room a few minutes later, caught her eye, and smiled, she felt her blush deepen.

Anna! she scolded herself again. Where had this schoolgirl streak come from?

Two nights ago, Anna had been on the Grahams' porch while

George played his fiddle and Nora led them in song. Mr. Lockwood sought her out, as he had seemed to do at every event that week, and stayed by her side for the rest of the evening.

Anna had continually reminded herself not to be taken in by his charm and humor, but all her primping and blushing suggested that her wiser angels were being quite overpowered. Feeling the need to breathe and gather her thoughts, she slipped into an adjoining room, which was mercifully empty.

In college, Anna was always surprised by her friends' occasional displays of romantic feeling. Though no more interested in marriage than Anna, they would still delightedly describe some tête-à-tête or rhapsodize over a handsome man. Anna had assumed she was born without this streak.

All right, so I have it, too, she thought. But this . . . flirtation (she supposed that was the term?) need not challenge that resolve. Besides, even if Anna had suddenly been transformed into one of the "marriage-bound," to borrow Irma's old term, which she definitely had not, she could never consider Mr. Lockwood suitable, given his relationship with Judith Fairchild.

Anna felt society was unfair to women, so it was not so much Judith's reputation with men that troubled her, but rather her desire to *make* trouble, specifically for Elizabeth. Anna was not sure of the present status of Mr. Lockwood's entanglement with Mrs. Fairchild, but that he'd had one, she had no doubt. At best, his being associated with such a schemer spoke poorly of his taste and judgment, and it was all too close for comfort.

Feeling calmer, she looked about the library. The Gilberts, their hosts this evening, were a harmless but rather formal couple, whose house looked as if it might have been lifted out of Back Bay and plunked down here. The stone mantel around the fireplace was carved with floral wreaths and a heraldic plaque. Above it hung a portrait of a woman, presumably an ancestor, in a gilded frame. Anna was gazing at it when she was startled by a voice behind her.

"The artist took some liberties with that painting."

She turned to see Mr. Lockwood, a twinkle in his eye.

"Oh? I did not know her."

"While not evident in this work, the elder Mrs. Gilbert had a terrible wandering eye."

Anna's reproachful look made him laugh. "I should not have mentioned it, of course, had she not also been such an old dragon, a quality the artist also failed to capture. As she was, I feel no scruple. I actually think a more faithful depiction would have been interesting. Like the *Mona Lisa* in reverse."

"So, no matter where you stood in the room . . ."

"She would *not* be looking at you."

"Angrily," Anna added.

He laughed again, then said, "So, Miss Bradley, what brings you in here by yourself? Are you hiding from someone?"

She returned her gaze to the portrait. "I am afraid I haven't much of a social appetite." She forced a smile then managed to meet his eye. "I require intermittent respite."

"And here I have interrupted. My apologies."

"It need not be a *long* respite."

"I understand the need for a break. The social calendar is quite full here on . . ." He paused for emphasis, then added, "Watery End."

Anna burst out laughing, in spite of herself.

"You laugh. I think it apt!" he said, with mock indignation.

"Very Shakespearean. Though I cannot help but note the promise of imminent death in your suggestions."

"You have discovered the morbidly grim streak masked by my jocund exterior."

She smiled again, then said, "I should be getting back to the party."

He offered his arm and escorted her back to the living room. Fortunately, Nora approached, and Mr. Lockwood was beckoned by a friend and excused himself.

"Anna, come talk for a moment," Nora said, then led her to a pair of chairs in a quieter corner of the room.

"Do you know what the girls have up their sleeve?"

"I was going to ask you the same question," Anna replied. That week, every moment the girls were not on the island they had spent in the Grahams' field, playing with the harbormaster's dog, Domino, an enormous creature of uncertain breeding ("half Newfoundland, half imbecile," according to Mr. Phillips). Julia was enormously fond of the dog, but her affection would not account for such commitment.

"Last week, Maudie asked if she could train one of our terriers. I asked, 'What for?' She would not tell me, so I refused, and they recruited Domino instead."

"I suppose we'll find out," Anna said, not sure if she should feel excitement or dread.

On Saturday, Letty Stinneford had arranged "Olympics" on the beach for the children, in honor of the real games underway in Paris. Anna and Mr. Lockwood sat on a bench at the beach club, watching the various competitions underway.

In one spot, children were tossing beanbags into brightly painted boards. Farther down, other children were engaged in some relay that involved running in a suit of men's clothes. Older children were racing in wooden tubs in the shallow surf.

"This is like a circus," Mr. Lockwood said.

"Several circuses, in fact."

"A competition! Which will be the official circus of Guillotine?"

The children gathered for the final contest, a game of Capture the Flag. At Julia's request, she, Maudie, and Ruthie were on one team, and their brothers on the other. Julia held Domino by the collar and called out to William, who was captain of the opposing team. "Domino's playing for us."

"Fine, Julia." He rolled his eyes. When Julia, Maudie, and Ruthie exchanged smiles, Anna knew she was about to discover what the girls had been doing all week.

George Graham blew the whistle to start the game. Maudie held something in front of Domino's nose; then Julia let go of his collar. The dog ran off in a zigzag pattern, moving with so little evident purpose that the opposing team, other than dodging him, paid the dog no attention.

That is, until Domino got behind the guard and grabbed the flag in his teeth.

Julia, Maudie, and Ruthie clapped their hands and yelled, "Here, Domino! Here, Domino!" The dog tore off in their direction. William and his teammates, having finally awakened to what had transpired, ran after him, but Domino, sensing danger, picked up speed. He crossed the line, flopped at the girls' feet, and began chewing on the flag.

By this point, Anna and Mr. Lockwood were laughing so hard, tears filled their eyes.

"How on earth . . . ?" he asked when he caught his breath.

"I haven't the slightest notion."

There was cheering and laughter, and the girls were surrounded by their teammates, clapping them on their backs and demanding to know how they had pulled off the trick. Anna wished she could hear the answer.

"That's not fair!" William yelled, a stormy look on his face. The fact that several of his own teammates were also laughing was probably not helping his temper. William Demarest had inherited his father's size, athletic ability, and overweening confidence, but deep down, he could not fail to recognize his younger sister's raw appeal.

Julia, on tiptoes, called out from inside the admiring throng. "You said he could play!"

Anna eventually caught Julia's attention and beckoned her over to ask how they had gotten Domino to do their bidding.

"Ruthie sewed pieces of bacon in the hem of the flag," Julia said, still beaming from the triumph. "Maudie dipped shells in bacon grease to make a scent trail for Domino to follow."

"What a brilliant ploy. What on earth gave you such an idea?" Mr. Lockwood asked.

"I read about it in a book. Maudie's the one who knows about training dogs, though," Julia said with a shrug, then ran back to her friends.

That evening, Jerome and Elizabeth invited a group over for an impromptu party on their back lawn, and the girls' stunt was the talk of the evening. Anna listened as George Graham, a marvelous storyteller, relayed the tale to Mary and Adam Francis, who were kicking themselves for being in Portland and missing it.

Jerome was laughing heartily throughout, as if hearing it all for the first time, though he had witnessed it himself. He was as engaged with his children as any father in his set (which was to say: not very), but he could be amused by, and even proud of, Julia's high spirits. In fact, when William grumbled on the way home earlier about the unfairness, Jerome had cut him off. "You're being a very poor sport, William. I, for one, thought it was a marvelous trick."

Anna wondered if Jerome would derive as much pleasure—or any at all—if his mother were here. Lillian certainly would have disapproved. Julia was too wild, too *pushing*; her competitive spirit was unladylike. *Just one woman's poison can get into the groundwater*, Nora had said about Vesta Sears, but it was equally true of Lillian.

Well, she isn't here, Anna reminded herself. For now, all was as it should be.

A few minutes later, she heard Letty Stinneford talking to Serena. "Too bad Mr. Lockwood returned to Boston."

Anna felt her mood plummet to earth, a sure sign that all was *not* as it should be.

CHAPTER ELEVEN

June 1918
Washington, DC

JULIA

Lucy cheered with great enthusiasm when, after at least a dozen attempts, Victoria finally managed to stand athwart the rowboat, one foot on each gunwale. (Lucy knew no self-respecting pirate would windmill his arms as Victoria did, but one did not wish to be discouraging.)

FROM *LIBERTY ISLAND*, BY MISS CRANE

Julia headed home, her spirits low. As she left the school building, she had spotted one of her students, Dieter Hoffman, hiding behind a low wall, tears running down his face. She urged him back inside, led him to the empty classroom, and gently encouraged him to tell her what was wrong.

Poor Dieter had been coming in for much abuse from his fellow students. His parents emigrated from Germany decades ago, and there was no reason to believe they were anything but loyal Americans, but life was difficult for little boys with German names these days. Julia would speak with the boys, but the term was almost over, and she doubted she could do much good. She was so tired of this awful war.

When she got inside her building, however, a letter was awaiting her on the hall table that pushed all other concerns aside.

Her name was scrawled on the envelope, which had been delivered by hand, but she thought she recognized the handwriting. When she turned over the envelope and saw Robert Seaborne's seal, her heart froze. She opened the envelope with shaking hands, terrified she was about to read the worst about Michael.

It was not the worst, but it was bad enough, and the worst could still come.

Dear Julia,

We have just gotten word that Michael was shot in France. We have little information at present, but I am going to the office to see what I might discover. If you have time, I feel sure Margaret would welcome your company.

Sincerely,
Robert Seaborne

The maid led Julia to the sitting room, where Margaret was pacing and twisting a handkerchief in her hands. She spun around, saw Julia, and immediately fell into her arms.

"Oh, Julia, dear . . ."

"Is he . . . Did you . . . ?"

"Robert is at the paper, trying to find out what he can. We know nothing about the injury, and only a little about the circumstances."

These she explained as best she could. The treaty with the new Bolshevik government in Russia enabled the Germans to move fifty units to the Western Front, and they had been pushing steadily toward Paris. Michael was with the marines, who were making a valiant stand in Belleau Wood, a few miles from Château-Thierry.

He had attached himself to an intelligence officer and headed into the woods, despite a battalion commander's warning that things were "awfully hot up there." When they entered one of the oat fields that broke up the forest, they were fired on by a nest of German soldiers. Michael was hit. They knew no more.

Julia sat with Margaret throughout that long afternoon and evening, during which every hour felt like a day. Just after midnight, they finally heard the door and raced to the front room. Mr. Seaborne, ordinarily neat as a pin, looked rumpled and tired, as if he had aged a decade in an evening.

Julia took hold of Margaret's arm. If her own legs felt weak, she was certain Margaret could not stand unassisted. Mr. Seaborne approached Margaret, his arms out. "He's alive. And they think he will be all right."

Now Margaret fell into his arms. "Oh, thank God. Thank you, God."

"There is more," Mr. Seaborne said, a note of warning in his voice.

Margaret pulled back. "What is it? You must tell me at once. I can bear anything if he will live."

Mr. Seaborne held his wife by the shoulder with one hand, and with the other brushed a lock of hair from her face. He looked at her so tenderly, Julia felt a catch at the back of her throat.

"It seems he lost an eye."

"Oh, an eye!" Margaret began to laugh and cry at the same time. "Who cares for an eye? I thought you were going to tell me he had lost his legs!"

Over the next few days, Mr. Seaborne was able to fill in a few more details, and they got more information in a letter from the intelligence officer who had been with Michael.

I am at the bedside of your son, who asked that I write to relieve what he imagines to be your great anxiety. He is recovering quite well, despite now being "cyclopic." (As I assume is obvious, I use this word at his insistence.)

The censors prohibit my sharing details, but having relented on the matter of "cyclopic," I will give myself license to relay what I am sure Michael will not: He proved himself as brave as any marine. I am certain his gallantry will earn him the Croix de Guerre. At some point you will know all.

He will be in the hospital for some time, after which he will likely be sent home. He says to prepare yourselves for his distinctly piratical appearance. He also requested that I pass along his apologies to Miss Demarest for "accidentally appropriating her childhood ambition."

Michael was in the hospital for more than a month, after which, to Margaret's dismay, he promptly returned to the front. As the weeks wore on, however, the American interest in the marines' bravery at Belleau Wood grew so keen, both the army and the paper agreed that Michael would be of the most use returning to America on "convalescent leave" and commencing a lecture tour.

In September, he sailed to New York on a military transport ship. Margaret, who had been at the pier when he arrived, later told Julia he was surprised by the honor guard that met him, and even more so when a reporter informed him that he had indeed been awarded the Croix de Guerre for his bravery.

"He seemed embarrassed by it all," Margaret said. "But he looked marvelous, and rather handsome with the patch over his eye."

Margaret also learned a bit more about what had transpired (though not, of course, from Michael). Michael entered the field behind the commander, who was hit as soon as the nest of soldiers began to fire on them. Armed only with his pencil and notepad, Michael had crawled forward to help him. A bullet ricocheted off a rock and hit him in the eye.

Julia thought it would be ages before she saw Michael, since he was leaving directly from New York to begin his lecture tour. But in October, the Spanish influenza epidemic hit. When Washington schools announced they would close for two weeks, Julia thought she would go out of her mind with boredom. Two days later, however, her telephone rang, and to her delight, she heard Michael's voice on the other end.

"Michael! Is it really you?"

"It is, and I'm back. My tour was cut short because of the epidemic."

"I'm sorry. You must be disappointed."

He barked out a laugh. "Not even a little. It's horrible of me, because I know people are suffering from this terrible disease, but I could not be happier. I enjoyed talking about the marines, but audience members invariably wanted me to talk about myself. Not my cup of tea. And speaking of tea, I've called to invite you to one . . ."

The First Lord of the British Admiralty had just arrived in Washington, and Vice Admiral Sir William Lowther Grant and his wife, Lady Grant, were hosting a reception for him the following afternoon.

"It's on their houseboat. I'm sure it will be dreadful, and we won't be able to hear each other talk, but I can bear it if you'll come with me."

"Of course!" Julia laughed at his referring to the HMS *Warrior* as a "houseboat." The Royal Navy had requisitioned the yacht, formerly owned by Frederick Vanderbilt, and sailed for Washington in March. It had been docked near the Washington Barracks ever since. That Lord and Lady Grant had made it their home struck Julia as a rather good answer to the housing shortage. She had been dying to get a peek at it.

The next afternoon, when Julia heard the knock and threw open her door, she felt as if her heart might burst with pride.

"Oh, Michael. Look at you!" As he was still ostensibly on convalescent leave from the correspondents' corps, in addition to his white eye patch, Michael wore his army-issued dress uniform, khaki breeches, and a belted jacket. "You're so dashing!"

"You are a feast for sore eyes yourself, no pun intended." He laughed. Julia had put on a blue brocade gown and a smart hat. Suitable for a diplomatic event, she thought, but cheerful.

"Is it hard adjusting to having only one eye?" Julia asked, as they headed outside.

"If I wink, I'm blind," Michael said, feigning sorrow.

Julia lifted a hand in front of her own eyes. "Just go like this," she said, smartly tapping her index finger to her thumb.

"An excellent plan," he said, and gave it a try.

The leaves in Washington turned later than in New England, but there was an autumn briskness in the air, and when they reached the "houseboat," Julia reveled in the breeze from the river. She had grown used to Washington, even the climate, but the city was not oriented toward the Potomac as Boston was to the Charles, and she missed the centrality of the water. It was a pleasant novelty to be at the confluence of the Potomac and Anacostia Rivers. And on the deck of the grand old steam yacht, too, while a band played from the dock.

The party was a colorful affair, with French, British, Italian, and even Brazilian diplomats, many in uniform. Spirits were high, as it seemed the tide of the war had truly and finally turned, and they had begun to believe that an Allied victory was imminent.

It was not over, of course. Territory continued to change hands, and every newspaper still brought fresh horrors. The country was recently gripped by the "Lost Battalion," boys of the 77th Division, mostly poor immigrants from New York City, trapped and surrounded in the Argonne Forest. They refused to surrender, and for six days fought so valiantly, even with their heavy losses, they had become a symbol of the bravery and tenacity that would bring an end to the war.

Michael was an object of great interest, but while he seemed embarrassed by the attention, Julia loved to see him so celebrated, especially among the many dignitaries. And while he did not seem to notice admiring glances from young women in attendance, Julia did.

Michael had been correct that it was not conducive to talking to each other, but at one point, they found themselves on a less crowded part of the deck.

"By the way, I saw Mr. Stewart, and he asked me to give you this." Michael bent and kissed her on the cheek.

"Oh . . ." Julia felt herself flush.

"Oh, no, you don't, Jules," he said, in a tone of gentle remonstrance. "I'm your friend always, remember."

"Well, then." Julia nodded. "Thank you."

Two weeks later, Julia sat in the parlor of Louisa's boardinghouse downtown, reading Pelham's latest letter aloud. She read it through without looking at Louisa's face, hoping that when she finally did, she would see a reassuring expression, or perhaps even puzzlement, as if Louisa could not understand why the letter had made her anxious.

When Julia looked up, however, what she saw was concern, not confusion, and the pause that followed made her heart sink. Louisa was as honest as the sun. The only conceivable reason for silence was the knowledge that her words would hurt.

Julia's shoulders slumped. "Just say it. He sounds impatient, doesn't he?"

"I'm not sure. I have never met the man." Louisa winced a little before adding, "Though I perceive he feels you are in need of . . . *instruction*."

"I hoped you would tell me I was crazy, but I sense that, too."

At Julia's request, Pelham had expanded upon lots of his theories, including about education. He saw American schools as little factories, churning out compliant workers, and believed teachers should seize on children's natural curiosity and encourage them to follow their interests.

Julia thought his ideas sounded marvelous, though in one of her letters, she mused that it was hard to imagine implementing them, with so many children of such different abilities in her classroom.

More recently, she had written about poor Dieter, her former student, now in fourth grade. Though the war was almost over, he was still being bullied by his classmates.

This letter in response felt like a scolding.

> *Conflict is eliminated when students are truly engaged, their minds and imaginations captivated. You are blessed to have the spirit of Brook Farm coursing through your veins! Bring it to the classroom, and I am persuaded you will win and hold your students' attention, and arouse in them a sense of personal responsibility.*
>
> *I realize there are many children in your charge, and the present system allows only a little latitude. Remember, though: Children learn to thrive and cooperate with* <u>*fewer*</u> *rules.*

"You do not actually believe him, do you?" Louisa asked. "Boys fight for lots of reasons, a chief one being that their fathers and brothers are at war. Besides, this boy isn't even in your classroom anymore!"

Seeing the uncertainty in Julia's eyes, Louisa added, with a touch of asperity, "Has Pelham had any teaching experience at all?"

"No," Julia said.

Louisa sighed. "It's like what people say about socialism. It would work if everyone just did it right. But lots of ideas that sound wonderful end up failing when people actually try them. His theories might work in some little experimental school, but hothouse flowers can't grow in any old soil."

"I know," Julia said sadly.

"You are a gifted teacher, Julia." Louisa's tone was gentle.

Julia tried to smile. "Thank you."

Louisa opened her mouth as if to say something, but she closed it again.

"What?"

"It's just that I would hate to think that Mr. Stewart is interested in your opinion only so long as it comports with his own," she said apologetically.

"Oh, I don't think it's that. It's hard to communicate just with letters."

"All right. I don't want you doubting yourself."

"Thank you. I won't, and I so appreciate your listening."

Julia pulled herself together and managed a cheerful goodbye. Once she was on the streetcar, though, she leaned her forehead against the window and tried to hold back the tears.

Pelham's early letters had made Julia feel like they were two people in a crowded café, so intent on getting to know each other, they took no notice of anything or anyone. Even in his shortest missives, she sensed that in the few minutes he snatched to write them, he was with her, just her.

Julia loved drawing Pelham out on his theories, and he said her openness and curiosity helped him clarify his thinking. Since these qualities were all she had ever felt like she had to offer, she was thrilled that they were finally of use to someone.

Julia could not possibly agree with all of his ideas, though. There were so many of them! Besides, Pelham and his fellow intellectuals often disagreed with each other. Until now, Julia had felt that what mattered was that they both wanted a better, freer, fairer world.

While Julia appreciated Louisa's steadfast defense of her teaching, it was not what troubled her. She had never rigidly followed prescribed texts or methods, and since her students invariably learned what they were meant to, she had earned even more latitude. She could probably win an argument with Pelham on points. She just did not expect to be having one.

Until now, their exchange had been cheerful, open, and frictionless. There was a presumption of good faith, in which they were both not just willing but eager to see each other in the most charitable light. Now she felt like she had failed a test she had not known she was taking.

However improbable, given that their entire relationship consisted of twenty-four hours together and nothing but letters since, Julia had fallen hopelessly in love for the first time in her life. She simply could not bear the thought of losing him.

A week or so later, Julia received a letter so sweet and sentimental, she concluded that she had imagined his impatience. But then that was followed by another discomfiting exchange, about a novel Pelham urged her to read, which he said revealed a "keen understanding of Freudianism."

After Julia read it, she wrote to Pelham, extolling the author's prose, and the way he depicted how secret desires, locked in the unconscious, affected human behavior. Her only ambivalent comment was that she struggled to sympathize with the characters: "I just found it hard, since they were driven by instincts they could not control."

His reply caused the same sinking feeling she experienced when she read his letter about her students' conflicts. "I suspect you are influenced by the old literary tradition," he said. "You should read it again."

Julia did not read this letter to Louisa. She did not need to be told Pelham was wrong. Julia loved books and had always read broadly. She was happy to cozy up with a Mary Roberts Rinehart mystery, but she also read classics and contemporary literary works, and her opinions were honest and considered. Once again, it was not the substance of his remarks, but rather what they indicated: that while Pelham might have once been enchanted, he was no longer.

Meanwhile, as letters between them slowly traveled across the Atlantic, Austria-Hungary surrendered, and then Turkey followed suit. The war was over, though it took until November 11 for the armistice to be signed.

The good news acted as a damper on Julia's despair. In addition to deep relief that this horrible war would soon be behind them, she felt sure that if the distance could finally be erased, she and Pelham could recapture what they had lost.

Pelham would stay to cover the peace negotiations, so she knew he would not return immediately, but over time, she began to wonder if he wanted to come back at all. She still heard from him, but his letters came more sporadically and were less personal.

They were still at the café together, still in conversation, but now his body was angled away from the table, his attention diverted. The new object of Pelham's consuming interest was Russia. He was deeply envious of Jack Reed, a member of the Greenwich Village set who was in Russia when the revolution broke out and wrote a riveting book on the subject: "What I would have given to see what he saw. Now it's almost impossible for American reporters to get into the country."

In February, three months after the armistice was signed, Julia received a rather cryptic letter.

I would like to see you again, Julia, to be together, face-to-face. There is a project here that interests me, and I believe it might be of interest to you, too. I will tell you more when I know more about it myself.

Julia had no idea what the "project" was, or if by her "interest," he meant for her to be involved somehow. Either way, it cemented what she had all but known before: Pelham Stewart was in no hurry to return to America—and in no hurry to return to her.

Part Two

Whenever the girls got up in time, they'd race to the cliff to watch Mr. Flannery pull in his lobster traps. When he finished, he'd raise a weathered hand in salute, and Lucy would shout down to him.

"Fire when ready, Gridley!" (She liked playing Admiral Dewey.)

"THREE . . . TWO . . . ONE . . . FIRE!" Mr. Flannery would yell back, and then slam an oar on the side of his boat, which made a terrific boom.

They'd send him off with a shout of "Remember the *Maine*!" to which he'd respond, "To hell with Spain!"

They knew Aunt Phillipa would not approve of their befriending lobstermen. "We don't even know who their people are!" she'd say.

"Knowing your people" meant being able to trace them back for generations, and Aunt Phillipa thought the musty portraits in the dining room were evidence of their being descended from "the best people."

Mr. Flannery was so wonderfully willing to pretend along with them, and the girls considered him to be the very best of men. They would never understand why they were supposed to care more about some ancestor in chain mail wearing a saucepan for a hat.

From *Liberty Island*, by Miss Crane

CHAPTER TWELVE

July 1900
Haven Point, Maine

ANNA

Elizabeth poked her head in Anna's door.

"Nora and Serena are downstairs. Mr. Lockwood is coming over to speak to all of us."

Anna's heart leapt at the news—*He's back!*—but she replied in a deliberately casual tone. "Oh? What does he wish to speak to us about?"

"It has to do with a child from Eugenia's settlement house. I'll let him explain." Elizabeth slipped out and went back downstairs.

Anna reached the bottom of the stairs just as Elizabeth's maid opened the front door to admit Mr. Lockwood. He smiled and greeted her with a warm handshake.

"It's so good to see you," he said.

Anna felt her face flush as she led Mr. Lockwood to the living room. Nora and Serena were already there, and tea was set out. A quick look at the seating arrangements revealed two options for Anna: sit beside Mr. Lockwood on the sofa, or on the ottoman beside Elizabeth's chair. She opted for the ottoman.

"Thank you all for coming," he said, once tea was poured. "My sister and I have rented the Grahams' cottage at the beach, and we will be bringing a recently orphaned girl named Louisa Murphy from the settlement house to stay with us. I particularly wanted to speak with all of you because she is of a similar age to your daughters."

Mr. Lockwood explained that Louisa suffered from poor health. Her late mother had managed to take her to the countryside every summer for the clean air the doctors recommended. She died recently, so he and Eugenia had stepped in to fill the gap.

"My sister has taken a particular interest in Louisa, who is a promising child. It was her sense, and mine, that your daughters would make her welcome."

"Of course, Mr. Lockwood," Serena said. Nora and Elizabeth nodded their agreement.

"I am sure the girls will be overjoyed to have a new friend," Anna said. "But I should mention that I have been taking them to Gunnison Island several days a week. If she is sickly . . ."

"Yes, Mrs. Graham told me as much. Louisa is quite small, but I do not think you would otherwise notice any impairment. In fact, I think it would do her a great deal of good to run about." He added, "I should mention, though, that Louisa has not spoken a word since her mother died. Eugenia has researched the phenomenon, and the muteness is thought to be temporary."

He turned to Anna. "If you are amenable, though, I think it would be best if I brought her myself at first, just to spend a few hours in the afternoons."

"Of course."

As they were all preparing to depart, Mr. Lockwood turned to Anna.

"I apologize for what must now seem like a mission of surveillance," he said. His eyes were kind, and she managed to summon the equanimity to tell him that she perfectly understood, but she returned to her room with an ache in her heart.

Mr. Lockwood's rationale for his "surveillance" was perfectly understandable. Anna would spend many long hours with a child in whom he and Eugenia had taken such an interest, so it was natural that he wanted to know her better.

Time to recover your wits, Anna, she told her reflection in the mirror.

She had tried to maintain a clinical interest in the connection she felt to Mr. Lockwood. He was intelligent, amusing, and he managed to bring out the humor Anna ordinarily only shared with her closest intimates. But as she lowered herself into the chair by the window and looked out at the bay, she was forced to acknowledge that she had not succeeded. A little seed of hope had been planted in her heart, though hope for what, exactly, she could not say.

Despite her heavy heart, she knew it was fortunate to have learned Mr. Lockwood's motive in seeking her out. Nothing good could have come from allowing that seed to take root and blossom. The most likely outcome would be disappointment, but the alternative, in its way, was even worse. After all, Anna's desire for independence—her drive to pursue a career, to make the most of her skills and talents—was not a decision she made, but a calling. It sprang from her very essence, and she had no desire to abandon herself for romance. And certainly not for Mr. Lockwood, of all people.

In addition to revealing a flaw in his character, his relationship with Judith Fairchild rendered it dangerous to have anything but the most superficial friendship with him. For evidence, Anna needed only recall her last encounter with Mrs. Fairchild.

A week before they left for Haven Point, Lillian came to dinner with Judith in tow. When they entered the parlor, where Elizabeth, Jerome, and Anna were gathered, Lillian had launched in immediately.

"Julia just told me she wants to go to the Philippines!" Lillian said, as if the very idea was offensive. "I asked where she got such a notion, and she said, 'From Beebe Bean'!"

The newspapers had gone wild over the exploits of Miss Bean, a young woman who had dressed as a boy and stowed away on a ship from San Francisco to Manila. Julia, naturally, had the deepest admiration for the woman. (Anna regretted not advising her niece to refrain from mentioning it to her grandmother.)

Jerome, impervious as always to his mother's disapproval, chuckled from behind his paper, but Lillian ignored him.

"Have you been letting the child read the newspapers?" she asked Elizabeth sharply.

"I believe the young woman has been the subject of discussion at school," Elizabeth replied.

Lillian sniffed. "I'm not surprised. It is not a fit subject for girls' ears, but that school is far too permissive, as I have repeatedly told you. I hope you have told Julia not to participate in any conversations about this Miss Bean. It is quite harmful!"

For the most part, Lillian aired her grievances about her granddaughter to Elizabeth, and merely threatened to speak to Jerome. She'd grown bolder lately, which Anna attributed to Judith's insidious encouragement.

Jerome folded down his newspaper and looked at his mother skeptically. "Oh, come now, Mother. That's a bit extreme, is it not?"

Though Judith had remained silent during the conversational tennis match, Anna knew she would see this as her cue.

"Oh, but Jerome, you cannot approve of the woman's deceit," Judith said, in the gentle tone she used to launder Lillian's harsh proclamations. "The glorification of women behaving like men, and trotting around the world having outrageous adventures, has a terrible influence on impressionable girls. Our daughters must be shielded from such stories if they are to grow up to become feminine and home-loving."

Jerome might not mind his daughter being an imp now, but Judith's cunningly painted picture of a masculine, bold *adult* Julia was too much for him to bear.

"I daresay you might be right," he said, sitting up a little straighter. "Liz, we ought not let Julia go on about that Miss Bee person."

Lillian nodded triumphantly. Anna knew what she was after. Lillian was determined to persuade her son that Julia was wayward, and that his wife was unsuited to the task of setting her straight. Then Lillian, with Judith's help, would swoop in and fill the child-rearing vacuum.

Anna sighed and picked up the letter she'd recently received from Sally.

We have already ordered another print run, and my uncle is speaking of an entire series! We have had complaints about Liberty Island from the usual corners, with one happy result. That pious windbag Mrs. Howland was so furious about the book, she told Fanning and Scott they would no longer have the pleasure of publishing her books. (As if it was a pleasure! Mr. Scott has only kept her on our list out of pure nostalgic sentiment.)

Anna could not help feeling gratified by the response of girl readers, and the added financial security that could come from a series was more than tempting.

Sally and her uncle would be delighted if *Liberty Island* appeared on lists like Judith Fairchild's "Books to Avoid." (According to Sally, they might as well be called shopping lists, for that is what they became in the hands of girl readers.) Anna, however, could not be so sanguine.

She recalled Lillian's words from last September: *I know Julia spends a good deal of time with Anna . . . I am increasingly concerned about her influence over my granddaughter . . . She has a secretive air about her.* She could only imagine the reaction if she was discovered to be the author of *Liberty Island.* Elizabeth had refused to defend herself against far lesser charges than "harboring an author of immoral literature."

Anna was finally able to support herself. Not in any luxury, granted, but she did not mind that. However, she hated the thought of a rupture with her sister if the identity of "Miss Crane" was revealed—and of not being there to support Julia, particularly if Lillian got her way and she was sent away to school.

Anna could not afford to draw attention to herself at present, particularly from Mr. Lockwood. She had enjoyed the witty banter, but it was useful to know that he had merely been evaluating her suitability to supervise Louisa Murphy. It would help her remember that he was, first and foremost, a friend of Judith Fairchild's.

And as everyone knows, the friend of one's enemy is an enemy.

When the girls spotted Duncan's boat coming around the tip of the island, with Mr. Lockwood and a little girl on board, they raced down to the beach to greet their new friend.

Duncan rowed his passengers ashore, and Mr. Lockwood got out of the dory, lifted the child out and placed her on the sand, then smiled kindly at Anna. She felt a flutter in her chest but dismissed it quickly, and turned her attention to the child.

Julia and Maudie were tall for their age (though Maudie was sturdy, and Julia lithe), but even Ruthie was at least two inches taller than the newcomer. Despite her diminutive stature, bow-shaped mouth, and small nose sprinkled with freckles, Louisa was quite striking. There was a suggestion of maturity in her face, a placidity in her expression, and eyes that seemed to take everything in.

Anna had told the girls that Louisa had been "very quiet since her mother died," and that she hoped they would be understanding. She introduced each girl in turn, and Louisa nodded soberly in response.

"Now, girls, Louisa might not wish to speak at present," Anna reminded them.

Maudie shook her head. "Oh, she doesn't have to speak," she said earnestly.

"That's right, because we talk a *lot*," Julia added. "Will you play with us, Louisa? We were kidnapped and got away, but now we're on a deserted island. You can be Mute Mary, and then you don't have to say anything at all."

Louisa paused for an instant, then shrugged. Julia, never one to test the ground before advancing, simply took Louisa's hand and led her up from the beach to the clearing, explaining where the game had left off. Maudie and Ruthie followed in their wake, and Anna and Mr. Lockwood brought up the rear.

As soon as the girls were out of sight, Mr. Lockwood looked at Anna and began to laugh.

Anna smiled. "Did something in particular tickle your funny bone?"

Mr. Lockwood held up his hands, as if helpless. "Where do I begin? The notion that talk is measured collectively and quantitatively?"

Now Anna chuckled, too. "Also that Louisa need not worry, as there is sufficient supply. Which, by the way, is probably true."

"And 'Mute Mary'?"

"She left before you could learn the rest of their names. Julia is the Red Rajah, Maudie is Captain Joker, and Ruthie is Selena, the nurse. Selena is also a princess, but she does not know that yet. It is a shame they were kidnapped, as their boat was 'as staunch and pretty a craft as ever sailed the blue waters.'"

"Eugenia clearly knew her business, bringing Louisa here," Mr. Lockwood said.

Anna walked him around the clearing, pointing out the various paths that the girls used and explaining where they led. The tour ended at the lean-to where two willow lawn chairs were stowed. Duncan had brought them, along with cotton duck cushions his wife, Mary, had sewn, when Anna finally admitted that it was uncomfortable to sit on the ground for hours.

Mr. Lockwood carried the chairs to the elm tree on the edge of the clearing. While careful not to reveal anything she had adapted for use in *Liberty Island*, Anna regaled him with stories about Jumaru. Mr. Lockwood was gratifyingly amused. He had been teaching for two years at Wendover, a boarding school for boys in New Hampshire, and had his own store of anecdotes to offer.

By the time Duncan came to pick them up, Anna felt she had managed things well with Mr. Lockwood. She could enjoy his company, and if they were to be thrown together for all these hours, at least his charm made the time go faster.

On Friday, they heard Louisa's voice for the first time.

There had been fog that morning—not enough to keep them from going to Jumaru, but damp and brooding enough to inspire Julia to concoct a game of detective. They had been standing around for a while, struggling to come up with a name for the criminal.

"Call him Split Ear," Louisa said.

Julia, Maudie, and Ruthie had been admirably nonchalant about Louisa's muteness, and while they looked surprised for an instant that she had finally spoken, they recovered quickly.

"That's a great name, Louisa," Julia said. "His ear is split open?"

"A dog bit him when he was trying to rob the grocery store," Louisa explained.

Though more of a listener than a talker, from that moment on, Louisa did not hesitate to speak when addressed, or if she had something to add to the proceedings. Her contributions were usually in the form of colorful characters, which it emerged were drawn not from her imagination but from her neighborhood. To their games, Louisa introduced a policeman known by local lawbreakers as "The Ghost," for his ability to appear out of nowhere; "Sally Stunner," a table girl at the corner saloon; and "Smoosh the Peddler," who sold oranges and knew all the neighborhood gossip.

The next day, when they returned from Jumaru, the girls stopped by the harbormaster's office to introduce Louisa to Domino. Mr. Phillips cheerfully let the brute out to play for a while. When they brought him back, Mr. Phillips, who also handled all the mail for Haven Point, was thumbing through envelopes.

"You know," he said, peering at the boxes and sliding an envelope into one of them, "they say there's treasure buried on some of these islands."

Julia's eyes flew open. "Really?"

He nodded, still sorting through mail. "Captain Kidd supposedly buried some treasure on Jewell Island, but they've never found it. But lots of other pirates roamed these waters, too. Who knows what's out there?"

In Julia's fertile imagination, possible treasure on some Casco Bay island quickly became actual treasure on Gunnison Island, and absolute certainty that they would find it. The next day, at Julia's request, Duncan brought shovels in the boat so the girls could get to digging.

"They think there was a farm on the island once," Duncan said, as he motored them to the island. Julia was rapt with attention. "The big clearing where you all play was probably the field. You've probably seen the smaller clearing just on the other side of the trees."

Julia nodded.

"That's where the little house stood. There's one more, though, you might not have gotten to yet, because I don't think any paths lead in that direction. Suspect it was where they had some little cellar or some such. If I were a pirate, that's where I would have hidden treasure."

When the girls began chatting excitedly, Anna gave Duncan a reproachful look.

"Oh, it won't do them any harm," he said.

"All right," Anna said with a sigh. They certainly would not find anything, and who knew how much they could even dig in this rocky soil? Duncan was right, however, that it would do no harm. Julia swung from disappointments like a weather vane in a brisk breeze.

By the time Mr. Lockwood arrived with Louisa that afternoon, the girls had found the spot, but Anna had been strictly forbidden from seeing it. She gave Louisa a general idea of where it was, told her they had a shovel waiting, and suggested that she call out when she got close and follow the girls' voices in.

"I am afraid we must resign ourselves to the fact that we will have no share in the booty," Anna said to Mr. Lockwood when Louisa had run off. "Though I'm not sure they realize that we can hear every word from here."

"Not to mention the clinking of shovels on rock," he said with a laugh.

A few hours later, Duncan returned them all to Haven Point, the girls covered in dirt and undeterred by their lack of success. Unfortunately, William and Owen Graham were on the dock when they arrived.

William looked at Julia, disgusted. "What did you do to get so filthy?"

"Wouldn't you like to know?" Julia said, lifting her dirt-smudged chin. Then an idea seemed to come to her. She turned back to Duncan. "Oh, Mr. Douglas! I forgot my shovel."

Julia had a gift for inspiring even the most honest adults to abet her schemes. Duncan feigned a look of confusion, and then began looking around, as if he did not know exactly where the shovels were, or that they were supposed to stay in the boat.

"So you did! Here it is."

Julia took the proffered shovel, put it over her shoulder, and marched down the dock like a railroad worker, followed by Maudie, Ruthie, and Louisa, wearing similarly haughty expressions.

"What is she on about?" William scowled. He was doing his best to sound disdainful, but Anna heard a hint of reluctant interest in his tone, which worried her.

"Leave her be, William." Anna sighed.

Even if Anna wished to tell William, Julia had sworn her to secrecy. "He'll go dig it up himself, if he knows it's there," she'd said.

Last summer, the boys had accepted with complacence what Nora told them about the girls' activities on the island. They were convinced that the girls spent their time sketching, listening to stories, and learning to cook outdoors. They liked having their sisters out of the way, and probably appreciated the sympathy implicit in their mothers having removed them.

William's newfound curiosity had the potential to be very unhelpful.

The next morning, they awakened to dark clouds, and the air was heavy with the possibility of rain. Jumaru was out of the question for the day, so Anna had a leisurely breakfast. Elizabeth lingered at the table, too, reading her letters, while Anna looked over the paper.

Elizabeth opened a large envelope. "I suppose I should give you this," she said, handing over Judith Fairchild's latest dispatch. Anna glanced at it and felt a twinge of anxiety, but Elizabeth certainly did not expect her to read it on the spot (if at all). Anna smiled, set it aside, waited for her sister to leave the table, then picked it up again.

Anna had been prepared for *Liberty Island* to appear on the "Books to Avoid" list, and since it was selling well and "Miss Crane" was a new author, she knew Judith might mention it in the letter that always appeared on the first page of *Our Daughters' Reading*. She was dismayed, however, to see just how much attention Mrs. Fairchild had given it.

Dear Christian Mothers,

I take great comfort in the pains so many of you are taking to choose reading materials that teach your girls to be noble, gentle, and self-sacrificing.

My regular book recommendations and warnings appear on the back pages, but I would like to highlight one book from the latter category: "Liberty Island," by a new author, Miss Crane, which is a pernicious example of all the damaging trends in girls' fiction.

The four girls in this book deceive their guardian in order to spend weeks on an island, unchaperoned. Far from using their deceit as a foundation for a moral lesson, the author celebrates it!

Rather than helping girls joyfully anticipate the day when they reign as moral guardians of their own homes, this is the sort of book that makes that great privilege seem like a punishment. In addition, the pacing is unhealthily stimulating and will exploit girls' temperaments, which tend toward the ardent.

I fear many girls will be clamoring for a copy, but I urge my readers in the strongest possible terms to ensure that "Liberty Island" does not get into their daughters' hands.

Though Anna knew this would please her publisher, it made her feel acutely uncomfortable. That was nothing, however, next to how she felt when she turned the page and read the closing paragraph.

"Liberty Island" is published by Fanning and Scott, which has published my sister-in-law's books for decades. Mrs. Howland is so

> *revolted by "Liberty Island," she has informed them that they will no longer have that privilege. If nothing else will persuade mothers to keep this book away from their daughters, surely the actions of this good Christian woman will!*

Anna's mind reeled. *Mrs. Howland is Judith's sister-in-law?* She must be the late Mr. Fairchild's sister. But then Anna recalled Lillian's birthday lunch two years ago, when Serena asked about books for Ruthie. *And when she's a bit older, I naturally recommend Mrs. Howland's books* . . . Anna had found it odd at the time—*"Naturally"?*—but it made perfect sense now.

She could only pray that Mrs. Howland was not overly curious about the identity of Miss Crane.

CHAPTER THIRTEEN

July 1920
Haven Point, Maine

JULIA

Sometimes they swapped breakfast and dinner. They called them "Fastbreak" and "Rennid." (They knew that these are different methods of backward-ing the words, but they did not think it mattered. The sort of person who insists on "Tsafkaerb" over "Fastbreak" just for consistency's sake is hardly likely to swap meals in the first place.)

FROM *LIBERTY ISLAND*, BY MISS CRANE

As she and Louisa arrived at Union Station in Washington, Julia was surprised at the feeling of pleasant anticipation that snuck up on her.

Neither she nor Louisa had been to Maine since America entered the war. Father and William had been deeply involved in war financing, so Julia's family had spent less time on Haven Point, and on top of travel challenges, Julia and Louisa had their own war work. Then, last summer, Morgan's school term went long to make up for time lost during the influenza epidemic.

In truth, Julia had been glad of the excuses. She had come to view her once beloved summer refuge with a vague sense of shame. Haven

Point was so resistant to change and modern ideas, so cut off from the real world—a "citadel," to use Mina's word from all those years ago.

But while Louisa would never admit it, Julia suspected that she missed Haven Point. The ghastly summer heat in Washington was hard on her, and while she would be welcome regardless, she'd never go without Julia. A few months ago, when Julia casually mentioned that they should go to Maine this summer, Louisa's eyes lit up, confirming Julia's suspicion.

Julia received what she felt was another auspicious sign when she and Louisa went to the dining car for lunch, and a girl at the next table was reading *Liberty Island.*

The girl's mother, evidently noticing the look Julia and Louisa exchanged, said, "Terrible, I know, letting her read at the table, but she won't put it down."

Louisa hastened to correct the misunderstanding. "Oh, no. Whatever makes the time go!" She gestured to Julia. "We only smiled at each other because her aunt wrote that book."

At this, the girl finally looked up. "She *did*?"

"Yes, and Lucy was based on her," Louisa said proudly.

Julia smiled and added her usual qualification: "Very loosely based."

They spent a pleasant hour with the girl and her mother. Julia had not shaken the feeling that the books, like Haven Point itself, were a bit of a relic, and she would never feel quite the same pride in them that she once had. Louisa, whose appreciation for *Liberty Island* was unimpeded by any ambivalence, answered most of the little girl's endless questions. Julia found there was something contagious in Louisa's enthusiasm as she described some of their real-life adventures, and as the train chugged north, Julia's own enthusiasm for their visit increased.

The trip could be made in a day, but with changing trains in New York and Boston, it was a very long day. They stayed over at a boardinghouse near South Station, run by Mrs. Keane, an old friend of Louisa's late grandmother, whom both Louisa and Julia adored. (Julia, in fact, had long expressed a wish to swap out Grandmother Lillian for Mrs. Keane.)

After a good night's sleep, they set off again, and by the afternoon, they were sitting on the back porch of Fourwinds with Mother, looking out at the water, which sparkled under a clear sky, and reveling in the cool air. Julia's heart was softened further when her nephews returned from the beach with their nurse.

"Aunt Julia! Aunt Louisa!" Daniel said, as he burst onto the back porch, full of chatter about his sailing proficiency and the big fish he caught off the rocks. At six, Daniel looked like a little William, handsome and large for his age, but he acted like a little Julia—boisterous and talkative, with no hidden depths.

Oliver, nearly five, was almost as tall as his brother, but leaner, with his mother's big brown eyes, fringed with long lashes. His greeting was less exuberant, but he followed it up by climbing on the wicker love seat and snuggling next to Julia, his head on her shoulder as if she were his oldest and dearest friend.

"A sad state of affairs that I was flattered by the attention of my four-year-old nephew," Julia said later, as she and Louisa changed for dinner.

"Are you kidding? That was a conquest! I was jealous," Louisa replied.

The dinner table looked lovely, decorated with pale red garden phlox in glass vases, and candles that flickered in the gentle breeze that came in through the open windows. Julia took in the familiar smell of salt and sea air—such a *sturdy* scent!—and the background music of the waves at low tide, crashing against the rocks below.

William and Pauline finally came downstairs. They sat. And thus commenced one of the least comfortable meals of Julia's life, the strain palpable enough to overpower every pleasant sensation.

It took little time to identify William as the source of the tension. Julia wished Father had not been away on business. He would have kept the conversation going, at least, even if it was only to talk about golf or sailing or stocks. Mother, reigning queen of domestic harmony, tried to smooth things over, but her attempts were too tepid to make a difference.

"The sunset was lovely," she ventured.

"Yes, it was," Pauline said, then added, with almost apologetic tentativeness, "Did . . . did you see it, William?"

William did not look up from his consommé. "No."

An awkward pause followed, the first of many. With his prized self-command, Julia knew William would never physically harm his wife, but his coldness was cruel enough, and she felt a ball of fury form inside her.

And I looked forward to this? In recent years, Julia had rarely seen Pauline and William together—only at Christmas, when any unpleasant undercurrents were hidden by the busyness of the season.

Pauline brought the boys to visit her family in Virginia once or twice a year, though, so Julia had actually seen more of them than anyone in her immediate family. It was jarring to note the difference between Pauline tonight and the version of her that Julia encountered when she called on the Powells in Alexandria.

Pauline's family no longer had to take in boarders, and two of her brothers fought in France, but their home was still always full to bursting. Julia would sit in the parlor with Pauline, Mrs. Powell, and some complement of friends, relations, and visitors. Pauline invariably had a child on her lap, her own or someone else's, and usually one or more crawling around the legs of her chair. They might as well have been in the middle of one of those busy traffic rotaries that so flummoxed drivers, but the happy chaos did nothing to stem the flow of conversation, mostly in pleasing Virginia accents.

Pauline was small and delicate, but in the bosom of her family, she did not appear vulnerable. Tonight, however, her eyes were cast down and shadowed. She seemed shaky and fragile.

William finally broke the awkward quiet, but unfortunately with a contentious subject.

"I saw that Delaware voted against suffrage."

"Yes," Julia replied. She knew he was baiting her. Congress's passage of the suffrage amendment last year had set off a long march through the states for the thirty-six needed for ratification. They had been stuck at thirty-five for ages. As William surely knew, it was a terrible blow when Delaware voted no.

"If it doesn't pass, you'll have that friend of yours, Miss Ellis, and her ilk to blame."

"Oh? Why is that?" Though Julia aimed for a bored tone, she could feel her irritation getting the better of her.

"Getting themselves thrown in jail, and then that appalling tour around the country. Despicable, attention-seeking behavior."

"To whose behavior are you referring—police who arrested the suffragists, supposedly for obstructing traffic, when they did no such thing? Or perhaps you are referring to the warden who force-fed them?"

"You can't tell me you approved of their comparing the president to the kaiser, our enemy, during wartime. Wilson himself said his support for suffrage was despite their actions, not because of them."

Julia and Louisa had continued to help with the suffrage effort whenever they could, without regard for which faction of the movement was involved, but William seemed to believe that any support of the National Woman's Party marked one as a radical, beyond the pale.

"They kept the issue alive. You're insane if you think that did not help."

Mina was indeed one of the formerly imprisoned suffragists who participated in the "Prison Special" train tour. They visited cities all across the country and spoke of their treatment in jail. Mina enjoyed the attention, of course, but attention was precisely what was needed.

"I suppose you support socialists now, too."

No. I hate them. Rational or not, Julia considered them at least partially responsible for the demise of her relationship with Pelham, which had ended in April with a devastating letter.

"I would appreciate it if you would refrain from arguing at the dinner table," Mother said, in that restrained tone that Julia found infuriating.

"Well, why don't you tell us what you think, Mother?"

"I have said I support suffrage," she replied with a hint of impatience.

It had taken Julia ages to drag that much out of her mother. For years, when Julia spoke of her suffrage work, Mother invariably replied with a trite remark: *I gather you have met inspiring people* or *That must have been exciting.* What Julia never heard was *I am glad you are engaged in this battle. We need it.*

Last year at Christmas, Julia decided to pin her down. When she mentioned an event she attended, Mother replied with her usual: "It sounds like you found it interesting. I'm glad."

"Just for me, Mother, or also glad *for you*?"

"If you're asking if I favor suffrage, Julia, I do," Mother had replied wearily.

"She gave you the answer you wanted," Louisa said later, when Julia relayed the conversation.

"Now that it's socially acceptable."

"You never asked her directly before."

True, but Julia was not inclined to give her mother the benefit of the doubt. The movement had gained so much momentum in Boston, it was backward to be an "anti." Before that was the case, Julia was sure Mother would have evaded the question. *Wait for the signal! One must not be right too soon!*

"I'm not asking if you support suffrage," Julia said now. "I'm wondering what you think about its chances." She knew she was not helping ease the strain, but she could not help herself.

"You know I don't care for politics, Julia."

What DO you care for, exactly? Julia felt like screaming.

As a girl, Julia had been in the habit of thinking of her mother as rather a good sort of person—elegant, an excellent athlete, and amusing at times. She had chalked up their differences to temperament: Julia was more open, whereas Mother was more contained.

She had given little thought to the differences between her mother and her aunt, but it was Anna who had defied society's expectations, and Anna who helped steer Julia to Barnard, her first real step off the straight and narrow path.

Was there a scrap of evidence that Mother, who had defied no expectations, would have been anything but delighted if Julia had taken the path she herself had—debutante season, marriage, and settling down to life in the shallow world of Boston society?

To the extent the meal was salvaged, it was thanks to Louisa, who redirected the conversation by asking Pauline if she had seen the new torpedo factory on the waterfront in Alexandria, Virginia. She had, and Louisa was able to draw her out on the subject. Pauline was not effusive, but Louisa's curiosity lent her some dignity, and required her to emerge from her shell sufficiently to provide more than one-word answers.

It also gave Julia's temper time to cool.

Maudie had invited Julia and Louisa to come over after dinner, so they fetched sweaters, said good night to the boys, and then returned to the living room, where William and Pauline sat on opposite ends of the sofa, William hidden behind a newspaper and Pauline embroidering a handkerchief.

"Pauline, would you like to come with us?" Julia asked.

William folded down the corner of his paper and looked at Pauline, eyebrows up and lips pursed, like a parent whose child is on the verge of doing something naughty.

"I think I will stay here with William," she said, her own expression blank, as William disappeared behind the paper again.

"My brother is a beast," Julia said, practically spitting, as they headed down the road toward Maudie's house.

"I suspect there is something we don't know, but he is behaving very badly," Louisa replied. Somewhere in the corner of her heart, Louisa had always harbored a little sympathy for William. Julia might have found this annoying, had Louisa not also been fully awake to his faults.

"What do you think it is?"

"I haven't the slightest notion," Louisa said sadly.

In the years since Maudie and John were married, their cottage had taken on the look of George and Nora Graham's house. The porch was lined with fishing poles and potted plants. Inside, things were homey and unfussy.

"I'm not getting up," Ruthie said, waving at them from the living room, where she sat in a comfortable chair, legs stretched out before her on an ottoman, a plate of crackers resting on her very large belly. She was well along in her first pregnancy, and amusingly grumpy.

"They call it an interesting condition. I've never been less interesting in my life," she grumbled, as they arrayed themselves around her.

"You're not what's interesting," Maudie replied.

"What is, then? Is it what led to this condition? If such discussion is a rite of passage of motherhood, somebody failed to tell me." They all laughed.

"It's not what led to it, but what it will lead *to*," Maudie said.

"Oh, I see. So, I'm just a vessel. How charming."

Julia found Ruthie's candor refreshing. While her friends on Haven Point were following in their mothers' footsteps, at least they were not stiff and repressed, like Julia's own family.

Ruthie and Maudie, eager to hear about life in Washington, asked lots of questions about Julia's students and Louisa's work in the labor movement. They even inquired about Mina, whom they remembered from her visit years ago. (Granted, Mina did tend to leave rather indelible impressions.) They were fascinated to learn that Mina had been one of the suffragists arrested and imprisoned.

"We were all devastated, of course, about Delaware failing to ratify the amendment," Julia said.

"Oh, they didn't ratify?" Ruthie replied. "What a shame."

She seemed genuinely chagrined, but Julia felt the balloon of charitable feelings deflate. She understood that Ruthie had other things on her mind, but Delaware's outcome had been so anticipated and the result so devastating, it was difficult to comprehend her missing this pivotal event.

When they returned to Fourwinds, Julia flopped on her bed, arms crossed behind her head. “I can’t believe Ruthie didn’t even know about Delaware.”

Louisa was putting her nightgown on, and when her head emerged, Julia saw her frown.

“That’s not fair. Ruthie worked for suffrage in Massachusetts. They were one of the first to ratify, and she and Maudie both canvassed in Maine last summer.”

“But she isn’t anxious about it!”

“What matters more? What they actually did, or how they regard it at this moment?”

“Both! We need action *and* urgency,” Julia insisted. “How will women ever get unstuck if people aren’t even paying attention? They’re all too content here, too sheltered from what’s going on in the world. They just get married, have babies, and never question themselves. It’s all so backward-looking.”

Julia knew she was being unreasonably harsh, but Ruthie’s ignorance was the final straw. She felt a bitterness setting in, a vague sense that all she feared about herself, her family, and Haven Point was being proved correct.

Louisa was quiet for a moment; then she sat on her bed and looked at Julia.

“I can’t help feeling that it’s not you talking, but Pelham Stewart,” she said finally. Her tone was gentle, but there was a hint of admonition in her eyes.

“It’s not. It’s me talking,” Julia insisted.

The words were hers now, but Louisa was not far off in that Pelham’s thoughts were behind them.

A year ago, Julia sat sweltering in her apartment, reading a letter from Pelham, in which he informed her that he would not be returning to America anytime soon. He had joined a group of young people in

France who were trying to set up agricultural communes in Russia, recruiting workers and experts in infrastructure and modern agricultural methods.

I feel I must do what I can for the Russian people, whom I am sure will soon show the world a new and better way of arranging society. Though the capitalist powers are threatened by this, and doing all in their power to thwart them, the Russians will prevail.

In the meantime, we are living as we mean to go on, in a small house in the French countryside. We share in cooking and cleaning. Each gives according to his or her own means and talents. We live simply, but our needs are simple, and as it is not far from Paris, I am able to write the occasional magazine story.

It is enthralling, Julia, like a miniature Brook Farm! Would you come? It is the chance to be at the vanguard of a new order, and Russia will need enlightened teachers. It is a good deal to ask, I know. How might I persuade you?

So keen was Julia to see him, she was briefly tempted. Had she not always loved the idea of being so . . . so *enmeshed*? Her happiest memories of Barnard were of her friends piled into Julia and Louisa's suite like pack animals.

It did not last long, of course. She could only imagine how friends and family would react. *I'm leaving my job and sailing to France to live on a commune . . . Do I know the people? Well, one of them. A man, in fact. We spent a few hours together two years ago, but we've been pen pals ever since!*

Besides, while Julia thought the idea of communism was interesting and, if pressed, could even admire the idea of experimenting with a different way of living, she had hardly embraced it! And while she felt deeply for the Russian people and admired Pelham and his compatriots' desire to help, she could not help wondering if it actually would.

That said, she had never felt about any man as she did about Pelham. Despite the years apart, the memory of his intense blue eyes, powerful frame, and rugged handsomeness could still make her heart beat faster, and their epistolary relationship had only deepened her fascination with the workings of his brilliant mind.

Julia had not forgotten the letters in which Pelham had seemed dismissive of her perspectives, but for the most part, he had been the one person who made her feel like she belonged—who spotted her on the outskirts of the crowd, pulled her in, and made her a part of his exhilarating world. It had affirmed something Julia saw in herself, or wanted to see. To lose him would be to lose that sense of validation.

Julia put off a firm no by saying she was obliged to finish the school year, but she confessed that she also found the idea a bit overwhelming.

At first, he seemed to take her resistance in stride. He sent sweet, cajoling letters, describing the beauty of the countryside and the world they would be creating. She generally responded as she always had to Pelham, by asking lots of questions and inviting him to tell her more. Only occasionally did she push back, and always gently.

"Is there nothing here that you miss?" she asked. "I know America is imperfect, but there is beauty here, too, and people I love. I cannot quite fathom leaving it all behind."

On this point, he was adamant.

> *America has lost something vital and primitive. That greed and acquisitiveness, the endless, hungry pursuit of money, of things—it makes for such a graceless life. If this war taught us nothing else, it is that we are all puppets of capital and militarism. Here everything is owned by everyone . . .*

Their back-and-forth continued for a few months, but toward the end of the year, his letters once again began to arrive more sporadically, and his efforts to entice her less emphatic. Julia grew increasingly anxious in response. By February, in a rather desperate state, she wrote to him, proposing that she visit over the summer. She was so uncertain even about this prospect, she felt some trepidation about his response.

As it turned out, she was correct to fear his reaction, but wrong—catastrophically wrong—about the reason why. Never for a moment did it occur to her that Pelham would see her suggestion as the final straw, but evidently that was what it had been.

As much as I relished the idea of seeing you, your proposal occasioned some thought on my part. I asked a lot of you, I know, and while I held out some hope that you would jump at the chance, I knew it was unlikely. Literally or figuratively, you will always have one foot planted on American soil. I feel we must accept that we are on different continents, an ocean apart, in more ways than one.

You have an inclination toward contentment, an ability to see beyond the base and vulgar and find beauty. These wonderful qualities helped see me through the war, and I feel like a wretch to be throwing them back at you.

I know you are not complacent, Julia, that you yearn for change. But the work we are doing here, the world we are preparing for (and, indeed, that we are living in a small way ourselves) is a wholehearted business. It requires not just willingness, but eagerness—a need, even—to cast off everything, to relinquish all attachments.

I suppose I hoped your Concord blood might win out, that it would transcend, to use their word. It did not, and in many ways I envy you. I suspect yours will be a happier life. I certainly wish you all happiness . . .

Julia did not know what she would have done without Louisa. For countless hours, her friend sat cross-legged on Julia's bed, handing her clean handkerchiefs and listening as nobody else could. Louisa frequently disagreed with Pelham, but she accepted that Julia loved him and sympathized on those grounds.

That said, she could not avoid the occasional comment. At one point, Julia declared that Pelham was right. "I'm like Mr. Carruthers. Too content."

"You mean the seal on Liberty Island?" Louisa replied, a smile teasing at the corner of her lips. "As you're neither fat nor lazy, I'm afraid I don't see it."

"That makes it even worse," Julia replied. "To my lack of seriousness, I add frenetic movement, in service of nothing important. And when it came to embracing big change, I balked."

"When you're on the wrong road, driving off a cliff is a change in direction," Louisa replied dryly. "Doesn't make it a good idea."

Louisa was right, of course. One could be committed to change without committing to *this* change. If joining a commune in France was a test, Julia knew almost no one who would have passed. Pelham had even acknowledged as much, in a way.

Somehow, though, that did little to diminish Julia's distress. She had lost not just someone she loved, but also a sense of who she was, or who she could be.

When Julia was little, Grandmother Lillian often derided her as "bold as brass," little knowing that what she meant pejoratively, Julia had considered high praise. Similarly, when Pelham described his image of Julia as a "liberty-loving" child, nothing could have touched her more. She had spent so many hours in her youth imagining herself as bold and freedom-seeking, different. *More.*

Pelham had seemed to see something in Julia that Mina and her friends never had. He treated her as a worthy companion on his adventure, simply by virtue of her curiosity and enthusiasm for learning. But in the end, he had concluded that she lacked the vital qualities of restless discontent and "wholeheartedness," and was thus ill-equipped for the journey.

Julia was evidently not worthy of his world, and now that she was back on Haven Point, she was reminded of how alienated she still felt from this one.

The following afternoon, Julia and Maudie sat on a blanket at the beach, watching Julia's nephew Oliver and Maudie's daughter, Georgina (already "Georgie," thanks to her brothers), as they built a sandcastle.

Julia had arranged the outing with two purposes in mind. The first was that she had resolved to spend more time with Oliver, the one inmate of Fourwinds, besides Louisa and Daniel, with whom Julia not only enjoyed unadulterated mutual admiration, but who also seemed genuinely attached to her, and eager for her company.

Though not quite four years old, Oliver and Georgie were already old friends. After much discussion of the relative merits of various spades, they had chosen their implements and were setting about their task with a level of industry that would have pleased the Victorians.

"I think I know who the foreman is on this construction site," Julia said. Georgie was standing over Oliver, hands on her hips, head tilted. The wind drowned out her words, but she was clearly conveying some vital piece of instruction.

"Oliver has ambitious ideas," Maudie said. "I think Georgie adds a practical touch."

"Sounds familiar." Julia laughed.

With the kids comfortably out of earshot, Julia turned to her other purpose, which was to learn what was amiss with William and Pauline. Anna was in Europe, and as dear as her aunt had always been to her, Julia was not sure how forthright she would have been. Maudie had been such a friend to Pauline, Julia hoped she might enlighten her.

"Maudie, I've been troubled by how William is treating Pauline. He seems so cold and angry. I wonder if you knew anything about it."

Maudie grimaced and her face clouded over. She was such an unsentimental New Englander, but just as Oliver touched a tender spot in Julia's heart, Julia knew Pauline had touched a tender spot in Maudie's.

"Pauline got a bit too jolly at the Ballantines' a while back. I'm not sure it was the first such incident. I gather William was quite bothered by it."

"How jolly?"

"Definitely worse for the wear, though nothing anyone here hasn't seen before."

"I see," Julia said, furious at the double standard. William and his friends could drink as much as they wished, but Pauline had to behave with perfect decorum.

Julia wondered what Mother had said or done about William's irrational anger, but she knew better than to ask Maudie. Haven Point women, regardless of generation, tended to circle the wagons. Julia's absence in recent years put her decidedly outside that circle.

They talked about other matters, as the children hastened to complete their castle before the tide came in. When water began to lick at their toes, Georgie placed a shell atop the tallest tower, evidently the crowning touch. They stood back and watched as the water rolled into the moat and began its inexorable erosion of the walls.

Julia was struck by the loveliness of it—the willingness children had to experiment, their comfort with the ephemeral nature of things. Oliver and Georgie might pretend to believe that this time they had finally constructed something that could survive the deluge, but it was belied by their delight in seeing the inevitable destruction.

It made Julia sad, thinking of the future, when these children would lose that comfort.

In the years ahead, Oliver might still come to Haven Point, but he would no longer build sandcastles just to watch them fall. His energies would go to protecting the sturdy walls of Fourwinds, or some other castle built on this mound of granite.

Julia's only hope was that he would not take after his father. She hated to think of this child spending his life as William did, maniacally trying to beat back the tide.

Julia wavered about how to speak to Mother about William, or even if she should. She expected it would be futile, and might just further drive the wedge between them. Pelham Stewart had abandoned his family long ago, but even if Julia were so inclined, she felt far too alone at present to take such dramatic action.

That evening, Julia was passing the children's room when she heard Pauline's voice. She could not see in, but it sounded like Oliver was curled up on the bed beside his mother.

"Make up one about an egret," Oliver said.

"All right, darling. Let me think." Pauline was quiet for a moment, then she said, "All right. Here's a poem about my favorite kind, the snowy egret."

It is from my color that I got my name
And the fluffy plumes, that are my fame.
The truth is, I don't care for snow.
When it gets cold, that's when I go.
I fly down South, where the weather is warm,
Where I'm with friends and safe from harm.

Julia's first reaction was to think it was a rather sweet poem to have made up on the spot. She knew her sister-in-law had a wit, albeit one she kept on a short leash, like a dog that is only let out in a fenced yard. (She probably never let William see it. He'd just try to train it out of her.)

It was only later, when Julia was in bed and the lights were out, that the last lines of the poem echoed in her mind: *I fly down South, where the weather is warm . . . Where I'm with friends and safe from harm.*

Pauline's poem was not about an egret. It was about herself.

The next morning, Julia resolved to approach Mother in a spirit of open inquiry. Unfortunately, Father had arrived for the weekend, and his demands on Mother's time made it difficult to get her alone.

Late in the afternoon, Julia was sitting on the porch that faced the front of the house when her father and mother came in from tennis.

"I should have gone back to the line," Julia heard her mother say. "That was my fault."

"Hindsight is twenty-twenty, Liz. You played so handsomely at the net, I would not have told you to do otherwise."

Something about the exchange irritated Julia. Her parents never spoke about politics, literature, feelings, or anything of substance. If not for golf, tennis, and sailing, they would live in near silence. Meanwhile, William was mistreating Pauline, who was in obvious distress, and Mother's biggest concern was that she failed to return to the line in her doubles match?

Julia knew it was unwise to speak with her mother before she got her temper in check. She slipped out and made her way to the cliff path, following it until she reached a spot with flat rocks that made a nice perch, took a deep breath, and tried to collect herself.

With more time, she might have done so, but only a few minutes later, she heard her name and turned to see that Mother had unfortunately chosen this moment for an amble. Julia sighed, got to her feet, and returned to the path to meet her.

"Hello there. I didn't know you were out here," Mother said pleasantly.

"I just came out," Julia replied, her own tone cold.

Mother was quiet a moment. Julia felt her eyes on her but did not wish to meet them. She crossed her arms over her chest and looked out at the water.

"Is something wrong, Julia?" Mother asked finally.

"Is anything *right*?" Julia replied, still refusing eye contact.

"I'm not sure what you're referring to, Julia. You'll have to fill me in." Her tone was even, and not unkind, but somehow her lack of emotion triggered the opposite in Julia. Her gaze snapped back to her mother.

"I am talking about our family, Mother." It occurred to Julia that they stood on almost the exact eastern tip of the peninsula, Julia facing south, Mother facing north. Points on a compass, opposite directions.

"What about it?"

"I have not failed to notice William's treatment of Pauline. I gather she has had a few drinks on occasion." She added, parenthetically, "A tendency I must say I sympathize with. I suspect I'd take to the bottle, too, if I were married to William Demarest."

Mother flushed slightly, then raised her eyebrows and tilted her head, as if to say, *And . . . ?* No reaction could have angered Julia more.

This was either the best place for this conversation or the very worst, depending on how you looked at it. In Fourwinds, anyone might be within earshot of an open window. Out here, Julia's words would reach her mother's ears, then be swallowed up by the wind and waves.

"And you are just going on!" she continued, volume rising. "Smoothing it all over, pretending nothing is amiss!"

Mother's jaw tightened, but other than an impatient little "Hmm," she offered no reply.

"Do you have nothing to say?" Julia yelled.

"You seem certain you have everything figured out, so what more is there to say?" Now Mother's expression was sardonic, and she mirrored Julia's posture, crossing her arms over her chest.

Julia uncrossed her own arms and leaned forward, a finger pointing west, toward Fourwinds.

"I cannot believe this!" she yelled. "A woman is living in your house, powerless, bullied by your brute of a son, and you have nothing to say? You are doing nothing to protect her?"

Mother paused, the strain now telling in her taut jaw. "A house you have not set foot in for years, Julia," she said finally. "Do you not think that renders you a bit ill-qualified to judge what happens beneath its roof?" She let out a huff of breath and looked away, obviously trying to rein in her temper. Meanwhile, Julia wanted nothing more than for her mother to unravel, to show some emotion, some passion—something!

That said, she did feel a small flash of compunction. It was possible, of course, that she was not in possession of all the facts. But was that any excuse? If Julia did not have the facts, it was because nobody had shared them with her. Her family was so unwilling to express themselves, so terrified of airing their dirty laundry. If Pauline was struggling, didn't Julia deserve to know the reason?

"And you wonder why I haven't been here," Julia said.

"You're an adult, Julia. You are free to come and go as you please."

"Yes. I am."

After a chilly goodbye to her family, Julia left the next day.

CHAPTER FOURTEEN

July 1900

Haven Point, Maine

ANNA

Anna sat on a blanket on the little beach, laughing immoderately, as Mr. Lockwood, in a pretentious, scholarly tone, entertained Anna with a rigorous analysis of the game the girls were playing.

"It is simply not credible that Buckskin Bill, a Rough Rider, would be in cahoots with Frontier Frank, a contemporary of Kit Carson's, whose epoch was nearly a half century earlier." He shook his head sorrowfully, as if terribly disappointed in Maudie and Julia, the respective actors. "I am pained by the historical inaccuracies."

Anna, mirthful, added, "Not to mention geographical!" She pointed to Louisa. "How did the Mad Ranchero of Texas happen to kidnap the Phantom Princess of the Everglades?"

"And terrible casting. A tiny, fair Irish girl as the Mad Ranchero?" He sighed and added, "And the costumes . . . I am not sure where to begin."

"They clearly didn't either," Anna said. Julia and Maudie had assembled whatever items they could locate that remotely suited the theme. Maudie had a fur pelt over her shoulders and a bandana around her neck. Julia wore a beaver hat and a leather holster. The cowboy hat they found for Louisa was so large it covered her eyes, and she had spent much of the day quite blind.

"Perhaps we should credit them for encompassing such a great swath of the country," Anna said. "I believe they have California, Montana, Texas, and Florida covered."

"Well, all right, then. We shall award points for regional ecumenicism."

Anna chuckled again. The day was warm, but there was a pleasant breeze, enough to stir the branches and make gentle ripples on the surface of the cove. Though Louisa was quieter than the other girls, she seemed game for anything. Mr. Lockwood had said that he and Eugenia agreed that the child was the happiest she had been since her mother died.

Mr. Lockwood was such easy, amusing company, Anna had struggled to maintain her resolve to be wary of him. The island felt like such an escape that even her anxiety about the possibility of Mrs. Howland discovering her identity had ebbed.

When Anna heard the sound of an outboard motor, she did not think much about it until it came into view, and she saw William and Owen Graham. They approached the shore, in clear view of the girls, who unfortunately had just picked up props: long branches, which they were using as guns.

William stood up in the boat, his face red with fury. "Those are my clothes, Julia!"

"Man the barricades!" Julia yelled. The girls lifted their fake guns and pretended to fire at the intruders.

"They seem to have skipped over the manning of the barricade," Mr. Lockwood said.

William continued shouting, and at some point, Julia evidently decided it was growing tedious. "Get out of here, William Demarest, or I'll break every bone in your unlucky carcass!"

"The cast has expanded," Mr. Lockwood said. "An Irishman has entered from stage left."

Julia, fascinated and endlessly amused by Louisa, was forever mining her for colorful turns of phrase. Yesterday, Julia came down to the breakfast table and announced she was "hungry as a saint's dog."

Amusing as the confrontation was, Anna worried that the timing of this spy mission was very inauspicious. Lillian, always a sympathetic audience for William's complaints about Julia, would arrive tomorrow for a week's visit on Haven Point.

Unfortunately, he now had plenty of fresh material.

As it happened, the first days of Lillian's visit passed without incident. The weather was good, so Anna had the girls on the island during the day, and Elizabeth kept Lillian busy, visiting her various friends on Haven Point.

On Saturday, Anna was in the dining room with Elizabeth and Lillian, when Rosemary brought Julia and Louisa home from the beach. She ushered them upstairs, but they did not escape Lillian's notice.

"Who was that child with Julia?"

"An orphan from the settlement house in South Boston," Elizabeth said. "Harley and Eugenia Lockwood have brought her to Haven Point because she is sickly."

Anna braced herself, but while Lillian's brow was wrinkled, it seemed to be as much in consideration as consternation, as if she was deciding how to react.

"Well, perhaps it will be good for Julia to attend to a sick child," she said (unaware that she was citing one of Julia's least favorite themes in children's literature).

Monday again brought rain, and Anna and Elizabeth were by the fireplace when Lillian came and stood over them, looking even more imperious than usual.

"Elizabeth, I should like to speak to you."

"All right," Elizabeth said. She set aside her magazine and folded her hands in her lap.

"I have been informed about what the girls have been doing on that island with your sister." Lillian cast Anna a narrow-eyed glance. "Running around like little savages, dressed in all manner of inappropriate costume, shrieking and generally behaving like little barbarians. I am truly appalled.

"That child is in desperate need of a civilizing influence. I have told you repeatedly that a girl, particularly one as wild as Julia, should be tethered to her mother's side, learning how to go on," Lillian continued, as usual making Julia sound like a colt that needed to be broken. "As you seem unwilling to take on that responsibility, it must fall to me. I would like to give you one more chance to change your mind about Newport."

"Julia does not wish to go to Newport this summer," Elizabeth said. Her tone, though as mild as ever, suggested that Lillian had already been informed of this.

"This is a decision for a responsible parent, not a child!" Lillian said shrilly. "I gather you have no intention of budging on the matter. I did not wish to take this up with Jerome, but I am afraid I will have to do so."

Elizabeth, whose cheeks flushed, clearly did not relish this prospect. But she merely nodded. "He will be here Friday, not long after you return from your night in Portland."

"I think you will regret this," Lillian said, and stormed up to her room.

The next afternoon, Rhinelander and Vesta Sears arrived on their yacht, along with a group of friends from Bar Harbor, all of whom were heading to a big society wedding in Newport. Ambrose and his friends were invited for cocktails and to tour the yacht that evening. *Again?* Anna thought. (Evidently there were many improvements.) Serena had seemed anxious for her friends to join, so Anna and Elizabeth had accepted.

Mr. Lockwood had been invited, too. "Will I see you on the yacht this evening?" he asked Anna that morning on Jumaru.

Anna was unable to suppress a sigh. "Yes, I'll be there."

Mr. Lockwood laughed. "I take it you're not itching to tour the craft?"

"As it happens, I had the pleasure years ago. I recall a riveting discussion about how they kept the sails so white."

"Perhaps I will come late," he replied. "I agree with whoever said yachts were 'holes in the water, surrounded by wood, into which one pours money.'"

"Oh, but speaking of wood," Anna said, with faux earnestness, "if you miss the tour, you will not learn of the many, many species represented on the interior."

He shuddered. "I will *definitely* come late."

After enduring the tour, and the company of the Searses' superficial friends, Anna could not help being pleased when she spotted Mr. Lockwood and a few other latecomers on the launch, heading toward the yacht.

Then, from a few feet away, Anna caught the voices of two friends of Vesta's.

"Did you see Harley Lockwood?" one of them remarked, evidently surprised. "What's he doing here?"

"He was visiting Ambrose, and then took a cottage," the other replied. Anna could not see them, but she practically heard the mystified shrug. The woman tittered and added, "I suppose the poor man must absent himself from Boston occasionally, if only to escape Mrs. Fairchild and her constant importunities."

"She does pester him so, does she not? I suppose it's not surprising that he simply gives in from time to time."

Anna felt a rush of heat to her face. Praying she did not appear as frantic as she felt, she looked around, desperate for escape. She moved toward the stern, away from the tables, from the people, and stood gripping the rail, looking out at the water.

Anna had known she was naive and inexperienced, and she had continually reminded herself about Mr. Lockwood and Mrs. Fairchild, but some part of her had stubbornly refused to believe it. How could someone so dedicated to a young orphan girl, so kind to Anna and engaged with Julia and the other girls, possibly be involved with such a horrible, hypocritical woman?

You foolish, foolish girl, Anna scolded herself.

"Miss Bradley!"

Anna turned to find herself face-to-face with Mr. Lockwood. He seemed genuinely pleased to see her.

"I have been looking for you. I was afraid you had begged off."

"Hello," she said coldly. She glanced at him, then looked away.

"Is something wrong?" he asked.

"No," Anna replied, feeling childish.

"You seem angry. Have I offended you in some way?"

"Not . . . not exactly," Anna said. She crossed her arms over her chest, her cheeks burning.

"Have I . . . have I *inexactly* offended you?"

Anna's mind was in such a muddle, she had no idea what to say, or what she even could say. It was not safe to mention Judith Fairchild's name. The woman was already too attuned to the tension in Elizabeth's family, and far too eager to make further trouble. Anna felt too hurt and humiliated, though, to speak to Mr. Lockwood with equanimity.

"There is something I had known about you, Mr. Lockwood," she said, unable to look him in the face. "We were to be thrown together so much, I pushed it from my mind for the sake of the children, but I was reminded by a chance comment I overheard a moment ago."

"Would you tell me what it is that you heard, or what you believe you know?"

Hearing a new stiffness in his tone, Anna finally glanced at him. His expression was inscrutable, and she suddenly felt irritated. Even in the unlikely event that the rumors about him and Mrs. Fairchild were unfounded, it strained credulity to think he had never heard them! If such gossip had reached Anna's ears, when she was barely in society and had no obvious interest in the matter, they had certainly reached Mr. Lockwood's. Even that ridiculous Mr. Wimborne had spoken of the two of them.

He needed only to acknowledge that he was aware of the rumors, and to say that they were unfounded. He would even be within his rights to tell Anna that it was unjust of her to have believed the gossip! That he was brazening it out instead told her all she needed to know.

"You must excuse me, Mr. Lockwood," she said. She left him then, snaked her way through the crowd, and slipped into the teak-paneled deckhouse. Not ten minutes later, she saw Mr. Lockwood on the launch, speeding away toward Haven Point.

She felt a tear form. *Just one tear. You're allowed to let one fall.*

It slid down her cheek; then she pulled a handkerchief from her reticule, dabbed at her eyes, and prepared to pretend.

CHAPTER FIFTEEN

August 1920
Washington, DC

JULIA

Sally was getting awfully attached to her plans. Lucy knew from experience that cuddling an idea like a kitten and refusing to let it go was a good way to get scratched in the face. Sally was fifteen months younger, though. She could not be expected to know everything.

FROM *LIBERTY ISLAND*, BY MISS CRANE

Julia and Michael headed down the narrow alley toward the Krazy Kat Club, where Mina and some others had gathered to celebrate the suffrage victory. Michael chuckled when he saw the message chalked above the door of the old livestock stable: "All Soap Abandon Ye Who Enter Here."

"They'll be out back," Julia said.

Julia found it aggravating that Mina insisted the Krazy Kat was the only worthwhile speakeasy in Washington. The city had a three-year jump on most of the country in going dry. As a result, it was wringing wet, with literally hundreds of speakeasies. It was a nice night to be here, though, an unusually mild evening for August in Washington, the temperature in the sixties.

Julia led Michael past the winding staircase that led upstairs to the bar and dance floor, around lumber and farm equipment, until they reached the back door. Ordinarily, the Krazy Kat's gravel courtyard was a bit seedy, but they had put clusters of candles on every table and strung Japanese lanterns on poles, which gave it a festive air.

"Duchess!" came a voice from above. Julia looked up and saw Mina leaning over the rail of the tree house. It was a simple structure, just a platform with a rickety railing built into the large oak in the center of the courtyard, but it had room for a small table and a few chairs.

"They're over there." Mina pointed to the corner, where Vera, Jane, Mitzy, and a few others were assembled around several wobbly tables. Mina came down to join them, and a waiter brought glasses of ice and tonic water.

"It's supposedly from an embassy, though I doubt it," Mitzy said, as she offered them the bottle of gin that was being passed around. Foreign diplomats, exempt from Prohibition rules, were allowed to import liquor, and Washington bootleggers all claimed to sell "embassy stuff."

Vera, who looked as if she'd had a bit too much not-from-an-embassy gin, pulled her head back and squinted at Michael.

"You have a patch on your eye!" she said, when her squint finally allowed her to focus on his face. Julia was unable to suppress a giggle.

"I do?" Michael reached up and touched it. "How odd."

Vera nodded earnestly, glad she had alerted him to this fact, and Michael thanked her for the information. A moment later, she began to wave her arms and sing, "*What do you do with a drunken sailor?*"

"Good God, Vera, shut up." Mitzy rolled her eyes.

"So, Duchess, how was the mods' celebration?" Mina asked, in a teasing tone.

"Packed, but fine." Julia sighed inwardly. Earlier that afternoon, she and Louisa had attended a celebration at Poli's Theater, sponsored by the moderate suffragists. Just as William believed women were tainted by any association with radical suffragists, Mina deemed any support of the moderates to be mildly traitorous.

When Tennessee had voted to ratify the Nineteenth Amendment eight days ago, it was a big moment, but last-minute maneuvers by the anti-suffragists created enough uncertainty to make full-throated celebration feel premature. They had been waiting for the main event: the arrival of Tennessee's certification, and its signature by the secretary of state.

Secretary Colby signed it at his home early that morning. It was disappointingly unceremonious, given that twenty-seven million American women had just been enfranchised. In part, the secretary was trying to stay ahead of an injunction, but the unwillingness of the factions to lay down their arms also played a role. Both groups, radicals and moderates, ferociously lobbied the secretary's office to be the only ones present at the signing. In the end, neither was.

Unsurprisingly, Mina's question about the Poli's event triggered grumbling.

"Have you heard what the moderates are saying?" Jane complained. "They've never understood this struggle. Just as we predicted, they're acting like it's done, like we've reached the destination, when it's only the beginning."

This, in turn, inspired everyone to name their favorite lingering inequities. As it was, admittedly, a very long list, the conversation went on for some time.

Julia turned to Michael and spoke quietly. "I'm sorry. I am afraid this is not what I advertised."

He had phoned earlier and asked if he could celebrate with her. She explained that Poli's would be mostly speechmaking, and suggested he come with her here instead.

"Don't be silly. It's actually interesting," he said.

"I wish we were allowed to enjoy one night." Julia sighed. On Haven Point, she had been frustrated by her friends' lack of investment in the suffragist cause, and her family's repressed emotions and unwillingness to speak openly. But the candor and free expression that Mina and her friends considered the highest virtues often came off as plain rudeness, and Julia was tired of the relentless complaining.

Michael smiled and lifted his glass. "Cheers."

Julia clinked her glass to his and took a sip of her not-from-an-embassy gin and tonic, grateful that Michael was with her. He had invited her to several parties since she returned from Maine, but she declined them, offering up alternatives instead—a ride in the park, a lecture, a film at the Knickerbocker.

Michael did not seem to understand that routinely having one girl on his arm was an impediment to his meeting another. The thought of someone taking her place made Julia feel wistful at times, but she still felt it was wrong to stand in the way.

Julia was only half listening to the wider conversation, but when she heard Jane the Socialist mention Pelham Stewart's name, both ears pricked up.

". . . and nobody seems to know when he'll come back."

Mina must have seen her look up. "It's a good thing you and Pelham never became an item, Julia."

Julia's curiosity got the better of her. "What's that? Sorry, I missed what Jane said."

"Pelham Stewart has taken up with some Russian woman."

Julia stiffened. Feeling Michael's eyes on her, she gave her head a slight shake she hoped was perceptible only to him. She had not told Michael that things were over between her and Pelham.

"Some Trotsky aide, I guess, who's now in France, trying to lure people to Russia to start up agricultural communes. I gather she's frighteningly beautiful."

Julia couldn't know whether Pelham "took up with" this woman before or after they broke up, but she had suspected something like this. Julia desperately wanted to escape, but she worried the ever-perceptive Mina would take note of the timing of her departure. For twenty long minutes she sat, pretending to be unbothered, until the conversation veered into other subjects, and she could finally ask Michael to take her home.

As they walked to his car, she tried to summon some topic of conversation to fill the pregnant silence, but she was not up to the task.

"Julia, are you all right?" Michael asked finally, as they made their way up Connecticut Avenue.

"Yes, thank you. Mina merely added details to what I already knew. If you do not mind, though, I would prefer not to speak of it."

"Of course." Michael rallied with some neutral subject to occupy them, and when they reached her home, he walked her to her door and took her hands.

"I will not speak of anything unpleasant, except to say that I wish you were happy."

She gave him a hug. "Thank you."

Julia did her best to distract herself over the following days, but she could not stop thinking about Pelham's "frighteningly beautiful" Trotskyite. Though not ordinarily inclined toward rumination, it proved an easy habit to pick up. Within a week, her imagination had conjured a full picture of the woman. She was of Nordic descent, with blond hair, light eyes, and a perfect complexion.

Julia imagined Pelham musing aloud to the woman, wondering how he ever got mixed up with a silly schoolteacher with no special talents, no willingness to *commit*. It was when Julia gave the mystery woman a name ("Svetlana") that she began to see how dispiriting a habit this could be.

The start of the school year was a blessing. Though her general dissatisfaction lingered, it had plagued her so long, she had grown sadly used to it, and she was busy, at least.

Days turned into weeks, and weeks into months. She went home for Christmas, and she and her family pretended everything was fine. Julia still felt adrift, but over time, it became an unpleasant background hum, and slowly the acuity of her grief over Pelham, and even her memories of him, began to fade.

On a Sunday evening in early March, Julia heard a knock at her door and opened it to find Mina, who had just returned from a weekend in New York.

"How was it?" Julia asked.

"Fine," Mina said, her tone clipped. Julia offered her a drink, but

Mina shook her head and walked around Julia's living room, idly picking things up and putting them down again.

Mina's entire bearing said, *You are in trouble, and we are going to have a talk, but only when I am ready.* Julia waited, feeling exasperated by the drama.

"So," Mina said, finally turning to face Julia. "You never told me you and Pelham Stewart were in correspondence."

"I told you I saw him at the Seabornes' house before he left for war." Julia was far less concerned about Mina's anger than she was about the context in which she had gathered this information.

"You didn't tell me you had written to one another."

"What was there to tell? I wrote lots of people."

Mina's chin went down, and her eyes narrowed, as if to say, *I know you are lying.* "From what Pelham said, there was quite the blossoming romance. He seems to think he wronged you somehow."

From what Pelham said . . . Did that mean he was in New York? Julia skipped right over wondering why he was there and went straight to a hot rush of humiliation. She imagined Pelham confessing to Mina about his abominable treatment of poor, naive Julia. *Oh, and have you met Svetlana . . . ?*

Mina's annoyance notwithstanding, Julia was glad she had never told her. Even if she had sworn Mina to secrecy, it was easy to imagine her scolding Pelham for his neglect, and then defending herself later on the grounds of her abiding loyalty. *How could I be silent when my friend was treated so poorly?* In the process, of course, she would have cemented the image of Julia pining away while Pelham and Svetlana romped about.

"Well, he told me he wants to see you. He'll be in Washington next week."

So, I must face this humiliating apology in person? Having already implied this was much ado about nothing, however, Julia could hardly say she had no desire to see him.

"That's fine." Julia shrugged.

"He is joining the civilized world again. I gather one of the men in that Bolshy French commune made off with all the money. He's taken a job with a magazine. The man will always be poor as a church mouse, not that that need weigh with you."

"What do you mean?"

"That if you agree to give this supposedly nonexistent romance another go, his bank book will not matter to you." Mina said, still using that deliberate *I will humor you, though I know you're lying* tone.

"Oh." Julia, who felt neither a need nor a desire to explain herself, changed the subject. Mina left soon after, having failed to extract information or an apology.

Julia thought it was possible, if not likely, that Mina was misinterpreting whatever Pelham had said to her, but at least it was not as bad as what she had imagined: Pelham commiserating with Mina about poor Julia, while Svetlana stood by, blond and bored, smoking a cigarette.

This image reminded Julia how much time she had already wasted thinking about Pelham. She decided to put him out of her mind until such time as she heard from him. When the week passed without a word, she concluded that Mina had indeed misunderstood matters.

She was completely unprepared, therefore, when she got home from school on Friday and found Pelham waiting on her front stoop. He rose and met her at the iron gate.

"Hello, Pelham." She stopped in front of him. He was not "old enough to be her grandfather," as he had joked in one of his letters, but there were lines in his forehead and around his eyes that had not been there before the war. Somehow, as was so maddeningly the way with men, they made him look more distinguished.

"I am sorry to surprise you like this, but I wanted so much to see you, and I thought you might not agree if I asked first. Will you let me take you to dinner?"

"Tonight? I have plans."

"Tomorrow?"

"All right." She could not hold back a weary sigh. "Tomorrow, then."

"Thank you, Julia." Pelham had the decency to look pathetically grateful.

As she got ready the next evening, Julia wished she had some guidebook for how to handle what she found to be a confusing situation. The old courtship rules were ridiculous, and she was glad her generation had tossed them out, but it would have been useful if they had replaced them with something else.

Given that she could not even categorize what they had, she had no idea what her attitude should be. They were two adults who spent one day together, had one kiss, and exchanged some letters that were intimate, in their way. None of that constituted anything like a promise. Did she even have a right to be angry?

He had offered to pick her up for dinner, but she declined, having no idea how things would go, and not wishing to be beholden to him for transportation home. By the time she met him outside Café St. Mark's downtown, she had come to no conclusions about how she should think about this encounter.

That said, she did put on a very pretty gown, dotted net over black satin, which he seemed to admire.

The café was in an old Presbyterian church that had been made over to look like an indoor Italian garden, with stucco walls, fountains, and a pergola below the sapphire blue ceiling.

She wondered at his selecting St. Mark's, which was popular with Washington's "residential set." Sure enough, as they walked to their table, Julia was hailed by a number of people she knew from that milieu. Pelham seemed amused by this, and she was secretly pleased. It seemed like compelling testimony to the full life she lived in Washington.

Julia knew that this was a meeting of sorts, and since Pelham was the one to call it, it was his responsibility to set the agenda. Still, she expected some small talk first and was disconcerted when he launched in as soon as they had ordered drinks.

"Julia, I wish I knew how to begin to tell you how sorry I am for breaking things off as I did. I was horribly wrong. I cringe whenever I think of the absurd things I said."

Julia paused and looked off for a moment, feeling flummoxed. "I don't know that you owe me an apology or explanation, Pelham," she said finally. She heard the uncertainty in her own voice.

"Of course I do." His own tone suggested far more certainty, and when she met his eyes, she saw chagrin. "I was horrible, and not that it should weigh with you, but I have been wretched about it for some time."

"I see."

"I hope you took none of my words to heart because they were perfectly backward. I disparaged your tendency toward cheer, toward joy, when those are the best things about you. And while I imagine it is hard for you to believe, I care so much for you. I would like another chance, if you would just allow me to explain."

Julia did not understand why it was that only now, after Pelham had acknowledged his error, she felt indignant about his treatment. It was as if she was deferring to his terms for her own feelings.

But when she looked at him and took in his gentle, beseeching expression, she experienced the same powerful tug of attraction that she had felt the first time she laid eyes on him. No other man had ever made her feel this way, and she had begun to wonder if one ever would. Though he seemed in earnest, he had indeed wronged her, and Julia knew she would have to tread more carefully this time.

However clarifying these feelings of aggrievement were, she found she had a desire neither to vent them nor to hear his explanation.

"Perhaps it would be best if we just began again, Pelham. We shall just see how things go." She smiled. It was a rather closed-mouth affair, that smile, and not particularly encouraging, but it was all she could manage.

"Beginning again," after all, did not mean *forgetting*.

CHAPTER SIXTEEN

July 1900
Haven Point, Maine

ANNA

The morning after her confrontation with Mr. Lockwood, Anna went for a walk into the woods at the center of the point. It was quiet, almost eerily so, and the air felt heavy. As she followed the rough trails that had been blazed by those who'd used the woods as a shortcut over the years, she tried to empty her mind, yet she kept coming back to the words she'd overheard on the Searses' yacht.

She does pester him so, does she not? I suppose it's not surprising that he simply gives in from time to time.

If she had more experience, Anna was sure she would have spotted the signs that must have been there, and been spared this disappointment and shame.

The thick tree canopy prevented her from seeing the leaden sky. It was not until she emerged onto the road near the Grahams' house that she looked up and saw the ominous storm clouds overhead. She heard a rumble of thunder, and then a heavy raindrop hit her face. She turned to head toward Fourwinds, but she had only made it a little way down the road when the sky opened up, and torrents of rain began to fall, punctuated by flashes of lightning and great claps of thunder.

Alarmed, she ran to Nora's. She climbed the porch stairs, and the door opened even before she reached it.

"I saw you through the window," Nora said, ushering her inside. "Thank goodness you didn't make for home. What a gully washer!"

She found a towel, helped Anna dry herself off, and sat her by the fire.

"What on earth were you doing out in this?"

"I went walking in the woods, like a perfect idiot."

"Well, you're safe now. You can wait it out here."

Nora had made some scones, and Anna, who had eaten little at breakfast, found that she was hungry. Nora's house was cozy, and her sensible chatter was comforting. And now that she was safe and dry, the storm made for an interesting show, with sheets of rain lashing at the windows, and the great booms of thunder overhead.

She had been there a half hour when they heard the sound of wheels and hoofbeats. Next thing they knew, the door was flung open, and Elizabeth stumbled in, soaking wet, her face red and streaked with tears.

"Please, please tell me Julia is here somewhere," she said, her expression beseeching, as Nora and Anna hastened to her side.

"She's not, Liz. Is she missing?" Anna asked.

"This was my last hope," Elizabeth wailed. She scrambled around her skirt until she found her pocket, and pulled out a piece of paper. She handed it to Anna. "I found this note this morning. She's run away."

The brief note offered little clue of the child's whereabouts.

I am going away becus I do not wish to go to New Port.

Sincerely yours, Julia

Anna's heart sank. She wondered where her niece had gotten this idea. Had Elizabeth given in to Lillian?

"When did you last see her?" Nora asked.

"A little over two hours ago. She said she was going to Louisa's.

When I saw the rain coming, I went to fetch her. Eugenia said she and Louisa had risen early to help Mr. Lockwood pack, as he had to leave for Boston at the last minute, and then they saw him to the steamer. They had neither seen nor heard from Julia."

Elizabeth explained that she had returned to Fourwinds after leaving Eugenia. Rosemary had the morning off and had taken the steamer to Portland, and Elizabeth thought Julia might have returned without her knowing. It was when she looked in Julia's room that she found the note on her dresser.

"I stopped by Serena's, but she hadn't seen her either. I cannot imagine where she has gone."

The news that Mr. Lockwood had left Haven Point had not escaped Anna's ears, but given the far more pressing concern, she pushed it aside.

Once again, they heard the sound of hoofbeats. Elizabeth raced to the door, Nora and Anna in her wake. A carriage pulled up, bearing Serena and Ruthie. Seeing Elizabeth at the door, Serena shook her head, her expression apologetic. They got out and dashed to the door.

"We have not found her, Elizabeth," Serena said, when they came in. "But Ruthie overheard us talking and thinks she might know where Julia has gone."

Elizabeth knelt before the child.

"Oh, do tell us what you know, Ruthie," she said gently.

Ruthie looked up at her mother, who nodded. "Julia once said that her grandma wanted her to go to Newport, but if you ever made her, she'd run away to Jumaru." She blushed and added, "I didn't think she would do it."

"Well, of course not. Who would think of her doing such a silly thing?" Elizabeth gave Ruthie a reassuring smile, then stood. "I wish we could be sure that's where she went."

"I think it is," Serena said, her tone apprehensive. "One of my servants told me that the rowboat we keep on the north side is missing."

Clever girl, Anna thought ruefully. Someone would have noticed if she took a boat from the wharf, but several families, including the

Lawrences, kept rowboats near the crossing to the mainland to make it easier to get back and forth. Once Julia passed the northwest corner of the peninsula, no one would have reason to know a passing boat was even from Haven Point. It could have come from anywhere.

"We must sail over and see," Elizabeth said. "Nora and Anna, will you come?"

They both nodded, though Anna felt more than a little alarmed about sailing in this weather. She comforted herself with the thought that Nora Graham surely knew how to navigate through a thunderstorm.

Elizabeth glanced out the door. "Serena, will you take us to the wharf, then distract Mr. Phillips? I'd prefer to avoid any questions, and he'd fuss about our going out in this."

At the wharf, Serena headed to the harbormaster's office. She felt certain that she could keep Mr. Phillips occupied with many confused and confusing questions about the mail. Anna agreed that she was the right woman for the job.

"Is this wise, Nora?" Anna asked under her breath, as they headed for the dock.

"We'll be fine in the catboat. The sloop would be faster, but the catboat is easier to rig, and it's broad-beamed, stable. We can tow the dory behind it so we'll have a tender when we get there. It'll be tricky once we get around to the other side of the island, but Elizabeth can handle it."

So Elizabeth is to be the captain? Anna was not sure why, but she had assumed Nora was the better sailor.

The rain was still very heavy, and there was nobody in sight, so Anna, Elizabeth, and Nora climbed into the Grahams' dory and rowed the short distance to the mooring. When they reached it, Elizabeth instructed Anna to get aboard, and then she and Nora followed.

Anna did not speak the language of sailboats. Or of sailing. Or even of wind, really. According to family lore, when she was little, she once refused to sail with Elizabeth because she did not like the wind's "pranks." She was a frequent passenger, however, and while otherwise useless, she generally knew how to stay out of the way.

The first leg, straight to the southwest tip of the island, was fairly straightforward, with a steady breeze, requiring only a few orders from Elizabeth to Nora to ease the sheet. The choppy water slapped against the side of the boat, and the rain and spray stung their faces, but they were soaked long before even getting into the boat. Anna found the thunder unnerving, but the flashes of lightning she saw were mostly over the mainland.

When they passed the tip of the island, Elizabeth said, "Ready about."

Anna ducked to avoid the swinging boom and scrambled rather ungracefully to the other side. The dory pulled hard to one side and made a sharp slapping sound against the waves.

"Sheet in! Sheet in hard!" Elizabeth said. A strong gust of wind heeled the boat, and the water seemed to rise up the deck toward them.

"Keep her full!"

They could see the cove now. The entrance looked threatening to Anna, the waves crashing on either side and the water churning menacingly. Elizabeth, however, was not looking in that direction. She was peering through the rain at something to their east.

Anna followed her gaze and spotted darkness on the water, and then a sudden rise, almost like a shelf on a canal, and with some alarm, she realized they were facing down a massive wave.

Everything seemed to happen at once. "Sea's building! Stand the sheet." Nora handled the sail, Elizabeth pushed hard on the tiller, and the boat swung away from the cove. The wave that Anna thought would capsize them was now beneath them. Rather than being directly hit, the boat rolled with the sea. Anna clung to the gunwale, feet braced on the deck, her stomach dropping uncomfortably.

She felt as if they had narrowly escaped complete disaster, but while Elizabeth and Nora were alert, neither seemed terrified, and she did her best to follow their lead.

"We'll come back up once this sea passes," Elizabeth said.

"Hardening up!" she said a moment later, and once again, they were turning back on course. Without incident, they navigated into the cove, the entrance of which had looked so perilous to Anna. Once the little beach was in sight, Nora pointed, and they saw the Lawrences' rowboat, pulled up on the shore.

Julia was nowhere to be seen, however, and the storm was not done with them. The thunder continued to rumble, and Anna saw a crack of lightning that was far too close for comfort. Elizabeth and Nora got the boat unrigged and attached to the mooring. Nora untied the dory and pulled it alongside the catboat, and they boarded it and rowed to shore.

Anna led them up to the clearing, and peered through the rain toward the lean-to, where she assumed Julia would have sought shelter, but she was not there. Her eyes scanned the clearing, and then they walked the perimeter, looking for any trace or clue, but there was no sign of her. They went to the other clearing, where a farmhouse had supposedly once stood, and she was not there either.

Anna was mystified. She had been sure they would find Julia in one of these familiar places where they had spent so many hours. Then she had a thought. *The treasure.*

The girls had never lifted the prohibition against Anna or Mr. Lockwood seeing the spot where they were digging, but they had also gone back and forth so often that they had trampled on the ferns and wild strawberry ground cover and created a path. It now led them to the edge of a small glade.

Anna took a few steps in, promptly lost her footing, and fell.

"Are you all right?" Elizabeth said. Anna looked at what had tripped her up and saw that she had stepped in a hole.

"Yes, I think so," she said. She took hold of Elizabeth's outstretched hand and let herself be pulled up. Her ankle was a bit sore, but she could walk. "Be careful. It's like a minefield, just without the explosives. The girls have been digging for treasure here."

Anna looked around, and through the rain, she saw a darker patch of ground on the far side. She pointed, and they picked their way across the clearing. The hole was almost four feet deep, and wide enough to fit Julia, who sat at the bottom, hugging her legs, her forehead on her knees.

Elizabeth knelt in the dirt by the side of the hole. "Hello, Julia," she said, kindly.

When Julia looked up, Anna saw that her eyes were swollen, her face dirty and smeared.

"Mama!" she cried. She unfolded herself and quickly scrambled out of the hole, as if afraid her mother would disappear, and then threw herself into Elizabeth's waiting arms. Elizabeth stroked the back of her head, and murmured to her that it was all right, she was quite safe, they would get her home.

CHAPTER SEVENTEEN

January 1922
Washington, DC

JULIA

When Victoria dug up the ceramic jug handle, the girls debated whether it counted as "treasure." Audrey said that without the jug attached, it shouldn't even be considered, but Victoria insisted it qualified.

After going round and round, Victoria said, with an air of finality, that "it's treasure because I treasure it." This seemed like a good rule of thumb.

FROM *LIBERTY ISLAND*, BY MISS CRANE

Lillian Demarest could not have died at a worse time had she selected it to spite her granddaughter.

She probably did, Julia thought bitterly.

The telegram was waiting when she arrived home from work: "Funeral Saturday at Trinity. Please advise as to arrival. Will have you picked up at North Station." It was not a complete surprise. Mother had informed Julia a week ago that Grandmother Lillian was quite ill.

As if to drive home the poor timing, the telegram was sitting atop a package that Julia knew contained Pelham's manuscript.

She went up to her apartment and slumped into a chair, head

swimming. Pelham's novel had just been accepted for publication, and he was eager for her reaction. She had been pleased it would arrive in time for her to read it before his planned visit the coming weekend.

She dragged herself to the telephone to break the news.

"Why are you expected to pay your respects?" Pelham said. "She didn't even like you!"

"I cannot skip my grandmother's funeral."

"Whyever not?"

"Because my absence would be remarked on, and it would create unpleasantness for my family." Julia was careful to use a matter-of-fact tone. "That unpleasantness would, in turn, be heaped upon my own head, a prospect I do not relish."

Julia felt neither angry nor defensive, but she was aware of a certain weariness that had been creeping up on her and was now settling into her bones. Evidently Pelham sensed this, because when he spoke again, his tone was gentler.

"Julia, I leave for Europe on assignment next week. I have no idea how long I will be over there. Please. Won't you consider begging off? Tell them you're ill."

"I won't lie."

Pelham sighed. "Julia . . ."

Julia wavered. Her last visit to New York had ended on a confusing note, and she had hoped to clear the air before he went abroad. He sounded so pathetic, too, that something in her melted. "I'll see what I can do."

Julia hung up the phone and paced about her apartment. She had known Pelham would not understand. He and his friends had no sense of filial obligation. The more she thought about it, though, the more she saw his point. Besides ill-considered Christmas gifts, all Lillian had ever given Julia was her firm and consistent disapproval.

Her attendance would spare her parents embarrassment, but why was that her responsibility? Julia's mind flashed to her last visit to Haven Point, images of William's cruel treatment of Pauline, and then that scene on the cliff, when Julia practically begged her mother to show some emotion, to let down her guard and just be *honest.*

Maybe it's time for some honesty of my own, she thought. Before she could talk herself out of it, Julia went to the telephone.

Needless to say, her mother was as appalled at the idea of Julia skipping the funeral as Pelham had been at her attending.

"Why should I go?" Julia argued. "Lillian never even liked me."

"Because she was your father's mother," Mother said, in a tone of utter mystification, as if she could not comprehend having to point this out. "You should be there for him."

Julia felt a pang of guilt. She had considered her parents' shame, but not her father's grief. She had gone this far, though. She was not going to turn back now.

"Lillian was horrible to me, Mother, and nobody ever said or did a thing about it. It was all just *repressed.* Brushed under the rug like everything else."

"So the opposite of repression is neglecting the most basic courtesy to your father?" There was an uncharacteristic twinge of contempt in her voice. "I wonder, should nothing be repressed? Should we utter every truth that comes into our minds, no matter who it hurts? If merely being civil is a sign of repression, then give me that any day, rather than this cruel rudeness that has come over you."

Despite mounting uncertainty, Julia tried to maintain her indignation. "It would be the height of hypocrisy to show my face at the funeral of a woman who despised me."

Mother was quiet for a moment. When she spoke, she sounded as weary as Julia felt.

"I don't know what is happening with you, Julia, but you don't seem happy, and you haven't for some time."

"I've never been happier, Mother. I have to go," Julia said. She hung up the phone and promptly burst into tears.

Julia could not remember when she last had a good cry, and a half hour later, she wondered if she should not engage in the practice more often. Once she'd "cried 'til her tears were gone," to borrow Louisa's term, she did feel a bit better.

She wrote a letter to Father, in which she managed to extend her genuine sympathy, and to apologize profusely for not attending the funeral, while omitting any mention of the reason for not being there. It would not erase the consequences, but it made her feel better, and might even make him feel better, too.

By the time Mina popped in to visit an hour later, she had somewhat recovered her equilibrium.

Mina's eye immediately caught the manuscript on the coffee table. "What's this?"

"Pelham sold a novel. It will be published a year from now," she replied. Seeing a shadow cross Mina's face, she added, "It was a great secret. He is terribly superstitious and would not speak of it until it was sold. He is only now allowing me to read it."

Julia ordinarily found it annoying that Mina believed herself entitled to all information about everyone she knew, but it was more understandable in this case. Since September, Mina had been seeing Gardiner Lide, one of Pelham's closest friends in New York. She eagerly coordinated trips with Julia, and the two couples had spent countless hours together.

Mina recovered somewhat. "Well, wonderful, then. Did he get a handsome sum?"

"I believe he did, yes."

"So, it's arrived just in time for his visit."

"Yes, which has caused a great row." Julia relayed the news of Lillian's death, and told her about the fallout from her announcement that she would not attend the funeral.

"This was an important stand to take, Julia. I'm proud of you," Mina said.

Julia found the comment a bit condescending, and Mina was grating on her already taut nerves. Plus, Louisa would be in the neighborhood and planned to stop by, and Julia needed every available minute to read the manuscript, so she was relieved when Mina left.

Julia brought the stack of pages to the wingback chair by her fireplace, and began to read.

Julia had known Pelham's lush prose would translate beautifully to a novel, and he had clearly marshaled every ounce of his tremendous talent for this story. That said, he had told Julia that "some of the material would be familiar," and by the time she heard a knock signaling Louisa's arrival, she understood what he meant and had begun to feel uneasy.

She felt uneasy again when she opened the door and took in her friend's appearance. Louisa was just getting over one of the infections she was susceptible to in winter, and it was not uncommon for her to huff a little after climbing the stairs to Julia's apartment, but she seemed more breathless than usual. She was pale, too, her normally clear eyes dimmer, like a watercolor painting left in the sun.

"Come in, Lou," Julia said. "I'll make you some tea."

When she returned with the mug, Louisa nodded at the manuscript on the table.

"Pelham sent his book?"

"He did." Louisa was the only person Julia had told about Pelham's novel. She was safe as houses with a secret, and also far outside Pelham's orbit.

"How is it?"

"I'm no literary critic, and I'm only a quarter of the way through, but it is quite good. Remarkable, even," Julia said with a sigh.

"Remarkable but . . . ?" Louisa said, evidently noting the incongruence between Julia's high praise and flat tone.

"It's about a utopian commune, clearly based on Brook Farm."

Pelham had set his novel, *The Schoolcraft Colony*, on the Upper Peninsula of Michigan, forty years after Brook Farm failed, but Julia recognized elements, including some characters.

"And his is a sympathetic perspective?"

"Quite sympathetic, as far as I can tell. I honestly thought his flirtation with Bolshevism was just that, a flirtation."

It was implicit between Julia and Pelham that his time in France after the war was a tender subject, and they never spoke of it. The subject of Russia came up, of course, given the terrible famine, and Mina's boyfriend even referred to Pelham's efforts in France once—"You were ahead of your time, I'm afraid"—but Pelham had merely nodded in response.

"I am not certain how this story unfolds," Julia continued. "But I have a suspicion that Pelham is writing an alternate history of Brook Farm, in which the commune somehow succeeds. Needless to say, it will be tricky to discuss."

"Is Pelham under the impression that you favor communism?" Evidently revived by the tea, Louisa looked amused.

"I'm not sure what impression he has. We talked about Brook Farm the very first time we met. He asked if my grandmother liked it there, and I said she did. But Winifred Newbold was just a little girl, romping through fields and making daisy chain crowns. He seemed so pleased, I didn't want to tell him that she ultimately concluded the concept was unworkable."

"Concluded *correctly*." Louisa favored government helping the working class, but she was skeptical of all forms of socialism. *Leaves far too much to people's decency, and most aren't so decent.* Given that one of the members of Pelham's little commune had made off with all the funds, Julia had thought he might have come to the same conclusion.

"I fear I am insufficiently proletarian or self-sacrificing to relish the idea of living on a commune," Julia said.

"You're selling yourself short." Louisa had the hint of a smile on her lips. "We lived on something like a commune ourselves, did we not?"

"I suppose. But we were never on Liberty Island for more than a few days. We always came back to Haven Point."

". . . for tennis," Louisa added. "Perhaps there's a compromise in the works."

"Part-time communism. With tennis," Julia replied.

"Monday through Friday in Siberia. Weekends at a hotel."

"With room service. Also good motorcars and moving pictures."

"You will scrub floors," Louisa said, then raised an admonitory finger and added, "But *not* if you must go without good hats."

They went back and forth for a while, until they were both laughing.

"I highly doubt he'll ask you to live on a commune, Julia," Louisa said finally.

"Well, he did once," Julia said, but then she began to chuckle again. "Though he was thrilled with his advance and is presently looking for a larger apartment. For a collectivist, he's rather obsessed with money."

Louisa had picked up the manuscript and was thumbing through it. When she reached the place that Julia had marked with Mother's telegram, she held it up, a question in her eyes.

"Oh, I forgot to tell you. Lillian died."

"Oh, my," Louisa said, crossing her heart. "When is the funeral?"

"Saturday."

"But wasn't Pelham supposed to come this weekend?"

"I'm not going to the funeral."

"What?" Louisa looked more confused than appalled, but even this was too much for Julia. The sensation of her mood crashing back to earth filled her with rebellious anger.

"Not you, too!" she snapped.

Louisa's face fell. "Julia, I am sorry. I'm just surprised."

"It's long past time for me to stand up to my parents. There's no reason for me to attend after the way Lillian treated me. You realize, don't you, that Liberty Island started in part because of her? They wanted to keep me out of her sight!"

"What a stroke of luck that was." Louisa's tone was gentle, but there was still a confused wrinkle in her brow.

"I know you are nostalgic for Liberty Island, Louisa, but I can't love the memory as you do. Think about it. My own family—my own *mother*—hid me away. It was all an elaborate way of saying, 'You cannot behave this way in public.'"

"Well, we couldn't. That's how things were. And it was hardly bondage. It was permission. Encouragement, even."

"You're being too generous," Julia scoffed. "How was Mother any different from Father or William? They hoped I'd get it out of my system and eventually do as they wished. Make my debut, marry, and settle down in Back Bay."

"And yet here you are, unmarried and not in Back Bay."

"*Despite* my family. And what did Mother ever do to protect me from Lillian? Nothing!"

"I don't recall your needing protection."

"Yes, because I repressed my feelings," Julia said, too annoyed to stop herself, even as she knew that, for the second time that evening, she was channeling Pelham (and therefore Sigmund Freud).

Louisa tilted her head and looked at Julia, as if she were seeing someone familiar on the street but could not quite place her face. As Julia had been struggling to recognize herself of late, this, too, hit a bit too close to the bone.

"Just say it. I'm spoiled. I was clothed and fed and had a very fine roof over my head."

"I was not thinking anything of the kind."

"Then what?"

"I suppose I don't understand what feelings you supposedly repressed. You were the most expressive person I'd ever met," Louisa said. She paused, then shook her head slowly. "You were a happy child, Julia."

"I just hadn't faced the truth. Pelham agrees I shouldn't go. So does Mina."

"Naturally." Louisa sighed wearily.

"What do you mean by that?"

"I mean that, according to their philosophy, we should do whatever our impulses say, with no limits or criticism. Pelham, in particular, seems to have a knack for concocting elaborate intellectual justifications that happen to serve him. They hate anything or anyone that tries to regulate their behavior, including families, and especially parents. And it's more fun when everyone else hates their parents, too." She shrugged and added, "It's a bit ungrateful, if you don't mind my saying."

Julia felt a spasm of compunction. Louisa never said a self-pitying word, but she was just a little girl when her mother died, and she never knew her father. Still, Julia had had a few too many home truths for one night. "I feel like you're taking what I've told you and throwing it back at me!"

Louisa closed her eyes, took a tired breath. "I'm sorry. Forgive me, Julia. I did not mean to speak of that."

Julia knew she was the one who should ask for forgiveness, but she was too agitated. When she said nothing, Louisa tiredly pushed herself up from her seat and left.

Unfortunately, finishing Pel's manuscript late that evening did nothing to improve Julia's mood. She was correct that Pelham had set out to rewrite the history of Brook Farm. In the eponymous "Schoolcraft Colony," two factions emerged, one of which he portrayed as responsible for the failure. The other split off to start a new commune. The reader was left with the impression that the new experiment would flourish.

By this time, however, Julia had a much bigger concern than having to feign enthusiasm for utopianism. From the first pages, she saw that one of Pelham's characters, Patience Turner, was based on Margaret Fuller.

In Pelham's interpretation, this beloved figure from Concord, idolized by three generations of Julia's family, teemed with neuroses and secret perverse yearnings. Patience Turner's father was devoted to her, just as Margaret Fuller's had been, but Pelham had interpreted it as a twisted devotion, resulting in Patience's perverse sexual desires. She repressed them, but as any believer in psychoanalysis would tell you, nothing is ever *really* suppressed, and they manifested in Patience's ill health, irregular behavior, and bizarre dreams.

Julia could have kicked herself for letting Pelham borrow her bound copy of Margaret Fuller's diaries, which Michael's mother had given her. They were her adolescent diaries, and as such contained dramatic flights of emotional fancy.

Worse, Margaret Fuller had suffered from nightmares and written about them. However forward-thinking, not even this brilliant woman could have predicted Freudians, who reacted to a description of a dream as a kitten responds to a ball of twine.

Julia put the manuscript down and stared into the dying embers in the fireplace.

Louisa's summary of Pelham and his comrades' beliefs was accurate. They disdained society's rules and held the "primitive" in great regard. Feelings and instincts were superior to logic and reason, and an authentic life required indulging one's impulses. The very reason they were so attached to Sigmund Freud was that he affirmed all these beliefs.

Julia had not forgotten Pelham's scolding letters during the war, or that horrible last letter, when he said her "inclination toward contentment," her naive optimism, made them incompatible.

When they reunited last spring, though, his system of beliefs manifested in ways that appealed to Julia's native spontaneity. "Following one's impulses" meant delightful hours spent walking aimlessly about New York, stopping when and where the mood struck.

They went to jazz clubs, art shows, and experimental theater productions. One evening, they saw a play at some makeshift theater near Hell's Kitchen. Julia found it bizarre and incomprehensible, but given Pelham's deeper appreciation for the avant-garde, she figured he might be enjoying it. But then he squeezed her hand, and she turned and saw amused horror on his face. With a jerk of his head toward the aisle, he signaled *Let's go.* They snuck out the back, managing to hold in their laughter until they were on the sidewalk.

He truly seemed to appreciate Julia's more cheerful disposition and more optimistic perspective. One warm midsummer night, a long ramble landed them near Morningside Heights, looking out on the Hudson, and Pelham turned to her suddenly.

"Julia, I've begun writing a novel." He spoke quickly, as if it was a confession he had been afraid to make.

"Oh, Pelham, I am so glad. Your writing is almost too beautiful for magazines."

"Do you really think so?"

"Of course! Your metaphors, your imagery and descriptive prose. You bring things to life, even in the letters you wrote me."

Just then, they heard the sound of a great deep horn from a boat on the river.

"Well, that's that, then," he said, and they both laughed.

"Literature really is the only real venue for primal creativity and authentic emotion," he added. (Pelham could still be a bit oratorical, but in those blissful days, Julia did not mind.)

He stuck to his rule of not speaking about the content of his novel, but that still left plenty to discuss. Julia found it enthralling to hear him speak about his inspirations, his writing process, and the exhilaration of coming up with ideas. He credited Julia with his completing it: "If not for my absolute faith in your intuition, I would never have pressed forward."

She was not sure what she had expected from this story, except that *The Schoolcraft Colony* was not it. That said, she had been picking up dissonant notes in the music of his ideas lately, though for the most part, she had responded by putting her fingers in her ears. She refused to see anything wrong when their reunion had felt so right. She reveled in the new vistas that were opening up to her, and of a sense that they were again traveling together on a great adventure. She could not bear the thought of it coming to an end.

It was a confusing tangle, but there was no time to unravel the threads now. Pelham would arrive in a few days. Julia needed to figure out how to manufacture enthusiasm for a book that genuinely repelled her.

Julia spent every free moment that week poring over Pelham's manuscript, finding aspects of the narrative she could praise, turns of phrase and metaphors she admired. By the time he arrived on Thursday, she felt prepared.

Pelham had a meeting downtown, so they had agreed to meet at the Willard Hotel. Julia dressed carefully, in a narrow black chiffon evening dress with silver beads, cut low in the back. She pulled her shoulder-length hair back on one side, and kept it in place with a rhinestone comb.

When she looked in the mirror, she chuckled. *Perhaps it will occur to Pelham that women in communes are unlikely to wear such frocks.*

She arrived to find Pelham waiting in the lobby. He approached, took her hands, and chafed them. "You poor soul, out in this dreadful cold." It had been a mild winter until earlier this week, when Arctic weather had set in.

"New Englander, recall!" Looking up at his bright eyes and dazzling smile cemented her resolve to set aside her misgivings. "You're brilliant, Pelham. I'm so proud of you."

He smiled and pulled her into an embrace, right there in the lobby.

The maître d' led them to a table by the window, which reflected their faces and the flickering candlelight. A tenor, accompanied by a ten-piece orchestra, was singing "I'm Always Chasing Rainbows."

"I want to hear about you, darling," he said. "How did your parents take the news of your not attending the funeral?"

"Not terribly well," she said, rather understating the matter. "But I wrote to Father, and I am certain it will be all right. Please, let us talk about your novel. It is marvelous, so beautifully written and engaging. I know it will be a great success."

"I hope so," Pelham replied, uncharacteristically humble.

"Oh, I am certain!" Julia said, and proceeded to spend an hour expounding upon the good points she had so carefully indexed, assiduously avoiding the trickier aspects. She thought she had managed it well, but as they were having coffee, he took her hand in his.

"I must ask what you thought of Patience Turner."

Julia's heart sank, but she smiled as brightly as she could. "I recognized her, of course, as Margaret Fuller. I thought she was interesting, a very . . . *textured* character."

"It's just, well . . . I wondered if it would be difficult for you to read," he said, his voice full of tender sympathy.

It isn't a biography! Julia felt like screaming. "I suppose it was a somewhat sordid interpretation," she said, her tone carefully neutral. Julia knew Pelham believed that he had been faithful in his portrayal of Margaret Fuller's inner life, and she never felt like she could argue with Pelham, especially on this subject.

"I was afraid you might see it that way. I hoped her happier ending was mitigating."

"Yes, you freed her," Julia replied, glad her own comment had not prompted a debate, as she was not sure she could restrain herself. She was relieved when she heard the band play the first strains of Al Jolson's "It's You."

"Can we, Pelham?" She nodded at the dance floor, filling up, as always, for this song.

He rose and took her hand, and Julia did her best to shake off her annoyance. Pelham was always at his most gallant and amusing when they danced, so by the time the orchestra stopped for the night, she felt more favorably disposed toward him.

As was his custom, Pelham was staying in a small hotel in Washington Heights, not far from her apartment. He asked if she would come over for a bit.

They went to the secluded reception room off the lobby, always deserted at this late hour. He removed her cloak and led her to the love seat near the rear of the room, out of view of the reception desk. He bent to kiss her, and she felt the familiar stirring thrill, the pull of attraction, of temptation.

He pulled back and looked at her. "Please, Julia, won't you come up?"

And there it was. One of the dissonant notes.

I am such a fool, she thought.

A few weeks earlier, during Julia's last visit to New York, she and Pelham met Mina and Gardiner at a basement speakeasy in lower Manhattan. They resurfaced at the end of the night to find it had begun to snow. It was like pixie dust, barely visible except in the streetlight, but Julia was enchanted.

"Rather anemic little snow, isn't it?" Gardiner said, breaking the spell as Pelham's friends so often did. He grabbed Mina's hand. "Well, good night, kids!"

As they trotted off hand in hand, on their way to Gardiner's apartment, Pelham let out a sigh that sounded very much like a huff.

"What?" she said.

"I can't say I don't envy them," he said.

Julia felt sands shift beneath her. The very first time they met, Pelham had told Julia he opposed the institution of marriage, and she knew his crowd put great stock in the idea of "free unions."

He had been so courtly, though, always taking it for granted that Julia would stay with a friend when she visited New York, and he would stay in a hotel in Washington. She took that to mean that he had abandoned his anti-marriage stance along with some of his other more extreme views.

In the much larger world beyond his very small one, relationships like theirs either ended in marriage or just *ended*. Julia felt misled somehow, but unsure if he had misled her or she had misled herself, she had stood mute and motionless under the streetlight. No longer enchanted by the pixie dust snow, she just felt cold and wet and foolish.

How Pelham took her silence, she could not say, but his slightly defiant look disappeared. He tilted his head and frowned in a rather sweet, reassuring way.

"Come on. Let's get you back." He took her hand and led her in the direction of the apartment where she was staying, and then said good night tenderly. A few days later, she received a nice letter, in which he apologized for his "little tantrum" at the end of her weekend.

Not long after, everything was eclipsed by the news of his novel being accepted for publication. He was so proud to send it, and Julia was so thrilled to read it, she had shoved the memory of that evening far in the back of her mind.

Julia felt no great moral impediment to going to bed with Pelham before they were married. She certainly desired him. But if marriage was off the table, foreclosed as an option, it felt reckless. More reckless, even, than if she did *not* love him, if he were just a casual fling of the sort Mina and her friends occasionally indulged in.

Until that night a few weeks ago, Pelham had not pressed her, and given his apology for it, Julia had assumed (rather blithely, she now realized) that some talk of their future would precede his doing so again. Yet here he was, with no preamble, looking down at her with that beseeching expression.

While she did not relish broaching the topic herself, it could be put off no longer.

"Pelham, where do you see this going, you and I?"

"I see us together, of course," he said, pulling her close.

"Going along as we are?"

"What are you suggesting, Julia?" Pelham pulled in his chin, a baffled expression on his face. "Are you talking about . . . about *marriage*?"

His confusion could not possibly be sincere. Julia might have talked herself into thinking they were of one mind, but only because his chivalrous behavior had suggested it. What hint had she ever given that she was in accord with his notions? Irritated, and disinclined to help him along, she raised her eyebrows and waited.

Pelham shook his head, as if to rid it of surprise. "I must say, I had not taken you for an institutionalist, Julia."

It was fortunate he followed up the charade with such an infuriating comment. A kinder response—*I'm so sorry, I fear we have misunderstood each other*—might not have overridden her dismay. As it was, his response sharpened her tongue.

"A helpful hint for the future, Pelham: When you meet people outside the tiny circle you have clearly been spending too much time in, you can safely bet they don't favor 'free unions.'"

He had the gall to appear stung. "But Julia, given all you have told me about your parents' passionless marriage, I don't understand how you couldn't!" Pelham replied. "Free unions are a more natural arrangement, far superior."

"You know what else is natural?" Julia snapped. "Snakebites. Snakebites are natural."

She pushed herself up from the love seat, crossed the room, and stood looking out the window, her back to him. Then she spun around again.

"Suppose I got pregnant?"

"Julia, I love you. I am committed to you, whatever comes! Why would you need some piece of paper to prove that? I think I've found an apartment. I want you to come to New York, for us to be together. And if this novel leads to another, just think what might lie ahead. We could go to Paris!"

She turned her back to him again and looked out at the darkness. He came up behind her, brushed her hair aside, and kissed the back of her neck.

"I know you, Julia. I know you yearn for freedom. It's as clear as the nose on your face. You could be someone's pretty wife in Back Bay at this very moment, with summers on that fortress erected by Boston's finest. But you aren't. Trust your instincts, what do they tell you?"

"That this is a bad idea," she said, flatly.

"That's not you talking. It's the censor."

Julia almost laughed at his evoking "the censor," Freud's term for society's expectations. "You ask me to tell you what my instincts are, and I do. And what is your response? *Oh, no. Not* those *instincts!*"

"Is it society's opinion you fear? Or perhaps your family, who would have cheerfully sold you to the highest bidder. Why you would ever submit to their codes, I cannot imagine."

"Then you should try a little harder," she said, turning to face him again, arms crossed over her chest. "And keep in mind while you do that I'm a woman, who would alone bear all the consequences for living with you without marriage. I would be utterly cast out, and not just by my family. Your friends might accept me, but once again, that's a mighty small world."

"But you're a part of it!" he argued.

No, I'm not, Julia thought, but she did not say it.

Pelham let out a frustrated groan. He turned and wandered aimlessly, rubbing the back of his neck.

"What, Pelham?" she asked wearily.

He glanced at her, hand still at his neck. "I cannot think of anyone who would benefit more from psychoanalysis than you."

"Oh? Am I so neurotic?"

"I did not say that. But there is freedom in awareness and self-understanding."

"Yes, and connecting to my inner libertine," Julia said dryly. Like all good Freudians, Pelham believed that sexual repression was behind all neuroses. Only in the free and open expression of her sexuality would she find true satisfaction.

"Please walk me home, Pelham," she said.

After a restless night in which her emotions swung back and forth between anger and despair, Julia struggled to drag herself out of bed in the morning to dress for work. She would have been grateful for the distraction of her students, but they were distracted themselves by the snowstorm that started up in the afternoon. It was a great deal of work to keep their attention, especially in her low mood. Only by recalling how she, too, had loved snow as a child was she able to maintain her patience and some semblance of order.

When she emerged from the school, she was surprised to see Pelham waiting for her on the sidewalk. He met her at the bottom of the stairs and took her gloved hands in his.

"I'm so sorry about last night, Julia. You have given me a great deal to think about. I am afraid I behaved like a brute, and a rather presumptuous one."

Surprised by the apology, Julia was not sure what to say.

"And now I must compound my sins. They say this snow won't let up, so I have to get back to New York. I can't get stuck here past the weekend when I sail for Europe next week."

"Oh . . . That is a shame, Pelham," she said, and in that moment, she meant it. He looked so fine in his dark woolen coat and black fedora, smiling down at her. He took her chin in his gloved hand, glanced around to ensure there were no eight-year-old witnesses, and kissed her on the forehead. She felt a catch at her heart.

"You're a darling, Julia. And I am sorry—both about last night, and that I must leave."

As she started for home, Julia initially felt encouraged, but as she neared her destination, relief began to give way to fatigue. It was as if she and Pelham had been acting out the same roles, repeating some version of the same scene, over and over. And hers was such a pathetic role, too, always asking herself the same question—*Does he like me enough?*—and alternating between despair and relief, depending upon the answer.

Well, she was off the stage for the time being, at least.

She found a note from Mina waiting for her in the vestibule:

Gardiner and I won't be able to see you and Pelham tomorrow night. He can't get down from New York because of this wretched snow, so I'm catching the last train to Charlottesville to see a friend. x, Mina.

Julia felt relieved. She had always tolerated Mina's personality quirks, but while she could not pinpoint when or why, at some point in recent months, she had begun to find her presence oppressive.

When Julia reached her apartment, her first thought was to call Louisa. She had meant to do so all week, but she had been too consumed with Pelham's manuscript. When she glanced at the clock, however, she realized Louisa would not be home from work for at least an hour.

Julia grabbed a blanket and went out to her sleeping porch. She did love snow. It was so quiet, so clean.

Like spreading a nice white blanket over all her troubles.

CHAPTER EIGHTEEN

July 1900
Haven Point, Maine

ANNA

The morning after Julia's daring, reckless escape dawned crisp and bright. The few clouds in the sky were perfectly defined, as if they had been pasted onto the bright blue sky.

Elizabeth and Anna sat in wicker chairs on the south porch, looking out at the bay, but the lovely view was doing little to dissipate the ominous feeling that had been dogging Anna.

Before Lillian left for Portland yesterday, Anna sensed she had something up her sleeve. Clarissa had written, and after Lillian read the letter, Anna detected a subtle shift in her expression, from its usual impatient sourness to something resembling satisfaction. This would be welcome in someone with less malevolent motivations, but it was not what one wished to see on Lillian's face.

Anna, preoccupied first with her own misery about Mr. Lockwood and then by the terrible apprehension about Julia, had pushed it from her mind until Lillian returned from Portland an hour ago with a malicious gleam in her eye.

When Anna finally heard Lillian's heavy footsteps in the living room, heading in their direction, she felt her heartbeat accelerate.

Lillian emerged on the porch and stood before them, her shoulders tight, her head jutting forward slightly, like a cat about to pounce.

"I am glad you are both here because I have come across some deeply disturbing information." She turned to Anna. "I will begin with what I learned most recently, which involves you. I will ask you a question, and I demand an honest answer."

Anna detected a glint of triumph in Lillian's eyes, and a bubble of anxiety formed in her chest. Not trusting her voice, she merely tilted her head and raised her brows. *Well, out with it, then.*

"Are you the author of that infernal book *Liberty Island*?"

The bubble burst, and regret spread through Anna's bloodstream like poison. She had never been a good liar, and she knew she would likely give herself away. Yet somewhere in the mix of chemicals coursing through her veins, she located one potentially helpful emotion: anger.

"What gave you that notion?" she replied coldly, though she knew the answer probably lay in the telegram on the hall table that had been waiting for Lillian when she returned.

"I learned it from Judith's sister-in-law, Mrs. Howland," Lillian said, confirming Anna's suspicion. "Furthermore, William got his hands on a copy and noticed similarities between what the girls in the book do and what Julia and her friends have been up to under your supervision on that island. Positively feral!"

Anna felt she had little to lose at this point. "If the book is so harmful, I wonder that you did not tear it from William's hands."

Lillian's face reddened. "You know as well as I do that girls are uniquely vulnerable to certain themes in literature," she spat. "Judith has already raised the alarm about this book, and for good reason. It is pernicious in every conceivable way. Now, I demand an answer."

Anna knew the residual heat in her face was telling on her, but unwilling to give Lillian the satisfaction of an answer, she rolled her eyes instead.

"I cannot say I'm surprised that you refuse to be forthright. You have showed yourself to be extremely underhanded in your dealings with my granddaughter." Anna sensed Elizabeth stiffening next to her, but whether she was offended on Anna's behalf or fearful of the truth of Lillian's accusations, she could not say.

Now Lillian turned to Elizabeth, the malicious gleam back in her eyes. "As reprehensibly as your sister has behaved, it is nothing to what I learned about you."

"Oh?" Elizabeth's tone was clipped.

"That guttersnipe Julia has been fraternizing with is not just some orphan. She is the daughter of your former lover, a man who was, from all accounts, entirely unsuitable.

Louisa is Calvin's daughter? Anna, stupefied, wondered briefly if she was not actually awake, but rather in the midst of a vivid and very unpleasant dream. Could this possibly be true?

"You have deceived my son in the most scandalous manner and have obviously consorted with this man since your marriage. And really, who knows if the child's mother is actually that Murphy woman? I have held my tongue through Julia's many transgressions, through all her outrageous behavior . . ."

When? Anna wanted to scream. *When have you* ever *held your tongue?*

"I remained silent because I did not wish to distress Jerome, but my hopes that you would heed my advice were obviously in vain. Given how little you have seen to her upbringing, I fear the child's character might well be beyond redemption."

She paused then, tilted her head, and looked at Elizabeth.

"I notice you have not spoken a word. Do you deny that this is the child of a man you once loved?"

"I do not." Elizabeth's tone was even, but Anna felt as if the world had tilted.

"Well, I am glad you are honest, at least," Lillian said with a patronizing nod. She continued with smug certainty, knowing she now held all the cards. "Now we can speak about what will come next. Julia will go to Newport with me, of course, but arrangements must also be made for September. I would have preferred to wait until Julia was old enough to attend Sacré Coeur or one of the better convent schools in Paris, but I am sure Jerome will agree that there can be no delay in removing her from unwholesome influences. I will consult with Judith at the first opportunity about a school that will accept her immediately."

Anna felt like her heart might break. She had never dreamed that Lillian would have this kind of leverage. Jerome was hardly likely to disagree with his mother's edicts once he discovered the secrets his wife had been keeping.

Would Elizabeth's marriage even survive? Ordinarily, the Demarests would not countenance a divorce, but suppose it freed Jerome to marry Judith? Either way, Anna was glad that *Liberty Island* was selling so well. At a minimum, her own tenancy in their home was certain to come to an end.

Throughout the diatribe, Elizabeth had sat still and silent. When it ended, she straightened.

"Are you quite finished, Lillian?" She spoke slowly, enunciating each word, as if she was only barely containing her temper.

"I am." Lillian's chin was up, but she seemed to be faltering slightly. She obviously had expected Elizabeth's total submission and seemed as surprised as Anna by her defiant posture.

Elizabeth gestured toward the chair opposite. "You have said a great many things. I will ask you to please sit, as I now have a few things to say to you."

Lillian hesitated before finally lowering herself into the chair with an exaggerated sigh. "All right, Elizabeth, I will hear your excuses."

"Thank you, Lillian." Elizabeth smiled falsely. "You are correct. Louisa Murphy is indeed the daughter of Calvin Stannarius, whom I—and indeed my entire family—once knew and loved. Until a chance encounter with Mr. Stannarius in Portland on the eve of his death, I had not laid eyes on him since the day I met Jerome.

"I told Jerome about Mr. Stannarius many years ago, and when I learned of his death, I asked if we might find a way to help his child. He readily agreed, though he asked that I not mention my family's relationship with Louisa's father, as he thought it might invite unwelcome questions." Elizabeth smiled thinly and added, "Though I feel certain he never imagined they would come from his own mother."

After a pause to let that sink in, Elizabeth continued. "Louisa's mother was a woman of great pride, but over the years, we helped the child in what small ways she would permit. When Louisa's mother died this spring and Eugenia indicated she would like to take her somewhere for her health, I asked Jerome if we might suggest Haven Point. Again, he agreed, with the same stipulation. You are welcome, of course, to say whatever you wish to your son regarding Louisa Murphy, but you will be telling him nothing he does not know."

Lillian huffed again, obviously flustered.

Elizabeth's brow wrinkled in a charade of thought. "Though I suppose it *might* surprise him to learn that you were prepared to disclose information he wished to remain private, and in the process accused him of being a fool, his wife a deceitful liar, and his daughter irredeemably awful."

Lillian sputtered, but Elizabeth put up a hand. "I have refrained from sharing with Jerome your countless criticisms of Julia over the years because I knew he would be displeased."

Lillian interrupted. "The same reason I have refrained!"

"You misunderstand me, Lillian. Jerome would not be displeased with Julia." Elizabeth's tone was steady but firm. "He would be displeased with *you*. I have spared him the knowledge of your unrelenting censure of his beloved daughter because I did not wish to cause a rift between the two of you."

Lillian interrupted again. "I believe you have spared him the *knowledge* of his daughter's behavior."

"You may say whatever you wish to Jerome. You should know, however, that he will not react kindly to the suggestion that he does not know his own child. He loves Julia as she is. You might consider following his example. I suspect you would be happier."

Lillian, not ready to accept that she had been bested, reverted to her earlier complaint. "I notice you have said nothing about this book of your sister's, which she wrote in secret, and which directly insults me!"

Elizabeth shrugged. "I have not read this book. How, precisely, were you insulted?"

"A character in the book is clearly based on me, and the portrayal is defamatory."

Elizabeth turned to look at Anna. Superficially, her expression was one of calm curiosity, but Anna saw something else in her sister's eyes: *No apologies. Give Lillian nothing.*

Anna turned to Lillian. "To what character are you referring?" she asked, as innocently as she could manage.

"The aunt!"

Anna feigned confusion. "What similarities did you note that led you to believe she was based on you?"

This left Lillian in rather a bind. Aunt Phillipa in *Liberty Island* was Lillian's physical opposite. To answer the question, Lillian would have to reveal the other ways she believed she resembled an extremely unlikable character.

"Oh, good heavens," Lillian spat. "This is insupportable."

"You have misread so many circumstances, Lillian, you might consider that you are misreading this, too," Elizabeth said, now utterly in command. "I believe it would be best if we both pretended that this conversation did not occur. Do you agree?"

Lillian took a breath, lifted her chin, and summoned what remained of her own dignity. "I apprehend that I was not in possession of all the facts." She rose and added, "Of course I had no way to know how many secrets you and my son were keeping from me. I will return to my room. I have delayed my rest long enough."

If Anna could have cheered out loud, she would have.

CHAPTER NINETEEN

January 1922
Washington, DC

JULIA

> Victoria said raw seaweed was good for one's blood, but the others thought that nothing so slimy and smelling of low tide could be good for anything. Audrey reminded her that scientists said all sorts of things that turned out to be wrong, but Victoria just said, loftily, "But this is *modern* science."
>
> Lucy thought for a moment, then said, "The Greeks and Romans and all the Whoevers of the Dark Ages thought they were modern, too, and that they'd figured things out, once and for all. But all modern really means is 'now.'"
>
> FROM *LIBERTY ISLAND*, BY MISS CRANE

Julia spent most of Friday afternoon reading on her porch and watching the heavy snow come down. When evening came, she went inside and tried to call Louisa, only to discover that the snow had caused trouble with the wires, and she could not get through.

She felt a twinge of despair. Julia, who had always been happiest when she was ensconced with people she loved, felt alienated from everyone, a pack animal without a pack. She did her best to shake it off. She found something in her cupboard to eat, then lit a fire in her fireplace and settled down again with her book. Meanwhile, the snow continued to pour down, inch after inch, hour after hour.

Boston generally got far more snow than Washington, but Julia could not remember ever seeing it snow so heavily for so long. By the time she woke up the next morning, eighteen inches had fallen, and it was still coming down.

Julia still could not get through to Louisa on the telephone. She wished she could go to her boardinghouse to apologize, but the city was paralyzed, and she could not possibly get there.

By the time the snow stopped late Saturday, more than two feet had fallen, and Julia was starved for company. She considered trying to get through to Michael, but she was trying not to monopolize his time. She had seen his name in the society pages linked with Genevieve Carter, an attractive, pleasant woman Julia had met at the Seabornes' country club. Julia needed to let Michael be.

Just as she had decided to walk over to Bess Riordan's house, a knock came at her door, and she opened it to find that very person, wearing khaki knickerbockers and several layers of clothing under her coat. Over all of it was a layer of snow, blown from the trees.

"Bess, you look like a snowman!" Julia laughed. "I was just about to go to your place. Are you as antsy as I am?"

"So antsy, but good news: *Get-Rich-Quick Wallingford* is playing at the Knickerbocker."

"The cinema is open?"

"Believe it or not, yes. I saw people going to the early show. Hurry up and get dressed, though. You can't imagine what slow going it is, walking in this mess."

Julia raced to her room and put on a thick sweater, trousers, and heavy boots. Washington had not entirely embraced trousers for women, but their acceptability for horseback riding had created a slippery slope for other activities. Julia did not feel an ounce of compunction for wearing them when she tramped through Rock Creek Park, and they were certainly sensible today.

Bess had not exaggerated. The sidewalks were mostly impassable, and none of the streets had been cleared. They laughed as they sank into the snow, over and over, and at the exaggerated climbing steps required to move down the sidewalk.

When they reached the theater, they bought their tickets, and Bess pointed at the little candy shop off the lobby. "You go find the seats, and I'll get us treats."

"I'll get them!"

"No, no. I saw the stage version of the film," Bess said, shooing her inside. "You go ahead. I won't miss but a minute."

The theater could seat more than a thousand people, and it usually did on a Saturday night, but it was only about a quarter occupied this evening. Julia went halfway down the aisle, and selected seats at the center of an empty row.

The audience was clearly ready to be amused. Almost as soon as the film started to roll, the crowd was laughing at the unscrupulous "Blackie" Daw, sidekick to con man J. Rufus Wallingford.

When the first round of laughter died down, though, Julia heard another layer of sound behind it, a hissing of sorts. It grew louder and louder, until it sounded like a great bedsheet being torn.

When dust fell over the orchestra pit, Julia looked up and, to her horror, saw a crack move across the ceiling, from the front of the theater to the back, as if someone were slicing through the roof like a piece of cake.

An instant later, there was a great blur of movement and sound, people yelling to get out. Julia began scrambling toward the aisle, but when she glanced up again, her heart seized. The cracks were spreading, like ice breaking on the surface of a frozen pond. Somehow she knew she was too far from the entrance, that she did not have time to escape.

She crouched down, hands over her head. Something hit her back, and instinct propelled her to drop to her side and push herself under the seat.

Just as she had curled herself into a ball, fitting as much of her body beneath the seat as she could, there was a great roar from above, followed by a deafening crash, and a searing pain shot through Julia's ankle.

Then came another sound, like a hurricane-force wind, mingled with screams from every direction. Almost immediately, another thunderous crash followed, this one from the back of the theater, followed by more agonizing screams. The balcony had fallen.

The pain in Julia's ankle was unbearable. She felt an almost overwhelming urge to coil into herself, to pull her leg in so she might cradle it, but she could not obey the summons. Her lower legs were completely immobilized by debris.

Julia's heart wrenched at the anguished cries coming from every direction. Then her mind registered another ominous sound, the creaks of shifting debris, and a horrible, cold dread ran through her. Nothing but a theater seat separated her from the load of concrete, metal, wood, ice, and snow above. She could not imagine it holding such a load for long.

If Bess had been in the theater, Julia prayed she had been killed instantly, rather than waiting, as she was, for her skull to be crushed. Every muscle was tensed against the pain in her ankle, and what she was sure was her imminent death.

She whimpered, overwhelmed by a terrible despair. She had heard of people's lives flashing before them, but what Julia saw was a kaleidoscope of images from what she was now sure were her last days on earth. The horrible phone call to Mother . . . *Because she was your father's mother . . . You should be there for him.* With blinding clarity she saw how feebly she had justified a terribly shabby act. Then she had lashed out at her dearest friend in the world, who had spoken nothing but the truth.

Her whole body trembled, and she cringed at every noise, certain the next would mark the moment when it all came crashing down upon her.

But after a time—five minutes? ten? she had no idea—she realized the sounds of shifting material were coming further apart. Somehow it seemed less ominous, as if this horrible demonic force had decided it had done what it came to do. She still heard moans and sobs, but those, too, grew fewer and farther between.

Then, finally, she heard new voices, coming from above the rubble, the words indecipherable but the tones imperative. Not the voices of the injured or dying, but of those who had come to help.

For the first time since she realized she could not move her legs, Julia thought she might have a prayer of getting out. The pain had settled into a numb ache, still beyond anything she had experienced in her life, but it was somehow less consuming. She listened, trying to make out the words, but the voices were too distant.

Then her ears picked up another sound, this one from under the rubble not far from where she lay. At first, it was a high-pitched whimper, almost like the mew of a cat, and then she heard words . . . "Mama? Mama?"

Julia tried to call out, but her throat was caked with plaster dust. It was everywhere, in the air, on her skin, in her nose, even in her closed eyes. She swallowed, wiped her dusty lips, and tried again.

"Is someone there?"

There was silence for a moment; then she heard a little boy's voice. He spoke haltingly. "I . . . can't . . . move."

"Are you hurt?"

"A little," he said, still laboring to speak. "My mama . . . is on top of me. She's not moving . . . won't say anything."

It had been dark when Julia took her seat, but she recalled two silhouetted figures, a woman and child, sitting a couple of rows behind her.

"She probably fainted," Julia lied, in her most reassuring teacher's tone. "My name is Julia Demarest. What's your name?"

His voice was so shaky, his answer came out like a question. "Peter . . . McCarthy?"

"You're very brave, Peter."

"What, what . . . happened?"

"I think the ceiling fell because of the snow on the roof," Julia said.

"I hear people walking and talking above now, so they'll be looking for us soon."

"It's so dark," Peter said, with another fearful whimper.

Julia's heart wrenched for this child, pinned under his mother's dead body. She, too, was pinned, and mostly helpless, but at least now there was something she could do. If nothing else, Julia knew how to talk to children.

"It *is* dark, Peter. Let's pretend we're camping at night."

"Do you go camping?"

"I used to," Julia said. "When I was a girl, I often camped on an island in Maine . . ."

Conscious of how hard it was for Peter to speak, Julia began to tell him about Liberty Island, about the three girls who started it, and how they became four with the addition of Louisa, who was, to this day, her very best friend in the world.

A few halting questions from Peter suggested she had captured his interest, so she plumbed her memory for stories. She told him of the imaginary games they played. ("Pirates?" he asked, managing to sound skeptical. "We were very unusual little girls," Julia replied with a little laugh.) She told him about Mr. Carruthers the seal, and finally about camping out under the stars when they were older.

"Were you scared?"

"No, Peter. I wasn't scared," Julia said. "I always felt quite safe."

As these words came out of her mouth, Julia felt a catch at her throat, and she was overcome by a wave of sorrow, and something very like regret.

Meanwhile, the imperative voices she had heard above were joined by banging and scraping. At first, the sounds were coming from the rear and perimeter, far enough away that Julia knew that even if she shouted, nobody would hear her.

After some time, however, she could tell that the activity had drawn nearer. Just as Julia was preparing to shout for help, she heard something fall near her legs, an alarming reminder of the precariousness of their shelter. Trying to keep her voice calm, she called out to Peter.

"We must yell, Peter, so they can find us." *So they don't kill us.* "I'll count to three, and then yell 'Help' as loud as you can."

"Okay," Peter said, a little uncertainly. Julia counted to three and tried to shout, but her mouth and lungs, while clear enough to speak, were still too dry to yell. She swallowed a few times, and then tried again. Peter tried to shout, too, but his voice was too small, his poor lungs impaired by the weight of his mother.

When another chunk of debris fell even closer to where she lay, Julia somehow found her voice. She was not sure what words came out of her mouth—some combination of *Help*, *We're down here!* and *God, please, help!*

There was a pause in the motion above, and Julia shouted again, as loud as she could: "PLEASE! HELP!"

The voices were still too muffled to make out the words, but she heard a man call out to someone else. There were creaks and thuds, more indecipherable shouts, and the sound of debris being dragged away. And then a tiny sliver of light pierced the darkness above her legs.

"Someone down there?"

"Yes! Please help!" Suddenly, tears threatened, and for a second, Julia was unable to speak. She took a deep breath. "I'm under a seat. My leg is trapped."

He called out to someone. "A woman's down here alive!" Indistinct voices responded.

"A little boy, too," Julia called. "He says he is all right, but his mother is on top of him. She seems to have . . . fainted."

"Where is he?"

"He was sitting about two rows behind me." She called out, "Peter?"

Peter was silent. Julia tried once more, and when he again failed to reply, she felt another surge of anxiety. Had Peter sustained some internal injury of which, in his shock, he had not been aware?

"I'm your teacher, calling roll. I say, 'Peter McCarthy,' and you say . . ."

"Here," Peter said.

"Louder, Peter. Your teacher can't hear you. She has a banana in her ear."

Peter, God bless him, actually giggled. "HERE!" he said, a little louder.

"Good job, young man," came the voice from above. "I'm going to find you some help."

"Are you a fireman?" Julia asked.

"A reporter, I'm afraid. It's a bit chaotic up here. Firemen are here, but they sent for the army, and the soldiers are just arriving. What's your name, ma'am?"

"Julia Demarest."

"Miss Julia Demarest?" There was a sudden excitement in his tone. "Oh, that *is* good news. Give me a moment, will you? I promise, I'll be right back."

The man seemed to have stood because his voice was farther away, but she heard him call to someone. A few minutes later, she again heard steps above. Then, through the hole in the debris above, came a familiar voice.

"Julia! My God, is it really you? Are you all right?" The tone was a mix of anguish and wonder.

"Michael!" Tears stung at Julia's eyes once more. She was confused for a moment about why he was there, but then she realized the place must be crawling with reporters. "My legs are trapped. I think my ankle is broken. How did you know I was here?"

"Miss Riordan found me as soon as I arrived."

"Bess is all right?" Julia's voice seized, and she choked back a sob. Since her first prayer that Bess might have been taken quickly, she had not allowed herself to think about her friend.

"She was in the lobby. The air compressed and blew her out the doors, but she landed in the snow. She is fine, except frantic about you.

I sent someone to find her and let her know you're alive." He paused for a second, then added, "I see soldiers arriving. The firemen have been doing their best, but the army has better equipment. We're going to get you out of here, Jules."

She heard more sounds above, banging and the dragging of debris, along with lots of shouting, but she sensed the operation was more careful, methodical. Another sliver of light appeared, closer to Peter. She could not hear the words over the noise, but someone was calling down to him, and he appeared to be answering.

Eventually, a larger hole opened, and Julia saw the figure of a man descend through it, then crouch in the small space. From what Julia could make out, Peter and his mother were in front of their seats, her body sheltering his. Then she saw Mrs. McCarthy's lifeless body being lifted out.

"Michael!" she called up.

"What is it? Are you all right?" Michael asked.

"Peter's mother *fainted*," she said, urgently. "Do you understand? Don't let anyone say otherwise in front of that poor boy. Not now."

"I understand. Give me a moment." She heard him speak to someone; then his disembodied voice returned. "I let them know. But Julia, it seems they need to cut through a metal beam in order to get you out of here. It's a bit tricky, so it might be a bit. Just . . . just hang on, will you?"

"I'm not going anywhere."

For three long hours, she stayed under that seat, while she grew progressively wearier, and the ache in her ankle returned with a vengeance, along with terrible cramping throughout her whole body. Julia told Michael more than once to go do his job, but he just laughed and stayed put.

Eventually, she heard voices directly above and smelled the acetylene from torches. There was a great deal of sound and movement, and a few scary moments when bits of debris fell around her, but finally, an opening appeared above her, and before long, she saw a man's face, peering at her beneath the seats.

"Are you all right? Doctors are up there waiting. We've got the steel moved, but now we have to get some concrete off your leg."

"I'm all right."

"Afraid it'll hurt like the devil when they lift it."

"Just . . . just be careful," Julia said. She heard machinery of some kind, and then felt the weight come off her ankle, and then a shot of agonizing pain traveled from her leg, up her arm.

"Can you move it?" someone asked.

Julia tried to answer, but everything went black.

The first thing Julia noticed when she awakened was the smell of carbolic soap. Then she saw light through her eyelids and tried to open her eyes, but she found she could not. She sensed a pillow under her head and space around her, though, and became aware of a feeling of relief. Finally, with what felt like superhuman effort, she pried her eyes open and saw a leg, encased in plaster, and realized it was her own.

And then she remembered.

She heard movement in the room and turned her head to see a nurse.

"Where am I?" she asked, her voice thin and raspy.

The nurse spun around and smiled. "Hello, Miss Demarest. I am Nurse Osgood. You're at Garfield Hospital, and you're a very lucky woman."

It was at that point that the pain in Julia's leg registered, but another worry superseded it.

"The little boy?" Julia struggled to get the words out. She was disoriented, and her throat was so dry. "Peter?"

"Peter McCarthy?"

Julia nodded.

"He is fine. A bit scraped up, but he is home with his father."

"His mother?"

The nurse shook her head sadly, and Julia lapsed back into sleep.

Those first days she would only ever remember as a series of discrete images. It was as if the hospital acted as an amnesiac. Relieved of all volition, she surrendered herself utterly. That her mind was superfluous came as a relief, as she did not wish to think. She slept a great deal. If visitors came when she was awake, she saw them. Somehow she knew they had come, but she remembered little about what was said.

She recalled Mina being there, holding her hand and urging her to talk, so as not to repress her memories. The tenderness was so un-Mina-like, Julia thought she must have dreamed it, but she remembered Mina pointing to a bowl of roses and telling her they were from Pelham. Later, she asked Nurse Osgood to hand her the card, which confirmed he had indeed sent them.

Her second day (or she thought it was her second day, at least), Julia awakened to feel another hand in hers. She opened her eyes and saw her mother, sitting in a chair beside her bed.

"Oh, Julia . . ." Mother managed a smile, but her voice was choked with emotion.

Julia tried to apologize, though she could not really say what for. She had a vague notion that this was all a nuisance, that lives were being upended, and another, even vaguer idea that she was in bad odor for something.

"Father was not able to come, but he sends his love and best wishes for your healing."

Father. The funeral. Julia squeezed her eyes shut. "I'm sorry." Her voice quavered.

"There is no need, Julia, I promise." Mother pressed her hand, and Julia opened her eyes again to see that her mother's eyes were damp, her expression one of gentle admonition.

More, please, Julia thought. *More of this.*

Though she was still in and out of sleep a great deal, it seemed as if whenever she woke up, Mother was there, either sitting by her bed or speaking to the doctors and nurses.

Eventually, after a few days, the fog began to lift, and Julia could at least carry on conversations. Unfortunately, this was when she began to notice that practically every person who entered her room wanted to talk about the disaster at the Knickerbocker, and to tell her how lucky she was.

Julia had spent hours beside a child lying under his mother's dead body. She had heard people scream, and then heard them fall silent. She knew she was fortunate, that she should be grateful, but for some reason, she found the talk unbearable.

After one of these exchanges, Michael popped into her room and found her near tears.

"What's wrong, Jules?"

"Nothing," she said.

"Come on. Tell me."

She shook her head. He plopped down in the chair and leaned forward, his arms folded on the side of her bed.

"Thing is, Julia, I'm a reporter, and an annoyingly persistent one." He looked at her sympathetically, as if his being nosy was an immutable quality beyond his control.

"Oh, all *right*." Julia let out an irritated sigh and looked up at the ceiling. "It's just that everyone who comes in here wants to talk about the theater. I know I'm lucky, and it makes me feel selfish, like a terrible ingrate . . ." She felt her throat tighten, and she struggled to complete the thought. "But I can't stand it. Not yet, at least." *Maybe not ever.*

In an instant, the smug reporter was gone, and in his place was good old Michael, with his gentle smile, and his one eye, kind enough for two. He shook his head, and with perfect, reassuring sympathy said, "It is not in the least selfish, Julia. Not even a bit."

From that point on, nobody spoke of the theater catastrophe in her presence. The omission was so pronounced, in fact, it actually became a source of amusement. Julia wondered if Michael had put a sign on the door. *Mention the Knickerbocker on penalty of death.*

Visitors were limited, and Julia was glad. The only person she wanted to see was Louisa, but to her dismay, Mother said she had been called to Boston for a work project. She sent flowers and a note, but when days went by with no more word, Julia asked for stationery and wrote a letter of apology, hoping to clear the air.

It was hard to keep track of time in the hospital, but the sense of being suspended somewhere between past and future suited her.

While she tried to avoid dwelling on the particulars, Julia knew her life had been in a sorry state when this accident happened. Like the person who goes on a trip without cleaning house first, she was not eager to return and face the mess.

Not all talk of the future could be avoided, of course. The doctors, Mother, and the Seabornes had many discussions about her progress. The break had been relatively clean, but she would need a good deal of rehabilitation once she was discharged.

Julia did not ask where this follow-up care would take place, and she did not find out until ten days or so into her stay at Garfield, when Mother and Margaret Seaborne came in to speak to her. Mother sat on the side of Julia's bed and took her hand.

"Julia, I must go back to Boston tomorrow," she said. "Mr. Seaborne has been in contact with an orthopedist at Walter Reed Army Hospital. They learned a great deal about physiotherapy treatments during the war, and he will oversee your case."

"You won't be able to manage the stairs at your apartment," Margaret added. "So you'll come stay in my studio."

"I am sorry it cannot be immediately," Mother said. "But we hoped this might give you something to look forward to."

Julia managed to say the right things to Mother and to thank Margaret. She realized, though, that despite her best efforts to remain glued to the present, once she had learned Louisa was in Boston, a vague notion had formed in the recesses of her mind that Mother would stay indefinitely and then take her home to Back Bay.

Now, not only was Mother leaving, but she seemed distracted, as if she had one foot on the train already, and Julia felt unaccountably hurt. Abandoned, even. But as with Louisa, who had yet to respond to her apology, Julia knew she bore a great deal of responsibility for any distance.

It was all part of the mess that the accident had interrupted, and which she still had no desire to face.

Three weeks later, Julia was installed in Margaret's studio. The space had been arranged so everything Julia needed was on the first floor—a bed and bath at the back, and the living room at the front, with its large fireplace, comfortable furniture, and pretty, diamond-shaped windowpanes, framed by curtains of ivy.

In a way, it was perfect. She was required to go neither backward in space and time to her childhood home nor ahead to her apartment and a resumption of her life. She would continue in her limbo state, but in a far more pleasant setting.

When she had been there a few days, Mina came for a visit. She tossed off her usual "How are you, Duchess?" and wandered about the room, flipping her hair. Julia found it intensely annoying.

Finally, she sat down. "How long will you be locked in the castle back here?"

Julia ignored the insult. "They think I'll be able to manage stairs by May. Before the end of the school year."

"Well, that's good. Will you go to Maine?"

"I haven't planned that far."

"Your parents have forgiven you, though?" When Julia nodded, Mina added, "Well, that's good. I suppose they think you were punished enough for not attending the funeral."

Julia looked at Mina for a second. "Is it good? You were so proud of me for taking a stand. I'd have thought you'd rather I fully renounced them."

Renouncing one's family was a rite of passage among Mina and Pelham's friends, practically a sacrament. (At any gathering, Julia half expected someone to stand up, tap a glass, and say, "I have a renouncement to make.")

In college, Julia had once spotted Mina and her mother having tea, and was struck by how such a supposedly monstrous woman could appear so normal and harmless. It occurred to her now that perhaps Mina's problem was not that her mother was extraordinary in her awfulness, but rather awful in her ordinariness.

"I think you might be too entwined for a renunciation," Mina said, completely missing Julia's meaning. "The important thing is, you let them know you wouldn't be bullied."

Bullied into being with my father when his mother was laid to rest, Julia thought, but she did not say it.

Mina inquired about Pelham, and Julia relayed some of what he had said in the few letters she had received. They were discouraging, but mostly because Europe was discouraging—border disputes from the Baltic to the Black Sea, Russian famine, German aggrievement—ominous signs that the "war to end all wars" had been no such thing. Another ideal dashed on the rocks of reality.

Pelham's correspondence was kind, and he always signed his missives "With love," but he made no reference to the unpleasantness before he departed. And as he had no idea when he would return, there was little reason to address the future. However unwittingly, he had written letters perfectly suited to Julia's suspended reality. She told Mina none of this, of course.

"Well, Duchess, I wanted to let you know, I've accepted a job in New York," Mina said. Her expression was apologetic, as if this would be a great loss to Julia.

Julia asked a few questions and wished her luck, but as she felt acutely uncomfortable with Mina, she was relieved when she moved to the door.

"It will be good to get back in the swing of things with everyone," Mina said, hand on the knob. "They all send their best, by the way. They were terribly worried about you."

"Oh, that's nice," Julia managed, though she knew Mina's friends would not have cared if she lived or died.

When she left, Julia grabbed her crutches, made her way to the window, then opened it and took in a great gulp of air. She wondered what it was about Mina's behavior that had irked her so much. From the moment she sashayed into the room, she had behaved as she always had. Julia knew she had not been herself since the Knickerbocker, but she remembered now how relieved she had been to learn that Mina would be in Charlottesville the weekend of the snowstorm. In fact, this discomfort had been building for months.

Julia recalled a night toward the end of last August. She and Pelham had come upon a street musician playing some Viennese waltz on his violin. Pelham pulled Julia into his arms and danced her around the sidewalk. The whole summer had been set to music like that—romantic waltzes and warm operatic recordings, alternating with ragtime's infectious call-and-response and popular foxtrot songs in brighter keys.

Pelham wanted Julia to himself, so they rarely saw his friends, but that changed when Mina started seeing Gardiner. At first, Julia thought it was sweet, how eagerly Mina coordinated her and Julia's visits to New York. Looking back, though, it was when the happy twosome became a foursome and then, inexorably, was grafted onto their larger group of friends that things started going wrong with Pelham. The musical accompaniment changed, and everything was in a minor key.

Pelham and Mina's friends were flamboyant in their pessimism. They were all dying to go to Paris (it was not for nothing Pelham mentioned that on his last night in Washington). Europe appreciated its intellectuals and literary men, whereas America was an irredeemable cultural wasteland, where the older generation controlled the youth.

Over the summer, Pelham had seemed to appreciate Julia's sunnier nature, but among his friends, he acted every bit as disillusioned. God was dead. Truth was dead. Faith and hope were for saps. The only permissible joy was in hedonistic rebellion. The only honest, courageous approach to life was to face its essential darkness, to look straight into the abyss.

Julia shared their disillusionment to some extent, but she could not bear to think as they did.

In October, they went to a party with Mina and Gardiner. Julia remembered walking in and hearing the strains of some dark, melancholic jazz recording. She was standing with Mina and some others, who were discussing a new novel by a British author, which Julia had read and hated. She found it relentlessly dark, lacking in any redemptive message. Naturally, they all loved it.

Julia felt eyes on her and turned to see that Mina was watching her, a little half smile on her face.

Say something, her eyes were saying. *Say something so I can pounce.*

Not all visitors to the studio were unwelcome. Bess came every week, bringing with her the youthful air of the classroom, along with tidings from and stories about her students, and when Pauline was in town visiting her family, she stopped by with a crate full of gifts from Boston.

Julia's aunt had put several books in it, including the latest in her new juvenile fiction series. ("I thought perhaps you would like some light reading," Anna's note said. How well she had always known her!) Father sent a box of Easter candy, and Mother added some spring frocks from her dressmaker, who, with inerrant taste, had continued outfitting the fashion-agnostic Julia all these years.

Since her own terrible visit to Haven Point two summers ago, Julia had seen little of her sister-in-law, but Pauline was in the pink of health now. William had seemed a touch less domineering at Christmas, too. Julia had a hope—a tiny hope, granted—that he had learned that his wife blossomed under kinder treatment.

Louisa occasionally sent letters from Boston, but they were short and oddly formal. In all their years of friendship, Louisa had never held a grudge against Julia. It seemed Julia had gone beyond the pale, something she had not thought was possible. Though Louisa's coldness pierced Julia's armor, for the most part, she continued to push aside any thought of what came before this accident, and what awaited her.

That said, she threw herself into the rehabilitation of her ankle with a vengeance. The doctor from Walter Reed had done a thorough examination and assigned a physiotherapist named Miss Quinn, whom he considered one of the best he had worked with during the war.

Though only thirty, Miss Quinn had all the command of a field general. Julia told her as much more than once, but she submitted to all of the treatments and did every exercise to the best of her ability.

The worst was the "circumductor," a pivoting iron brace attached to a wheel that dragged on the turn, forcing her to use all the muscles and ligaments around her ankle. Though Julia asked Miss Quinn where she had managed to procure this medieval torture device, she did as she was bid and received so much praise for her tenacity, she was sure she was disguising her low spirits, and that nobody had guessed that part of her still felt lodged under that seat, waiting to be crushed by the weight of everything.

Not everybody was fooled, it seemed. One day, a month after she had moved to the studio, Michael came out to visit.

"It's very fine weather. I'm taking you for a drive."

"I am tired."

"So? You'll be a passenger. You don't have to do anything but . . . *passenge*. You need it."

"Why?"

"Novelty. You needn't see people, but you must see something besides these four walls."

"I've sat outside!" Julia objected.

"Forgive me. I did not count the back of my parents' house. Five walls."

"And a fence."

"Congratulations. Now get up."

She grumbled, but she got her cloak and the cane to which she had graduated and hobbled beside him through the side garden gate to his roadster. He took her around the speedway in East Potomac Park, and she did find that there was something brightening about being outside, away from her place of convalescence. After that, Michael took her out almost every day. They drove out the old Conduit Road toward Great Falls, around the grounds of the Soldiers' Home, and through Rock Creek and Meridian Parks.

Julia appreciated everyone who had helped her and every kind gesture, but she had learned over these months how much easier some people made it to accept their help.

Michael was the easiest. He was like Louisa in his utter lack of self-consciousness. Mina left a residue behind, but Michael always left the air cleaner after he visited. With him, she sensed no anxiety or unspoken needs or expectations. And like Louisa, while Michael saw Julia quite clearly, he did not subject her to endless analysis. His cajoling her into taking a drive with him was so typical. He discerned what she needed, and issued his demand with his usual cheer and directness, and without judgment.

Michael would marry someday, and Julia knew he would be a wonderful husband and father, and she wanted that for him. At least in theory she did. When she once again saw his name and Genevieve Carter's linked in the social news, it gave her a terrible pang. She knew no wife would allow them to be as close as they had been. She resolved to enjoy what time with him she had left.

One Saturday in late March, Julia sat on a comfortable cushion in the bow of a canoe, while Michael paddled her upriver.

"I feel like I'm in a gondola in Venice," she said, then laughed as Michael began whistling "O Sole Mio."

Years ago, when Julia was Michael's partner for a Washington Canoe Club mixed event, he mentioned that when he was young, he and his friends had camped out on an island off the Maryland shore a little farther up the Potomac.

"Our own Liberty Island," he called it.

She had always wanted to see it, so after a thorough interrogation by Julia's doctor, Michael obtained permission to take her out. She was cleared neither for paddling nor for disembarking and tramping about, but on this marvelously crisp spring afternoon, reminiscent of the Maine coast in midsummer, it was a treat just to have Michael navigate her around the perimeter.

"What did you name it again?" she asked.

"Whoop Whoop," Michael said with a groan. "I don't know what it's called now, but needless to say, that didn't stick."

When they returned home, Margaret was in the back garden, pruning shears in hand and an old straw hat on her head. She stood up and waved, then peeled off her garden gloves and beckoned them over, eager to hear about the adventure.

"I'm glad Julia saw your little island, Michael," she said, after they told her about the excursion. "She's responsible for it, in a way."

"How so?" he asked.

"I'd actually forgotten this until you mentioned the plans, but it was Julia's mother who persuaded me to let you camp out on the river. She said I was being silly."

"She did?" Julia asked, barely able to keep her jaw from dropping.

"I wasn't usually a nervous Nellie with Michael, because his brothers had broken me in." Margaret shrugged. "It's just that none of them had ever proposed such a daring scheme."

Later, when Julia was alone in the studio, she had a strange feeling that something inside her had been out of alignment, like an off-track drawer scraping against its runners, and had suddenly slid back into place.

"It was hardly bondage," Louisa had said of Liberty Island that night, when Julia had railed against her mother for "hiding her away." "It was permission. Encouragement, even."

Louisa had looked so confused, as if she were speaking to a stranger. Looking back at the person she was just three short months ago, Julia was not sure she recognized her either.

CHAPTER TWENTY

July 1900
Haven Point, Maine

ANNA

In the silence that followed Lillian storming upstairs, Elizabeth let out a great sigh. She shook her head slightly before turning to Anna. "I am sorry I did not tell you about Louisa. I assumed you had discerned who she was."

"I'm embarrassed to say that I did not," Anna replied. She was still processing all that had just been revealed. "So, Jerome knew all of it?"

"Of course." Elizabeth's tone implied this should be obvious.

Of course nothing! Anna thought, but she was mortified by how deeply she had misunderstood her sister's marriage. "I'm sorry I did not tell you about *Liberty Island.* I expected Judith would react as she did, and I thought it would be easier if you did not know."

"That's all right. I am proud of you, Anna! I have not read it, of course, but I must." She smiled and added, "I did read Judith's newsletter. Her comments made it sound very appealing, and also suggested it's been a success. I am so pleased for you."

Anna asked some more questions, carefully worded so as not to apprise Elizabeth as to the full extent of her own ignorance. From Elizabeth's answers, she learned that, contrary to her own belief, Elizabeth had told Jerome about Calvin Stannarius before they married, and informed him immediately about the shipwreck and what she and Nora planned to do for Johanna.

Elizabeth had visited Johanna over the years, and though hesitant to accept help, she was open to advice. It was evident early on that Louisa was a quick learner, and Elizabeth urged her to look into the programs at the settlement house. Eugenia immediately noticed that the child was intelligent and mature beyond her years.

"I am sorry, Anna, for not telling you," Elizabeth said again. "Jerome felt very strongly about it."

"That's all right. I certainly will not breathe a word of this to anyone, so he need not know that his mother spilled the secret." Anna paused for a moment, still digesting it all and trying to square it with what she had understood. She was still unclear on a few points. "Where did Julia get the idea that she was going to Newport?"

"Before Lillian left for Portland, she told Rosemary to pack for Julia's stay in Newport, and Julia overheard her. Dear, brave Rosemary said that it was her understanding that Julia would not be going. In reply, Lillian said, 'I know that's what Mrs. Demarest thinks, but Mr. Demarest will set her straight when he returns on Friday,' and it would not leave much time to get her things together.

"Rosemary agreed, but only to humor her. She thought it was ridiculous, not even worth mentioning before she left for Portland. Of course she had no idea that Julia was eavesdropping. If only Julia had told me what she heard . . ." Elizabeth's face fell, and she shuddered. "If I had just *known*."

"You didn't, though, Liz. And you couldn't," Anna said, then added, "I gather you've taken an awful lot of slings and arrows over the years." She saw quite clearly now how her sister had absorbed all of Lillian's criticisms.

"Better that she vent her spleen with me than with Jerome."

"It still seems rather heroic," Anna said.

Elizabeth shrugged. "Well, as you and I know, there are two choices. You can promote good relations among the members of a family you marry into. Or you can be like Clarissa."

"Speaking of Clarissa, I assume she is the one who informed Lillian of Louisa's identity. How did she know?"

"Probably from Bertie," Elizabeth said. Bertie was Clarissa's maid, who had been almost as unpleasant an addition to the household as Clarissa herself. "Her family belongs to the same parish in South Boston. Johanna gave Louisa her own surname, as unmarried mothers often do, but I do not think the father's identity was a great secret."

"I know why you did not think it would be fruitful to confront Clarissa about intercepting Calvin's letters," Anna said. "But what about now?"

Elizabeth looked up, thinking, and then a sly smile appeared on her face. "At the very least, Clarissa should know how shortsighted she was with this recent transgression."

"How so?"

"Lillian knows nothing about Clarissa's interference all those years ago. Would she be pleased to know that, if not for Clarissa, Jerome might not have married me?"

Anna smiled; then Elizabeth looked off for a second, as if remembering something, and began to laugh.

"What's funny?" Anna asked.

"I was just thinking about something Lillian said, about not even being sure if Johanna Murphy really was the child's mother. Was she implying what I think she was implying?"

"That you are Louisa's mother? Probably. Though it's hard to say if her problem is math or biology. Louisa is only a little older."

They laughed again; then Anna put her hand on Elizabeth's forearm. "I admire how you handled Lillian, how I now realize you have always handled her. You're a good mother, a good wife. Mother would be proud of you."

"I hope so," Elizabeth said. "I've tried to do as she asked, to keep up the Newbold traditions, but nobody could live up to her example."

Anna felt a jolt at the familiar words—the request that she had long believed her mother had made of her, specifically.

"Well, you have done a fine job," Anna managed. "Among many

things, Mother's gift to us was summers. You have given Julia the same."

"She gave us one thing I could never give Julia, though."

"What's that?"

"A sister," Elizabeth replied, once again sounding as if this were an obvious answer. "I wanted to help Calvin's daughter, of course, but I own I was also a bit selfish. Once I got to know her, I had a sense that Louisa and Julia would be . . . I don't know . . . *comfortable* together." She looked at Anna hopefully. "And they do seem to be, don't they?"

Anna felt tears threaten, but she suspected such a display would embarrass Elizabeth, so she just smiled and nodded.

Overwhelmed and in need of time to think, Anna got her shawl and went outside. There was no danger of a walk being interrupted by weather on this bright day, so she headed back into the woods.

I hope the traditions live on. And that you will help Elizabeth . . . Anna had always believed that Mother had anointed her the heir to the Newbold traditions, the Concord traditions. Now she understood that she had passed them down to both daughters, and wanted them to help each other.

And who had done the better job with that legacy? Anna recalled her frustration with her sister's response whenever she suggested that they stand up to Clarissa, or urged Elizabeth to resist Lillian's incessant demands. *What good would that do?* Elizabeth invariably replied.

That five-word question, which Anna had always considered a symptom of her sister's passivity, her aversion to difficult conversations, she now saw in an entirely new light. It was, in fact, the distillation of a code of conduct as profound as it was simple: If it will not do good, why do it?

And Elizabeth did not merely say it. She lived it.

With some shame, Anna realized how consumed she had always been by the question of *rightness*. Clarissa was quite often wrong, but once she and Father were married, there was no turning back the clock. There was no profit in arguing with Clarissa. The goal was to preserve what relationship they had with Father, which required not caring who was right or wrong.

Anna had thought her sister was powerless in her marriage, but now she saw that she had simply picked her battles carefully. She would not fuss about the Demarests' furniture, but when something mattered, she took it up privately with Jerome.

Anna had thought Elizabeth "lucked into" Haven Point, but she would bet her last dime now that she had a hand on the tiller all along, helping to navigate away from Newport, just as she expertly steered the catboat yesterday. Fourwinds was not a replica of their old cottage by the lake, but while willing to relent on matters of taste, Elizabeth would not do so on matters of community. She ensured they would be among good people, solid and reliable.

And none finer than Elizabeth herself.

Later, Anna and Nora stood on the Grahams' lawn, overlooking the water, where the Searses' yacht looked like an oversized, overdressed giant amid the humbler craft moored in the harbor.

"I was thinking about that act you put on years ago, when you persuaded Rhinelander and Vesta Sears that this place was too boring for words."

"And yet, there they are," Nora said wryly, gesturing toward the harbor.

"Do you recall me asking if Elizabeth knew about the scheme? You said it was better not to tell people what would be uncomfortable to know."

Nora nodded.

"I wondered what you meant by that. At the time, I thought it had something to do with Elizabeth and Jerome's relationship."

"Oh, no. It was just that the party was at Fourwinds. It would not be right to ask her, or any wife, to join in some scheme under her own roof without her husband's knowledge."

"Oh, I see. That seems like a good way of thinking," Anna said.

"A way of thinking for which your sister is largely responsible, in fact."

"How so?"

"Elizabeth just has a good instinct for where to draw the lines, how the women here can be supportive of each other, while also being respectful of marriages that could be strained by husbands being gone all week," Nora said. "I've always thought she was the wisest wife on Haven Point."

And the wisest mother, sister, and daughter, Anna thought.

Jerome would be arriving late, so after dinner, Elizabeth asked Anna if she'd like to take a walk and see how the cliff path was coming along. Ambrose had hired some men to cut through the brush along the edge of the cliff so that residents would be able to enjoy a scenic walk between the yacht club and the beach. They had been working on it all summer.

Elizabeth was civil to her mother-in-law during dinner, but Lillian's defeat had put her in a rather sour mood, so Anna was glad to get out of the house. Apparently Elizabeth was, too. As soon as they reached the rough path, she let loose a sigh of relief so loud, it made Anna laugh.

"I really think Lillian should be grateful," Anna said, as they walked along the rough dirt path. "I am not sure she understands how fortunate she is that she chose to confront you first."

"Fortunate indeed. She was probably so thrilled with her supposed discoveries, she simply could not hold off until Jerome arrived. Whether she realizes it or not, she saved herself a good deal of heartache."

Elizabeth had never confided in Anna about her marriage, though she understood now why that had been the case. She had been holding everything together all these years, striking a careful balance. Since Lillian had chosen to air it all in front of Anna, Elizabeth evidently felt she could now speak freely.

"Did you perceive that Lillian wanted Jerome to marry Judith?" Anna asked. She had always wondered.

"I did not have to perceive it. Jerome told me as much," Elizabeth said with a laugh. "Honestly, though, I doubt Lillian would have been happy with anyone he married. She was too desperate for Jerome's attention, too anxious about losing her place in his life. I just tried to ensure she felt welcome so that she would not suffer so much."

For an instant, Anna felt a surge of the old, habitual exasperation at her sister's willingness to tolerate such an unreasonable demand, but she quickly corrected herself. *You can promote good relations among the members of a family you marry into. Or you can be like Clarissa.*

Elizabeth had sensed that Lillian, in her desperation, was in danger of irreparably harming her relationship with her son, and she did what she could to prevent it.

"That was good of you," Anna said.

"I once hoped I might bring them closer together," Elizabeth said with a sigh. "In the end, I realized that the best I could do was try to keep Lillian from driving them farther apart."

Anna nodded. She had observed how impatient Jerome was with his mother at times, but she had been far more focused on his casual deference to his mother's opinion, and what she perceived was her sister's unconditional surrender. In the meantime, Elizabeth had been keeping an eye on what really mattered.

"How much did Jerome know about Lillian's threats?"

"I shared what was necessary, though stripped of her vitriol. He knew his mother was eager for Julia to go to Newport and agreed that the decision should be Julia's. As you heard, that was not well received," Elizabeth said with a wry laugh. "There were other occasions. Last fall, Lillian demanded that we attend some talk Judith was delivering about that convent school in Paris. Jerome scoffed, so I had the pleasure of informing his mother that he had declined."

Anna knew about that demand, of course, but she could hardly say that she had been listening at the door. "I wonder that she did not appeal to him directly about these matters."

"I think she was always a little afraid to," Elizabeth said.

"I suppose she was waiting until she had what she thought was an airtight case," Anna said.

"Exactly. Hopefully she sees now that she will get nowhere."

They walked for a while, and then Elizabeth stopped and looked at Anna.

"There is something I feel I should say, Anna, and that I probably should have said long ago."

She paused, looked out at the water, and took a breath before continuing. "It was such a remarkable coincidence, my seeing Calvin just before he died, I cannot help but believe we were brought together so we could both know that what we had was good and true, and so I might have a chance to redeem my part in what happened. I have, in turn, been richly rewarded, knowing Louisa, and having known Johanna.

"I have Clarissa and Lillian as living examples of the corrosive effects of bitterness, and I made a firm decision to not look back with regret. It would have hurt Jerome to learn what Clarissa did, so I have not told him. If he ever found out, however, I could tell him in perfect honesty that I love him, and that I have never regretted marrying him.

"In my resolution to not dwell on the past, though, I realize that I utterly neglected you. I should have told you what I felt, how I had chosen to move forward. I am sorry for keeping all of that from you."

Once again, Anna felt tears sting, but she held them back. "But you did tell me, Elizabeth. You said it in your love for your family, including me."

Anna reached out and pulled her sister into a hug. It was through actions and not words, and Anna had not always chosen to listen, but Elizabeth had indeed spoken clearly.

CHAPTER TWENTY-ONE

April 1922

Washington, DC

JULIA

> Climbing trees left their hands covered with sap, but then they realized how easily they could pick up dried leaves and pine needles. They played at being a new sort of forest creature, half person and half tree. (All sorts of unpleasant things can be turned to good account with a little determination.)
>
> FROM *LIBERTY ISLAND*, BY MISS CRANE

In late April, Julia could finally walk without a cane and manage the steps to her apartment. According to the doctor, Julia was ready to reenter the world. According to Julia, she was not, but everyone was pleased for her, so she made a great show of also being pleased.

She could not expect anyone else to understand that she dreaded the thought of returning to the life interrupted by the Knickerbocker disaster, since she did not even understand it herself. Nor could she continue to impose on the Seabornes. She could only keep pretending.

A few days after Morgan School's principal accepted with alacrity her offer to return for the last weeks of the school year, Bess came by the studio to fill her in on where her students were with their lessons.

"I should warn you that the children have *lots* of questions," Bess said with a little grimace. "I told them all I could, but since I was not in the theater, I could only partially satisfy their curiosity. Which, I must say, is a bit morbid."

"That's all right. I expected as much." Julia had indeed anticipated this, but as soon as Bess left, she burst into tears.

What is wrong with me? For the thousandth time, she wished Louisa were there.

Julia looked out the window and was alarmed to see Michael heading for the studio. She dried her eyes and tried to disguise her dismay, but given his own alarmed expression upon entering, it seemed she had not succeeded.

"Jules, what is it?" He sat on the little sofa by her side and looked at her with such concern, tears welled up again.

She covered her face. "Don't be nice."

"Shall I throw a dead fish at you?"

She managed a sniffly laugh. "Bess came by and gave me an update on the students, and for some reason, it just sent me."

"I wonder why?" His tone was of genuine inquiry.

She finally removed her hands from her face and looked at him. "Thank you for being curious."

He looked affronted. "A fine man I'd be if I wasn't curious when you're obviously overset."

"I don't mean curious as opposed to uncaring or indifferent. I mean curious as opposed to already knowing. I'm sick to death of people thinking they know me better than I know myself, and patiently guiding me to the truth." Julia surprised herself with this outburst, but it was something that had been simmering under the surface during her convalescence.

Though Michael had the decency not to mention it, he had probably long observed what Julia herself had only just begun to recognize: In her romantic drama, Pelham was cast as the master, with Julia in the role of eager, ingenuous pupil.

She continued. "I suppose what sent me was that Bess mentioned that my students will have lots of questions, and I cannot answer them." Julia had avoided reading anything about the accounts of the Knickerbocker disaster, and knew little beyond her own experience. "I guess I should look at the papers."

"Are you sure?"

When Julia nodded, Michael stood. "We have them saved. I'll be right back." He soon returned with a box, filled to the brim with newspapers and magazines. "Shall I stay, in case *you* have questions?"

"You wouldn't mind?" In reply, Michael held up a magazine he had brought for his own entertainment, then plopped into a comfortable chair, feet on an ottoman.

Since the most recent papers were at the top of the pile in the box, the exercise was like starting with a toe in the water and slowly immersing oneself. The latest stories were about grand jury indictments against the architects and builders involved with the construction of the theater, followed by stories about the investigations that led to those proceedings.

By the time she reached the profiles of the dead, Julia thought she was acclimated. Besides, she had not been able to avoid all knowledge of who lost their lives that night. Margaret had told Julia about several families she was acquainted with who had lost loved ones in the disaster so Julia could write and express her sympathy.

As it turned out, she was not at all prepared. As she read about the many brilliant, worthy people whose lives had been cut short, she felt as if a great weight were pressing on her chest. Musicians and diplomats, politicians and veterans, young people who were engaged to be married, four women who worked in the War Office. And children, so many children. Before long, she was crying again.

Michael rose, pulled the ottoman over, gently removed the paper from her hands, and waited patiently.

"Why am I alive?" she asked finally.

"Do you mean why did you survive instead of them?"

"Children, Michael! They had their whole lives ahead of them. And the others, people doing such valuable work, parents who left their children orphans . . ."

Michael took her hand in his. "Soldiers who survived and made it home from the war speak of the anguish of believing they did not deserve to live. You are no less worthy than anyone, of course, but more importantly, Julia, your survival defied no principle of fairness or justice. No one died so you could live. The fact is, nobody deserved to die in that theater."

She was quiet for a moment, then said, "I suppose I feel like I have been too lucky all my life. That I have had so much when others have so little."

Michael smiled. "There are wretched souls who have far more, and happy people with less. As to your advantages, you are generous with people in need. Not just materially, but spiritually, too. You have always been a light in the darkness, Julia. The world is better for you still being in it."

"Thank you, Michael," Julia said with a watery smile. It had helped just to bring her thoughts into the light and expose the flaws. Though she was not entirely relieved of her feelings, what Michael had said was sensible, and she felt she might eventually embrace the idea that she was not chosen to live, that none were chosen to perish. And while she considered his other comments too generous, she was grateful for them.

She returned to the papers. By the time she reached the stories that were published closer to the event, she had already absorbed much of what was in them. She was almost to the bottom when she came across a story containing her own statement. She had forgotten that Michael had coaxed it out of her at the hospital.

> I am so grateful to those who worked so hard to free me, and to the doctors and nurses at the scene and here at the hospital. I know how very fortunate I am, that it was by the barest chance that I survived. I am heartsick for those who did not, and I extend my deepest sympathies to their loved ones.

She smiled at how rational it was, compared to how she had felt just moments ago. She also saw that it appeared in several papers simultaneously. Michael had ignored his job and stayed by her for hours that night, and then shared with the wire services the one tidbit that could have been his exclusively.

It was when Julia picked up one of the last papers, *The Washington Herald*, that she got a terrible, confusing shock. It did not contain the statement from her, but to her dismay, it did have one about her, from Miss Mina Ellis, "a close friend of Miss Julia Demarest."

> I hope the men who were responsible for this disaster are soon brought to justice. Nobody should have to endure what Miss Demarest did. Long, harrowing hours in total darkness, entombed by debris, her ankle crushed. Yet even when rescuers finally discovered she was alive beneath the rubble, she insisted they first help a young boy, also trapped, whose spirits she had kept up throughout the ordeal.

Julia recoiled in horror. "Oh, no!"

"Is that the *Herald*? I wondered if I should show it to you."

"How could she?" She was horrified by the low note Mina's words struck. Nearly a hundred people died in that theater. Even in her pain-addled state, Julia had known the only appropriate sentiments were gratitude and sympathy. Not only did Mina's words savor of self-pity, but they depicted her as some sort of heroine, simply for comforting a child trapped under his dead mother's body.

Then Julia noticed something else. The paper, an early edition, was dated Monday, January 30.

"Do you remember Mina visiting me soon after I was admitted?"

"She came the very next day. I was in the room."

"She said she was going to Charlottesville for the weekend."

"She couldn't have gone and gotten back. The trains weren't running."

"I know I was muddled, but I feel like I would remember her telling me she had not gone after all. I recall feeling relieved she had gotten back safely."

"You did not just feel that. You *said* it," Michael replied. "You were so groggy, and I didn't know she was supposedly in Charlottesville. I figured you were referring to her being stuck across town or something."

"And she did not correct me?" Julia asked.

Michael shook his head.

Mina was hiding something, and Julia bet it was a love affair, probably with someone married and prominent. "Why would she dare come to the hospital, knowing I could catch her lying?"

"Most people take the *Herald* in the afternoon, so she probably forgot they even had a morning edition. She could have returned by rail on Monday and given them the statement for the late edition." He added with a hint of apology, "It might be unfair, but from what I know of Miss Ellis, I suspect she could not stay away."

"I am sure you don't mean because she was so worried about me," Julia said dryly.

"You know this was a big story, but being in the hospital all those weeks, I'm not sure you know how big. It was in the papers all over the world."

"And she couldn't stand not being close to it," Julia said.

"Not just close to it." Michael nodded at the paper still in Julia's hands. "Part of it."

When Julia returned home on Sunday, she felt a brief surge of joy at being in her lovely apartment, among her own things. But fairly soon, she found herself yearning to return to the cocoon of Margaret's studio, to the months-long pause in her life. If not for her eagerness to see her students, she might have fled back there again.

Julia knew the children would be curious, but reading the papers had given her a better sense of just how intense and consuming the interest had been in Washington, especially in her neighborhood. Many Morgan School students walked by the wreckage of the theater every day.

Bess had said the children's curiosity was morbid. Julia understood, and had no wish to moralize or make the children feel ashamed, even for any perverse pleasure they might have experienced, having such a big, interesting thing happen so near them.

That said, she thought she might be able to direct their thoughts in a less macabre direction, and she put her mind toward preparing to do so.

On her first morning back, the children greeted her with hugs and kind words, and their sweet welcome was a tonic. When they were all seated, she stood and told them how glad she was to see them, and thanked them for all the dear cards and pictures they sent.

"I know you probably have many questions. I thought I might just tell you my story. Would you like that?" The nearly forty sets of eager eyes gave her the answer.

In a matter-of-fact tone, she told them where she sat in the theater, and about the sound she heard from above, soon after the film began.

"The cracks on the ceiling looked very much like cracks on the surface of a pond when it is about to break. I was very lucky to have seen such a thing before. It made me realize the ceiling might fall, so I got under a seat and curled myself into a tight ball.

"My lower legs could not fit, which is why my ankle was broken when something fell on it, but the rest of me was protected." (Not wanting the children to focus on the horrifying aspects of her experience, she skipped over the terrible period during which she had not been at all confident that was the case.)

"I called for help until someone heard me, and because of the debris, it took a long time to get me out, but eventually, they did."

She gestured out the window, at the green grass, the leaves on the trees, the flowers in bloom. "I know it's hard to picture, looking outside on a day like today, but does anyone remember how much snow there was on the ground?"

As she expected, many hands went up, and children excitedly recalled snow-covered motorcars, fathers who shoveled walks only to realize an hour later that they had to be shoveled again. When one of the children mentioned how difficult it had been to get around, it gave Julia the opening she sought.

"Yet despite how hard it was, people came from everywhere to help, some from miles and miles away. Would you like to hear about some of them?"

Julia, whose childhood love of sensational tales was equaled only by her love of heroic ones, knew they would say yes. She relayed story after story of bravery, benevolence, and sacrifice that she had culled from the press accounts. She told them about the quick-thinking telephone operator who got the first call from the theater and assigned other operators to call every doctor in the area, so that in minutes, seventy-two doctors had been phoned. And about mechanics who appeared with tools and torches, and men with shovels who cleared snow for fire trucks and ambulances. She spoke of the Red Cross nurses and volunteers who brought warm blankets and socks, and administered first aid.

She shared the story of the hotel manager who ordered everyone on his staff, no matter their job, to make sandwiches for the injured and the rescue workers, and somehow got them to the theater, along with urns of hot coffee.

She spoke of the many neighbors who opened their homes late that night to give refuge to the wounded and their families, like the two elderly women who lived above their hat shop across the street and saw what happened out their window. They raced down to their shop, cleared the counters, and opened the doors so injured people could be treated there.

She recounted the story of the woman beneath the rubble, singing songs to cheer people up, and the little boy who was rescued but would not leave for the hospital until his younger sister was rescued, too. And about policemen and firemen, soldiers and marines who brought equipment and helped free Julia and many others.

"It was a horrible thing that happened that night, but it reminded me that the world is full of people who are good and brave, and who are willing to help each other."

Julia went to the chalkboard and asked her students to think of all the jobs they could. She soon had a long list. Doctor, police officer, fireman, nurse, banker, librarian, reporter, baker, mayor, soldier, hotelier, janitor, pharmacist . . .

Then she asked them to imagine something like the theater disaster happening, and went through the various occupations. "If you had this job, how might you help?"

For the next half hour, with their youthful creativity and boundless sense of possibility, thirty-seven children imagined themselves as librarians bringing books to hospitals to entertain injured patients, bankers giving money to orphans, policemen clearing the road for ambulances, and so much more.

One warm, rainy afternoon in early June, Julia returned to her apartment to find a letter from Mother. It opened with the usual inquiries about her ankle and her return to work, and updates on how her nephews were getting along in school, but she closed it with a request that surprised her.

> *I would very much appreciate your coming to Haven Point as soon as possible after the school year has ended. Both your father and I would like you to be here, particularly as you did not visit last summer.*

Julia had given little thought to her summer plans, besides a vague idea of accepting the Seabornes' open invitation to Gibson Island. Her first instinct was to decline the summons. Mother's tone was oddly peremptory (really not like Mother at all), and the mention of Father struck her as faintly retrograde. *The paterfamilias commands your presence . . .*

She could only imagine how Pelham or Mina would laugh at the letter. *Luring you back to the lost tribe, to the land that time has not touched!*

The immediate decision—go, don't go?—was small, but it felt like a concrete version of an existential question she had, in some way, been asking herself ever since she got out from under the rubble in the theater: *Where do I go from here?*

Or even one she had been asking for much longer: *Where do I belong?*

For so long, she had wanted to escape the constraints of Boston Brahmin society, but she'd flung herself into another world that was, in its way, just as constraining. Worse, it was one she had never truly been part of. Her only connections were Mina and Pelham, and both those threads felt thin and frayed.

In the end, she decided to go, but not because of Mother's command or her guilt about Father. It was because looking ahead, and asking herself what came next, had naturally made her look back—to when she had felt most content, most free to be completely herself.

And her mind kept returning to Liberty Island.

A week before the end of the school term, as Julia made her way home from school, she ran into Emmeline, the servant from Mrs. Palmer's, where Mina had lived.

"So good to see you, Emmeline," Julia said warmly.

"Why, it's good to see you, too, Miss Demarest. And up and walking! I was so worried when I heard you'd been in that theater."

Emmeline asked a few questions about Julia's condition; then she looked off, a thoughtful expression on her face. Her eyes returned to Julia, and she opened her mouth as if she was about to say something, but then closed it again.

"What is it, Emmeline?"

She hesitated, then said, "I been wanting to talk to you about something, Miss Demarest. The day after the accident, I went over to the theater to see if I could do anything. When I came back, I saw your friend Miss Ellis coming out of Mrs. Palmer's house . . ."

"And?" Julia braced herself.

"And she had that fellow of yours with her."

"Mr. Stewart, you mean?" Julia had introduced Pelham to Emmeline once when they saw each other on the street, but there was still a faint hope that Emmeline could be referring to someone else.

"Yes, him that I'd seen you with before," Emmeline said. She frowned sadly. "I wondered if maybe he was s'posed to be there or something?"

Julia smiled ruefully and shook her head.

"That's what I thought somehow. I don't know what it was, but something about it looked . . ."

"Clandestine?"

"I think that's it, yes. I'm sorry if this comes as a shock, but I thought you should know."

"It's all right, Emmeline," Julia said, not wishing to make the woman feel worse. "And did they see you?"

Emmeline barked out a wry laugh. "That Miss Ellis never really saw me."

Julia knew Emmeline had not been confused about what she saw. In a way, it affirmed the vague mistrust she had been harboring toward both Pelham and Mina.

That said, her stomach turned at the image of them together in Mina's apartment, planning their deception. She wondered what had gone through their minds when they learned Julia was in the Knickerbocker Theatre, if Pelham was still there when Mina came to the hospital to insert herself in the drama.

Julia had just enough self-respect to know that she would have to confront each of them in person at some point, but she was glad Mina was in New York and Pelham on another continent, as she felt far from ready to have those conversations.

Unfortunately, the gods had other plans. A week later, as Julia was packing to leave for Maine, she heard a knock at her door. She opened it to find Mina, in a smart scarlet day dress, belted at the hips, and a little matching cap over her bobbed hair.

"Hello, Duchess," Mina said, entering without invitation. "I'm in town for Vera's birthday. How are you getting around?"

"I'm fine," Julia said coldly.

Mina peeled off her gloves and was doing her usual act of sniffing around the perimeter, like a dog. She stopped when she reached the framed *Liberty Island* illustration of the four girls looking up at the night sky. Margaret had given it to Julia before she moved back to her apartment.

"This really belongs to you," Margaret had said, while Julia struggled to hold back her tears.

Mina cocked her head. "Hmm," she said with a condescending smile. It was just a little sound, but like Grandmother Lillian's half "ugh," one that said so much. It occurred to Julia that Mina and Lillian actually had a good deal in common.

Julia still had said nothing, and Mina finally seemed to sense something amiss. She turned away from the picture. "Are you going to ask me if I'd like something to drink?"

"I learned that Pelham did not go back to New York the weekend of the Knickerbocker disaster. He stayed here with you."

Julia did her best to appear calm, but her heart was beating wildly. Mina knew how to give the appearance of owning up to faults and errors, but only with sufficient time to script her careless, tossed-off lines. *You know how dreadfully unreliable I am, duckie* . . . It was a dangerous business, confronting her unprepared.

Mina flushed, but she recovered quickly. "Julia, dear, you really must get past your absurd hang-ups about sex."

"Being bothered about your friend going to bed with your boyfriend is a *hang-up*?"

"No, Duchess." Mina smiled contemptuously. "I mean that one led to the other."

"Ah! I would not go to bed with him, so you had to." Louisa's words echoed in her mind: *They hate anything or anyone that tries to regulate their behavior.*

"Julia, what did you think? You are very pretty, of course, and I am sure your hero worship was great fun for Pelham, but did you actually think the man would marry a spoiled, wealthy child? You could never be any sort of companion to him. If you were smart, you'd stop the playacting and find some nice fellow to marry." She nodded at the trunks on the floor. "Maybe up at the citadel."

Julia held the door open. "Goodbye, Mina."

After Mina left, Julia lowered herself into a chair and sat looking at Margaret's beautiful illustration, wondering how she had gotten so off track.

She had gone to Barnard in hopes of immersing herself in the world of ideas. How thrilling it had been to learn that many people were asking the very same questions she had. *But why? Why not?*

Those early days, following Mina around Greenwich Village, had been all she hoped for. It was a wonderful spectacle, a joyful, boisterous exploration. People were open-minded, open-hearted.

Not all had taken the same dark turn that Mina and Pelham did, but Julia had never been more than a guest of one or the other. She was so dazzled by them, she failed to notice when their curiosity and exploration hardened into a dogma that was every bit as rigid as that which they had rejected.

By their unwritten rules, this beautiful illustration, and any pleasant thought Julia had about her own childhood, must be written off as naive and sentimental. Under Pelham's chosen theory, Julia was irreparably harmed by her family. It was awfully convenient. What better way to get what he wanted from her than by casting a shadow over her childhood, over everyone she had known and loved?

No, Peter. I wasn't scared, Julia had said that night in the Knickerbocker. *I always felt quite safe.* She recalled now the wave of sorrow she had felt upon uttering those words. Peter was talking about camping under the stars, but Julia was talking about much more than that.

Louisa, dear Louisa, had tried to set her straight. *I don't recall your needing protection*, Louisa had said. *You were a happy child.* All children need protection, of course, but she was right that Julia had never felt a lack of it.

Father was set in his ways, and William and Grandmother Lillian had always been derisive, yet Julia had been a happy, thriving child. She was overwhelmed by the sense that the person responsible for that was the very one she had been hardest on in recent years: her mother.

CHAPTER TWENTY-TWO

August 1900

Haven Point, Maine

ANNA

Anna was at the steamship landing, fetching the mail, when she met Serena Lawrence, attired perfectly in a tightly corseted white flannel morning dress. She greeted Anna warmly.

"It's a shame that Mr. Lockwood departed, is it not?" Serena asked.

In all the upheaval, Anna had had little time to think about Mr. Lockwood, and she felt a twinge of self-consciousness, wondering if Serena's inquiry contained any hidden meaning. Had people been speaking about her and Mr. Lockwood's flirtation? (And had it even been a "flirtation"? Anna felt horribly ignorant.)

She quickly dismissed this as silly. Serena had always been guileless. Mr. Lockwood had been with the girls on Jumaru almost every day, and they adored him. It was natural for her to feel his departure was unfortunate.

"Yes, it is a shame," she replied.

Serena rolled her eyes. "Perhaps he was summoned by Mrs. Fairchild."

Anna was so flabbergasted by this comment, it rendered her speechless. Guileless Serena was now trafficking in salacious gossip?

"I don't know how he stands it," Serena continued, shaking her head.

Now Anna began to feel annoyed. "If it is so distasteful, why does he permit it?"

Now Serena looked at Anna strangely. "Well, he cannot just go back on his promise to Mr. Fairchild!"

Anna's mind was now in a scramble as she tried to fit this comment into her present understanding, but doing so required a deathbed conversation between Mr. Fairchild and Mr. Lockwood that was beyond her imagination. Finally, she relented.

"To what promise are you referring?"

Serena looked at her in bewilderment. "Acting as the trustee for his fortune, of course."

"He is Judith Fairchild's *trustee*?"

"Did you not know that?"

Anna shook her head slowly.

"Mr. Fairchild wanted someone of integrity who was also young enough to see things through for his son."

"Ah, very wise," Anna managed. Fortunately, Serena did not ask what Anna's prior assumption about Mr. Lockwood and Mrs. Fairchild had been. Anna bade Serena farewell and set off for Fourwinds, her mind swimming.

When Anna, on the last night of her debutante season, saw Mrs. Fairchild clutching at Mr. Lockwood, her beseeching expression had reflected her desire for *money*. The "wiles" that Mr. Wimborne said Mrs. Fairchild used were to extract *money*, as was the "pestering" of Mr. Lockwood that Vesta's friends referred to. Whenever Anna heard the two names whispered together, she was hearing people gossip about Judith Fairchild's incessant requests for *money*.

Anna had thought herself a woman of reason and science, yet she had refused to question her own opinion, even when faced with evidence that Mr. Lockwood was not actually a person of irredeemable character.

It was in a very downcast state that she walked in the front door of Fourwinds. As it happened, Elizabeth was descending the stairs at that very moment, her eyes swollen with fatigue. "I did not sleep a wink last night, and it is all your fault."

"What do you mean?" Anna asked wearily. Her list of errors was already so long, she was not sure she could bear adding another to it.

"I stayed up reading *Liberty Island*."

By this time, Elizabeth had reached the bottom of the stairs. She took Anna's hands in her own. "It is splendid, Anna. Absolutely splendid."

Anna's heart swelled. She had believed her sister was in earnest when she expressed a desire to read *Liberty Island*, but Elizabeth had never been a reader. Anna certainly did not expect her sister to pester her for a copy, as she had, or that she would read it immediately.

She smiled. "I'm sorry it cost you sleep."

"I cannot allow you to hide this light under a barrel. You must let people know that you wrote this wonderful book. I am going to have a party here on Haven Point. We have to celebrate."

"Oh, I don't know . . ."

"Tell me one reason why you must remain anonymous."

"Lillian Demarest? Judith Fairchild?"

Elizabeth scoffed. "You do not think I subscribe to Judith's notions about children's literature, do you?"

"No," Anna conceded. Elizabeth had never said a word on the subject. And Lillian was hardly a threat, now that she knew she did not have the power to turn Jerome against Julia.

"Any other objections?" Elizabeth asked.

Anna shrugged. "I am drawing a blank."

"Excellent." Elizabeth nodded triumphantly. "Because I have already sent to Portland for copies to give to all our friends."

Two days later, Anna was in the living room when Eugenia brought Louisa to Fourwinds to play with Julia. Louisa trotted up the stairs, and Anna asked if Eugenia would like to come sit for a moment. To her surprise, Eugenia accepted.

"Anna, your sister gave me a copy of your book, and I thoroughly enjoyed it!"

"Thank you," Anna replied, then looked down, prepared for the inevitable lecture about how she should not have taken time away from the Margaret Fuller book. It would be nothing she had not already said to herself.

"You seem rather subdued. Is there something wrong?"

Anna looked up and saw a confused expression on Eugenia's face.

"Oh. Well, I appreciate the compliment, but I suppose I saw it as a bit, well . . . *unserious*. It was such a dashed-off thing, and it took me away from the other book, of course."

"You mean the Margaret Fuller book?" Eugenia paused for a moment, thinking. "As much as I would personally welcome a biography of Fuller, the most important thing is that her ideas live on. And the girls in *Liberty Island* are so Concordian! They love beauty, simplicity, nature. They're independent and adventurous. And through their adventures, they discover their affinities. I think such stories have a great deal of power in working on children's imaginations."

"That's interesting," Anna said. She had not thought about her book in this light.

"We wonder why women have not made more progress since Margaret Fuller's time. I cannot help but conclude that, to some extent, it comes down to simple lack of imagination."

"Thank you, Eugenia. That is a very nice way of looking at it."

"As for it being a 'dashed-off thing,' as you put it, if you found it easy to write, perhaps it is because you have found *your* affinity. A scholarly work is not inherently better, only different. Personally, I'd rather see you write more books like this than a hundred tomes on Margaret Fuller."

Anna felt something slacken inside her. She could not quite tease out why, but Eugenia's perspective was obviously something she had needed very much to hear. "Thank you again. I am pleased you see this as worthy."

Eugenia smiled, but it faded, and she looked at Anna carefully, as if trying to figure something out. When she sat up straighter, Anna braced herself for the impending change of subject.

"On another note, I have to ask: What did you say to my brother that made him leave Haven Point in such haste?"

Anna could feel her face grow warm. She knew she had to explain, as difficult and embarrassing as it would be. Whether Mr. Lockwood forgave her or not, she at least wanted him to know why she had been so ungenerous to him, and Eugenia was the best person to convey that to him.

She took a breath, then told Eugenia everything—what she saw on the last night of her debutante season, when he did not appear for the dance, and all the comments she had heard over the years, up to the most recent ones on Rhinelander Sears's yacht.

"I was stupid and stubborn, but given my ignorance of your brother's role as Mrs. Fairchild's trustee, perhaps you can see how I might have misread things."

Eugenia kept a straight face throughout the confession, but when Anna was finished, she began to laugh, and once she started, she struggled to stop. The confession, and Eugenia's amusement at it, came as such a relief, Anna could not help joining in.

"Oh, Anna, that is the funniest thing I've ever heard!" she said finally, wiping her eyes.

"Well, not so funny, when you consider how abominably I behaved toward your brother!" Anna said ruefully.

Eugenia collected herself. "No, no . . . I understand how uncomfortable it must be for you. But I would like you and my brother to be friends again. I will see what I can do."

Later that week, Anna was on the island with the girls. She sat beneath a pine tree, legs stretched out before her, reflecting on Eugenia's comments about *Liberty Island.*

If you found it easy to write, perhaps it is because you have found your *affinity.*

Anna thought back to her mother's words during their last conversation. *Only if it is your inclination, Anna,* she had said, referring to Anna working with Father. *I want you to follow your own affinity.*

At the time, Anna had thought she understood the worried expression on her mother's face: She wanted Father and Anna to complete the Fuller biography, but she did not want Anna to feel she had made a deathbed promise.

Now Anna wondered if that was the future her mother really had envisioned for her. Mother had been so perspicacious. Perhaps she had always known it was not her daughter's affinity.

When Eugenia suggested that *Liberty Island* served a similar and equally valuable goal, Anna had instantly felt relieved. She had found it easy to write—enjoyable, even. She had never been able to summon the same motivation for the Fuller biography.

Anna had been feeling that her personal horizon was looking a bit gray. Perhaps allowing herself to more fully embrace this new direction would brighten it.

A little. Maybe.

She heard a noise behind her and turned to see Harley Lockwood approaching from the direction of the cove. Her heart leapt at the sight of him, but as he drew closer, she felt a sudden rush of shame and hid her face behind her hands.

"May I join you?" he asked.

Anna removed her hands from her face. She knew she was blushing furiously. "Of course," she managed, and scooted over to make room for him.

He sat, arms around his legs. The girls were sitting astride the branches of two pine trees, weaving and yelling. Mr. Lockwood looked at Anna, amusement in his eyes.

"Can you fill me in?"

So, we are just picking up where we left off?

"They have been captured by pookahs."

"Pookahs?"

"Irish fairy creatures. They can assume any shape, but Louisa tells us they prefer to be horses. When in such form, they have a bad habit of luring people on their backs and then taking them on death-defying rides."

The girls, having finally noticed Mr. Lockwood's arrival, climbed out of the trees and came over to greet him. He rose and gave them all hugs.

"I must apologize. My arrival seems to have broken the pookahs' spell. I do not like to have deprived you from what seemed to be a most exhilarating ride."

"Oh, it's all right," Julia said reassuringly. "We were going to go dig for treasure anyway."

The girls ran off, and Mr. Lockwood resumed his place beside Anna. He was quiet, and she wondered if he was preparing to dress her down. It might be a relief. A kindness, really, to be offered the chance to explain, and to tell him how sorry she was.

She was astonished, therefore, when he turned to her and said, "I owe you an apology, Miss Bradley."

"How could that possibly be, Mr. Lockwood, when I have done you the most terrible injustice?"

"But you had a reason, did you not? My sister has told me how you came by your misperceptions. She also informed me that the first offense was my own, when I failed to show up for a dance. I confess I do not remember the evening in question, but I was a rather selfish young man, and I am sorry for that."

Anna felt her face grow red. "It was one silly dance. It does not excuse my assumptions."

"It was an honest mistake. I feel terrible regret for how I behaved on the boat. I knew something must have caused the change in your manner, and if I had not been so cold and stiff, perhaps you would have told me," he said. "I'm afraid I've learned that I can be devilishly prideful. I was wounded, you see, that you might think so little of me. In case you had not noticed, I had fallen quite in love with you."

With effort, Anna kept her jaw from dropping, but she could not prevent her heart from hammering, or her soul from singing. "You . . . you *had*?"

"I had. I have, rather. And the reason I came back here, besides to apologize, was to ask you if there was the smallest chance of your ever feeling the same."

She sighed and looked up at him, unable to keep the smile from spreading across her face.

"I think the chances are quite good, Mr. Lockwood."

He reached for her hand and threaded his fingers through hers.

"I will try my best to be worthy, for I am determined to marry you, if you'll have me."

"You wish to marry me, Mr. Lockwood?" she asked, astonished again.

He pulled her closer, took her face in his free hand, then kissed her. She returned the kiss, most enthusiastically.

"I do wish to marry you," he said, when he finally pulled away. "And I also wish you would stop with this 'Mr. Lockwood' business and call me Harley."

"I will, if you would call me Anna."

"With pleasure. I confess I've been calling you Anna in my mind for the longest time. I have also read *Liberty Island*, and I think it's an absolute marvel."

"Thank you," Anna said.

"In fact, it was to be my consolation if you did not accept me. If nothing else, I knew I would always have your book."

"What do you mean?"

"I was reading a story inspired by a world I had come to know and love, written by a woman I had come to know and love. I felt keenly the privilege of having immersed myself in all of this," he said, with a sweep of his arm taking in the island. "I was so engaged, I read it once without stopping, but then I read it again, awed by the way you created different characters and stories, but still captured so perfectly what was best and truest about Jumaru."

He was looking around at the clearing, but then he turned to Anna again. "I knew, if nothing else, I could always pick up *Liberty Island*, and it would transport me back to what had been some of the happiest days of my life."

Anna beamed up at him.

"Do you want to write more such stories?" he asked.

Anna picked up a dry pine needle and twirled it in her fingers. She recalled earlier, when she became aware of a seed of hope that had been planted in her heart. She had dared not identify it, but now she knew that this was what it was. She wanted to marry this man, but she also wanted to write more books.

Women almost always had to make a hard choice between marriage and career. Perhaps a marriage to Mr. Lockwood would be the exception that proved the rule, but she could not be sure.

"Yes, I would like to write more such stories," she said finally.

He nodded. "I believe you would enjoy living at Wendover, and I can promise you would have the quiet and the time to write. That said, I am willing to live wherever you would like." She must have looked astonished because he looked at her a little more closely and added, "You would have my full support, of course."

Support. It was amazing how easily this rolled off his tongue, as if her continuing to write after they were married was perfectly natural and expected. Of course he was Eugenia's brother, and she had taught him well.

"I am sure I would like it very much."

"I should tell you, too, that I am thinking about buying the Grahams' cottage. I wonder if you'd like that."

"A house?" Anna said, putting her hands to her cheeks in mock surprise. "A house of our own, on *Guillotine*?"

"It's just a cottage," he said, waving a hand. "Nothing to lose your head over!"

She threw back that very head and laughed; then he pulled her closer so it could rest on his shoulder.

CHAPTER TWENTY-THREE

July 1922
Haven Point, Maine

JULIA

The girls had meant to learn the constellations, but they'd been so busy, and now they were almost out of time. They decided they would each pick a favorite star and name it. (Lucy's was in the southern sky. She called it Bertram.) Afterward, they lay on their backs, gazing up at the vast night sky.

"I want the world to be better," Lucy said, thinking about their fathers and war and suffering. "Right now the world seems awfully big, though, and I feel like I'm just one little person on a tiny island."

"Seems to me things would be much better if people paid attention to their tiny islands first," Audrey said. She was thinking about fathers and wars and suffering, too.

FROM *LIBERTY ISLAND*, BY MISS CRANE

Julia made the trip in a day and arrived on Haven Point so late, Mother was the only one up. She greeted Julia with a hug and said all the proper, civil things, but she seemed distracted, and Julia felt a twinge of disappointment. She had hoped to make a fresh start with her mother, and that during this visit, she would disabuse herself of her false impressions.

We're both exhausted, she told herself. *We'll have a proper greeting in the morning.*

Not long after dawn, Julia was awakened by the sound of voices downstairs. She pushed herself up on one elbow and reflexively looked to the bed next to her, prepared to exchange a *What is happening?* glance with Louisa. But she was not there, of course.

She could make out no words, just William's angry staccato tones, alternating with Pauline's higher-pitched pleading. It sounded as if Pauline was crying. When the front door slammed, Julia threw off her covers, quietly opened her bedroom door, and crept to the staircase landing, where a window looked out on the front of the house.

The causeway had finally been built, and William's motorcar was in the drive with the passenger door open. Jaw set, face red with fury, William led Pauline to the car, his hand gripping her upper arm. He shut her door, stomped around to the driver's side, started the engine, and they were off.

Julia dressed quietly, thinking she was the only one awake. As she descended the stairs, however, she saw Mother in the living room, staring at the empty fireplace, a stricken look on her face. A stair creaked, and Mother hastily rearranged her expression into something like a smile, then turned to her.

"Good morning, Julia. Did you sleep well?" Evidently she was prepared to act as if nothing had happened.

Julia stopped before reaching the bottom step.

"Mother, please. I saw that scene out the window." In coming to Haven Point, Julia had thought she was pulling herself from the edge of the abyss. Now she felt like she was staring right into it.

Mother let out a weary breath, closed her eyes, then opened them again and stared into the middle distance. She was obviously not going to take Julia into her confidence. But while harsh thoughts arranged themselves into words, Julia held them back for once. She still was not sure about the extent to which she had misjudged her mother, or in exactly what ways, but she knew she had been unfair.

This time, at least, she would gather the facts first, and as Mother would not be forthcoming, she would have to look elsewhere.

"I'm going to Anna's," Julia said, and walked out the door.

An hour later, Julia sat on Anna's sofa, staring out the window, processing what her aunt had just told her.

Anna had welcomed her warmly, as she always did, and not asked what Julia was doing at her house at such an ungodly hour. Fortunately, they were alone. Julia's uncle Harley was away somewhere, and their two boys had jobs in Boston for the summer. (Though they were hardly "boys" now. Julia's Lockwood cousins were both strapping college men.)

Anna went to the kitchen to get them both coffee, and when she returned, Julia asked the question that so pressed on her.

"Anna, what is going on with William and Pauline?"

Anna hesitated, but she must have seen something in Julia's eyes—a need, perhaps, or maybe even just a simple willingness to listen with an open mind—because she decided to give her an honest answer.

What Anna shared with Julia did not excuse William's behavior, but it did help explain it. Pauline, it seemed, had developed a very severe problem with alcohol, and the repercussions had been devastating.

Julia was horrified by the stories Anna told. When Daniel was three years old, he pulled a hot iron onto himself while his mother was passed out drunk on the couch. On another occasion, Pauline got horribly drunk at a party, and when William tried to gently steer her out, she lashed out at him in front of everyone.

When William stopped keeping liquor in the house, Pauline began sneaking out to find it. One night, he hunted her down in a speakeasy and had to practically carry her home. Just as he was helping her up the stairs, Oliver came out of his room, and was terrified by the spectacle of his mother, stumbling and slurring nonsensically.

Over the past few years, Pauline had been to several sanitariums. A period of temperance would follow, but it never lasted long.

Now Julia surveyed her memories, trying to fit them to this new information.

"What was happening two summers ago?" she asked, recalling her last visit to Haven Point, when William treated Pauline so harshly.

"She was fresh out of another sanitarium," Anna said. "Your uncle and I were abroad with the boys that summer, as you know, but if my memory of events is correct, she had just fallen off the wagon again. His harshness was likely a fruitless attempt to shame her back to sobriety. She was back in another institution before the end of summer."

"She seemed so well when I saw her this spring."

"She had a nice long stretch." Anna sighed. "While we cannot know for sure what led to the scene this morning, I think we can safely guess. It's terribly sad."

"I can't imagine William's anger helps, though," Julia said.

"I am sure it doesn't. You might find it hard to believe, but he was very tender and encouraging at first when Pauline would have a period of temperance. I confess it even surprised me. I'm not sure I knew before how much he truly loved Pauline. I suspect some of his anger is disappointment, a feeling that the woman he loved has left him."

"Why did no one tell me?"

"William did not want you to know. He did not think you would respond well." Anna looked apologetic, but Julia was not angry. These secrets were not ideal, but she knew she had not exactly earned anyone's trust in recent years.

"I cannot imagine your mother is pleased with William's behavior, and I would be shocked if she had not spoken to him privately about it," Anna said. "The plain fact is, we can hardly expect William or your mother to know how to solve the problem when the best and most reputable institutions haven't been able to do so. Your mother is trying to stay close, to be there for the boys. I credit her with understanding what it is that she can actually do."

"I'm not sure I've given Mother credit for all she does know," Julia said, relieved she had restrained herself earlier.

"I'm familiar with that," Anna said. "I thought she was the pretty, athletic sister, while I was the smart one. I devalued not only her mind but also her accomplishments."

"Such as?" Julia asked.

"I never appreciated what a study she made of her athletic pursuits, for example, or the relationships she built and sustained around them. Your father spotted more than a pretty girl on a tennis court that fateful day in Newport. He saw her keen interest, her desire for mastery."

Julia's mind flashed to the last summer she was on Haven Point. She had been so annoyed when she heard her parents talking about a tennis game, thinking it was frivolous. Now she recalled her father's earnest compliments, how much he appreciated her skill. With the fresh memory of the failure of her own overly complicated romance, Julia had a new appreciation for her parents' shared pastimes and simple enjoyment of each other's company.

"It took me a long time to recognize that my sister was far wiser than me," Anna continued. "I was consumed with who was right and who was wrong. Your mother focused on *what* was right, and she had far more power than I realized to bring about the right outcome.

"Power . . ." Julia mused. "I confess it's not a word I associated with my mother."

"That's because your mother wields it judiciously, in a way that allows everyone to maintain their dignity. She is remarkably discerning, though, about what matters and what is trivial. She knew what mattered. Especially what mattered for you, Julia."

"I learned something recently about Mother that surprised me." Julia relayed what Margaret Seaborne had told her, that it had been Mother who persuaded her to let Michael camp out on the island in the Potomac River. "I confess, I always associated Liberty Island with you."

"Your mother knew your imagination needed room to run, that *you* needed room to run. I took you to Liberty Island, but it was her gift. It was a great tradition she was passing along, a very enlightened sense of possibility."

Julia was so deep in thought, she jumped when the telephone in Anna's kitchen jangled.

"Sorry. That old telephone bell is so loud, they could use it at a fire station. Excuse me a moment."

Julia could only hear half of the conversation, Anna saying "yes" and "no," but she knew Mother was on the other end.

"Your mother is coming over," Anna said when she returned to the living room. "We have something we need to talk to you about."

Julia felt a bit wary suddenly, wondering what more they could possibly have to tell her, but when she heard her mother's bicycle on the pebbles outside, she rose to meet her at the door, resolved to be more generous, less hasty.

"I'm so sorry, Mother," Julia said, as she hugged her.

"I'm sure I have much to apologize for, too, Julia. We can have a long talk later, but there's something Anna and I need to speak to you about." She nodded toward the living room. "Let's sit."

Julia curled up beside Mother on the sofa, with Anna opposite. When Mother and Anna exchanged a glance, Julia detected grimness in it and felt a surge of anxiety. "Is everyone okay?" Julia asked anxiously. "You? Father?"

"We are fine, Julia. But Louisa is not."

"What do you mean?" Julia had a strange feeling in her limbs, a presentiment of something terrible.

"Louisa has a weak heart, and her condition has worsened in recent months. I know she told you she was in Boston for work, but she was actually there receiving treatment. The doctors have done all they can, however, so she is coming here to Haven Point tomorrow."

"But isn't that good? She can rest and recover here, can she not?" Julia said, but then her mind flew to Mother's strange peremptoriness in asking her to come to Haven Point, and she had a dreadful feeling that she was wrong.

"No, she is not coming here to recover." Mother paused and looked down, as if to gather herself. When she lifted her face again, Julia saw sorrow etched in every line. "Louisa is coming here to die."

Julia snatched her hands away and stood. She took a few steps back, holding her arms out before her, as if to ward off this news. Then a bubble of anger rose up, not a pleasant feeling but preferable.

"Everyone is just giving up, then? There must be someone, something that can be done!"

"She has seen the best doctors there are, Julia," Anna said.

"When did this happen?"

Mother looked down again. "She was not well at Christmas. When I came to see you in January, she was worse. I brought her back to Boston with me."

"If it just happened, can't it get better?" Julia said, though she knew she sounded desperate and childish.

"But you see, it did not just happen, Julia," Anna said gently. "When Louisa was a child, she had a very bad case of rheumatic fever. We have always known it compromised her heart. She lived much longer than anyone expected."

"Why did no one tell me?" Julia screamed. "I might have taken better care of her!"

Mother shook her head. "Nobody but your father, your uncle and Eugenia, and the two of us ever knew. Louisa wanted to live her life, to do as much as she could for as long as she had, and for no one to hold her back. We had to respect her wish."

"But why did you not tell me in January?"

"I wanted to, and I felt terrible leaving you when you were still in the hospital, but she was in very bad shape. Louisa wanted *you* to heal, though, and not be worried about her. She hoped to wait until it was time for her to come to Haven Point, but if things had progressed more rapidly, we would have brought you to her."

Julia looked from Mother to Anna, hoping she might see some cause for hope, or even something else she might lash out at. There was nothing. She was unarmed, undefended, utterly exposed to this terrible, terrible truth. She felt her legs weaken, and she sank back into the sofa next to her mother, her face in her trembling hands.

"I don't think I can do this."

"I know," Mother said, her tone at once resigned and also perfectly in sympathy. Julia looked up. Mother's eyes were damp. However blind Julia had been to her mother all these years, she could see her clearly now. *I know how you feel*, she was saying. *I don't know how to do this either.*

"Oh, Mother . . ." Julia took a shuddering breath, and then the tears came, great heaving sobs.

"I saw Louisa before the Knickerbocker," Julia said, when she could finally speak. "We had argued and parted on chilly terms. Her letters after were so distant. I thought she must still be angry or she would have found some way to come see me."

"She couldn't be angry at you. Never."

Julia pushed herself up, put her hands on her knees, and took a deep breath.

"So when is she coming?"

"Your uncle is bringing her in two days. She will need you to be strong, Julia. We all do."

Louisa spent the last ten days of her life on Haven Point.

It was raining when she arrived, and they set her up in Julia's bedroom. Anna had warned her about how Louisa looked. Julia hoped she did a creditable job, but it cut her to the quick to see her friend's once lustrous hair so thin, her pale skin so gray.

"I'm sorry. I didn't want you to know until you had to," Louisa said, once she was comfortably ensconced, blankets to her chin.

"I know, Lou. It's all right." Julia climbed onto the bed beside her.

Louisa's breath did not come as easily, but she was, as always, peaceful.

"Julia, I want you to know that I am all right. I want us to have this time together and not tiptoe. Do you understand?"

Though Julia did not want to say the words, she knew she must. "You mean you know you are going to die, and you don't want us to pretend you're not."

"Thank you. Yes."

"Can we pretend to be rumrunners, though?"

Louisa laughed weakly.

"I just found out about my mother and your father," Julia said. After sharing the terrible news about Louisa, Mother had finally told Julia about her relationship with Calvin Stannarius. She had told Louisa, too, though evidently only a few months ago. "I wondered what you thought when you heard, if you felt deceived."

"Not at all," Louisa said. She turned to look at Julia. "I thought it was sweet."

"I did, too." Julia took Louisa's hand. "It made you feel even more like my sister than you already did."

It was Julia's idea to take Louisa to Liberty Island. She spoke to Mother first, who agreed, then to Maudie and Ruthie, and finally to Duncan Douglas. On a bright morning, a few days after Louisa's arrival, Julia and Duncan went out to Gunnison Island to get things ready. Julia had been trying not to cry, but when she looked at Duncan and saw his tears falling, she let her own fall, too.

In addition to a comfortable chair for Louisa with blankets, pillows, and a footstool, they set up a few other chairs and a table, and Julia helped Duncan put up two hammocks. They worked steadily, silent tears streaming down their faces the entire time. Other than Duncan offering a handkerchief, they did not say a word. There was no need.

An hour later, Duncan and Julia fetched Louisa in his boat, while Maudie brought Ruthie in her own. Maudie had packed a big picnic, and they arrayed themselves around Louisa, who sat on the comfortable chair, blankets tucked about her, declaring she felt "like an old grandma."

They had a lovely time, reminiscing about Clem the bootlegger, and all the idyllic days they had spent running around this island. After Maudie and Ruthie left to return to their families, Julia picked up Louisa, who was as light as a small child, and moved her to one of the hammocks, tucked the blankets around her once more, and put a soft pillow behind her head. She climbed into the other hammock, facing the opposite direction, so she could see her friend's lovely face.

"Now will you finally tell me what happened with Pelham?" Louisa asked.

"Are you sure you want to talk about such rubbish?" Julia had only told her it was over.

"Yes, I *do* want to talk about such rubbish," Louisa said. Her voice was thin, but she had not lost her command. "You have spent days keeping me comfortable, doting on me, and telling me you love me. I'm tired of it. I demand to hear about you."

"All right!" Julia said, a warning look in her eye. She told Louisa everything—about Pelham's novel, her reaction to his sordid interpretation of Margaret Fuller's life, and then about the discovery of his and Mina's betrayal.

"You knew he wasn't right for me, didn't you?" she said, when she finished.

Louisa looked off for a moment. She was very still, lost in thought.

"When I heard you had been in the Knickerbocker Theatre," she said finally, "I thought of you, stuck under that seat in the pitch dark. It was the very worst thing I could imagine for you. In a way, I felt similarly about you and Pelham. You need light and open space, and he seemed so . . . so cramped and dark."

"How so?"

"So many things. All those ideas about psychology, for example. We are controlled by our unconscious selves, and there's no escaping terrible harms from our childhoods, even if we don't remember them. It's the worst kind of bondage that I can imagine. There's no room for transcendence, or even a soul."

"I had some hope last summer, when Pelham and I got back together," Julia said. "He seemed to like my more optimistic nature. But when we were around his friends, he was just as miserable. In the end, I realized that what he liked about me wasn't that I believed in a better tomorrow. It was just that I believed in *him*."

"They're all very intelligent," Louisa said. "But not smart enough to know they've made a religion of their ideas, or to see what a miserable corner those ideas have painted them into."

“And Mina?” Julia asked.

“I felt like whatever you had that she did not, or could not, have, she didn’t want you to have either. I felt at times like she was taking a blacking brush to everything people love about you—your enthusiasm, curiosity, openness, candor, humor.” Louisa paused, frowning. “Maybe I am saying too much?”

Julia shook her head. “No, no . . . not at all. I am so grateful. And of course, hearing you say this, I do see how she tried to diminish everything, everyone in my eyes. She wanted me to dislike my mother, my friends, this place.”

“Haven Point or Liberty Island?”

“Both.” In an imitation of that lazy drawl of Mina’s, which she had once thought sounded sophisticated, Julia said, “*Haven Point is cut off from the world, you know. The old Protestant aristocracy keeping the barbarians at bay.* And you know how dismissive she always was of the *Liberty Island* books.”

“I never felt anything but welcome on Haven Point,” Louisa said. “And Mina knew *Liberty Island* marked you as special. As well it should. I came here as a little girl so grief-stricken I could not even speak. But you just took my hand and folded me into the magical world you had created. With that accepting, confiding way of yours, you healed me, Julia.”

“Thank you,” Julia said, feeling as if she might cry.

They were quiet for a while, and Julia assumed Louisa had grown too weary to talk more. But then she spoke again.

“I am glad Margaret gave you that illustration from *Liberty Island.* She was right that it belongs to you. That’s you, Julia, always pointing at the light.”

Seeing the question in Julia’s eye, Louisa searched for more words.

“My Irish grandmother used to say, ‘Open the curtains and let out the dark.’” She smiled, her expression sweetly tender. “You don’t need to look to anyone else for answers, Julia. The fact is, you are meant to love. You’re made *for* love. All you need to do is let out the dark.”

• • •

Eight days later, just after dawn, Julia went downstairs and found her mother sitting on the porch. She sank into the wicker love seat next to her.

Mother took her hand. "Do you feel all right? I know it is a lot to ask of you, speaking today."

"I wrote something, finally. It might not be enough, but I did my best."

"It will be enough. And Julia—I have not forgotten that I promised we would talk."

"There's nothing you need to say, Mother," Julia said. The past few weeks had revealed Elizabeth to her daughter in a new light. "I'm the one who owes you an apology. I am sorry for how much and how long I so willfully misunderstood you."

"I know I do not try hard enough to make myself understood." Mother gave her a wry smile. "I have been reliably informed that I assume too much."

"You assume everyone means well, and expect the same in return. You deserve that, especially from me. I won't forget it again."

Julia felt anxious as she sat in the front pew of the little church on Haven Point. Anna had come by Fourwinds yesterday and found Julia in her room, weeping over a nearly blank sheet of paper.

"I am no writer. I can't do this. There are no words that can properly honor her."

"We are all more than what can be captured on a page," Anna replied. "Even a full biography is inevitably inadequate, never mind a eulogy. Your love for Louisa will come through, whatever you say."

Julia hoped so, but she was not at all sure. When the time came, she rose from the pew and approached the lectern, her legs wobbly. She got encouraging smiles from her family—Father and Mother, who had Julia's nephews by their side, and from her aunt and Uncle Harley, and their sons, who had come up for the service.

Tomorrow they would all go to Boston for the full Mass at Louisa's church, where she would be buried beside her mother. Louisa had not lived in South Boston for years, but she never lost ties with her old neighborhood. Friends from Washington were also traveling up for the service. Her life would be well celebrated there. Yet when Julia glanced up, she saw that this little church was full, too.

Most people gathered here did not know Louisa's history, that Haven Point was not just where she died but also where she was born. They knew nothing of the bittersweet ties that bound her to this place. They came because here, as everywhere, Louisa had touched many lives in her quiet way.

As Julia scanned the faces, she spotted one that surprised her. It was Michael, sitting on the aisle, halfway back. She smiled at him, and he lifted his hand and touched his index finger to his thumb. *His wink.*

Julia's tremors eased. With more confidence, she looked down at her paper and began to read.

> Louisa was eight years old when she was first brought to us here, for the benefit of her health. Once, when we were still very young, she told me that Haven Point was a bath for her lungs, that she could feel the air washing her breath.
>
> She was so independent, it was hard for her to let us take her in, no matter how often we told her how much we loved and needed her. She only relented because she knew, although I did not, that she had only so many breaths to spare. She wanted to do as much good as she could before they were depleted. If being here on Haven Point would help her save them up—to bank them, if you will—it was a bargain she was willing to strike.
>
> Louisa saw us as giving her the gift of breath, but the truth is, that is what she gave to everyone else.
>
> I used to feel about Louisa as I imagined a boat feels about its mooring. I often tugged at the line, yearning to enter the current. But if it was dark, or the current was too swift and dangerous, she kept me anchored. When I did wander, I knew I could return, and that she would hold me fast.
>
> I have come to think of her in a more elemental way. When

we were in college, we attended the suffrage march in Washington. A crowd of rough men swarmed the parade route, and Louisa was knocked to the ground unconscious, with a wound on her head. I remember thinking she needed a circle of space around her so that she could breathe.

Louisa was the figurative version of the circle I literally sought that day. Everyone who entered Louisa's circle breathed more easily. You could tell her your secrets, and she would keep them. You could betray your idiosyncrasies, and she would accept them. You could come to her with your sorrows, and she would listen.

Oh, how she would listen.

Louisa's serenity was such that she was hardly ever roused to anger, and on the rare times she was, it was almost always directed at those who exploited the poor working women to whose needs and interests she dedicated her life.

She helped them breathe more easily, too. Literally, in fighting for better ventilation and fire protection in factories, and figuratively, in pressing for better wages and shorter hours.

Louisa used to say that people were too enamored of the idea of what could be. She could not think about an imagined, idyllic tomorrow. She was far too concerned with what is.

When I first learned she was coming here to die, I remembered that and thought, "The reason she must think about what is, and not what could be, was that she only had so many remaining breaths."

The truth, though, has since hit me quite forcefully. What was true for her is true for all of us. We all have only so many breaths.

In that bargain Louisa struck all those years ago, I got the better end. She might have been small, humble, and frail, but she had more strength and courage in her little finger than I have in my whole body. She did more with her short life than most do with a long one. I only hope that with my own remaining breaths, I will remember her goodness and follow the example of the life she lived.

Mother had planned a luncheon reception, but after the service, Julia had to navigate a gauntlet of people offering kind words and sympathy, and by the time she was through, her family had already left for Fourwinds.

As she walked back alone, her mind returned to that moment when she had spotted Michael in the church. She'd had no idea he was coming, and seeing him there had steadied her instantly.

The day before Louisa died, she had taken Julia's hand. "I have a confession to make."

"For me or a priest?"

Louisa smiled. "This one's for you."

"All right. I can handle it."

"I always wished you could love Michael."

"Me, too," Julia had said sadly.

Michael was the one person who knew Julia almost as well as Louisa had, and who, like Louisa, had never tried to change her, who wanted nothing but her happiness. Suddenly, Julia felt keen to see him. She had no idea what his plans were, but she picked up her pace, hoping he would be at Fourwinds.

She entered the house and paused in the hall, where she could see into the living room. To her relief, she spotted Michael talking to Anna. When he caught her eye, he excused himself and came to meet her, his smile kind and sympathetic.

He is so handsome! Why had she never seen that? Julia felt something stir inside her, something tentative and tender. And for some strange reason, she began to cry.

Michael pulled her into a hug. "You were perfect," he said into her hair.

When he pulled back, he kept one hand on her shoulder, brought the other to her face, and brushed a tear away with his thumb.

"You were good to come, Michael. I felt all right when I saw you there."

"You did, Jules? I'm glad."

"How long are you staying?"

"I have to leave Haven Point this afternoon, but as it happens, I won't be going far. I know you're going to Boston tomorrow. I can meet you back here in a week if you would like?"

"I would. Very much," Julia said, though her heart sank. Genevieve Carter's family had a house in Bar Harbor. Other than seeing her, Julia could not imagine what other business he would have in Maine.

Julia already felt as if her heart had been cracked wide open. She was not sure it could take another blow.

Julia had thought her time after the Knickerbocker disaster might prepare her somewhat for living without Louisa. Had it not been good practice, those long months when she had felt so bereft of her presence?

She learned that grief and sorrow do not get easier with practice. It was familiar, yes, that feeling when she saw something amusing and wanted to tell her friend about it but realized she could not. But it hurt so much more, now that she knew she never would.

As Michael's return visit approached, she thought she should prepare herself for the likelihood that he might be newly engaged to Genevieve Carter. Unfortunately, her preparations, such as they were, consisted of many hours contemplating if and how she might tell Michael that Miss Carter was a simpering ninny and not nearly good enough for him.

He arrived in the late afternoon in a cheerful humor, which naturally made Julia suspicious. She cursed whoever decided that only women should wear engagement rings. If she saw one on his hand, it would at least give her time to prepare herself before the words came out of his mouth.

It was a clear day, a bit warm, but there was a breeze coming from the north, so they headed out on the cliff path in the direction of the beach.

Despite a resolution to be cool and nonchalant, Julia yammered. She described Louisa's funeral Mass in far greater detail than was warranted, and then began ticking off the names of every person in attendance whom she thought Michael might know from college or Washington.

At one point, Michael pointed at a sailboat in the distance. "Is that your parents?"

She squinted. "I think it is."

Her parents sailed together often, but Julia felt unexpected pleasure at seeing them do so today. Julia still saw her parents' marriage as rather Victorian, but while Mother might be a wife in the old tradition, that did not mean that she was powerless, or that her marriage was without passion.

"How is work, Michael?" she asked finally. Surely Miss Carter's name would not arise in a conversation about his professional life.

"I actually have an announcement on that front. I find I'm tired of the news game. I am glad I did it, but I'm awfully sick of petty political battles. I have decided to make a change."

"What will you do?"

"I was speaking with my father about some projects that I thought our family foundation should support, and he asked if I would consider running it. I said I would."

The Seabornes were so human, so earthbound, Julia often forgot how wealthy they were. "That sounds wonderful, Michael. What sorts of projects?"

"We have something in the works for wounded veterans, though I'm still figuring out what is most needed, where we can be most helpful. And I would like to start fresh air camps for boys and girls who live in the city."

"Oh, how marvelous! Where will they be?"

"Up here, in fact. I've been scouting sites over the past few days."

So, was he not with Genevieve Carter? Julia's heart lightened.

"Since you are available in the summers, I actually wondered if you might be interested in helping," he said, casting her a sideways glance.

"But I was not sure if your relationship with Mr. Stewart might be an impediment."

"That's over."

"Oh. I'm sorry."

"Are you? I'm not."

"Then I take it back. I'm thrilled!"

"So, you did not like him either?" Julia sighed.

"I didn't like him for you."

"Don't let anyone tell you that you see less with one eye than two." Julia took a deep breath and decided it was time to face her fate. "And what about Miss Carter?"

"Engaged!" he said, cheerfully.

Julia felt like crying and wondered how she could get through the rest of the walk without doing so. She managed to say, "My felicitations," though she knew her words sounded terribly hollow.

He laughed. "Not to me, you goose. To Hank Duvall."

"Oh!" Julia felt a jolt of hope. "Were you upset? I wasn't sure if you . . ."

Michael stopped, looked down, and idly kicked at a clump of weeds. "No, I never was."

"Why not?"

He looked up at her, smiled, and then shook his head slowly. "It's always just been you, Julia." He spoke gently, as always letting her know that whatever she wanted, or did not, was all right.

Julia felt a flutter in her chest, and a pleasant chill that left goose bumps on her arms. And then, suddenly, she began to laugh.

"Oh, Michael, I cannot tell you how much I had come to detest Genevieve Carter. I have had the most uncharitable thoughts about her."

Michael peered at her closely, as if he thought he might not be hearing her properly. "Julia, are you saying . . ."

She smiled up at him. "I am saying it's always been just you, too, Michael, only I was too stupid to know it."

He put his hands on the side of her face and looked into her eyes, his expression a mixture of joy and astonishment. He leaned in then and kissed her, and Julia felt as if she might melt.

He pulled back but kept his hands on her face, his thumbs stroking her cheeks. His eyes had always been so kind, so soulful. Truly, he did not need them both. One really did do the work of two.

Then, as if he could read her thoughts, he moved his hands to her shoulders and said, in a businesslike tone, "So, what do you think, Jules? Could you marry a cyclops?"

"No, I could not marry a cyclops." Julia shook her head and frowned. She paused, as if considering the matter, then added, "But I *could* marry a pirate."

He laughed, then took her hand, and they resumed their walk, stopping occasionally to kiss, or just to look at each other like fools. They spoke about the fresh air camps, when they might marry, and where in Washington they might live.

They made it to the beach and then turned to head back toward Fourwinds, but they stopped before they took the path up to the house.

The strains of the sunset orchestra wafted over from the west side of the peninsula, and they watched as a few soft clouds over the island turned pale pink, and a lavender gray spread over the water like a blanket. Julia felt tears sting at her eyes.

I opened the curtains, Louisa. I let out the dark.

AUTHOR'S NOTE

I have long been fascinated by hidebound New England summer colonies, which are uniquely well-suited to family sagas. When I decided this book would be partially set on the same fictional summer community as my debut novel, *Haven Point*, I was eager to once again explore the themes of intergenerational conflict.

The question was, what period?

The 1920s, which epitomizes "rebellious youth" as well as any decade but the 1960s, might have seemed an obvious choice for Julia's coming of age. However, I found myself intrigued by the 1910s, a period that reads almost like a skipped beat in the rhythm of history—a brief, fervent moment when many seeds of social revolution were sowed, only to be buried for decades by backlash, two world wars, and the Great Depression. It is one of the few spans of time in which one could imagine a novel being denounced as dangerously radical upon publication, and then, within one generation, being dismissed as reactionary.

I am indebted to a number of scholars and writers for their insights into the various currents of thought that thrived during this time, and the young intellectuals who promulgated them. Steven Biel's *Independent Intellectuals in the United States, 1910–1945* was enormously valuable, as were *A Woman of the Nation*, Sara Alpern's biography of Freda Kirchway, and *Young Radicals: In the War for American Ideals*, by Jeremy McCarter. Though the 1920s are the subject of Frederick Lewis Allen's *Only Yesterday*, the book contained useful perspectives about the period that led into that seminal decade, as did *The Modern Temper: American Culture and Society in the 1920s*, by Lynn Dumenil, and historian George Santayana's *Winds of Doctrine: Studies in Contemporary Opinion*.

Republic of Dreams: Greenwich Village: The American Bohemia, 1910–1960, by Ross Wetzsteon, and *The Village: 400 Years of Beats and Bohemians*, by John Strausbaugh, provided background on the colorful history of Greenwich Village. *American Moderns: Bohemian New York and the Creation of a New Century*, by Christine Stansell, performed a similar service for New York City more generally. Though published after my research was largely concluded, I also commend to interested readers Lottie Whalen's *Radicals and Rogues: The Women Who Made New York Modern*.

I did not craft the character of Pelham Stewart with any one writer in mind, but the sentiments he expressed in the talk Julia attends her freshman year echo those of Randolph Bourne, an influential member of that generation of young social critics. In addition to Bruce Clayton's biography, *Forgotten Prophet: The Life of Randolph Bourne*, I also relied on Bourne's articles in the archives of *The Atlantic*.

The idea for Pelham Stewart's *Schoolcraft Colony* grew out of a 1921 *New York Times* book review of *Margaret Fuller: A Psychological Biography*, whose author, Katharine Anthony, subjected Fuller to posthumous psychoanalysis. (Spoiler: The reviewer was not impressed.)

In conceptualizing Anna's approach to writing *Liberty Island*, and in writing the excerpts, I did have a specific writer in mind: Edith Nesbit, one of my favorite authors of children's literature. As the late British librarian Marcus Crouch put it, Nesbit stood "squarely at the doorway between the nineteenth and the twentieth century. . . . No writer today is free of debt to this remarkable woman." In her relatable characters and conversational narrative style, Nesbit broke from the idealized young characters, and the safe, moralizing tales of her predecessors.

In addition to Crouch's works, *Treasure Seekers and Borrowers:*

Children's Books in Britain 1900–1960 and *The Nesbit Tradition: The Children's Novel 1945–1970*, I found much useful information in Eleanor Fitzsimon's *The Life and Loves of Edith Nesbit* and Julia Briggs's *A Woman of Passion*.

In learning about the history of children's literature, particularly books for girl readers, I relied on *What Katy Read: Feminist Re-Readings of Classic Stories for Girls, 1850–1920*, by Shirley Foster and Jodi Simons; *The Rise of American Girls' Literature*, by Ashley Reese; and *Learning from the Left: Children's Literature, the Cold War, and Radical Politics in the United States*, by Julia L. Mickenberg. Useful resources for information about the general history of girlhood included *Transforming Girls: The Work of Nineteenth-Century Adolescence*, by Julia Pfeiffer; *The New Girl: Girls' Culture in England 1880–1915*, by Sally Mitchell; and *The Girl: Constructions of the Girl in Contemporary Fiction by Women*, by Ruth O. Saxton.

I drew much inspiration for young Julia's imaginary games from "Nickels and Dimes," an archive of dime novels maintained by Northern Illinois University libraries, and the "Edward T. Leblanc Dime Novel Bibliography," hosted by Villanova University's Falvey Library.

I am also indebted to Barnard College's excellent archives, which include yearbooks, photographs, and other artifacts from the 1910s. In the historical archives of *The Barnard Bulletin*, which are available on Newspapers.com, I found an April 1912 issue containing a letter to the editor, arguing that freshmen should be permitted to join the Suffrage Club, though needless to say, it was not written by Julia Demarest.

My understanding of nineteenth-century utopianism in America was enhanced by Richard Francis's *Transcendental Utopias: Individual and Community at Brook Farm, Fruitlands, and Walden*. To readers interested in the remarkable life of Margaret Fuller, I highly recommend Alison Pataki's work of biographical fiction, *Finding Margaret Fuller*.

Elite Families: Class and Power in Nineteenth-Century Boston, by Betty G. Farrell, and *The Proper Bostonians*, by Cleveland Amory, are very different books, but both provided an understanding of elite Boston families of the era. Between Amory's description of the Chilton

Club and the observations of friend and fellow author Laura Munson, I could not resist the temptation of mentioning that august institution, though it required my taking a liberty: Judith Fairchild could not have presented a pamphlet at the Chilton Club in 1899, as that precedes its founding.

Research often yields unexpected delights. One of those was *Washington Wife: Journal of Ellen Maury Slayden from 1897–1919*. I thoroughly enjoyed her observations of official Washington, DC, in the early twentieth century. Mrs. Slayden was active in the peace movement, and her journal entries describing war-mad Washington are evidence that social media is not, actually, required for an idea to become so firmly entrenched that dissent is rendered nearly impossible.

A number of additional sources illuminated life in the capital during this period. I learned of the event hosted by Vice Admiral and Lady Grant in the historical archives of *The Washington Post*. (They really did make the yacht their home.) Garrett Peck's *Prohibition in Washington, D.C.: How Dry We Weren't* and Paul Kelsey Williams's *Lost Washington* brought to life the Prohibition era in Washington, and introduced me to the Krazy Kat Club, which thrived from 1918 until about 1925.

I have family lore to thank for two additional Washington locations that appear in *Liberty Island*. Café St. Mark's, where Julia and Pelham reunite in 1921, was indeed popular with the "residential set," but unfortunately for my great-grandfather, who was one of its owners, it was not popular enough, and evidently closed within a year. "Whoop Whoop" was the name my great uncle Smoke and his friends gave to the island in the Potomac where they camped out for the entirety of several summers.

In addition to contemporaneous newspaper stories, I am indebted to Kevin Ambrose for his book *The Knickerbocker Storm*, which offers a comprehensive account of the collapse of the roof of the Knickerbocker Theatre, as well as numerous photographs. The theater collapse remains the deadliest disaster in the city's history, and the "Knickerbocker storm," with its twenty-eight inches of snow, still holds the record for Washington's largest single snowstorm.

Finally, Michael Seaborne's injury at Belleau Wood was based on the real-life experiences of *Chicago Tribune* reporter Floyd Gibbons. I read about this colorful, swashbuckling character in *American Journalists in the Great War: Rewriting the Rules of Reporting*, by Chris Dubbs. Additional details were in an article on WorldWar1.com by his great niece, Shelley Mitchell-Schaaf, which was condensed from *Floyd Gibbons, Your Headline Hunter*, a 1953 biography by Gibbons's brother, Edward Gibbons. More information is available in an April 2024 story in the *Army Times*, "The Man Who Made Belleau Wood—and the Marine Corps—Immortal."

ACKNOWLEDGMENTS

This book would not be in your hands without the work of an incredibly talented team. In the acknowledgments of my debut novel, I referred to my "unflappable" agent, Susanna Einstein. Five years later, and reader, she still has not flapped! Many thanks, Susanna, for your wise and steady counsel.

Sarah Cantin's consummate skills at every level of the editing process are reflected on every page of this novel. I am so fortunate that she saw the potential in this story, and gave me the gentle guidance (and time!) to ensure that I reached it.

Many thanks to the whip-smart team at St. Martin's Press: Jennifer Enderlin, Drue VanDuker, Erica Bartiramo, Jessica Zimmerman, Anne Marie Tallberg, Michelle McMillian, Michael Clark, and Michael Storrings. Thanks, too, to Susie Stangland, Anna Lawrence, and Grace McGovern, who help to keep me in the social media swim, even when I don't feel like getting in the water.

A special shout-out to Dana Perino, who not only was a great champion of *Haven Point* but also emailed many encouraging words during the (unexpectedly epic) "Interbook Period," and was an early reader of *Liberty Island.* Thank you, Dana.

I get by with a *lot* of help from my friends, particularly Beth Rives Chesterton, Jo-Anne Goldman Chase, and Hilary Brandt, each of whom has been making me laugh for more than forty years.

I would be nowhere without my family. I am blessed every day by Brit and Kim Hume's wisdom, love, and unflagging support. My husband, Drew Onufer, is not only decency defined but also a source of constant encouragement, even in this rather mad career choice of mine. Our daughters, Mary Clare and Helen, cheer me on, cheer me up, make me laugh, and make me proud.

I am eternally thankful to my mother, Clare Hume, to whom this book is dedicated. Thank you, Mom, for always believing in me.

Last but not least: Thank you, readers. Your time is precious, and I am so grateful that you chose to spend it with Anna and Julia.